The Handbook for
Lightning Strike Survivors

The

Handbook for
Lightning Strike
Survivors

a novel

MICHELE YOUNG-STONE

Shaye Areheart Books   New York

Published in the United States by Shaye Areheart Books, an imprint of the Crown Publishing Group, a division of Random House, Inc., New York.
www.crownpublishing.com

SHAYE AREHEART BOOKS with colophon is a registered trademark of Random House, Inc.

Library of Congress Cataloging-in-Publication Data

Young-Stone, Michele.
    The handbook for lightning strike survivors : a novel / by Michele Young-Stone. — 1st ed.
        p. cm.
    1. Lightning—Fiction.   2. Life change events—Fiction.   I. Title.
    PS3625.O975H36 2010
    813'.6—dc22

                                                    2009016611

ISBN 978-0-307-46447-7

Printed in the United States of America

Design by Lauren Dong

10 9 8 7 6 5 4 3 2 1

First Edition

For Rosemary Young

90% of lightning strike victims survive.

—THE HANDBOOK FOR LIGHTNING STRIKE SURVIVORS

The Handbook for
Lightning Strike Survivors

A fish . . .

She was a girl like you or like someone you knew—from a cracked home, a fault line between her parents, for which she felt responsible. A pretty girl with red hair: too curly to contain in barrettes or under headbands, twisting free, needing to spiral and curl like the ocean waves to her right.

The sun was hot, turning her back pink. She took great strides, walking faster, nearly running, her shadow mixed with the surf. Sanderlings scurrying to and fro mixed with her shadow. Except for the birds, she was alone with her thoughts, with hopes to caulk the crevice between her mother and father, the way she'd seen her mother do, wearing latex gloves, smoothing slow-drying putty around the bathtub's perimeter. How she set her highball on the tub's edge, digging out the old grout using a flat-head screwdriver. Mother was always drinking, and Dad was always working, but cracks can be mended so long as you let the caulk dry. They were here at the beach, weren't they? There was plenty of time to let that stuff dry. At home, Becca would mess it up, running the bathwater too soon, but here, she had hope. Here, she spotted a live fish with a fanlike tail, its gills opening and shutting, silver window blinds. Maybe the fish-on-the-sand happened to you or to someone you knew, but for Becca, it cemented her belief that anything is possible. She carried the fish through Atlantic surf, watching it swim away, running to tell her parents she had saved a life.

. . . out of water

Buckley loved everything about his mother, from the strawberry bumps on her legs where she dry-shaved with her Gillette to the way her black hair knotted at the nape of her neck. When the mean boys, the ones with fathers who taught them to fight before they could walk, jumped him from behind or from the front, Buckley counted himself a survivor. Knocked hard to the dirt, he got back up. It had everything to do with his mother. She was there for him, and he'd always be there for her. He could run fast.

It seemed that he was always running from someone stronger, bigger, and meaner—but not faster, and that was a very good thing. Today he was tired of running. The angry boys called, "Bastard!" That word didn't touch him anymore. He'd heard it so often, it'd lost its meaning. He walked, hearing footsteps at his heels and falling to the dirt. Maybe he needed a beating. Covering his head with his hands, he felt the blows to his ribs and legs. *Always protect the head.* He breathed in the dirt.

Much later, when he was sixteen, he met Clementine. She smelled like dirt too. Like the earth. Like he could bury his face there between chin and collarbone and be protected. Maybe that's why he loved her.

. . .

When the beating was over, the bullies toed dirt on Buckley's backside and touted, "Crybaby." As they left, he struggled to his feet.

The thing was, he didn't cry. Not then. Hardly ever. They could've kicked and punched until his ribs cracked and his lip split. It didn't make a difference. He wouldn't have cried for them. Maybe that was part of what was wrong with him. He was eleven years old, unable to cry, trying not to run from the world.

Lightning, 1977

The wind shifted and Becca stopped running. Her dad was taking her for a chocolate-dipped soft serve, but first she needed a bath. He wouldn't be seen with her this way. Her knee, bloody from tripping over a knobby root during hide-and-seek, had that sticky-tight feeling, and the other knee, scraped from tumbling on the sidewalk, burned. She needed to be more careful. How many times had her dad told her "Stop picking those scabs or you will scar, and scars last forever"?

The wind picked up—a rare cold wind. From her driveway, she watched the willow tree's branches, like charm-laden arms, sway back and forth, and thought about her ice cream, about her dad. She thought about the summer's end, another boring school year about to begin, about the dried blood caked on her knee— and her world exploded. It cracked open and Becca fell inside a whiteness that erased everything: the driveway, the tree, the long summer's day, the blood, the ice cream. For a time, the world was blank. She was still.

She woke up, her fingertips tingling, her head full of static, raindrops only now wetting her legs. She knew she'd been struck by lightning. There was never a question. She stood up, feeling peculiar, seeing herself from a distance as someone else might: wild hair, freckled nose, pink lips, pony T-shirt, corduroy shorts and gray sneakers; gangly arms and legs.

She hobbled inside to the den. With blood trickling down

her shin, her voice shaky, she said, "Dad, I got struck by lightning."

He sat on the sofa. "If you got struck by lightning, you'd be dead." He didn't look up.

The den's gold drapes were parted. The sky was black. Becca shivered, waiting for her dad to say something more like *We need to get you to the hospital!* or *Oh my God! I'll call an ambulance!*, but instead he picked up *Yachting Today.* He was in love with sailing then. He was in love with all things that required large sums of money, and Becca was in love with him.

Becca said, "It knocked me down."

"Who knocked you down? Did you knock them down first?" He looked at her then. Finally.

The rain streaked the front window. She said, "I think I got struck by lightning."

"Well, you seem fine now." He was used to seeing her bloodied and bruised. Like her mother, she lacked balance. "Get cleaned up." He returned to his magazine.

Upstairs, she undressed, leaving the bathroom door open. She looked at her watch before stepping in the tub. The hands had stopped at five-fourteen. *That must've been when the lightning struck. Or, maybe Dad is right: Who gets struck by lightning and walks away?* She knew the answer: *Me. I do.*

In the bathtub, with her big toe up the spigot, the water turned gray. Becca smelled bleach. She was trembling again. Shutting off the cold, she turned up the hot. She closed her eyes and took deep breaths to stop from shaking. She imagined hovering, twirling in the sky, shooting lightning bolts from her fingertips like a gunslinger before dropping, landing cold and wet in the driveway. She opened her eyes and felt sick. Her hands and feet ached. She used to ask her mother, "How can I turn off my imagination?" Back then, she didn't pronounce the *i*, saying, " 'magination" instead. It was back then that she'd started painting, to give her " 'magination" something to do. Maybe the prickling in her feet and the headache were imagination. Maybe she'd bumped her head falling down somewhere earlier today but didn't remember. More deep breaths. Her mother, who took smoke-filled breaths, said that deep breaths calmed the nerves. Becca, taking the deepest breaths possible, felt light-headed. She pulled the tub's stopper.

Looking at herself in the mirror, she decided to curb the breathing. She was pale. She might pass out, and she'd been through enough today.

Downstairs, she toweled her hair and waited for her dad to get off the phone. He said, "I'll be there," smiling at Becca, holding up his pointer finger to indicate *Be with you in a second.* He often held up his pointer finger. Sometimes when he wanted Becca to do something like fold laundry, he'd look at her and point to the full basket. He was a man of few words. Into the phone he said, "I told you: I'll be there."

Becca, having waited patiently, said, "I'm ready."

Covering the mouthpiece, he said, "Ready for what?"

"Ice cream. We're supposed to—"

He didn't let her finish. "Sorry. Another night." Returning to his phone conversation, he said, "I won't be later than eight."

Becca pulled the towel from her head and dropped it on the kitchen floor. She went upstairs to her room to paint a picture of a girl getting struck by lightning. She was certain that her father was in the kitchen pointing at the wet towel and waiting for someone to pick it up. Later, when he'd gone, she'd come back downstairs and the towel would still be there. It wasn't his responsibility to clean up after them.

An estimated 80% of people struck by
lightning are men. This is not, as you
might think, because men are too
stubborn to come in out of the rain;
rather, it's because men tend to engage
in outdoor sports and professions more
than women.

Regardless of a victim's gender,
doctors and scientists concur that the
surviving victim needs support from
family and friends to recover.

Immediate effects include cardiac
arrest and brain damage. Chronic effects
include anxiety disorders, memory loss,
stiff joints, numbness, and insomnia. For
years following a strike, the victim
might feel tingling throughout his body.
Because it's often difficult for a
victim to describe what happened, it's
important that there is a support group
to listen.

A good boy, 1967

Buckley R. Pitank imagined himself Jesse James, even as his jaw was pressed into the red clay roads of Mont Blanc, Arkansas. He spat and tried not to swallow the dirt that swirled into his eyes and nose. He'd eaten enough of this dirt. He choked on it and cried out, but that only made the other boy push his face harder into the cracked earth. The other boy was not one boy, but one of many.

Buckley was *one* boy born on his mother's mattress in Mont Blanc, Arkansas, in 1959. Raised by his mother, Abigail, and his grandmother, Winter, he never knew his father.

Mont Blanc, despite its name, had no mountains, not even snow-topped hills. It was a desolate wasteland for Buckley, with buzzing mosquitoes and snakes and jumping spiders the size of his fist. He was miserable, born to these two women: his grandmother, who said there was no time and no need for a hospital—she could manage quite well—and his mother, who said his birth was the worst experience of her life, everything bloody and slimy, her insides torn out, and she might never have recovered were it not for Buckley himself. Her joy.

Even as he struggled under the weight of a shoe in his back and a hand on his neck, he thought his future would be great. He had hopes and dreams, spawned by TV shows like *Bonanza*—espousing the world's fairness. In due time, Buckley thought that he would have his reward.

With the red clay of Mont Blanc caked on his two front teeth, Buckley invented epic tales about his father: He was an FBI agent working undercover, and if Buckley knew of his identity, the safety of America and the world would be at stake. He was a ship's captain who'd met Abigail in port (though when questioned by Buckley, Abigail reported to have never seen the ocean). Returning to sea, the captain promised to write, to come back for Abigail, but he was killed, ambushed by the Reds.

There were stories, endless possibilities. Buckley had faith that all would turn out right with the world. Later, he would stop believing in heroics and let the world do with him what it would.

One man who contributed to Buckley's loss of faith was the Reverend John Whitehouse. For two years in a row, Buckley had seen Reverend Whitehouse erect tents on Mrs. Catawall's overgrown acreage and Buckley had stayed clear, but on this Saturday night, red dirt under his fingernails, Buckley hid behind a dying magnolia, catching bits of the reverend's sermon.

Reverend Whitehouse preached about hellfire, the wages of sin, and the rewards for living a Christ-loving life. Buckley, Abigail, and Winter Pitank did not attend church, but that night, restless and curious about God, Buckley listened to those who filed out of the blue tent. They talked of being filled with the spirit: "I was sad when we got here. You saw me! I was as down as the dirt under these old heels, and now I'm changed! Look at me." He saw the flock's bright faces, seemingly oiled by God's own hands. "I never imagined," said a squat, freckled woman, her face slick with tears. "I should've made John come. He would've been glad he did." Her friend, holding a buckled purse at her breasts, said, "You'd think more people would turn out, but they're afraid of Jesus' love. I know if Jerry would've come, he'd have stopped the drink tonight. I know it." Buckley wanted desperately to be changed.

The revivalists lingered before driving away to their respective sinful spouses and neighbors—those who hadn't met Reverend

Whitehouse. They drove with their windows down, the dry Arkansas heat kissing their faces, calling to one another, "You should come for coffee tomorrow," feeling this kindred spirit that would dwindle as quickly as it came. Mont Blanc was not a friendly town.

Buckley caught the Reverend Whitehouse after the service; or rather the reverend caught Buckley. "What are you doing over there? Come out here, son." Buckley thought about making a run for it. Instead, he slunk from behind the tree, both hands deep in his pockets. "I said come here." Reverend Whitehouse was a lanky man in a black suit. He had long arms and a nose bumpy like a summer squash.

The reverend pulled a handkerchief from his pocket and blotted his forehead. "You want to make some money?"

It was rare that a grown man took an interest in Buckley. In fact, it had never happened.

"I asked you a question."

Buckley shrugged.

"Do you or don't you? This ain't a trick question. Can't you speak?"

"I can speak."

"So what'll it be? Do you want to make some money?" The reverend blotted his forehead again, leaving a beige stain on the folded kerchief.

"Yeah, I want to."

"Smart boy."

Buckley wanted a lot of things, but at the top of his list was for his mother to be happy. It seemed to him that she was always sad. She was a good mom—never a mean word crossed her lips—but like Buckley, she seldom smiled. She was fat, and it was hard for Buckley when they went places to hear people snicker and know she heard it too.

The first night Buckley met the reverend, he tromped along in scuffed cowboy boots beside the towering man over to a Chevy pickup. He could hear people inside the tent and wondered if they were the reverend's wife and children. The reverend stuffed a bunch of slick folded garbage bags into Buckley's hands. "Start over there. I didn't catch your name."

"Buckley, sir."

"All right, Buck." He handed Buckley a flashlight. Looking down at a grease-smeared popcorn container, the reverend said, "Good Christians don't litter. They know that I, the Lord's servant, have more important things to do than pick up their garbage." The reverend looked to Mrs. Catawall's big house. "The nice lady who owns this land don't abide trash in any form."

"Yes, sir." Buckley fumbled with the trash bags and the light, leaving all but one bag on the ground beside the truck's tire so he could find them in the dark.

The reverend shook his head. "I do God's work. What do you do? Are you in school?"

"Yes, sir."

"When I was a boy, I missed a lot of school. I spent October and November pulling tobacco, and then it was hard to catch up. Education can spoil a boy."

"Yes, sir, but our teacher says that . . ."

The reverend held up his hand. "Don't back-talk me. I'm hiring you to work. Let's get to it."

"Yes, sir."

In truth, Buckley's teacher didn't say much to him. It was actually Buckley's mother who told him, "Education makes a man. Ignorant people don't count for much." Buckley's teacher wrote math problems and vocabulary words on the chalkboard. She collected papers, most of which she never marked, and sat at her desk filing her nails.

Buckley couldn't even fill the first garbage bag, finding two deflated balloons, thirty or so cigarette butts (some stained with lipstick), and a few hard candy wrappers. He said, "This is all I can find."

"Keep looking."

For good measure, Buckley threw some twigs and dead brush in the bag. He didn't want to disappoint the reverend.

"Let's get out of here," the reverend said.

Buckley picked up the leftover garbage bags, wondering if despite his light trash haul this man was going to pay him as he'd said he would. Then again, it didn't really matter. He hadn't had anything better to do. It was August. There was no school. Still, his mom had taught him that *you judge a man by his word,* and the man had sure enough mentioned money.

"I'll give you a lift home," the reverend said.

"That's all right. I don't live far." Buckley hiked up his pants. They were from a secondhand shop his grandmother frequented. She bought everything two sizes too big, thinking the clothes would last longer, not caring that Buckley looked like a clown.

"Get in." The Reverend Whitehouse climbed into the pickup, and Buckley, who did as he was told, followed suit. "So how old are you?"

"Eight, sir. I don't live far. I can walk."

"Nonsense."

Buckley pulled the door shut. He did not want the reverend to come to his house. Even if he was getting paid, he didn't want the reverend to see his mother. Somehow seeing her gave strangers an advantage over him. He wondered if the empty blue and orange boxes of Kraft macaroni and cheese were still stacked in a pyramid on the kitchen table, a testament to her obesity. His grandmother had said last night, "I've had enough of this, Abby," and then his mother had boiled another pot of water on the old gas stove with the timer that no longer timed, and his grandmother swiped the box, adding it to her pyramid. Buckley couldn't help but think his Grandmother Winter liked his mom fat. Even if she said different, it gave her an advantage.

"You can drop me here."

"Is that your house?"

"It's not far."

"Nonsense, son. I'll drive you home." The Reverend White-house tousled Buckley's coarse locks. His hair was dark like his mother's.

"Please just drop me here."

Reverend Whitehouse pulled the truck over in front of a white cinder-block house—Mrs. Smith's house, not Buckley's. His house was a pea green cinder block. Mrs. Smith was on the front porch, smoking a cigarette. "Is that you, Buckley?"

"Yes, ma'am." Sweating, he turned to the reverend. "Thanks."

"No, son. Thank you. Hope you and yours can make it next Saturday." The reverend reached under the seat for his wallet. He pulled out one crisp dollar bill, then another, popping each one like the money was precious to him, like it had to be displayed. "It'd be good to see you there," he said, laying each bill out on the passenger's seat side by side, like a game of solitaire. "You take that, all right?"

Did this man expect him *not* to take the money, to offer it back to God? Was this some kind of test? "Thank you, sir. Thank you very much." Buckley crammed the bills into his pants pocket and ran from the truck. He saw the light from the truck illumi-nating the black road, his baggy shadow, the diamonds in the road, the trees far up ahead, his own house. He ran as fast as he could. Breathless, with his two dollars tucked away, he pulled open the screen door. He might buy a new GI Joe. He might buy a whole slew of balsa-wood planes and crash them. He liked the sound of the cracking wood, and when they didn't break, which was rare, he smashed them with his palm or his cowboy boot. *Man down. There's a man down.*

"What's with you?" his grandmother asked.

His mother sat in front of the TV. "You missed *Hogan's Heroes.* There's ice cream."

Buckley loved ice cream, but if he had to choose between his mother and ice cream, he'd never eat another spoonful. No contest. He'd decided that long ago, back when he first started weighing how much he loved his mother against everything else in the world. She came first. He went to the cupboard for a bowl.

She said, "It's after ten," and then Buckley heard a knock at the screen door, his mother struggling to rise from the tattered recliner, the twang of springs, his grandmother saying, "Oh, we didn't know Buckley got a ride home this evening." Buckley, frozen in the kitchen with an empty brown bowl in his hand, knew the reverend was at his door, and he knew this gave the man an advantage.

Geography plays a big role in
lightning strike frequency. Although some
contend that those struck are more likely
to be struck again, scientists argue that
it's not because the individual person
attracts the lightning; it's because the
geographical area is more prone to
strikes.

After reading multiple accounts of
repeat victims, I disagree with the
scientists. It doesn't make sense that
one person should get struck twelve
times just because he lives at a high
altitude prone to thunderstorms. Not
everyone who lives in that geographical
area has been struck twelve times. I
don't like to disagree with experts, but
on this point, I must, and I'm sure that
if you've been struck more than once,
you agree with me.

3

When making new friends . . .
1977

Becca's mother was drinking more than ever, smoking skinny brown cigarettes, forgetting whole conversations. Her dad stayed late in the garage. He had a passion for cars—which was one of the best things about him. Becca liked the heat from the engines on her knees and the wind tangling her hair. Everybody said her dad looked like Cary Grant. Even her mom. Her dad said Becca's mother was from Podunk so she was lucky to have landed him. He had heritage and good taste.

They fought a lot. According to her dad, he was being "screwed." Her mom was "a sot," and he nightly complained about a man, Mark Cusemeo, whom Becca didn't know. This man was "getting tenure" and he was a "moron from Plano, Texas." Becca knew what the word *moron* meant, but she didn't know about tenure or why her dad wanted it.

Becca's father was a Burke: Rowan Augustus Burke. Having ties and roots, Rowan didn't like anything nouveau. He counted Dr. Cusemeo "nouveau academic." Becca knew a little French, including *nouveau* is "new" because her babysitter Millie taught her. She knew too that her grandmother had "family" money. It was spent now, but her dad said that wealth was about attitude: a man's social standing, his home, his history. Mark Cusemeo, according to Rowan, had no history. Becca guessed her dad liked old British cars because they weren't nouveau.

Becca's mother disagreed with Rowan about Mark Cusemeo.

She said that Rowan spent too much time "chasing skirts" when he should be schmoozing the department chair. Becca knew what chasing a skirt meant, like Fonzie on *Happy Days*, but pretended not to know. It was better that way.

Today her dad drove Becca to Bobbie's department store to buy a new watch. She picked a Winnie-the-Pooh watch with flowers for hands. She also selected a brown and beige dog from the shelves of stuffed animals. Then she saw Colin Atwell and turned away. She knew him from first grade, where, on a double dare, he'd eaten glue on his hot dog. Then she heard that he was put in a special class. For glue eaters, social misfits, she supposed. Colin still had crazy blond hair, like he'd stuck his finger in a light socket.

"Hi, Rebecca," he said.

She looked at her shoes. He ate glue! Who knew what else he ate?

He grabbed the stuffed dog from her arms—"You still have a lot of freckles"—and tossed it in the air like a football.

"Who's your little boyfriend?" her dad asked.

"He's not my boyfriend."

Colin said, "I'm nobody's boyfriend." He held the stuffed dog out for Becca to see. "The nose is ripped. Get a different one."

"I don't want a different one." She reached for the dog.

"He's right," her dad said. "Pick a different one."

"I want him!" She grabbed the dog from Colin. "Mom can fix him."

"Get a different one," her dad said. "The paw is ripped too. There's stuffing coming out."

Becca said, "But if I don't buy him, who will? I want him." She held the stuffed dog to her chest.

Colin said, "You're spoiled."

"No, I'm not." She looked around, wondering why Colin seemed to be alone. "Where's your mom?"

Colin yanked the dog from Becca, throwing it to the retail

carpeting. "You're stupid!" With his knockoff Nikes, he stomped the stuffed dog. Becca picked the animal up. *What is wrong with that boy?* She and her dad watched Colin Atwell run away, tumbling into a rack of clothes and sending blouse hangers clacking to the floor.

Brushing off the dog, Becca said, "We have to get this stuffed animal."

Rowan said, "Your little friend is odd."

"He's not my friend."

"You said that before. That's good." Inspecting the stuffed dog, he said, "Sure, we can get him."

Becca was happy. Later, she'd recall this day as one of her fondest childhood memories.

Carrie Drinkwater rang the Burkes' doorbell at seven-thirty in the morning. She had straggly blond hair and a grape Kool-Aid smile. She wore cutoff Levi's and a San Francisco 49ers T-shirt with a faded tomato stain. She'd been going from house to house since sunrise, looking for kids her own age. Like Becca, she was lonely, dependent on her imagination for company.

Standing on the front stoop in her pajamas, Becca said, "Do you want some Frosted Flakes?"

Carrie didn't particularly like cold breakfast cereal, but said sure. At the table, she explained, "We moved here a month ago." Milk dripped down her chin.

"Have you met anybody?"

"Colin Atwell."

Becca said, "I hate Colin Atwell." Then, trying to impress Carrie, she said, "My neighbor Bob has a cheating whore wife. That's what my mom calls her."

"Your mom said that to her face?"

"Not to her face."

"Do whores get money?"

"I think so. But sluts don't."

"I can't believe you said you hate Colin Atwell. His mom ran away with a Harley-Davidson biker." Changing the subject, she said, "I moved here from Florida."

Becca said, "She couldn't have run away." *Grown-ups don't run away.*

"It's true. Colin's dad told my dad. They work together, and when we went to their house for this barbecue, there were pictures of her everywhere. Colin's dad thinks she's going to come back, but she's been gone for two years, so my dad said she isn't coming back. Anyway, my dad said I have to be nice to Colin, and when I asked Colin if his mom really ran away from home, he said yes. He was sad."

"I'll get dressed." Becca left her cornflakes on the table. She felt guilty. If she'd known about Colin's mom, she never would've asked him "Where's your mom?" How could she have known? She didn't think adults did such things. "Come on," she said to Carrie, who followed her upstairs. As an afterthought, Becca said, "Hey, I got struck by lightning."

"Lots of people do. It happens all the time in Florida. There was this man who got struck thirty times." In Becca's room, Carrie knelt on the flower rug, flipping through Becca's Mead sketchbooks—bright flowers and rainbows—while Becca put on a T-shirt and shorts. Carrie said, "You're like the best artist I've ever met."

"Not really."

"You are! What's this?"

"It's supposed to be a picture of lightning."

"It's neat. How'd you make it?"

Becca remembered: She'd painted the sheet white and waited, watching paint dry, but it wasn't right. It wasn't lightning. It wasn't white enough and it wasn't loud enough. She slid open the set of oil pastels her art teacher gave her for Christmas. There were twenty-four colors, and Becca chose titanium white. She started gingerly dotting and streaking the paint with the crayon. The oil pastel was whiter than the paint. She could see a slight difference, but it wasn't lightning. She circled and zigzagged the crayon, and it still wasn't right. She peeled the paper off the oil pastel and broke a sweat scribbling. *You can't paint lightning.* At least, Becca couldn't paint lightning. Not then.

Becca took the painting from Carrie. "Let's get out of here."

Outside, Bob's cheating whore wife rushed down the paved drive to her car and waved to Becca. Becca whispered to Carrie, "That's her: the lady I was telling you about." Bob's cheating whore wife drove away, her coffee cup forgotten on the car's roof.

Carrie said, "She's kind of pretty."

"Her boobs are too big."

Kevin Richfield, a blond, blue-eyed fifth-grader, rode past on his BMX racing bike.

Becca said, "Have you met him?"

"No."

"He's my destiny. If I decide to get married, I'm going to marry him. Otherwise, we might just live together. Do they do that in Florida? Do people live together without getting married?"

"Some people."

"I would," Becca said, "but I'd need my own bedroom and my own art room."

"Of course," Carrie said.

"I'm very creative."

"You are."

"What do *you* like to do?"

Carrie said, "Everything."

Becca stared curiously. "Like what?"

"Ride bikes. Draw and paint like you, and my favorite thing is Barbie. I have a Barbie Dream House. I love Barbies. I have the Cadillac."

"Hmm . . ." Becca had to think. She wasn't sure how she felt about Barbies. She confessed, "My mom hates Barbies, but I don't. Not really, even though I'm supposed to. I've never played with them. I'd like to play with them, but I'm not supposed to."

"How come?"

"It's an unreal imagination or image or something of women."

"I don't know what that means."

"My parents are strange about some things."

"I have a lot of Barbie clothes, and my mom makes them clothes too. You'll have to come over."

"Hmm?" Becca liked Carrie. There was possibility here.

The following weekend, Carrie spent the night at Becca's. The Burkes were going to dinner with the chemistry chair, and Mary was in a tizzy (Rowan's word) looking for her purple butterfly brooch. The babysitter Millie, standing by the sofa, was on the phone.

To Becca, Mary said, "Did you take it? Don't lie!"

"I'm not lying." Becca felt embarrassed. *She's already drinking.*

"That's my mother's brooch."

"I didn't take it! Why would I take it?" *You hate your mother.*

Carrie said, "I'll help you look for it, Mrs. Burke."

Mary didn't respond. "I can't find shit in this house." She picked up Rowan's denim jacket from the sofa and threw it to the floor. A bottle cap spilled from the breast pocket, and there, poking out of the pocket, was something pink. Something with strawberries, faded reds and greens visible through folded stationery.

Rowan shouted from upstairs, "Your brooch is in your jewelry box."

Millie the babysitter laughed—Mary presumed from something funny that someone had said on the telephone, but Millie was laughing at Mary.

Becca watched her mother pick up the strawberry note and slip it into her skirt pocket. Rowan descended the stairs dressed in a tweed blazer, white oxford shirt, and blue jeans. He held the purple brooch. Seeing Mary, he said, "With a closet full of clothes, you're wearing that?"

She looked down at her green pleated skirt and black boots. "I look nice."

"Let's go."

From the sofa Millie said, "Have fun."

Later, while Millie talked on the phone, Becca and Carrie ate popcorn and watched the *Late Night Friday Scarefest*. Becca showed Carrie her drawer of discarded watches. She said, "Sometimes I lose time—like, it should be five o'clock, but my watch says four forty-five, so I'm late, and it's not my fault. Every day I lose a little more time, and then the watch just stops. It's because of the lightning. No one cares. I get another watch."

"Your parents know?"

"My dad says it's something to do with the Communists. Did you see that note in my dad's pocket?"

"What note?"

"It looked like there were strawberries on it."

"I didn't see it."

"My mom took it."

"Whose note is it?"

"It was in my dad's pocket."

"She shouldn't have taken it if it wasn't hers." Carrie had that morality, that sensibility that Becca's parents lacked. Becca stuffed a handful of popcorn in her mouth. She didn't want to talk anymore.

Carrie was Becca's first love. She counted Carrie's eyelashes while she slept. She borrowed her striped tube socks. She asked a lot of questions, like "What did you do for your birthday last year?" to hear the sound of Carrie's voice. *Never stop talking to me.*

She told her mother, "Carrie is Sally, and I'm the girl with the naturally curly red hair. It's hard to believe Peppermint Patty's a girl, *sir*. Carrie thinks so too. Carrie thinks the Dallas Cowboys are the best football team in the world because of Tom Landry. She also likes the San Francisco 49ers, who have something to do with gold."

Becca's mother said, "Carrie sounds very smart."

"She is."

Despite their family differences (Carrie's parents were "blue collar"), the girls were, to quote Carrie's dad, "two peas in a pod," like "Martin and Lewis." The girls said, "More like Sonny and Cher."

Carrie's parents rented a bungalow close to campus, and before they'd even finished unpacking, Carrie was begging her parents to let her play soccer and take ballet. Becca, hopeful that Carrie's parents would say yes, stood at her side. They held hands.

Carrie's dad, Pete, said, "I can't be running you all over hell and creation."

Her mom said, "Your dad's right, Carrie. Pick one thing. We both work, and there's just not time. Pick one."

Carrie looked at Becca. "I don't know. What do you think?"

"Ballet. The clothes are better."

Carrie said, "Ballet," and squeezed Becca's hand. She squeezed back.

Her dad said, "I'm glad that's settled. Now go play in traffic."

All was fine and good with the Burkes and the Drinkwaters until the following March when talk of Chapel Hill's annual dance recital intensified. It was a big deal. There were sequined costumes and shoes and pictures to be bought. The Drinkwaters couldn't afford the costumes or the shoes. Carrie said, "My mom says a yellow sequined leotard is a waste. It's ridiculously expensive." Becca and Carrie sat at Mario's Pizzeria eating pizza bread—bigger than a regular slice and cheaper too. Carrie was explaining that she couldn't dance, not with how much everything cost; she was sorry, but she wasn't going to be able to participate in the recital. Becca was listening, feeling sorry for Carrie—who always worried about her parents' money situation—happy to get her school clothes from Goodwill or her nicer things from Kmart. Becca's clothes came from Bobbie's, which was more of a boutique, and locally owned. She shuddered at the thought of wearing someone else's discarded pants or sweaters. Becca was listening, waiting for her chance to say *Maybe my dad could help out* or *Maybe Mrs. Hogg has extra costumes?* when she spotted her dad through the restaurant's parted curtains. He was walking with the babysitter Millie, his fingers grazing the teen's forearm. Surely it meant nothing. But something, something warm and spreading in Becca's gut, told her otherwise.

"Are you going to finish that?" Carrie asked, pointing to Becca's pizza bread.

Becca stared at the black institution-style clock above the door. She saw the minute hand move two clicks counterclockwise. No one else saw.

Carrie said, "Are you upset because I can't dance in the recital?"

"No." The recital didn't mean anything in the larger scheme of things. Even at her age, Becca knew that. Feeling nauseated, she looked at Carrie. "Can we go?"

Carrie grabbed her book bag. "You didn't eat—"

"I don't want it."

Carrie snatched Becca's pizza bread off her plate. "Are you okay?"

"I'm okay." After all, her parents were simply going through a rough spot. She saw similar stories on *The Phil Donahue Show*. Certainly they wouldn't get divorced. Her dad said divorce was tacky. Things would get better.

Carrie danced that May.

Rowan saw to it. He thought the recital was important to Becca because it was important to him.

That April, he drove to Mrs. Drinkwater's office with the yellow sequined costume, the green tutu, and shoes for Carrie. Mrs. Drinkwater worked as an office assistant for Dr. Calhoun, a neurosurgeon. At three in the afternoon, she sat transcribing a recording of Dr. Calhoun's diagnosis of a twelve-year-old boy with a brain tumor. She typed wearing headphones. Professor Burke entered the office in jeans and a polo shirt.

Carrying two bags from Dance Girl, he was there to "save the day." Mrs. Drinkwater had barely gotten her headphones down around her neck when he swung the plastic bags onto her desk and said, "I'm really in a hurry, Belinda. These are for Carrie. So the girls can dance." He winked. He smiled.

She said, "I can't . . ." but he was gone. *Who the hell do you think you are?* Belinda Drinkwater did not like Rowan Burke.

What wasn't to like? Rowan would want to know. He was intelligent and handsome and soon he'd have tenure, and one day he'd buy that yacht. Come hell or high water, he'd find a way to regain the wealth the Burkes had lost.

He wasn't about to let Carrie Drinkwater drop out of the May recital. Not while he resided in Chapel Hill. Not while appearances mattered. If that little girl was his daughter's best friend, she would dance.

The recital was, as always, a success. Along with thirty other girls, Becca and Carrie, dressed like yellow tulips, dipping and twirling in first, second, and fifth positions, flitted across the stage.

After the recital, Mrs. Hogg curtsied onstage with an armful of jonquils. The crowd was on its feet, impressed with the performing eight- and nine-year-olds, their poise and pirouettes.

Becca's parents sat proudly in the front row. Belinda Drinkwater sat three rows back. Carrie's dad had to work late, which was actually a relief to Belinda, who didn't want him insulting Rowan Burke. She could imagine him saying, *Who the hell do you think you are, showing up at my wife's job? Do you think you're better than me? Because, Goddamn it, you're not! You're not better than me.* Chapel Hill was like no place the Drinkwaters had ever lived, and except for a handful of snobs, Belinda liked the town. It was charming—"beautified," the realtor said—a college town with safe schools and art venues. And amid this culture, the Drinkwaters were making ends meet.

After the seats had emptied, the cicadas screeching, the black trees seeming to close around the spotlighted girls in their sequins and bright tutus, the parents paced and chatted while the well-respected photographer posed their daughters for posterity.

The next week, Mary drove to Mrs. Hogg's school to pick up the ballet pictures she'd purchased. The photographer, known for his skill with shadow and light, was quoted as saying, "Pictures aren't necessarily about the subject but what surrounds that subject." This was never truer than at the Forest Theater, where the yearly recital was held. The long branches of the trees, although not visible in the pictures, were felt in the position and eyes of the ballerinas. For two decades, Wallace's photographs, documenting Chapel Hill's graceful ballerinas and genteel citizenry, lined the walls of a dozen downtown eateries and shops. Wallace, the gentry agreed, was a rare orchid among the window-boxed roses and daisies lining Franklin Street.

Mrs. Hogg, a stout woman with a squeaky voice, handed the envelope of Wallace's photographs to Mary.

Mrs. Hogg shuffled and straightened folders, walking back and forth to her metal file cabinet. "It was one of our greatest nights," she said. Mary slid the first eight-by-ten from the envelope, dropping her keys. As they clanked to the floor, Mrs. Hogg continued: "We couldn't have asked for better weather, and the girls danced divinely." In Wallace's photograph, Becca's head was crowned with an iridescent orange-and-yellow-tipped light. Mary's anticipation turned to irritation. She'd envisioned a portrait reflecting her daughter's grace and strength. "Look at this," she said, showing the eight-by-ten to Mrs. Hogg.

"I'm afraid they're all like that." Mrs. Hogg bent down for Mary's keys. Setting them on her desk, she said, "It's unusual."

Mary said, "Is it some kind of effect? Why did he do this? Are all the girls haloed? What was he thinking?"

"No," Mrs. Hogg interrupted. "All of *Becca's* pictures are like this. The other photographs are as splendid as ever." She took the photo from Mary. "I don't understand it. Neither did Wallace." Mrs. Hogg pulled eight more photographs from the packet, laying them out for Mary to see. "Here the light is reddish, but here it's rather blue." She pointed to another picture. "Most of the halos are yellow."

"There's something wrong with the film."

"You can call Wallace. He said that Becca was an anomaly. He wants to photograph her again."

Mary folded her arms at her waist, studying the pictures. Becca's toes were pointed, her hands in arabesque. She was a beautiful girl.

Mrs. Hogg opened the squeaking file cabinet. "My masseuse says it could be her aura. I don't know that I believe in such mumbo jumbo."

"I'm not paying for these." Mary tossed the envelope on Mrs. Hogg's desk and grabbed her keys.

"You've already paid for them, Mrs. Burke."

Mary crammed the envelope in her purse.

Mrs. Hogg said, "At least the orange light kind of matches her hair."

Mary drove home, the envelope in the passenger's seat, remembering Becca's assertion: "I was struck by lightning." She remembered Rowan countering, "If you were struck by lightning, you'd be dead." This disagreement had continued for weeks, with Rowan finally telling Becca, "Do not go around saying that you were hit by lightning or you're going to end up on a couch with a funny head doctor asking you how many times a day you go to the bathroom."

Mary tended to believe Becca's lightning story. What reason did she have to lie? Rowan asserted, "Giving credence to a preposterous story will only encourage further fabrication. Like you, she'll want to be a victim."

Mary reached into her purse, gripping the envelope. The strange light Wallace had photographed must be a result of the lightning strike. Maybe it was some sort of residual energy. Rowan would disagree. He'd say something like *You can take the girl (referring to Mary) out of Podunk, but you can't take the Podunk out of the girl.* He'd laugh at Mary's suggestion.

Driving home, she decided she'd keep the pictures in the bottom of her underwear drawer. Whenever Becca doubted herself, whether it was about the lightning or something else, she'd show them to her. *There's something very special about you*, she'd say. There was no reason for Rowan to see these photographs.

Victims report feeling an "other-worldliness" when struck.

Most surprising: 10% of lightning strike victims die, while just 50% seek medical attention.

. . . be on your best
behavior, 1967

The reverend leaned forward, his black boot on the sill of the Pitank's front door. "Reverend John Whitehouse." He shook Winter's hand.

"Evening."

Behind his grandmother, Buckley held an empty brown bowl cupped to his chest, a bent spoon protruding from his mouth.

"Good evening," said Abigail. The three Pitanks squeezed in the front hall. "Can we help you? Buckley, take the spoon out of your mouth."

Buckley bounced the spoon off his hip. "This is the reverend from that revival on Mrs. Catawall's land."

"Nice to meet you, Reverend."

"Call me John."

"Nice to meet you, John."

"I'm Buckley's grandmother, Winter Pitank."

He took her right hand, cupping it between his own two. "Buckley was helping me out tonight, and I got to thinking I should pay y'all a visit and see personally if you wouldn't be interested in joining us next Saturday. I hope I'm not calling too late. I saw the light on." He gestured to nothing in particular. "The flock's trying to build a church here in Mont Blanc. The tents get right drafty. I'm hoping the good Mrs. Catawall is going to donate a parcel of land. I told her that the Lord appreciates when those who can give, give generously." He handed a postcard-sized pamphlet to each woman that read, *The Holy Redeemer, a place where all are welcome regardless of denomination. Come and worshipp in the name of the Lord. Come All. Be Filled With the Spirit.*

"*Worship's* misspelled," Abigail said.

"Where?"

She held the pamphlet out for him to see.

"You're right. Awful glad you caught that." He laughed. "It looks to me like Buck's got two sisters."

"I don't go in for that kind of talk, Reverend," Winter said. "I'm an old woman."

"I don't lie."

"You most certainly do."

"All God's children are beautiful." He bowed his head, looking up, his eyes dark and piercing. "As you are eternally young to the Lord, you are the same to me."

Winter said, "That's a nice thought."

Buckley feared the reverend was going to mention the two dollars he'd rightfully earned, but instead the man pulled three gold foiled chocolates from his coat pocket and held them in his palm. He bowed his head once more. "I'm sure I've seen you ladies at services before, but I certainly do hope to see you again Saturday with Buck."

Winter said, "Thank you for the invitation, but we're terribly busy."

"No one's too busy to know God." He pointed to the candies in his palm. "It's chocolate and toffee from Hershey, Pennsylvania, where I spent time spreading His word. It's an indulgence of mine, this sweet tooth."

Abigail and Winter took their toffees, but Buckley left his gold foiled candy in the reverend's palm. Reverend Whitehouse slipped it back in his suit pocket. "It was a pleasure," he said. Winter held the screen door open and the reverend descended the steps. "I'm sure you know already, but five o'clock on Saturday, and nine on Sunday."

"Thank you," Abigail said. She unwrapped the gold foil.

Winter said, "We'll try."

"Bye, Buck."

"Bye, sir."

The screen door clacked shut. "What's wrong with you?" Winter said to Buckley. "That man offered you a candy. You say no thank you if you don't want it. You don't just leave it in his hand. You're ungrateful."

As the reverend drove away from the Pitanks', Buckley set his empty bowl on the kitchen counter. He wasn't hungry anymore. He was mad. He pulled one of his Sears and Roebuck cowboy boots off and flung it against a bottom kitchen cabinet. He threw the other one thumping against the cabinet and waited for his grandmother to shout at him. Instead, the metallic pipes shuddered and squeaked. She was already running water for her bath.

That same night, he asked his mother, "Why are there blind people and deaf people if there's a god? Why would God do that to someone?"

His mother said, "I think *Perry Mason* is on."

Buckley changed the TV station.

Abigail said, "If you read Job, it's to test a person's faith, but that's Old Testament. I think more likely it's to work miracles through people, to show what they can do in spite of their setbacks." She clicked on her table lamp. "We've got a Bible, Buckley." She pivoted in the recliner. "Somewhere."

That night, Buckley found the King James Bible stacked under a pile of old phone books. He took the Bible to bed and read the book of Job, but he still didn't understand. There was something very wrong with this god and with Job. This god was petty. This god wagered on a man's life as if it didn't matter. Buckley didn't think the reverend's and Job's god was his god. He placed his two dollars in the Bible and slid the book under his bed.

The Pitanks did not go to the Holy Redeemer revival on Saturday or on Sunday, but in a month's time the reverend came back to them to tell them that work was under way to erect God's own house.

Abigail, who had always been leery of preachers, instinctually thought to turn this preacher man away, but she had recently been to see Buckley's teacher. At the teacher's request, she had gone to the five-room clapboard school, where she could not sit down because the chairs were too small. She had heard her own heavy breathing trapped within the thin walls, the concrete floor, and the low ceiling.

The skinny Miss Johnson was holding detention. Two boys, both Buckley's age, but neither of them resembling her pale, wide-hipped son, were washing Miss Johnson's faded chalkboard. They dipped their foamy yellow sponges in a bucket of gray water as Miss Johnson, sitting in a student's desk, insisted that a male influence was what Buckley needed. She said, "He needs a father figure. Plain and simple." Abigail did not agree, but she didn't speak up either. She would do whatever was necessary to help Buckley grow up to be a good man. *Teacher knows best.*

Of course, Miss Johnson had no children of her own and only one degree in home economics with a minor in art history from a rural women's college in Mississippi. Abigail did not know that Miss Johnson had every intention of leaving teaching after she was married.

So, at his mother's urging, Buckley helped the reverend pick up trash on Saturday nights and Sunday afternoons, and Abigail promised herself and Reverend Whitehouse that she would attend the Holy Redeemer services after the real church was finished, and thus, Abigail, Winter, and Buckley got to know the reverend.

Part of getting to know Reverend John Whitehouse was getting to know what he liked to eat, which included pork chops and buttered corn on the cob, fried chicken and macaroni and cheese, deviled eggs sprinkled with paprika, cornbread, biscuits with thick, heavily salted slabs of ham, Vienna sausages, iced oatmeal cookies, cherry Kool-Aid, white rolls, the number-five-dyed red sausages you fish from a jar with your fingers, fried bologna, meat loaf made with six eggs and a half a bottle of ketchup, tuna fish sandwiches with Miracle Whip and relish, homemade apple pie, and green bean casserole made with Campbell's cream of mushroom soup. He didn't care for lettuce or fresh vegetables or any other kind of pie but apple.

The reverend slept, snoring, his right foot in spasm, on the Pitanks' sofa after Sunday dinner. Buckley saw his bumpy zucchini nose growing bigger and bumpier with each Sunday meal. There had been four in a row now. The reverend's right foot jerked and fell, jerked and fell on the arm of the sofa.

Excerpt from
THE HANDBOOK FOR LIGHTNING STRIKE SURVIVORS

Danny Jones, pitcher for the Jolly Indians, stood under a tree with the rest of his team waiting out a rain delay when lightning struck the tree. Danny and his teammates were rushed to the emergency room. Danny remained conscious, saying, "It felt like a train hit me. Everything was white and loud." For two days, Danny was numb from the waist down. Skipper McAdams and Jackson Feeley died.

Danny, in addition to suffering anxiety, also suffers survivor's guilt.

According to Danny, "We [he and his former teammates] don't talk about what happened. We just can't."

5

My mother's father, 1978

Becca

Becca's mother, Mary, drummed her fingers on the table. She didn't like fried chicken, so of course her mother, Edna Wickle, had fried chicken for dinner. Mary didn't want to be here, but Edna had telephoned and said, "I'd like you to come home. I think if you talk to your sister, it'll make a difference. Plus, I'm getting up there in years. I'd like to see my granddaughter."

Mary's younger sister, Claire, was depressed and fat.

Her father used to say, "You're lucky, Mary. You have a nice figure. Not like Claire." He somehow thought things between them were good and normal, while every day Mary imagined the horses trampling him, an accidental shooting, a tractor mishap.

There was a scar on her lower back—the imprint of his belt buckle.

"I think if you talk to Claire, she'll listen. She admires you."

He lost his head. He didn't mean it. That's what her mother had said.

Now Edna wiped the countertop with a dishrag and opened the freezer. "Do you think Becca will want strawberry or vanilla?"

Mary brushed a few crumbs from the table into her palm.

"I've always liked strawberry," Edna said.

"Are you even going to ask how I'm doing?"

"How are you?"

"Rowe's in the garage most nights." Mary tossed the crumbs in the trash.

"Becca's not allergic to strawberry, is she? My aunt Lucille was allergic. It could run in the family. I hear a good many people have strawberry allergies. I can't imagine."

"You're not listening."

"No, Mary. I hear you. Your husband spends a lot of time in the garage." Edna shut the freezer. "He likes cars, right? Fancy cars?"

"Right."

"And I asked you: What do you think I should do about Claire? She's my daughter who lives here with me, and she's very sad."

"I think Claire's depressed because you let Dad treat us like dogs. She fell in love with that idiot Tom because he's worthless like Dad was."

Edna opened the freezer again. "I guess Becca could have strawberry *and* vanilla."

"Mom!"

Edna thought that Mary's confrontations were annoying. "And your husband spends his time in the garage because of your father? Why do you do this, Mary?"

"Because he was a bastard and you didn't do anything."

"Your father wasn't perfect, but he never claimed to be. Is Rowan? Men aren't angels, Mary. Strawberry or vanilla?" Edna set two half-gallons of ice cream on the table. "I don't have chocolate. I can't stand it. You ought to try talking to Claire in the morning. Be subtle, I think. She's better-spirited in the morning."

"Why didn't you stop Dad?"

Edna put her hands on her hips and faced Mary. "I didn't know you were coming home for this. Your father's buried. You can't blame him for *your* life. You'd think with all that schooling you'd know that."

"Dad was a bastard. That's what's wrong with Claire."

"How long has your father been dead? I haven't seen you in four years!"

"Six!"

Edna put the vanilla and strawberry back in the freezer. "See that Becca gets some ice cream. I'm going to bed." She was tired, and there wasn't time for regret. Since her husband passed, her story had changed. She prayed every morning and played the organ at church. She believed that a kitchen should be the center of things, and kept busy canning and cooking for church dinners and invalids. She'd long ago left the bigger upstairs kitchen to the cobwebs. *It's not functional.* She slept in a room adjoining the basement kitchen. There was hardly reason to go upstairs these days. Too many rooms to clean.

On his deathbed, fearing God, her husband, Clayton Wickle, had said, "I was tough on the girls because I wanted them to be tough. The world's not an easy place." He'd had good intentions. Still, he'd been wrong—the way he treated them was wrong. Flinging that stupid belt around. Bullying Mary. Neither of his daughters was tough. If anything, they were weak. Always desperate and pleading, the two of them. Poor Mary couldn't let the past go. If only she understood how short life is.

Edna left Mary and Mary's resentment in the kitchen. She shouldn't have asked her to come home. Still, she'd wanted to know her only grandchild, and she was short on time. Tomorrow she'd talk to Mary. She'd try again to tell her daughter, *I love you. Please stop blaming me for what your father did. We did the best we could.* Edna wanted resolution. She wanted peace. It was the Lord's way. It was her way.

She went to bed to dream. Nearly every night now for weeks, she dreamed of her own mother, young and beautiful, and in the dream Edna was a girl, and she could smell lavender. Her mother had always kept satchels of dried lavender in the folded laundry. When Edna woke, she caught whiffs of lavender. She was sleeping more and more.

Mary didn't want Becca fat. She didn't offer her strawberry or vanilla. Instead she went to bed on a cot in the basement den.

Attached to the kitchen, the room smelled like fried chicken. There was a low ceiling with exposed wood beams, and a brick floor. Except for Claire's bedroom, the upstairs rooms were shut up. After her father's death, her mother moved into the basement where the farmhands and Willis, her mother's domestic helper, had slept. Willis used to say, "I'm nobody's maid. I'm a cook and a dishwasher." She'd worked for them three days a week, eight a.m. to six p.m., before going to bed in the same room where Edna now slept. Mary felt sick being here. She wished she'd never brought Becca to Prospect, Virginia. The sooner the days passed, the sooner she'd be driving home to Chapel Hill. She closed her eyes, desperate for sleep, picturing her old brown work boots worn thin at the ankles, heels touching, just inside the main door upstairs. She remembered stuffing her socks inside and tiptoeing to her bedroom. Always trying to be invisible.

She remembered the feel of her bare toes on the cold floor; hanging her winter coat with the soiled black sleeves on the pine rack her father made. Sometimes the coat dropped to the floor in a foul-smelling heap and she wanted to leave it right there, but she'd bend down to pick it up. She remembered being afraid. He would yell, "Girl, what are you up to?"

Don't think about it, Mary, she thought. *There's no one yelling anything anymore. There's only the whisper of Claire's TV.* But her mind wouldn't listen: *If there's a hell, I hope he's rotting there. I hope he's suffering.* Mary's rage kept her up most of the night.

At nearly nine o'clock, the sun was only now setting. Becca kissed her grandma's dog, Bo, on the nose. "Good night."

The house was quiet; everyone in bed. Becca went to her grandma's room and undressed quickly. She hadn't expected to like her mother's mother, having heard from her father that Edna was "a simpleton," and "a real pain in the rear," but Grandma Edna was hard not to like. Becca pulled the covers back and climbed into the twin bed across from her grandma's. According to her mother, a long time ago slaves had slept in this room. The room had a dank smell. The plaster walls were lumpy and the exposed bricks were faded and nicked. Grandma Edna was talking in her sleep! She was so different from Becca's other grandmother. Neither woman, she knew, had attended her mom and dad's wedding. *People are stupid.*

Becca felt sorry for Aunt Claire, who was sad and fat, reminding Becca of the ladies she saw at the Piggly Wiggly, their hair in pink curlers, their carts full of Twinkies and potato chips. It was hard to believe her mother and Aunt Claire were related. Aunt Claire was the kind of woman who disgusted Becca's dad. He said that fat people had no excuse. "Stop eating cheeseburgers."

Upstairs, Claire watched an episode of *The Love Boat*. She tried calling her ex-boyfriend Tom twenty-six times (using a rotary phone). His line was busy.

Carlos Lemon, ten years old, was struck while riding his bike. CPR was administered by paramedics, but there was no heartbeat. A shot of epinephrine was administered. After twenty minutes, his heart resumed beating and he breathed on his own.

Carlos does not remember his time in the hospital, riding his bike, or being struck. For eight days, he did not speak. After one month, he resumed his life before the strike. The local newspaper called Carlos's survival "a miracle." I tend to agree.

My mother's father, 1967

Buckley

"I had this key lime skirt I had to be careful not to get dirty, which was hard."

Buckley said, "Was Winter nicer back then?"

"No. Mama was never a warm person. I told you: I was Daddy's girl."

"Did Winter yell and scream when you were a kid?"

"Yep. She's always been a screamer. When Daddy was alive, he'd ignore her when she got uppity like that. He'd tell a joke to make me laugh, which would only infuriate Mama. She'd keep screaming about whatever had upset her. It could be anything: if you left a sock on the floor or if you forgot to ask to be excused from the table. She yelled about everything, and this one time Daddy and I were ignoring her, and Daddy was telling silly knock-knock jokes he memorized out of this children's book, and Mama got so hot, she exploded. She cried. Mama never cried. That's why we called it an explosion. She cried and cried, carrying on that no one loved her—not her husband, not her one and only daughter, who she'd brought into the world. If it'd been up to me, I would've let her cry. I would've kept ignoring her. I thought it was good to see her boo-hoo. Daddy stopped telling jokes and went to her then, calling her Winnie, a nickname he had for her. I was Abby, the apple of his eye." Tears welled in Abigail's eyes. "I don't know why he married Mama. She was never kind to him, and he was kind to everyone. He'd give the shirt off his back.

Every person in Mont Blanc owed him for some favor, but he never wanted payback for anything. He wanted people to be happy. I remember when the old train tunnel at Beckett collapsed; Daddy worked alongside the volunteer firefighters digging for two days just in case there was someone trapped inside. They found someone: a little boy. There was a picture of Daddy holding his dead body. The boy's parents brought a peach pie to our house. Being too sad to eat, they wanted us to have it. It's funny how when people die everyone brings food, and no one can stomach eating. Daddy didn't eat for four days."

"You ought to tell Winter to move out and get her own place."

"She's my mother, Buckley. You don't tell your mother to get out. Would you throw me out?"

"Of course not." He rested his head on her lap. "But you're not like her."

"Well, that's true."

"Tell me about my dad." He never stopped trying.

"I can't."

He sat up. "Why not? You knew your father. Why can't I know mine?"

"He's not worth knowing."

"I can be the judge."

"No, Buckley, you can't." Her voice faltered. Buckley couldn't mention his father without her falling apart. "Listen," she said, "I've told you before and I'll tell you again: when you're older, I'll explain and tell you who he is, but not now, because you can't be the judge. Not yet. You're too young." She pulled his head back to her lap, twirling her fingers in his thick hair. Her black hair, slick and plentiful, fell, tickling his cheek.

"Tell me more stories about your dad."

"I'm sleepy." She ran her fingers through Buckley's locks, knowing that he too was tired. It'd been a long day. Mont Blanc was too hot and too dusty, and they'd spent the morning scrubbing the dust off the cinder blocks and porch. *What kind of person asks you to scrub cinder blocks? Winter Pitank.*

Even though she was just twenty-five, Abigail knew that Buckley would be her only child. (No man wanted her, and she didn't want any man.) She wanted Buckley to be *good,* something he was born to.

When she remembered her own childhood—at least when she thought of her father—that's what she remembered: goodness. Her father said, "Who's the best little girl in the world?"

"Who?" she'd play.

"Well, I do believe it's Miss Abigail Pitank."

She'd coyly ask, "Do you really think so?" If she was within his reach, he'd hold her by the wrists, kissing both cheeks until she giggled hysterically.

Another reason that she would not have more children was her mother. There was too great a chance that her next child could be born with a disposition similar to Winter's. As it was now, Abigail detected her father and herself in Buckley, but more and more she saw Buckley separate from them, from every Pitank, becoming his own person.

Closing her eyes, she remembered the key lime skirt she'd worn to Ida's Luncheonette on Saturdays. She'd seen that skirt in a storefront on Main Street. She'd admired it. She didn't *need* it, but her dad told Winter to buy it.

"With *what* money?" Winter had complained.

"The laundry money."

"That's *my* money."

"It's ours. Buy Abby that skirt."

"I'm not buying it."

"Use my check." It was her father's money from the army.

Winter said, "And groceries will magically appear how?"

Winter did not buy the skirt, but Abigail's father acquired it through an exchange. Mrs. Madison, the store's owner, needed a fence built, and Mr. Pitank needed an expensive key lime skirt for his daughter. Mrs. Madison, knowing a fence required post digging, which is hard work, threw in a pair of key lime shoes and a polka-dot blouse. Abigail was in heaven, and her dad never told her how he got the skirt. Only after his death did Winter throw the story in her face. "Your father spoiled you. He let you take advantage of him. The man worked like a dog so you could have some stupid skirt. He was in no shape to build a fence."

Abigail knew what her father would say: *Don't listen to her*. And she didn't. She couldn't. It's funny how there are times when a girl gets knocked down and she thinks she'll never get up again, but she gets up quicker and stronger, and she survives things she couldn't have imagined surviving.

Abigail, grinning, wore her hair in pigtails. Holding the door to Ida's Luncheonette open, her dad grinned too, even letting the gap between his front teeth show.

Taking a seat at one of Ida's booths, Joe Pitank told Ida, "It seems only fitting that we have two slices of key lime pie and—"

Abigail interrupted him. "Two limeades."

"You took the words right out of my mouth."

Ida said, "Very nice. What's the occasion?" She brushed her hand against the lapel of Joe Pitank's suit.

"We're sharp, ain't we?" he said.

"I'll say."

"Abigail got new threads." In her white gloves, Abigail twirled for Ida to admire her outfit.

"You look very pretty."

She blushed. "Thank you!"

"Two limeades and two slices of pie coming right up."

Winter was home doing other people's laundry.

Winter was always doing laundry, and she was always nagging Joe: "You need to get a job. You need to get off your behind and put a decent meal on the table. You need to stop babying that girl. You need to teach her to respect her elders."

Abigail didn't know that there was anything wrong with her father until after he died, when Winter confessed to the town of Mont Blanc that Joe had been a shell and not a man. "Why do you think there's just Abigail? The man lived with demons. He got up with them and he went to bed with them. He couldn't hold a job, and he wasn't a proper husband to me."

Until her father died, when his burial was paid for by the county and there was no proper funeral, just a gathering on the scarce brown lawn outside their cinder-block house, Abigail didn't know that a man could go to war for his country and come home but still have the war with him. She heard her neighbors say that he was addicted to painkillers. She heard them say that he was depressed. He'd never recovered from his demons. Abigail imagined monsters walking the earth. The neighbors said, "Joe Pitank mistreated his family."

This awful man was not the man Abigail knew.

No one seemed to notice her that hot June day, watching her mother tug at the breast of her black sleeveless shirt. She was sweating. They were all sweating. Despite the occasion, only a few women wore stockings. It was just too hot. Abigail was thirteen. She sat in the dirt, waiting for the day to end. When it was dark it'd be cooler, and maybe her dad would come see her. Maybe she'd wake up tomorrow and he'd be home, and her mother would be dead in his place. *Don't ever think such things.* Her father would be disappointed.

Normally someone would've told her to get out of the dirt. Not today. Except for when her mom's friend Violet offered her a piece of cake, Abigail was invisible. They all said his death was unbearable for poor Winter—left practically penniless with a child. If it weren't for the army check, the Pitanks would be on welfare like the Negroes. Other mourners, including Abigail's mother, whispered that as awful as it was, it might be for the best. Joe Pitank was a sick man. Now he could rest.

Abigail needed reassurance from her dad. Days and weeks passed slowly, miserably, and then years. Abigail's father sent no word from his grave. She often thought that if it weren't for Buckley, she'd get herself addicted to some kind of painkiller. She remembered her father as happy and soft-spoken. She remembered his kisses. She was lucky to have known him.

Buckley slept, his head on his mother's lap. Abigail, hearing the Reverend Whitehouse at the front door speaking to Winter, set down her hairbrush and shifted to rise from the bed. There was something unsettling about that man. He was certainly no Joe Pitank. And what did he want with her family?

Victims may suffer symptoms similar to shell-shock, recently named post-traumatic stress disorder, turning to narcotics and other drugs to cope with their fears.

This disorder is most likely due to the trauma of being struck, but there is also a suggestion that the brain has been altered by exposure to high volts of electricity, rewiring the body to reexperience the event through flashbacks and irrational fears.

7

Ashes to ashes, 1978

Grandma Edna told bizarre stories with punch lines only Grandma Edna understood. Becca thought she might be senile, but Becca's mom said, "She's always been that way. I've never understood half of what she says."

"It's funny," Becca said.

This morning, Grandma Edna climbed into Becca's bed. She said, "I don't know what I'm going to do."

"About what?"

"My doctor. The medical profession is some kind of racket." Grandma Edna told Becca that she was thinking of leaving her local Prospect doctor because she had to wait too long. "It's me and the coloreds sitting there. I think the young people are treating old people like coloreds now. Like I've got nothing better to do. It'd be easy enough driving to Farmville to see a doctor there, but no one will let me."

"Why not?"

"Good question. I guess they think I'm too old. They're all full of it." Grandma Edna's dog, Bo, a half-blind Labrador mix, slunk into the room. Grandma Edna shooed him. "Get out of here!"

Becca looked at her grandmother's wrinkled face. There was something pretty about it. "Can I draw you?"

"Draw my picture?"

Becca nodded.

"No one told me you were an artist."

"I am."

"Smart and creative. I should've known."

Becca retrieved her sketchbook.

"I should change into something nice."

"I like your nightgown. Just stay there."

As Becca sketched her grandma, Edna told a long, nonsensical story with an eccentric cast of characters, speaking as if Becca had a history with each person, including Aubrey, "a sailor and fisherman, bird-watcher, dog lover, with eyes like pennies, big and round, who says 'Jesus' every other word, like he doesn't know what it means to take the Lord's name in vain, and he died of lung cancer, breaking Marianne's heart, who's a fine baker, but a terrible cook. I doubt she can boil water. She married Dr. Carl. He's not a real doctor. He's the kind of fellow who says 'How did that make you feel?,' wanting to know what you dreamed and if you got along with your mother. Dr. Carl is good enough for Marianne. Hell, it's hard to find a man alive over sixty anymore. He would've been good enough for me." As Becca finished her drawing, Grandma Edna finished her story. Taking the sketchbook from Becca's hands, she said, "Can I keep it? Could I?"

For Becca, that was the greatest compliment. She knew it wasn't her best rendering. She'd used a stick of charcoal, focusing on the lines in her grandmother's face, on the crow's-feet around the eyes. Her grandma's face was like her stories, the lines branching in a hundred directions, disconnected.

"Can I play with the dog?"

"You can play with that mutt to your heart's content. I'd let you take him home with you, but he's no city dog. He's used to country, like me."

Getting dressed, Becca said, "Did Mom tell you I got struck by lightning?"

"No. What's that do to you?"

"It makes you special."

"That's obvious."

"Thanks, Grandma."

"For what?"

"Believing me."

"Don't be ridiculous. Of course I believe you."

Her grandma's farm was big: a green lawn surrounded by bluebells, stinging nettles, and wild berries enclosed in barbed wire. Beyond the wire, the land sloped to a pasture where horses grazed. Becca held on to a fence post, looking out at the green mountains, dizzying in the distance. To the west she saw an old silo and barn bulging with hay.

All day into night, she played with the mutt Bo. When darkness fell, she and the old dog had a parade with fireflies. Becca thought the fireflies were drawn to her because she'd been struck by lightning. Bo played every animal, from Clydesdale to elephant, and every performer, from drum major to baton twirler, while Becca was the grand marshal. Grandma Edna came outside with a mason jar ("So you can catch one") but Becca left the jar in the grass. She didn't want to trap the fireflies' light—like putting them in prison. They might not like her anymore if she did.

After the fireflies had gone to wherever they go when it gets really dark, Becca and Bo settled beneath an oak, his snout on her thigh. She told him about the note she swiped from her mother's jewelry box. "It's not a big deal, except that it says 'Rowe.' That's my dad's nickname. His mother called him that." Bo grunted as though he understood.

THE STRAWBERRY NOTE:

Rowe,

I'll be a half hour late.

Patty

"It's nothing really," she told Bo, "but I wanted to read it. Carrie says that no one should read another person's private letters, but I wonder if that's true when the other person is your husband."

Understandably, Bo had no comment.

Becca said, "I have the letter now."

The next day, Becca and Grandma Edna heard Mary scream. Becca said, "What was that?" They were in Grandma Edna's bedroom. The scream came from upstairs. Becca led Edna up the rickety basement steps to the dining room. The heavy red curtains were ripped from their hooks. The room filled with sunlight, making it hard to see.

Mary looked up at the young Becca and the old Edna. "I think she's overdosed. Call an ambulance!" Claire sat listless, wrapped in one of the drapes, dust particles rising into the summer light.

At Farmville General, the hospital people in mint green scrubs measured from Aunt Claire's nose to her ear, from her ear to her breastbone. They marked a tube and guided it through her nostril, farther and farther, and they ordered, "Swallow. Don't fight this."

Aunt Claire gagged and choked. She fought. "Go on and swallow," they said. They slid a syringe into the end of the tube and plunged something down the line. They said, "You're doing just fine." With another syringe, they drew fluid out. There was another syringe and another, and Aunt Claire coughed. She jerked right and left, shaking the gurney and spattering chalky vomit onto a male nurse and the institutional tile. She cried. Then, soon after, she was quiet.

Becca was there, invisible to the nurses and doctor, her back pressed against the wall, one hand covering her mouth. She wasn't scared exactly. She was shocked at the physicality, the force it took, to empty someone's stomach. She felt nauseated, like she might never eat again.

Grandma Edna and Becca's mother were in the waiting room, filling out paperwork. They'd misplaced Becca, who was down the corridor in a curtained room, waving to Claire, who'd been wheeled down the hall to some new place with an institutional floor and the smell of disinfectant. There was a man mopping the vomit. There were two nurses dropping tubing and syringes into stainless-steel boxes marked with skulls and crossbones.

Despite Becca's wild red hair and Holly Hobbie shirt and matching jeans, no one saw her. She listened as one of the nurses, the skinnier of the two, said, "She's going to be fine. She's lucky she has some meat on her bones. Her metabolism saved her life. Not like this case I worked in Arkansas, in this little town, Mont Blanc. You wouldn't have heard of it. There was this girl, a bean-pole, with black hair and doe eyes. She was such a pretty thing. A young girl with so much potential. I still remember her name: Clementine. She shook me up. I wondered if I was in the wrong profession. Anyway, this poor girl was basically homeless, living in this god-awful commune, Drop Out City. Some people never give up trying to die. She was one of them."

The nurses spotted Becca. "You're not supposed to be in here."

"I'm lost."

"The waiting room's down there."

The other nurse said, "I need a smoke."

Becca left to find her mother and grandma, to tell them that Claire would be okay—at least for now. She hoped that Claire wasn't one of those girls who'd never give up trying to die.

That night the wind gusted. It rattled the chairs on the side porch and knocked a wind chime to the concrete. The rain came in spurts. Bo whined outside and pawed at the screen of the basement window. Grandma Edna shut the window and went back to her bedroom to watch TV.

Becca went upstairs and watched the storm through the curtainless dining room windows. She was sweating badly, and as the thunder grew louder, she worried that the lightning had come for her. Was that possible? She needed Bo. She needed him safe.

The lightning lit the mountains a soft purple and split the sky in two. Becca's hands were clammy and cold. She wiped the sweat from her lip and moved a few feet back from the window. There had been thunderstorms and lightning since the day she was struck, but nothing like this. With a sharp cracking sound, the lightning parted the sky, illuminating the barbed-wire fence in the distance.

The front door to the farmhouse had double doors and required a skeleton key. She needed that key. Becca found her mother in the abandoned kitchen, reading a book. She said, "Mom, I need your help."

"I love a good thunderstorm," she said, "though I know you're not a big fan." Her mother put down the book. "Aunt Claire's going to be all right, Becca. Don't worry. Everything's going to be fine." Mary seemed gleeful sitting in an old recliner with her calves tucked under her thighs. Now it was clear that Aunt Claire was the crazy one. Not her. She continued: "Claire will need someone to talk to, a therapist . . . what your dad calls a head doctor. But that's nothing to be ashamed of. It doesn't mean that she's weak-minded. Not really." Mary smiled. "It's understandable, when you think about it, considering she's a grown woman still living with her mother in the middle of nowhere with no job."

Becca had other concerns. "Do you know where the key that unlocks the front door is?"

"Why?"

"I don't know."

Mary rolled her eyes and picked up her book.

"Because Bo needs to come inside."

"Bo will be fine, Becca. He's weathered plenty of storms." Mary turned the page.

"No. He's not safe. I can feel it."

"I'm trying to read, honey. Find something to do."

"Mom, please."

"Bo can't come inside, Becca. Your grandma doesn't want a wet dog in her house, not even in her basement kitchen."

"But I've seen him in the house."

"On rare occasions. He's an outside dog, a country dog."

"Please, Mom. Please."

Mary sighed. "All right." She set down her book.

Becca followed her mother to the library, where Mary pulled a skeleton key off a gold hook. Mary said, "If your grandmother asks, I had nothing to do with this." Mary unlocked the double doors where the pine coat rack once stood—where her work boots had once rested. She hated this place.

No one used this main door anymore, and when Mary pushed the one door open, there was a loud sucking noise. Mother and daughter stood in the cramped doorway, Becca calling for Bo, the rain beating down. She walked out onto the covered porch to look for him. "Maybe he's still by the kitchen window." The wind gusted and swirled, lifting a pointed holly leaf off the porch. She called his name again: nothing. "Come on, Bo. Come on."

"He's got sense, Becca. He's probably under the house or under a tree or something."

Becca paced the porch. The bursts of rain blew sideways, sprinkling her shirt. "Bo!" Lightning touched down across the yard, and she spotted Bo heading their way. "Good boy. Here he comes." Her mother patted the pockets of her jeans, feeling for her lighter.

As Mary turned the lighter's flint, thunder exploded and the black sky flared white. Becca did not see the lightning clobber his head, but as she rushed toward Bo in that second of white stillness, never pausing, not suspended this time, not in shock this time, refusing to lose time *again,* she knew he was hit. Her mother was fixed on the porch, leaning with her shoulder against a column, the lighter in her right hand, an unlit cigarette dangling from her mouth. How could this have happened? Bo's fur sizzled in spots. His skull was split open and blood trickled over his left eye onto his nose. Becca touched his wet nose, soft and cool despite the steam rising from his burned body. Becca, struggling to breathe, lay on top of him. The heat from his fur blackened her T-shirt. She saw one of his paws twitch. She tried lifting him, to carry him inside where it was dry and he might live, but she couldn't. He wouldn't budge. She covered him with her body, protecting him from the new burst of rain and exploding light. Holding him, wishing he would live.

Becca's mother grabbed Becca from behind, sliding her hands under Becca's arms, pulling her off the dog. Becca hung like a puppet in her mother's arms. Her shirt was splotched with blood and smelled of burnt hair. Her mother said, "Walk. There's nothing we can do. Walk!" Becca wouldn't walk, and only ten feet from Bo's burned body, her mother dropped Becca on the wet grass. She couldn't carry her any farther.

Becca crawled back through the rain to Bo. "Don't die." She knew he was gone, but she still hoped for a miracle.

Her mother ran for the house. "Mom, I need your help! Mom!"

Becca felt the old woman's hand on her back. The rain beating down. The old woman's hand so unlike the feel of the lifeless, the dead. The old woman's hand so unlike the feel of electricity moving through arms and legs. "Come on," Grandma Edna said. "It's time to go inside."

Becca looked up, the rain striking her face. "I killed Bo."

"Oh, sugar," Grandma Edna said. "You didn't kill Bo. No one killed Bo. The Lord took him from us."

Becca rose from the ground. "We can't just leave him out here."

"We won't," Grandma Edna said. "I'll get the wheelbarrow and we'll make sure he has a burial that befits him."

Becca grudgingly obeyed, sobbing as she left Bo in the grass, beneath black skies and pouring rain.

Later that night, sitting in the bathtub, rubbing a bar of Safeguard on her knees, washing away the caked dirt and dried blood, Becca thought about Aunt Claire—trying to kill herself when life is so precious; when zap, in an instant, someone can die. She thought, *I will never be like Aunt Claire.*

Old Man John, who lived in one of the trailers up the road, "a good colored man," according to Grandma Edna, dug a grave for Bo. Becca chose the spot—close to the barbed wire, where Bo could look out and see the mountains. Old Man John wrapped Bo in a sheet, and Becca snuck an Oscar Mayer hot dog from the refrigerator. She gave it to Old Man John to stash inside the sheet. The four Wickle women along with Old Man John held a service early in the morning. Becca said, "Ashes to ashes, dust to dust, we'll miss you," and Mary thought, *Ashes to ashes, funk to funky, we know Major Tom's a junkie.* Claire wondered if the love of her life, Tom, knew she had tried to commit suicide. She wondered if he'd call. Grandma Edna envied the youth all around her and thought, *Goodbye, Bo. You were a good and loyal dog. I think that's Clayton's favorite sheet. God rest that SOB.* Edna clutched the handkerchief her mother had given her on her wedding day. Mary decided she'd buy Becca a dog to make up for all this death, and Old Man John, who stood a few feet back because he didn't know Bo all that well, thought about his own dog, Sadie, who was getting up there in years. He thought about one day having to dig Sadie's grave and then dismissed those awful thoughts. Instead, he remembered that he had to replace one of his gutters that'd gotten knocked loose in the storm. He'd start on that gutter first thing.

Grandma Edna sat in a straight-backed chair, pulling green beans from a paper bag. "Your mom's in the den."

Reaching into the bag, Becca took a seat.

The kitchen was cool, a breeze blowing through the tiny window above the sink. Becca said, "I miss Bo."

"Me too. He was old like me, you know. He had a good long life. He used to sleep right outside that window with his head on his paw. I can still see him there. That's the funny thing about memory." Grandma Edna's narrow shoulders were hunched, her bright silver hair lit up like tinsel by the spot of morning sun that seeped through the cinder-block-sized window. She wore blue polyester slacks and a matching shirt.

Becca said, "My mom has bad memories."

Grandma Edna changed the subject as she was apt to do— quickly. She said, "Marianne Pamplin brought the worst potato salad you've ever tasted to the church dinner last Wednesday. I expected the reverend to eat it, but dear Lord, they all ate it. Everybody went on and on about the stuff and how delicious it was." Grandma Edna laughed. "The poor dear has no idea how bad it is. I told them, the lot of 'em, that they shouldn't have gone on so about it, not with how awful it tasted. Not with them being in God's house." Grandma Edna wiped two tears from her high cheekbones. "I'll be," she said, having brought herself to hysterics.

"Which one is she?" Becca asked.

"She's Marianne."

They snapped the tips off the beans, dropping them in the colander. Grandma Edna told stories about more people Becca didn't know. She talked about a man named Freddie. Blond and blue-eyed, he was tan from working in the sun. "He worked for the Civilian Conservation Corps. He built the cabins and trails at

Twin Lakes. One night, he showed up here. Clayton was in Norfolk."

Grandma Edna never referenced time when she spoke, which made her stories even more confusing. Becca said, "And what happened?"

"Nothing. We ate what I had: snaps, cured ham, and biscuits. Lord, he was a fine-looking man. Hardworking too; he smelled like the earth. Spent enough days digging in the dirt." Grandma Edna seemed far away. "I let him clean up. Just as times were different then, people were different too. I guess we rise or sink according to our times."

"Are we still talking about Freddie?"

Grandma Edna popped a bean into her mouth. "His hair was the color of sand."

Becca felt the smoothness of the bean between her fingers. "And we're still talking about Freddie?"

"We are."

Becca said, "Can I show you a trick?"

"I don't see why not."

"I need your watch."

Grandma Edna got her timepiece from the sink's edge and handed it to Becca, who slipped the braided watch onto her wrist.

"Don't break my watch!"

"I'm not." She said, "Just wait. Watch the hands."

Grandma Edna leaned in close. "What am I seeing?"

"Just watch."

Nothing happened.

"Has it happened yet?"

"No. Keep looking!"

"I thought maybe I was supposed to be seeing something but with these grandma eyes I was missing whatever it was."

"Wait, Grandma. You'll see."

Grandma Edna stared at the gold hands of her own wristwatch, waiting for time to do what it always does: tick away. But that isn't what she saw. She saw what Becca saw. She saw the second hand move counterclockwise: one second, two seconds. Grandma Edna sat up straighter in her chair.

"Did you see it?"

"I did! I do!" Grandma Edna was book-learned, no "simpleton" as Rowan Burke assumed. Remembering a quote she'd years ago forgotten, *Clocks slay time . . . time is dead as long as it is being clicked off by little wheels; only when the clock stops does time come to life,* she smiled. Becca was a smart girl. Edna couldn't remember the author of the quote, but he was someone important.

Whether or not the second hand actually moved counterclockwise was in the eye of the beholder, as with all things, but what's certain is that the old, like the young, can sometimes see shades and nuances that those who are too busy with life's minutiae, too busy rifling through the past and seeking blame, fail to see. Grandma Edna saw the fingertips of a child propel time backward. The old, like the young, feel time slipping away. Grandma Edna felt her life was like flour in a sieve, the last bits of white dust clinging to mesh. *Hold on.*

Hearing the bad news about Bo, Becca's dad adopted a black mutt called Whiskers. Although he was not fond of domesticated animals because of the dirt and hair, this was a great opportunity to turn a negative situation into a positive one, making him look good.

When moisture is present, victims are visibly burned. Oftentimes, a strike will occur before it starts raining, in which case the current travels through the victim's cardiovascular system. In these occurrences, there may be entry and exit wounds without severe burns.

Because lightning seeks the path of least resistance, the worst place to seek shelter during a thunderstorm is under a tree. If you can't find adequate shelter, like a house or car, crouch close to the ground, covering your head with your hands, allowing only your feet to touch the ground. You're less likely to suffer a direct hit, and if the current spreads and travels through your body, it may be less devastating by entering through the feet.

Farm animals tend to gather under trees to avoid the pelting rain. If the tree is struck, the animals fall like dominoes. I've never witnessed this event, but I've heard accounts from farmers. One man, Jackie Garlad, lost ten cows and three sheep from one strike.

8

Funk to funky, 1970

A tiger-striped butterfly flew through the magistrate's open window, alighting on the corner of his mahogany desk. Buckley watched the butterfly, her wings closed, throwing a dandelion hue on the leather desk pad. He watched her wings open and close again, and for the life of him, he didn't hear his mother and the reverend say "I do." He was their witness, but he'd missed it. He was eleven years old. It was August 1970. It'd taken the reverend three years to talk his mother into marriage. Buckley didn't understand his mother's decision. They'd been fine without Reverend John Whitehouse sharing their home, sharing his mother's bed.

After the marriage license was signed and dated, his new stepfather drove them to Shoney's Big Boy on Route 54. Buckley ate a hot fudge sundae while the reverend took advantage of the "sweet buffet deal," filling four scratched and sweaty plates.

Buckley never remembered his mother being there. He wasn't much of a witness.

No one in middle school chased or hit Buckley. Coach Flanagan warned from the start that physical contact belonged in physical sports. "Energy expended outside practice is wasteful." He also said many less practical things like, "When you boys grow into men, the girls will squeeze your balls in a vise."

No one hit Buckley and no one squeezed his balls.

Between September and Christmas break, someone stole his gym shoes and science report, but no one cared. Then someone urinated in Buckley's locker. Buckley imagined this someone laughing as he zipped his pants, pulling a can of spray paint from his back pocket and tagging the locker *BASTARD*. The incident was not easy for Mont Blanc middle to ignore, especially since Buckley now had a father—a reverend, no less. Principal Clark called Buckley to his office. "Was the locker locked? Do you have a lock? Did you lose your lock?" Principal Clark was frustrated by Buckley's apathy.

"It was my third lock this year," Buckley said.

"Do you know who's pulling this nonsense?"

"No, sir."

"Me either, and I wouldn't particularly give a crap, except that it needs to stop, and it needs to stop today. The Women's Auxiliary has already gotten word of this. It's an embarrassment."

Buckley had no idea who disliked him so much that they'd go to this trouble. No one knew him well enough to hate him.

Janitor Jackson, like Buckley, stood before the principal. Principal Clark continued: "This kind of vandalism won't be tolerated. I've told J.J. here to clean up the urine and to let the librarian know if any of your books need replacing. If J.J. can't read the titles, he's to ask you or the nurse to write them down." Buckley rolled his eyes. He knew that Janitor Jackson was a smart man. He'd fought in World War II. He'd been a reporter for a black newspaper somewhere up north. According to Janitor Jackson, he'd fallen on hard times. It was "women and drink." He told Buckley, "Show me a good-looking woman and I'll show you a heap of sad men. There's a big difference between a good woman and a good-looking one. I seem to prefer the latter." Buckley knew Janitor Jackson fairly well, as Buckley had a tendency to hide in the bathrooms that J.J. cleaned between classes.

After school, Buckley preferred helping Janitor Jackson lug

trash to the dumpsters to going home to Reverend Whitehouse, who was always picking at him: "Do you think you're smarter than me? You'll never be smarter than me, boy." Hell, his stepfather hated Buckley more than anyone. Maybe Reverend Whitehouse had pissed in his locker.

Principal Clark continued: "When the piss is gone, J.J. is gonna scrub *bastard* off the locker. If it won't come off, he'll paint the locker brown. We're out of yellow paint."

Buckley and Janitor Jackson stood side by side. Principal Clark said, "What's the problem, Buckley? What do you expect me to do?"

Buckley didn't answer.

Principal Clark looked at Janitor Jackson and back at Buckley. "Don't worry, son: J.J.'s used to cleaning up piss. He's good at what he does."

Buckley didn't like Principal Clark. It was no secret that he was in the Ku Klux Klan, annually parading, his white hood starched, down Main Street. Some educated people, Buckley had come to understand, were still ignorant.

By the sixth grade, Buckley was trying to survive—nothing more. With the reverend living in his house, *sleeping with his mother,* Buckley understood that Reginald Jackson, just like him, was trying to survive. There were those who endured and those who thrived. He and Janitor Jackson would probably never thrive. Some men are born to eke by, and Buckley, having no interest in good-looking women or whiskey, had no one and nothing to blame for his predicament.

Class was in session. Buckley, a foot shorter than Janitor Jackson, stood outside his locker. Janitor Jackson plunged his mop into a rolling bucket of gray water. Buckley said, "I can clean up my own piss."

"Suit yourself."

Fortunately, finding solace in cleanliness and organization, Buckley kept things tidy. His books were neatly arranged on the top shelf, unmarred by the urine, nearly dry, that formed a yellow ring in the bottom of his locker.

Buckley handed one of the textbooks, *The Earth and You*, to Janitor Jackson. "Sorry," Buckley said, "that you can't read the important works of this century."

Janitor Jackson said, "Maybe I should take this to Miss Beverly in the infirmary and ask her what it says."

Buckley laughed. "I think you ought to."

"It's a shame us black folks can't read good. It's why we is always using the whites-only bathrooms and water fountains. You can't blame us for being dumb."

"Of course not."

Buckley dunked the mop into the gray water.

"I'll spray some bleach in there later," Janitor Jackson said, "and I'll get you a new lock—one that James Bond couldn't bust."

When the bell rang, the hall filled with onlookers, girls and boys snickering, concealing their smiles behind books such as *Mathematics Today* and *Grammar for Girls*. Ignoring the jeers, Buckley asked Janitor Jackson, "Anybody ever piss in your locker?"

"We didn't have lockers where I went to school. All we had were desks."

"And I bet you walked ten miles to school in the snow."

Janitor Jackson said, "I like you." He took the mop from Buckley. "Clark is an idiot, but I am good at my job. Don't attempt to get rid of the spray paint. It's not going anywhere. I've got a can of yellow paint stashed in the closet. I'll take care of it." As the hallway emptied, students rushing to their respective classes, Buckley felt fortunate to know Janitor Jackson. It was rare that he got to know someone.

Buckley said, "Are the women and the drink still hounding you?"

Janitor Jackson laughed. "We need more boys like you, boys who listen. And as a matter of fact, those good-looking women won't ever let me be. Day and night they hound me—a curse and a blessing. How can I live without them?"

"Wisely."

"Your father's done a good job raising you."

"You can read, Mr. Jackson. It says 'bastard.' It's no lie. I don't have a father."

When he got home from school, the reverend said, "You need to wise up and stop being a pantywaist."

His mother, looking heavy and sad in her recliner, beckoned, "Come here." Buckley was almost as tall as she was now. He leaned down. She pressed his head against her shoulder. Gangly and disheveled with unmanageable hair, he was uncomfortable in his own skin.

She said, "How was school today?"

The reverend said to Abigail, "Don't baby the boy."

Winter smiled. Her thoughts exactly.

Abigail said to Buckley, "Tell me what happened."

"Nothing." He pulled away.

"We need to talk about it."

The reverend added, "And we're going to talk about it."

Buckley walked toward his bedroom, hearing the reverend's boots at his heels. Tired of running, he waited for the reverend to take him from behind—which he did, being a reliable sort—grabbing Buckley's T-shirt and pinning his head against the cream-colored cinder blocks. "What's the matter with you?" the reverend demanded.

"Everything." Buckley's head hurt. He'd been through enough today. When he was older and taller, he'd hold the reverend's head with his feeble brain against this block and see how he liked it. Or would he? Men like the reverend aren't pinned. They don't eke by or survive. They thrive. The reverend had wanted Abigail and he got her. The reverend had wanted to rule

Buckley and that's what he was doing. Buckley said, "I'm worth-less."

The reverend said, "Pray through the night. When I come in your room at two o'clock, I want to see you on your knees; three o'clock, prostrate before our Lord; four o'clock, praying to Jesus for strength." The reverend stepped back. Buckley heard his mother breathing. She'd risen, but only in time to see the reverend's retreat.

This same year, Buckley's mom got a job at Roger's Gourmet Pork 'n' Beans.

On her first official day, Tarry Quince, a coworker, showed Abigail where their boss's office was located. She said, "The best thing about the man is we don't never see his ugly face." Mr. Peebles had hired Abigail. He'd seemed like a nice man, but it made no difference. She needed the money. "Drop your time card here on Friday," Tarry instructed.

Downstairs, Tarry pointed to the women on the steel ladders, working the vats. The vats seemed larger today than last Tuesday when Mr. Peebles had asked, "When can you start?" Tarry shouted over the noisy compressors and vacuum sealers, "Sheila, Laurie, Katrina, and Tracie." Sheila and Katrina noticed Tarry and Abigail over the rumble of the machines and waved, and one woman, Sandy Burkhaulter, who worked at the end of the line, climbed down. She wiped one hand on her tomato-and-bean-spotted smock before taking off her glove. She mouthed the phrase *good to meet you* and extended her hand to Abigail, who felt so overwhelmed, she left Sandy's hand where it was. Sandy climbed back up the silver ladder to her vat.

Abigail was hired to work the line inspecting cans of Roger's Gourmet Pork 'n' Beans, an Arkansas favorite, and according to Mr. Peebles, a soon-to-be national favorite. "We're going to put Hormel out of business."

Standing at the conveyor belt, Abigail wore a clean but orange-stained smock and a hairnet, as did the other two women who worked the line alongside her. The three inspectors were to ensure that cans of Roger's Gourmet Pork 'n' Beans were filled to the third line (counting down from the top of the can, Mr. Peebles explained, as if she were an idiot), no more and no less, before they entered the sealer. "It's the most important job," Mr. Peebles had stressed. "Imagine: You're about to feed your family dinner. You open up the can and there's a white sticky mold because there was too much air in the can. It's about consistency and quality. You work quality control."

In the last year, Abigail had lost one hundred and twenty pounds. One year married, she was miserable. She wore long-sleeved shirts and long pants despite the Arkansas heat to hide her sagging skin, and she was determined more than ever to save enough money to leave John Whitehouse and her mother, Winter Pitank, behind. She was going to take Buckley and move away from Mont Blanc, Arkansas. She wanted to see the ocean.

When her mother asked her why she wouldn't eat, why she'd lost so much weight so quickly—"Are you sick? Do you have a tapeworm?"—Abigail didn't have the courage to tell her that it was John, that she had made a huge mistake—that watching him hoard tuna-noodle casserole, the noodles sopping and dripping down his chin, had made her nauseated. It just happened one day: She sat across from him at the kitchen table, and she lost her appetite. She looked down at her own plate of casserole, the noodles like fat white worms, and felt sick.

Working the inspection line at Roger's, there was a lot of time to think about the mistakes she'd made, what she might have done differently. The past, like the slop she inspected, sped by, can after can and memory after memory, making her wonder if forgetfulness wasn't a blessing. She remembered her wedding night, John saying, "Tell me you like it. Tell me you like it," and she whispered back, "I like it," wishing the mattress springs wouldn't creak so. He said, "I know your fat ass does. I know it." Later, he said he'd been in the throes. He hadn't meant nothing hateful by what he said. She hadn't always had a fat ass, as John would say. She'd been slim before Buckley. Before Richard, Buckley's biological father, went away to the University of Florida to play football and study medicine.

Buckley R. Pitank is Buckley Richard Pitank.

Watching the cans rush past, she thought, *John is not a bad man, not as far as I can tell, and I can stomach him on top of me, inside me, calling me "fat ass" and "big girl" in the bed, and he treats Buckley like a son.* But therein lay the problem: That first week after they married, John taught Buckley to shoot. He taught Buckley to drive his truck and to lay brick and to hang drywall. He told him that Job had betrayed God, that he got what he deserved. John had even thrown a football with Buckley in the Holy Redeemer churchyard. The churchgoers were watching the stepfather and son, and John was encouraging Buckley, saying, "You got a good arm, Buck." When Buckley fumbled and dropped the ball, John said, "The boy's hands are greasy from the chicken." John's face had turned red. Buckley had embarrassed him, and John carried the football away, tossing it in his truck.

Shifting her weight from left to right, her back hurting, Abigail remembered her mother's face, pleased as punch, when Abigail told her that she was marrying the reverend. She would finally be somewhat respectable, a little less white trash. But now Abigail didn't want the husband. She never had wanted him, but now she didn't want the father for her son either. She had married John for Buckley and because John had proposed. He liked her cooking. He liked her fat ass, and he was quickly turning her only son into a young man doomed to lay bricks, hang drywall, shoot guns, drive pickup trucks, and probably pick up whores and gamble. She didn't know where it would lead, but shooting and whoring was not what she'd intended for her only son. She wanted him to go to college and read books and be a professional. She knew what John was about, and it wasn't about God. It was about scheming and living lazy. Despite all his promises, they still lived in Winter's pea green cinder-block house, and John's congregation was fewer than thirty. She had hoped John might just up and leave, but he licked his fingers at the dinner table, put his boots on the furniture, and smacked her on the behind in front of Buckley and Winter. He wasn't leaving any time soon.

The conveyor belt jerked and stopped. Pork 'n' beans slopped the belt and Abigail's smock. "Wake up," said Linda, who worked the line, and who for some reason didn't like Abigail. "I'll get Horace. Clean that up." Abigail tossed the nine slopped cans and wiped the belt with her rag. She wiped the sauce from her cheek with the back of her hand. Samantha, the other inspector, said, "I'll be back." She was going for a smoke.

Abigail's own daddy had taught her that a man or woman doesn't have anything if they don't have their word. *If you can't keep your word, you can't keep nothing.* And she had certainly kept her word. Maybe that was a mistake. The line started moving again, and she was alone at the conveyor belt. Samantha took long smoke breaks, and Linda was always looking for an excuse to leave the line. Abigail knew from experience that Linda wouldn't be back for at least twenty minutes. The balls of Abigail's feet ached. She wished she smoked or had some reason to leave the line, but she couldn't go anywhere with those two gone. It was two o'clock. She had three more hours to go. Mr. Peebles had reminded her this morning, "No break this afternoon. I let you leave early yesterday."

"My son was sick. It was a half hour."

He hadn't answered.

It was a mindless job and so her mind wandered. She thought on Richard and the promise she'd kept, not even telling her own mother his name. When Richard had said, "You tricked me. My daddy's right about you. You're a whore," she had said, "I would never trick you. Never. I love you. I won't ever tell anybody this is your baby if you don't want me to."

"How do I know it is?" He was handsome, with a golden crew cut. At his hairline, he had fine tufts of hair like a baby's first hairs, and he had the shiniest green eyes. In one more year he was leaving for the University of Florida to play football. She remembered him saying something like *I should've known you'd try something like this. In another year, I'm getting out of here. Nothing you can say will change that.* That's what she remembered, and she'd thought then, at three months pregnant, that despite what he said, he wouldn't really leave. That if he did leave, his conscience would bring him back. He would want to know his child.

In her mind she could still see him there behind Moore's Grocery. She remembered saying, "I was a virgin." It was August 8, 1958. She remembered writing the date in her diary. She had left the whole page blank to fill in later when he changed his mind, when he said *I want us to be a family. That page is still blank*, she thought. It would remain forever blank.

What had she looked like then? She tried to picture herself, the two of them standing with their backs up against the bricks, him hardly looking at her. She kept moving in front of him, trying to make eye contact, to see into his heart. She was so naive.

"I'll deny it's mine."

"No, you won't." *What did I look like then?* She let a can of Roger's Gourmet Pork 'n' Beans pass at the sixth line. *White mold. Some woman is going to be entirely destroyed in another year's time when she opens this slop to feed her family. How terrible. Mr. Peebles won't approve.*

I was thin then, she remembered, *and I had on that white skirt I bought in Fayetteville, the one patterned with French ladies and parasols. I had washed and pressed it, and it got dirty against the bricks. Stained forever. Pretty means pretty and nothing more. It doesn't pay.*

"I gotta go" is what he'd said.

Didn't he know Jiminy Cricket's "Always Let Your Conscience Be Your Guide"? If Richard doesn't want to know Buckley, then Buckley doesn't want to know him. She let another can pass, this one at the tenth line. *Richard got out of here. No doubt about that.* He left Mont Blanc for good, but not before he saw Abigail wheeling her baby boy down Main Street. She remembered walking proudly, trying not to seem obvious, but eyeing him. He crossed the street. He hadn't even tried to sneak a peek at his own son. *He's your baby,* she'd thought. She wanted to scream, *He's your son. You need to claim him!* But who was she to him? *A good time. An easy lay. What did her mother say?* "Why pay for the cow when you can get the milk for free." "Pretty's just pretty. It doesn't pay."

When Buckley was four or five, she ran into Richard at Bronco Billy's Drive-in. He was in town for the holidays, visiting his folks. She was fat then, and Richard hadn't recognized her, but she knew him. He looked the exact same, except his hair was long down his back, which suited him. Had she been thinner then . . . had her hair been washed . . . had she been nicely dressed . . . had she had more confidence, she might've approached him then to tell him how amazing his son was. She wanted to say, *It's me! Abigail.* She wanted to tell him about Buckley Richard Pitank.

Instead, she drove away with her cheeseburger and milk shake, her palms sweaty on the steering wheel.

Linda came up behind Abigail. "What the hell is going on?"

Abigail said, "I'm doing my job. I'm checking the cans."

"Has Mr. Peebles seen this mess?"

Abigail shook her head that no, he had not, thinking that if Linda and Samantha weren't always wandering off, this type of thing wouldn't happen in the first place.

"Thank God," Linda said. "And Horace didn't come by?"

"No."

"When the line started back up, did you check each can?"

"Not really." Abigail didn't lie. She kept secrets, but she didn't lie.

"Why not?"

"My mind wandered."

Excerpt from
THE HANDBOOK FOR LIGHTNING STRIKE SURVIVORS

A farmer from Waryo, Montana, struck thirteen times in the last ten years, told reporters, "I don't feel nothing. I'm numb. I won't run from a storm. I ain't seeking no shelter. I think it's God's way of letting me know he's here. He's waiting for me, but it's not my time. I've been to the hospital every time I got hit, and every time I tell them, 'Listen to my heart. Hook me up to one of them machines you got,' and every single time, we look at that monitor thing and there's my heart, still ticking, all crazy fast and slow and fast and slow, and they keep me there until my ticker settles down again, and then I go home. I guess I've had a dozen cardiac arrests and somehow she keeps on ticking. I'm like Timex."

9

This mortal coil, 1979

Grandma Edna goes to bed at quarter past nine. She unfastens her watch and drops it on the nightstand. She tucks the heavy knotted quilt under her arms and, anxious to dream, forgets what she should remember: forgets that tomorrow she has to buy tracing paper, red construction paper, snowflake paper, and tubes of silver glitter for the Sunday school Valentines; forgets to take her antacid (her stomach bubbled after supper); forgets the back porch light and the four pills in the white plastic Friday slot of her pill bin; forgets to defrost the chicken.

Tonight the February wind squalls. It clatters the chairs on the side porch and tears the wind chimes from their metal hooks. They clank on the concrete and thud to the grass. The wind rattles the storm windows. She thinks someone is trying to get in. She thinks, *Come on. I don't care.* She has gone to bed to dream and so she does.

In the dream, her mother is young, washing petticoats in the sunlight. Wisps of hair fall from her bun and she catches them with the back of her wrist, pinning them to her face. She laughs. Edna smells lavender mixed with lye. Beneath the covers, Edna's right hand opens and her fingers wiggle. She sees her mother's teeth, including the chipped one, and her mother's hands, wet and coarse from scrubbing clothes on the washboard. Her mother gathers her top skirt, drying her hands, calling, "Ed," but Edna's right there within reach. "Ed," she calls again. Edna says, "I'm right here, Mom." Every night her mother smiles or waves and the dream ends, but tonight Edna feels the sunlight on her arms and after reaching for her mother's skirt, feels the fabric. Both of her old feet kick beneath the tucked sheet. When Edna's fingers touch the suds on her mother's skirt, her right hand spasms under the covers. She hasn't touched her before. She feels her mother's wet fingertips on her forehead, sees the glowing red blur of sunlit skin. Her mother pushes a strand of hair from Edna's eyes.

Edna dies in her sleep at seventy-seven years old. Her mother, Rosemary, died at the same age.

Five years ago, Edna had prepared for death. She counted crisp twenty-dollar bills into the palm of Morton Spank, Prospect's sole funeral director, and waited for a receipt. Edna had never been a slouch. She took to heart the TV commercials that reminded her, *You shouldn't burden your loved ones, nor should you suffer their whims.* They might cremate her!

Her affairs were in order. She wasn't much looking forward to seeing old Clayton. There were things she'd done since his death that he wouldn't approve of. There was Old Man John, for one—who was colored. If Clayton knew about the kiss—even though it was on the cheek, just near the lips, and even though there'd been gin involved . . . Oh, never mind. If Clayton knew about the gin, he'd be upset. It was all right for men to drink, Clayton said, but not women. She wouldn't worry about seeing him. She had missed him, but he had been hard to swallow, like castor oil, and she wouldn't have known how difficult he was if he hadn't died so many years before her, opening her eyes to all the kind people close by. Well, there were plenty of other people up there she'd be happy to see, like her mother.

Rowan drove the Volvo to Prospect while Mary slept in the backseat and Becca told him about her grandmother. "She could see the watch hand go counterclockwise, and she wrote that I was blessed. I can't believe she died. I can't believe she's gone."

"Everybody dies."

Becca's neck, splotched red since her mother had told her about her grandmother's passing, felt hot. "I don't want to die. I don't want Grandma Edna to be dead."

"She's in our hearts," he said, adjusting the side mirror.

"Can you turn down the heat? I'm burning up." Becca slid off her shoes and tried looking for stars, but there were none to see. There were the headlights and the black trees. "I just got to know her, and she's gone."

"I'm sorry."

"Do you believe in ghosts?"

He squeezed her shoulder. "What do you think about going to Richmond with me next month? I've got a couple meetings, but we could sightsee in between."

"Sure." Even with her shoes off, her feet were sweating. She propped them on the leather console between the seats and thought, *When I get to the farm I'll look for Grandma Edna sitting at the kitchen table, standing at the sink, shuffling up the concrete steps. I'll listen for her laugh and her Marianne Pamplin potato salad stories.*

The next morning, Mary couldn't decide what to wear to her mother's funeral. Already quarter to nine, with the service supposed to start at nine-thirty, and Mary, still wearing her slip, tossed the dresses she'd brought from home, one after another, the wooden hangers clacking, onto her dead mother's bed.

Wearing a blue velveteen dress, black tights, and Mary Janes, Becca stood in the doorway, watching. She said, "What about that one?"

"What did you say?" Mary stopped, dress hanger in hand, staring hard at Becca.

"That one. The green one."

"Could you please get out of here? Am I asking too much of you?"

Becca went to her father and they waited together in the red dust, and he took her hand and squeezed.

In her dead mother's bedroom, Mary adjusted the wide-brimmed hat. She bobby-pinned it to her curls, checking the mirror to make sure the bobby pins weren't showing. She looked good and thought that if she were thinner, if she had dark hair, and if she weren't going to her mother's funeral, she could pass for Audrey Hepburn in *Breakfast at Tiffany's*.

Who will be there? she wondered, pulling on her black coat, adorned with the purple butterfly brooch—her mother's, and her grandmother's before that, and one day she'd pass it on to Becca. *When Becca's older and more responsible. Will I know anyone at the service?* she wondered. *What will they think of me? The daughter who never came to visit. Will Old Man John be there? He's a nice man. Is it an open casket?* She hadn't thought to ask. *I can't handle seeing her dead. She shouldn't be dead.*

Mary sat in the front pew, head bowed, concentrating on her black pumps. She didn't want anyone to see her face. She didn't want to see Claire, who sat on her left. The sisters had hardly spoken. Claire, with her ex-boyfriend Tom's help, made the arrangements. There wasn't much to arrange. Edna had taken care of everything. "Tom has been a big help," Claire whispered as the eulogist walked to the pulpit.

"What happened with his girlfriend Betsy?"

"It's over between them."

Mary thought, *That's convenient, since our mother is dead and there's inheritance and a farmhouse.*

Mary shifted in her seat, crossed her right leg over her left. There was a small snag in her stocking. She fingered it. Claire cried. Becca cried. She should be crying, but she had taken a Valium and sipped from Rowan's flask in the car. She hoped the snag didn't spread. *This must be Hank at the pulpit, one of the men from church that Mother was talking about last summer. He's also been crying. What is he saying?* As Hank said, "I never met a nicer, more generous woman, and I don't think I ever will. Make you laugh. Lord, she made me laugh," Mary thought, *I hate you!* Full of rage, she squirmed again. Hank told one story after another about a woman Mary didn't know. "I can't tell you how many times . . ." He wiped his nose with a handkerchief. "I can't say she'll be missed. That doesn't do her justice." *On and on. Shut up!* She shouldn't think that. She decided that she shouldn't have worn black. *It's too depressing.* She should've bought a new dress, but there wasn't time.

Her right foot was asleep. She shifted again and looked to Becca, whose face was swollen with tears, her green eyes flooded, almost transparent. Mary squeezed Becca's thigh to express to her daughter that it'd be all right. Becca gasped for breath and cupped her face in her hands. Mary tried to take Becca's hand as Rowan, seated beside Mary with his legs crossed, leaned in. He put his hand on Mary's shoulder and whispered, "It's all right."

Mary was relieved at his concern. *Maybe we'll make love tonight. It's been so long.*

Rowan thought about his meeting next month with Atkins and Thames. The additive he'd created. The money he might make.

After the service, the mourners drove to the farmhouse. They parked their boxy American cars in a row at the side of the house and down the dirt drive. The bare trees and brown grasses framed the crisp blue sky. It was a cold February day. Inside, Tom, who'd already removed the boxes from the living room and the upstairs kitchen, played host. He pulled back the curtains and distributed plates of food. Forks clanked on plates. Conversation hummed. Mary overheard Tom tell Old Man John, "We're staying here." Mary thought, *Who is "we"? He's a fool*, and she poured a glass of scotch. People she hardly knew patted her shoulder and embraced her, paying their condolences.

Marianne Pamplin said to the reverend, "I brought the potato salad and the cherry pie."

Becca scanned the buffet, crowded with the standard meatballs, platter of fried chicken, tray of ham biscuits, and casseroles with thick cheesy tops. Spotting Marianne Pamplin's famous potato salad, she heaped the mayonnaise-rich potatoes onto her plate. Becca took a large bite and laughed at how awful it was, spraying the potato salad onto the rug. Grandma Edna was right. It was by far the worst potato salad Becca had ever tasted. The mayonnaise was warm. She announced, "This is delicious," spilling her food on the rug. She laughed, and the mourners averted their eyes. *Someone ought to do something about that child* was the general consensus, she knew. Her father, who loathed a scene, took her by the elbow and reached for her plate. Becca, wriggling loose, saw Grandma Edna rocking heel to toe by the newly hung curtains. Grandma Edna's blue eyes were moist, the way they'd been the day the two of them had snapped beans. Becca heard her grandma laugh. "Grandma," Becca said, and the conversational hum stopped. "Grandma."

Everyone looked at Becca.

"Come on, Bec." Her father and Claire's boyfriend, Tom, lifted Becca from the rug. Tom wiped at the spilled potato salad with a frayed napkin. Becca hung limply, both knees on the rug. Her father's hands were under her elbows. "Mary," he called for help. "Come on, Becca. Don't make a scene."

Becca couldn't resist. "Your potato salad's delicious." She smiled at Grandma Edna, who still rocked heel to toe by the curtains. Becca knew her grandma would be here. Of course, no one else could see her. That's the way it is with these things—or is it? Marianne Pamplin, not long for the world, looked to the curtains. Becca watched as she put one hand on her hip and shook her head, as if to say, *Get out of here, you. You're dead.* Then Grandma Edna was gone.

Marianne Pamplin said, "I'll send the recipe to your mother." Holding her pearls against her bottom lip, she dropped them to her blouse, smiling at the odd little girl on the floor, who she presumed would grow up to have mental problems like the youngest Wickle girl, Claire. Then, finding the two sisters in separate rooms, she whispered to one and then the other the standard "I'm so sorry for your loss."

Claire said, "Thank you for coming, Marianne," but Mary was drunk and responded, "Why?" Mary tottered onto the front porch in front of the reverend and Marianne Pamplin with her glass of scotch, the ice cubes tinkling. The reverend was driving Marianne Pamplin home. He tried to shake Mary's hand on the porch, but Mary had a cigarette in the one hand and her scotch in the other. *Maybe another time, preacher man.*

"It felt like I died. I told my son, 'I'm dead,' and he said, 'No, Mama, you got struck by lightning, but you're not dead.'

"I said, 'Nobody gets struck by lightning.' We were on the beach, and there was only one black cloud. Even with my son right there and the lifeguard running toward us, I thought I was dead. I don't remember the next few days. Still, today, ten years later, I think I died that day. My husband and son are always reminding me how lucky I am to be alive."

Account by Margaret M.

10

Galveston, 1972

In 1972, with the money she'd earned at Roger's Gourmet Pork 'n' Beans, Abigail bought a yellow Vega hatchback. She and Buckley packed it with their scant belongings, mostly clothes, but Abigail also took the electric griddle because she'd bought that too with her money from Roger's. She packed her diaries—five total—and her photo album.

It was mid-August, and so hot in Mont Blanc that the red clay roads, dusty and cracked in the sun, were bleached pink and seemed to want to give way, to split open and swallow the pair. Buckley feared it could happen. How could it be possible to leave this place? He'd packed nothing but his clothes, and if it weren't for necessity, he would've left them behind too. He didn't want anything reminding him of Mont Blanc.

It was a Tuesday. The reverend was at the Holy Redeemer Church, and Winter was in town at her friend Violet's house. Violet had recently lost her cat, Twinkle, and as a result she refused to eat. Winter had baked Violet a pie. Winter didn't like cats, and it seemed ridiculous that anyone should carry on so, refusing to eat over a missing cat, but Winter believed in charity. She could count this visit as a good deed. Since the reverend had married her only daughter and moved into her home, she thought more on good deeds and heaven, and what it might take to enter heaven if heaven was a real option. What did she have to lose? An hour

baking a pie. A morning listening to Violet's woeful kitty-cat tale.
It was worth it.

Winter was already an hour at Violet's when Abigail and Buckley
left Mont Blanc. The Vega had no seat belts, but it did have a radio,
and as Abigail and Buckley drove west on I-40, Abigail turned up
the song "A Horse with No Name." She smiled. "We're going to see
the ocean!"

When Buckley was older, he would remember the brown vinyl
interior of the little car, the yellow foam bunching out of his
mother's seat where the vinyl was torn, the cigarette burn on the
dashboard, the song lyrics "I've been through the desert on a horse
with no name," and the skin hanging from his mother's right arm.
It was too much to hope that things would turn out right for them.
But now he was hopeful, imagining a blue ocean. Counting cars
and splintered mailboxes. Wondering about his new school. Would
he keep his name Buckley or change it to something cool like Keith
or Cliff?

As they drove farther away from Mont Blanc, Abigail wrestled
with whether or not she was doing the right thing. Would Buckley be all right? Would she be all right? Was it possible to start life
over? She'd never been anywhere.

When they crossed the state line into Oklahoma, Buckley sighed.
The radio newsman said, "The last American combat ground troops
are leaving Vietnam."

Abigail said, "About time."

"Do you think we'll live near the ocean?"

"That's the idea. You can't help but live near the ocean there. It's
an island. Did you know that the man who invented condensed
milk, something Borden, was one of the founders?"

"Who likes condensed milk?"

"I think it'll be a nice place. There's the ocean and it's an island, and—"

"Who told you that? About the milk?"

"I read it in the encyclopedia."

"Are you going to be able to get a job? Where are we going to live?"

"Oh, honey, don't worry so much. I already have a job. Sandy Burkhaulter's sister Jeanette lives in Galveston. She owns a restaurant, and she told Sandy she could use an extra hand. Everything's going to be okay."

It was hard to believe, but he wanted to believe. The farther south they drove, the dusty wind tangling his brown hair, the oppressive heat rising up through the Vega's floorboard, the more animated he became. The more questions he had. Each time they stopped for gas, Abigail added a quart of oil, and the little Vega didn't want to start. But Abigail pleaded, "You can do it. I know you can," and as luck or fate or God would have it, the car started.

Before falling asleep, Buckley thought about starting over. He thought about being one of the cool kids. He could reinvent himself. He could be any kind of boy he wanted. He'd learn about the sea. He'd learn to swim. He'd get a tan and the red bumps on his face would disappear, and he'd let his hair grow longer because girls liked long hair and boys thought it was cool. Maybe he'd wear a headband.

He slept grinning. Abigail drove across the state line into Texas, and when she saw the billboard WELCOME TO TEXAS, HOME OF THE DALLAS COWBOYS, she too grinned. The next billboard was shaped like a ten-gallon cowboy hat, and the one after that was a red, orange, and green sombrero. It read MEXICO IS CLOSER THAN YOU THINK. The billboard for Roy's Steakhouse had a smiling cow, its tail oscillating in the heat. Abigail was having fun. Then the billboards were gone and there was more road. More heat. Three hundred miles of I-45 South leading her closer to Galveston. Abigail couldn't find a radio station. She tried to picture the ocean. Could it be as beautiful as she'd always imagined? Her father had seen the ocean. He'd said, "Sometimes it's green and calm. Sometimes blue and gentle. Other times she's spitting and gray. Stormy. The sand gets into everything. It's gritty between your toes, letting you know you're alive. I'll never understand a person who walks the beach in shoes."

She'd told him, "I wouldn't."

"At night," he said, "the sand is cool, and the water serenades the moon."

Oh, he told stories. "The water doesn't sing, Daddy."

She felt as if he were with them now. He'd be proud. She should've made this move sooner, but her dad always said, "You don't step up to the plate until you're ready to swing." Boy, she was swinging now. She'd better keep her eye on the ball.

When Buckley awoke, they were pulling into the driveway of a small house on Sealy Street. Abigail cut the ignition. "We're here." Buckley looked at his mother, at the sleeveless canary yellow blouse she wore, at the pinkish white skin hanging off her arms, and hoped she'd put on a jacket or a long-sleeved shirt. It was hard to look at all that empty skin. He *personally* didn't mind. Of course not. But he worried what others would think. Abigail stood in the driveway and said, "You coming?" She hadn't put on a jacket.

"Where are we? Is this house ours?" It was a three-story row house fronted with two columns and a wide porch. The house was painted lavender with white shutters. There was a red swing on the front porch, and seven pots of ivy hung from the lintel. Their vines curtained part of the front door, which was painted eggplant.

Buckley rubbed at his eyes. The wind had knotted his hair on the right side, and the hair on the left side was greasy and matted. As they stood waiting on the front porch, Buckley noticed the tiny hearts cut from the corners of the white shutters. He thought about the story of Hansel and Gretel. This place was like a gingerbread house. He moved an ivy leaf off his shoulder and yawned. Abigail said, "Smile."

Mrs. Joan Holt opened the door. She was an old woman with downy snowflake hair worn loosely in a bun. Around her eyes were deep crow's-feet. She had smile wrinkles too. "You must be Abigail." Buckley looked again at his mother's uncovered arms, grateful that she hadn't worn shorts.

"This is Buckley," Abigail said.

"Hello, young man. Come in, come in."

"What about our stuff, Mom?"

"I'm just making lemonade," Joan Holt said.

"We'll get our things later."

"Where's the ocean?" Buckley asked.

"Five blocks that-a-way." Joan Holt pointed.

"I can't wait to see the ocean."

Abigail smiled at Joan Holt, who poured lemonade from a clear pitcher into three blue-tinted glasses in the dim light of the kitchen. The window-unit air conditioner buzzed and surged.

"Did you drive straight through?"

"We did," Abigail said.

"Did you have a good trip?"

"We did."

"Well, let's get a few things straight now," she said. "I know from Jeanette Burkhaulter that you know Sandy Burkhaulter, and that you probably don't have a lot of money saved. Don't worry. You ought to make good money at Jeanette's—not so good in the winter, but when school's out, you'll rake in the bucks. I am not one to believe charity is a bad thing. I am for charity. I am not for pride. If you've come here with too much pride, know that I will wear you down. My house is your house. I have heard kind things about both of you, and I won't have you running off or crying if you're short on rent one month. Another thing: I am old and lonely and done with eating by myself. I enjoy cooking, and I hope that we can have our meals together like a family. If you prefer not, I understand."

"Oh, no," Abigail said. "That'll be lovely."

"Can we see the ocean now?" Buckley asked.

"Another thing: call me Joan."

"If it's just five blocks, can I walk to the ocean?"

"After we bring our things inside and get settled."

"But Mom . . ." Buckley chugged his lemonade. He was ready to see the ocean *now*. The glass, perspiring and slick, slipped between his thumb and forefinger, shattering on the green tiled floor.

Joan Holt wiped a splash of lemonade off her cheek. "Well, now you've done it. You've really gone and done it."

"I'm so sorry, ma'am. I'm sorry."

"I'm sorry, Mrs. Holt," Abigail said. "Do you have a towel? I'll clean it up."

"For the love of Jesus, I'm just joshing you. I'll get the mop."

Abigail searched the counter for a rag, and Buckley picked up large shards of tinted blue glass.

"I'm sorry, Mom. It slipped," he said.

"It was an accident."

Joan came back with a broom and a mop. "Excuse me," she said to Buckley. She nudged him in the thigh with the broom. He couldn't help but notice her breasts through the sheer cotton blouse she wore, how they hung the way his mother's skin hung. He watched her sweep, her breasts lolling back and forth, how he imagined the women's boobs in *National Geographic* probably lolled. She said, "There's a good picture show this weekend. *Diamonds Are Forever.* Have you seen it?"

Abigail said, "No, ma'am."

Buckley realized that Joan Holt probably hadn't even noticed his mother's sagging skin. He felt ashamed for noticing her saggy breasts. It wasn't as if he was excited by them. It was just that his grandmother and all the grown women he knew had always worn brassieres.

Joan swept and Buckley mopped. He said, "I'm sorry for breaking your glass."

"There's nothing to be sorry about. Accidents happen." Her breasts swung back and forth.

Abigail wasn't sure what word she might use to describe Joan Holt: maybe *screwball*. But she sure was nice.

"Can we go to the ocean?" Buckley asked.

"Let's go," Joan said. "I haven't had my exercise yet." To Abigail, she said, "Come with us. There's always work to be done. It doesn't go anywhere."

There's no point in describing what they felt. If you remember seeing the ocean for the first time, you know what they felt, and if you don't remember, try to remember. It'll come back to you. If you've never seen the ocean, board a plane, train, bus, or car and go now, today. If you've seen the ocean and walked a sandy beach or rocky cliff, you'll be familiar with the ocean's powers, how it washes things away, how it erodes minerals, shells, and glass, reducing them to sand. The ocean also erodes the past, and already, with Buckley's bare feet and toes digging into wet sand, the water lapping up to his waist, he forgot, albeit briefly, the pea green cinder-block house, the book of Job, Reverend Whitehouse, Winter, and the bullies at Mont Blanc middle school.

Abigail worked at Jeanette's Pier Restaurant at Stewart Beach Park. In the mornings, she served eggs sunny-side up, scrambled, or fried, with toasted Wonder Bread and gold packets of margarine. She served pancakes and sausage links, and every few minutes, slipping her pen and order pad in her apron pocket, she looked up to see the green waves sweep white and foamy across the gold sand. Mesmerized and daydreaming, sometimes she forgot the customers sitting, eating the food she'd just set before them, and Jeanette would call to her, "I think they got it, honey," meaning, *Back away from the table and let them eat in peace.*

At lunch and in the afternoons, Abigail served Jeanette's

specials, her meat loaf, mostly, and the catch of the day, bottles of Budweiser, and greasy french fries. When it was slow, she watched surfboarders paddle through the breaking waves. She was in awe of them, these boys walking on water. These boys in their bright swim trunks swallowed by the waves, only to reappear and paddle out again.

Jeanette's Pier Restaurant had two sections, Sec One and Sec Two. "It's not very original," Jeanette had said on Abigail's first day. "Sec One's in here." And then, pointing, "Sec Two's out there." Sec One was the area connected directly to the pier. Entering Sec One, there was a beige sign with brown lettering that read PLEASE WAIT TO BE SEATED, but no one did. There was a bar with six stools, the cash register, and eight tabletops. Sec Two, on the other hand, was basically outside, so there was a lot of room and a lot of salty air.

Sec Two extended out over the dune. Exposed to the elements, the cedar walls only reached as high as the tabletops. The rest of the walls were rectangular frames stretched with metallic screens. The ocean was never out of sight. There were wooden shutters to protect the restaurant when storms blew through, but most of the time Abigail kept the shutters open. Like Abigail, her customers wanted to feel the salty air. Sec Two was her Sec. She had picked it even though Jeanette had warned her that the tips weren't as good: "The locals don't give a lick about listening to or staring at the ocean in this heat. Most of them is bored of it, and some of them are the best tippers."

Jeanette explained that there were a lot of tourist folks and teenagers in Sec Two who just wanted to sit, have a beer and a plate of conch fritters, and watch the waves curl and lick the sand. Abigail wasn't concerned. The folks who were new to the ocean were just like her.

After only two days at Jeanette's, Abigail was happy with her decision. It was never oppressively hot. There was always some breeze blowing off the water, and her customers, their hands on the thin screen between them and the dune, stared out at the waves—just like her.

Abigail met Padraig John McGowan, Galway born and American bred, in Sec Two. Abigail's new friend Sissy had decided to play matchmaker. Sissy was a full-time political activist. She lobbied for the Equal Rights Amendment, and she was "damn proud," as she liked to say, that her amendment had finally been sent to the states for ratification. She said, "Five years. No more, no less, and we'll be guaranteed equality. And I'm part of it. Women make things happen, Abigail. You and me. All of us, and it's overdue we got a fair shake." She bragged that she'd met Alice Paul. She told Abigail, "I'm changing the world. It starts with one."

Abigail was unconcerned with changing the world, but Sissy was extremely entertaining to be around. Like Joan Holt, she didn't wear a bra. She was brash, and she liked to brag about all the good work she did for the poor, the disenfranchised, and the downtrodden. She herself was disenfranchised, although she claimed her poverty was a personal choice in protest to the corruption that wealth breeds.

Today she was going to help Abigail. "I found a man for you. Because I'm intuitive, I'm skilled at this type of thing. I've known him a long time, and after you and I met, I just knew you two should be together."

"Please tell me you're kidding."

"You have to meet him. That's all I ask."

"No way. I am done with men."

"Fine, Abigail," Sissy said, "but men have to eat too, and I'm not kidding when I say that I'm gifted at matchmaking."

"Please don't bring any men in here to meet me. I'm serious."

"Men have to eat. That's all I'm saying."

Two days later, Padraig John sat across from Sissy at one of

Abigail's tables. He had boot black shoulder-length hair and a full mustache. It was October, but ninety-two degrees. He fanned himself with the greasy menu. "I don't know what I want," he said when Abigail came to take their order.

"Take your time."

"Why don't you sit down?" Sissy said—immediately clueing Abigail in that this was the man she wanted her to meet. He was weathered; his nose angled slightly to the left, as if maybe it'd been broken once or twice.

"I'm working."

"There's no one else here."

"I need to fill the saltshakers."

Sissy said, "Do it later."

"Sit," said Padraig John, still fanning himself. "You're making me nervous."

Abigail sat in the rickety plastic chair beside Sissy. She smoothed her green apron over her thighs.

"Sissy tells me you're new to town."

Abigail thought, *He's put the menu down. He's never going to order. I'm going to have to sit and make small talk.* "I'm from Arkansas." *How can he order with the menu under his elbow?*

"Whereabouts?"

"It doesn't matter."

"Jesus god, Abby," Sissy said.

"What?"

"It's a reasonable enough question."

"Mont Blanc," Abigail said.

"Never heard of it."

"No one has."

"Abigail loves the ocean," Sissy said. "She'd never seen it until she moved here two months ago. Paddy John loves the ocean too."

"I have a son named Buckley," Abigail said. She hoped it

would discourage Paddy John. He might order sooner than later. Besides, she liked putting her cards on the table.

"My boy's name is Tide," Padraig John said.

"How old is he?"

"Five. He was born when I was over there."

"Over where?"

Sissy said, "Paddy John was in 'Nam. I thought I told you that."

"How old is your boy?" Paddy John asked.

"Buckley's thirteen."

"Sadly," Paddy John said, "I've only known my boy a year."

"Your wife must like the ocean to name your son Tide."

"My wife's a loony hippie."

"She's his ex-wife, and she's not a loony hippie. She's a drug addict. There's nothing wrong with hippies, and there's everything wrong with drug addicts."

"I'm sorry."

"Me too." Padraig John picked up the menu again and began fanning himself. A bluish-gray seagull flew past close to their window.

Abigail said, "I love birds."

"I told you Abigail was far out."

"Are you ready to order?" She hadn't intended to be "far out."

Paddy John set the menu back down and rested his head in his hand. "It was nice to meet you. I don't want to bother you, and I have more baggage than any woman need carry." He turned to Sissy. "Let's go."

"Why?"

"Don't go," Abigail said, feeling sorry for the man. "What can I get you?"

Paddy John scanned the menu. "What do you recommend?" While Abigail thought about it, Paddy John said, "Can you do something about that?"

"About what?" Abigail asked, pencil and pad in hand. She was going to recommend the meat loaf. It was spectacular, and he looked like a meat loaf kind of guy. She smiled.

"Can you do anything about the skin hanging at your neck and off your arms?"

"What do you want to order? I have work to do."

"Jesus god, Paddy. What the fuck's wrong with you?" Sissy asked.

"It's a question. I'm asking a question. Is it some kind of disease? I don't mean any harm."

Abigail slipped her pad and pencil in her front apron pocket and said, "I don't have any disease. I lost one hundred and sixty pounds and I didn't lose the skin. Skin doesn't miraculously disappear along with the fat when you've spent ten years eating macaroni and cheese and Oreos." She grabbed Sissy and Paddy John's menus. "I recommend the meat loaf." A strand of Abigail's dark hair, red in the light, fell across her eye, and she tucked it behind her ear. "I don't have all day."

"I didn't mean no offense to you. I didn't know you used to be big. I wouldn't have known."

Abigail repeated, "The meat loaf's on special."

Padraig John said, "I'll have a High Life."

"And you, Sissy? Do you want anything?"

"The same, I guess."

The beers were not delivered to Sec Two by Abigail, but instead by Jeanette. She slammed both bottles down. "I don't know you," she said to Padraig John, "but you, Sissy, with your 'sisterhood' mumbo jumbo, ought to think twice before making one of my waitresses, one of my friends, upset."

Sissy chugged her beer and slunk from Jeanette's. She hadn't meant to upset Abigail. She really did have a gift for matchmaking. Her mother had been a matchmaker. It was a real calling. Padraig John told Sissy, "I'm staying."

"Suit yourself."

He drank four more beers and ate the meat loaf—as

suggested—until Abigail's shift ended. When she departed, he departed, following her home, keeping his distance, to make sure she was safe.

As Abigail met the locals and breathed in salt spray at Jeanette's, Buckley and Joan Holt got acquainted. She took him shopping for school clothes at Morton's department store on Rosenburg Street. (It was their secret. "Don't tell your mom," she said. "She'll try and pay me back.") As they walked past the palm trees lining the snug street with its shops in pastel pinks, blues, and greens, Joan said, "I didn't have any children. We didn't think we wanted any. My husband didn't think he wanted any, but now he's dead and it's just me. You can't have any grandkids if you don't have any kids." She reached for Buckley's hand.

"I guess not," Buckley said, stuffing his hands in his jeans' pockets.

"Where are your grandparents?"

"I only have one. Grandma Winter."

"Is she good to you?"

"I don't like her. She's not like a real grandmother. You know . . . she's not nice. She wouldn't think of spoiling anyone. Spare the rod and spoil the child. That sort of thing."

Joan pulled a folded paper fan from her purse. Opening it, revealing yellow butterflies, she asked, "Do you like it here?"

"Yes, ma'am."

"What did I tell you?"

"Yes, ma'am, Joan."

"Just Joan." Fanning herself, she added, "Maybe I could be your surrogate grandmother."

"What's that?"

"A step-in. A replacement, so to speak."

"If you want." Buckley frog-jumped over the cracks in the sidewalk.

"Careful."

He couldn't remember anyone but his mother ever saying "Be careful" to him and meaning it—until now. When he forgot and let his hand fall loose from his pocket, Joan Holt snatched it up. He couldn't hold hands with an old woman—he was thirteen! But he did anyway.

For the rest of the afternoon, Joan Holt talked about her dead husband, how he had been her best friend in the whole world, practically her only friend. That's how it was with them. They did everything together. They never got sick of each other. "Well, maybe on occasion," she said, "and then he got sick, really sick, and I took care of him until the end, until he died. Since then, I've been alone. Some days," she told Buckley, "I don't want to get out of bed." She coughed. "After he passed, I wanted to die."

Buckley said, "I'm sorry."

"Don't be. I understand now that God has His plan. He brought you and your mother to me."

God? Buckley thought of the reverend and of Job, but he didn't back-talk. *Let people believe what they will.* "What was your husband's name?" Buckley asked.

"Wally. His name was Wally Holt. He was a good man. Wally is short for Wallace. Sometimes I called him Walrus. He would've liked you, and you would've liked him. He was intelligent and kind, with a sharp wit."

Buckley squeezed Joan Holt's hand.

Padraig John was stuffed full on breaded shrimp and beer. He'd been to Jeanette's every evening for the past three days. When Abigail got off work, he left too. Jeanette told Abigail, "You ought to call the police if he doesn't leave you alone." The last thing Abigail wanted to do was file a police report. She was frightened that John Whitehouse and Winter would find them.

Tonight, Padraig John followed a few steps behind Abigail. The wind gusted. His boot black hair rose like wings from his part.

"Stop following me!"

"Maybe I live this way."

She rolled her eyes. "No, you don't."

"Does your boy like the ocean?"

She wasn't saying another word. She was done with men. It was mid-October.

Paddy John kept eating at Jeanette's. Every so often, he apologized for asking about her skin. "I didn't mean nothing."

She nodded and smiled that it was all right but she didn't have time for his silliness. "Stop following me."

In mid-November, Paddy John was still following a few paces behind. He took his dinner regularly at Jeanette's. *Clearly*, Abigail thought, *the man's got a screw loose.* Some nights he ate steak, sometimes shrimp, but always beer. *Just like a man,* she thought. *A worthless, no-good man.* He left better-than-average tips—always twenty percent—but that was no reason to talk to him. She was civil in Jeanette's. Outside the restaurant, she would not speak to him. Then he left a bunch of daisies—her favorite flower—with her tip. Still, she thought he was no good. Then he brought his son Tide to Jeanette's. He explained to Abigail, "His mom's not doing so good." That wasn't *Abigail's* problem.

The boy wrung his hands and stared at his lap. Padraig John said, "There's nothing to be afraid of. Have some." Tide prodded his tuna steak with a knife and shook his head no. They sat there, Padraig John eating his fish, telling the boy how good it was. "Do you want something else?"

Tide didn't speak. He moved his french fries around with a butter knife.

Abigail came to the table with a bowl of ice cream. "When Buckley is sad, ice cream cheers him up." She smiled at Padraig John.

Padraig John said, "Thank you."

"Where's his mom?"

"We don't know."

Abigail sat down beside Tide. She said, "Ice cream is cold so it makes you feel better inside. It's like medicine. How old are you?"

Padraig John said, "He's five."

"I asked Tide, not you."

Tide picked up the spoon Abigail had brought. She smiled. *Stupid! This little boy's happiness isn't your responsibility.* Padraig John smiled. Tide took a bite. Then another. Then he ate his french fries cold.

"I can get you some new fries," Abigail offered.

"Can I have more ice cream?"

He ate a second bowl.

Padraig John confided to Abigail, "He doesn't talk much."

"His dad makes up for that, I guess." She cleared away the dishes.

"Tide looks like his mom," he said.

"He's got your dark hair," Abigail said, "and kids switch. He might look like you next year."

"Does Buckley look like his dad?"

"I don't remember." The ocean had kindly eroded her memories of Richard, reducing them to sand.

"I have to take Tide home."

"It was nice to meet you," Abigail said.

Tide didn't speak, but shook her hand.

"He seems smart," she said.

No one had ever said that to Padraig John about his son.

The next night, Padraig John trailed Abigail again. "I'll probably give up soon," he said, "but Sissy said she was sure we'd hit it off. I don't know how well you know Sissy, but she's never wrong about a thing like this. She and I went to school together. I don't know if you know, but she's psychic."

Abigail heard his shoes on the sandy road and thought, *Your psychic needs to wear a bra. All of Galveston needs to wear a bra.*

Joan Holt was an old woman and her boobs were like something out of a geriatric *Playboy*. Abigail could see the woman's nipples, the size of half-dollars, through her blouse.

Paddy John said, "I don't guess I'm going to convince you to go out with me."

You're not. She turned to him. "Just leave me alone."

"I don't know why, but I can't do it."

She let her head fall back, her face to the moon. Paddy John stood behind her. Without turning around, she said, "I don't need a man in my life. I don't want a man in my life. I am content for the first time in my life." The moon was full. It was beautiful, and she heard the hush of the ocean. She righted her shoulders, adjusting her purse strap, and said, "Just stop." Turning to see him, his face pensive, she added, "Please."

He didn't say it, but he thought, *That's not what you want. It isn't. You want to be pursued. You need to be pursued.* The next night at Jeanette's, Paddy John was absent. The following night as well. Abigail even looked for him. On the third night, she received a dozen yellow roses. The note said: *Do you know "The Yellow Rose of Texas"? I'd like to play it for you.*

Padraig John hadn't given up, and to quote Sissy, "No living person can give up on love and keep living." She shook Abigail by the elbows. "I see it. You're in love!" Abigail stiffened in Sissy's hippie embrace. "I told you! I told you!"

Abigail freed herself. "I'm not in love." Her face told a different story. All night, she glanced at those roses, admiring them, their orange and red tips. They were the first roses she'd ever received. That same night, walking home, carrying her flowers, Paddy John walked behind, following the small of her back, her shoulder blades, her dark hair trailing in the wind. She was about to ask him to walk beside her when he said, "I've been having bad times. I think you've had the same. I get that sense. Sissy says so too." He paused, thinking what else to say without begging. If she wouldn't let him take her on a date after tonight, he was throwing in the towel. He'd never bought his ex-wife a dozen roses. Not that it made any difference. He continued, "I always say what I mean. Sometimes to a fault, but that's who I am. You'll never have to worry that I'm lying to you or telling you something I don't mean. Since I got back from over there, I've been bad off, and my ex-wife has been bad off for more years than my son's been alive, and you, Miss Abigail Pitank, give me hope. You are a raven-haired beauty, and I know a little poetry, like Poe, and I know a little music, mostly folk, and I'd like to get to know you—if I haven't made that clear enough." He cleared his throat. "I think Sissy's right about us. I think we were destined to meet. I think we need to know each other."

No one had ever said anything like that to Abigail. She answered quickly, instinctually: "You're right." Rushing to him, the flowers at her side, she kissed him. It felt like her first kiss. She got to experience the flutter of butterflies in her gut. She got to experience warmth brewing and spreading through her legs. She got to experience the things that some of us take for granted. If fireworks had exploded, she wouldn't have been surprised.

"I like being with you," he said, "even if it's just watching you watch the ocean."

"You don't have to talk so much." Abigail grabbed on to his windbreaker. "Kiss me again."

As he walked her the rest of the way home, she said, "You're right. I've had bad times, and so has Buckley." She looked at her freckled shins, her brown sneakers. "My skin's getting better. The doctor says I need to keep exercising." The wind blew from the south, lifting her hair.

"I was hoping you might have a beer with me?"

A beer? After following me for two months? A beer? "I like beer okay."

"Or we could get a milk shake?"

"I love milk shakes."

"And I'll play 'The Yellow Rose of Texas' for you."

"I would like that."

"And I'll make the milk shakes at my place, and you can invite Buckley, and Tide will be there, and I won't kiss you until late, and then only if you ask me to."

"Uh." She shook her head.

"What's the matter?"

"You," she said. "Do you do this to all the girls?"

"First time in my life that I bought any woman roses. I think you bring out the romantic in me." He crossed his heart.

"I better keep playing hard to get."

"That's what I'm trying to tell you: You don't have to do that with me. You never had to. It's exhausting."

The best way to reduce your chance of being struck is to avoid the following activities when there is even the slightest chance of bad weather:

a. Boating, fishing, or swimming
b. Working on heavy farm or road equipment
c. Playing golf
d. Talking on the telephone
e. Using or repairing electrical appliances

11

St. Patrick's Day, 1979

There was no wind on St. Patrick's Day. It was a humid day with highs in the eighties. A month had passed since Edna's funeral. It was a school day for Becca.

Mary had planned a shopping trip to Raleigh with her friend Laura.

Plans change. Nine-year-old girls get sick. School nurses track down mothers at their friends' homes at nine o'clock in the morning, and mothers, who'd prefer to spend the day shopping in Raleigh with their friends, cancel their plans and drive to Chapel Hill Elementary to pick up their fourth-grader.

Mary parks her car on the street because her husband's and her babysitter's cars are in the driveway. She tiptoes inside and then thinks better of tiptoeing because there's a sick daughter to think about. The sick daughter turns on the TV. She wants some soda. *Daughters are selfish.*

Mary opens her bedroom door and sees Millie sitting naked on *her* bed. Millie says, "Oh my God! Oh, shit! Oh, Mary, I'm sorry. Oh, fuck," and fumbles to pull on her jeans, one foot in, one out, tripping across the floor into a tower of glossy *Yachting Today* magazines that slide and spread reds, whites, and blues across the hardwood floor. Mary sees Millie's thighs, the young pink goose-bumpy flesh, her flat stomach, her pink fingernails covering her perky little breasts, then tugging the waist of her jeans, hopping, her breasts bouncing, to cover up. Then Mary sees Rowan, shirtless, exiting their bathroom in a pair of khaki shorts. He stands beside their rumpled bed, silent, while Millie continues to fumble across the bedroom floor. Rowan bends down and slides a copy of *Yachting Today* from the feathered pile. Why is he picking up a magazine? Why is he doing this to her?

Rowan says to Millie, "The joint's in the bathroom." Sloppily dressed, Millie goes to the bathroom. Rowan says, "You were right. It's good shit."

Mary says, "Becca's downstairs. The nurse telephoned. She's sick." She doesn't know what else to say. In shock, she stands there, watching Millie exit the bathroom. Millie smells of marijuana. Mary remembers when she and Rowan smoked pot together. It was before Becca.

Rowan tosses the magazine on the bed and pulls his polo shirt over his head.

Mary leaves the room, shutting the door on the husband and the babysitter because she can't think. She knows about the affairs, but suspected someone named Patty—from the strawberry note. She's known about the affairs for years, but not in her own bed, not with the babysitter, who isn't so smart. *Why her? Do you like stupid? Why here? Why not in her dorm? Why does it have to be in my face? In my home?*

Mary is only thirty-two, but already she feels old. It's St. Patrick's Day today. She remembers another St. Patrick's Day when they first met, when they were in love. There's a picture of the two of them on a parade float. She's wearing a top hat and he's kissing her. She's looking at the camera, knowing he can't keep his hands or his eyes off her. He loved her. It's past tense, isn't it? *Where's that picture?*

She thinks about taking Becca into the bathroom, or asking Becca to stay in her room so she won't see Millie come down the stairs, but she doesn't. She leaves Becca right where she is so Becca can see Millie leave. Maybe Becca will put two and two together and know that her father is a real shit. *Where is that picture?*

Becca says, "Hey, what are you doing here?" when Millie descends the steps.

"Nothing."

"Happy St. Patrick's Day."

"Yeah."

"I'm sick."

"Yeah. Your dad was helping me with school stuff." She leaves. She didn't say "Feel better" or "What's wrong?"

Becca hears the squeak of the liquor cabinet's antique door, she hears an irritating, breathless moan, and when she thinks about the midday highball her mother is about to mix, about the two cars in the driveway, about Millie's shirt untucked and her hair mussed, she understands. Having a fever of one hundred and two degrees, Becca stays put. She's too sick to do anything. She wishes someone would bring her some juice and some baby aspirin, but she's been forgotten. She remembers the day she saw Millie and her dad walking outside Mario's, his hand grazing Millie's arm, and it makes her feel sicker, knowing what he's doing. She wishes she were naive. She doesn't want to know about her dad's philandering. (Last year, Aunt Claire called Becca's dad a philanderer. Becca had assumed it was a good thing, but wrote the word down to look it up. It's not a good thing.) Why can't she fix her parents? Why can't they get along?

That afternoon into evening, Mary sits on the den floor, flipping through photo albums, dumping shoe boxes of pictures between her legs. Sorting through pictures and drinking, saying, "I don't know where that picture is. It's got to be here." She says it over and over before making another drink. Becca is too sick to get up, but her mother does bring juice and aspirin. She also brings apple wedges and sliced cheddar. Becca is grateful, but sad for her mother. "You know what picture I'm talking about, right?" Mary asks.

"I don't think so," Becca admits.

"It's got to be here."

"Maybe look for it tomorrow."

"Today is St. Patrick's Day. Not tomorrow, Rebecca."

"Oh, right." It's best not to disagree with her mother when she drinks this much. It's best to keep quiet or say what Mary wants to hear.

Becca's father stays upstairs.

Becca goes upstairs to bed, tiptoeing past her parents' door. She can't see her father, not now. She just can't. She didn't have dinner, but she goes to bed with a stack of Chips Ahoy cookies wrapped in a paper towel, leaving her mother passed out downstairs, a pile of wrinkled photographs under her cheek.

No one yells—not that night, the next day, or the next week. No one speaks.

Rowan parks the Austin Healey in the backyard and sleeps in the garage on an old army cot. Becca's birthday is April first. Carrie spends the night, and they eat cake with Becca's mom. Later, they play the board game Life in the garage with Becca's dad. After the house is dark, Carrie whispers, "This must be the worst."

Becca says, "It is." She had one wish on her birthday. *I want my parents to love each other again.*

Carrie asks, "What did you wish for? Did you wish for Kevin Richfield to like you?"

"I can't tell or it won't come true."

Throughout April, Becca's dad stays in the garage, smelling of kerosene and lying to Becca, telling her that sleeping in the garage is fun, just like camping out. She ought to spend a Friday night camping out in the garage with him. She tries. She doesn't want to hurt his feelings. They play six hands of gin rummy. Becca loses every time. In the middle of the night, she goes back inside to use the bathroom and falls asleep in her own bed.

Losing at cards isn't fun and neither is sleeping in the garage.

The world can be fuzzy or sharp or somewhere in between. After Bo was struck by lightning and Grandma Edna died, things were painfully sharp for Becca. When it thundered, she worried that she would bring the lightning to her house and accidentally kill her own dog, Whiskers. She didn't want to hurt or kill anyone, and even if she'd had nothing to do with Bo's death, she nonetheless felt responsible. She took precautions: staying clear of windows, water, and electrical wires during thunderstorms; bathing in the morning when storms are less likely; and wearing only rubber-soled shoes.

Sitting crouched in the den with Whiskers curled between her legs, she checked the bottoms of her shoes for sticky bits of metallic bubble gum wrappers, pennies, and paper clips. When it wasn't storming, she had other things to worry about. There were the bombs and the Russians and the whales being brutally harpooned. There were seals being clubbed and foxes being trapped. She worried that Whiskers was aging prematurely. She worried that her mother would pass out one night and never wake up. She worried that her father would leave the garage and she'd never see him again. She worried that if it weren't for her escapes—TV, books, and art—she'd go crazy. She was too young to go crazy. When she worried, she drew pretty pictures. Like in *Mary Poppins*, she jumped into those pictures, imagining bright sunny places without sticky liquor drinks and cheating husbands. Her other escapes included *The Wonderful World of Disney* and *The Six Million Dollar Man*, praying to Grandma Edna in heaven, and eating Chips Ahoy chocolate chip cookies for dinner. Becca's world, she knew, was sharp. It had a point, and she'd prefer a dull edge—like a butter knife's.

That summer, Becca and Carrie straddled their bikes outside the 7-Eleven, counting change to buy Coca-Cola–flavored Slurpees. They watched the comings and goings of the Chapel Hillians. Sometimes Becca saw things that weren't there and had to look twice. She saw a twenty-something man in dark sunglasses leaving the store with a six pack of Budweiser and an arm full of red roses. She asked Carrie, "They sell roses at 7-Eleven?"

"What are you talking about?"

"The roses."

"You need glasses, Bec."

Becca looked again and saw that the roses were a crinkly bag of pork rinds. She had to look twice at a lot of things. Sometimes at night, as she sat in the den with Whiskers, the door leading to the backyard flew open. Whiskers started barking. Once, Becca saw Grandma Edna and Bo. When she looked again, they were gone. She shut and locked the door, marching upstairs to tell her mother.

"You shouldn't have gone to see that scary movie. I told you."

"It wasn't like that. It wasn't scary. It was Grandma and Bo."

"Please leave me alone."

Becca shut her mother's door and went back downstairs to the TV.

In early July, Becca's dad moved back into the house. Becca wasn't sure what it meant exactly but hoped that the philandering would stop. She hoped that her parents would reconcile. They might fall in love again. As sharp-edged as her life was, there were nuanced things she remembered and mentally cataloged. For instance, she took haloed photographs. She saw roses instead of pork rinds. Once in a while, she propelled the second hand on a random timepiece to tick counterclockwise. Truthfully, Becca couldn't live in the world without hope. She was a girl. She was not a disbeliever, a naysayer, or a cynic. She was a girl with her whole life ahead of her.

Mary Wickle Burke, saving crumpled photographs of an unrecognizable life, decided to extricate herself from this life too: First, she quit chemistry socials on Thursdays; next, her Wednesday-night card game. She boxed her most expensive gowns and donated them to the Salvation Army. She resigned from the Garden Club board and the Historic Preservation Society.

When she'd quit everything that occupied her time, she took her calendar off the wall, crammed it into the garbage, and in permanent black marker wrote *I QUIT* where the calendar had hung.

She drank her cocktails at home and smoked cigarettes in the backyard. Rowan slept in their "marital" bed, but he didn't touch her. He wouldn't say he was sorry about the babysitter, just "It didn't mean anything" and "You're being ridiculous."

"I'm being ridiculous," she muttered. "I'm being ridiculous," she said again, her voice louder. "Me! I'm ridiculous!"

He told her, "Settle down. What is it with you that everything has to be dramatic?"

He had no idea that what he'd done did mean something. It meant that he didn't respect her. It meant that he didn't love her.

Pathetically, she still loved him.

Absolutely, she was ridiculous.

Victims who don't suffer post-
traumatic stress can still suffer acute
unreasonable fears of lightning,
partly due to a natural response, but
equally due to the damaged nervous
system, responding to both internal and
external stimuli. For example, if
a victim gets goose bumps or feels a
tingling sensation, he may relive the
strike, reacting with trepidation even
when there's not a cloud in the sky.

12

Barbi Benton, 1972

Buckley's first day of eighth grade at Galveston Junior High was like fifth grade show-and-tell in Mont Blanc, except that Buckley was the purple-spotted lizard scooped out of the shoebox, and Buckley, like the lizard, was a huge hit in his new hip-hugger jeans and eagle-patterned shirt. He didn't know how to act in the odd campus-styled school where he walked from one class to the next outside in the sunshine and girls smiled and giggled behind their notebooks, and a group of boys, dressed much like himself, huddled around Buckley, asking him if he knew how to surf, if he'd seen the Barbi Benton shots in *Playboy*. Charlie said, "My dad collects them. Barbi's the best." Buckley didn't say much for fear of fouling everything up, and surprisingly, his quietness made him cool.

Marty Bascott, a flame-headed girl, fittingly nicknamed Flame-head, pinned Buckley with his back to the red-brick school at three-thirty. He'd been going to school in Galveston for two months. She said, "I don't know if Theresa said she likes you, but she's a lesbian. If you don't know what that means, it means she likes girls. She likes doing *it* with them."

"I know lesbians."

"Your sister?"

"I don't have a sister."

"I do. She's a bitch. Do you want to come over?"

"What?"

"Do you want to come over?"

"Now?"

"No. In fifty years."

"I can't. I want to, but I'm going over to Charlie's."

"To look at *Playboy*?"

"I don't know."

"He's only got that one issue."

In fact, Charlie Zuchowski, a dark-headed thirteen-year-old boy with premature stubble on his chin, had far more than the March 1970 Barbi Benton pictorial. He had every *Playboy* from 1968 to the current October issue. His father was a *Playboy* collector. Charlie said his dad was a connoisseur of the ladies. Buckley pretended to know what that meant. Charlie pulled three issues, including his favorite, from his dad's bedside drawer. "My dad said I can look whenever I want."

They drank Cokes in Charlie's faux-wood-paneled den. They crouched on the shag carpeting. Charlie, Buckley, and Charlie's best friend, Eddie Smart, flipped from one page to the next until Buckley had seen all nine amazing, beauteous shots of Barbi Benton, including the centerfold. "She is the most beautiful girl I've ever seen."

"Yeah," agreed Charlie.

"I'd do it to her," said Eddie. Eddie said he'd do it to everybody.

"No you wouldn't." Charlie got up from the shag and walked into the adjoining sunroom. "Buckley, Eddie says he's not a virgin."

"Because I'm not."

"Eddie said he did it with Theresa's mom." Charlie began to laugh.

"I did."

"Did you?" asked Buckley, pulling at the waist loop of his hip-hugger jeans.

"Yeah, I did. I gave it to her." Eddie thrust his hips forward. "And she was screaming, 'Oh, Eddie. Oh, Eddie!' "

"Tell Buckley the rest." Charlie stood in the doorway between the sunroom and the den, his pinkish hands pressed into the sides of the archway. The afternoon sun lit the top of his chestnut hair, casting Buckley and Eddie in shadow.

Eddie rolled his eyes. "Theresa's mom had been drinking."

"Tell Buckley how much she'd been drinking."

"She was drunk. So what! It still counts."

Charlie laughed again, and Buckley joined in, smacking his palm on the carpeting for emphasis. It was funny. "Does she remember doing it with you?" Buckley guessed Mrs. Cormier, Theresa's mom, was no Barbi Benton. Buckley rose from the shag and high-fived Charlie.

"I'm no virgin."

"I'd rather be a virgin." Charlie shook his head in disgust.

Eddie said, "Flamehead's got a thing for Buckley."

"Marty Bascott?" Buckley asked.

"I heard she was going to invite you over today."

"She did, but I told her I was coming over here."

Charlie and Eddie both said, "You should've gone there. She goes to second base." Buckley felt ignorant. He didn't know what second base was.

Eddie said, "I like older, more experienced girls."

"Like old ladies," Charlie added. "Old, drunk ladies."

Buckley had no retort, only regret. Flamehead was pretty. Maybe she'd ask him over again.

Mr. Zuchowski, Charlie's dad, arrived home at six, and after his standard martini (the man was a big Hugh Hefner fan), he took the boys to Tony's Pizzeria on Seawall Boulevard.

Buckley stuffed his face with pepperoni pizza.

Mr. Zuchowski ate a salad. He said, "What did you boys do today?"

Charlie said, "I told Buckley about Eddie's drunk sex with Mrs. Cormier."

Mr. Zuchowski nodded. "It's a good story." Buckley felt queasy. It seemed weird that a grown man should know about a boy having sex with a divorcée and act like it was no big deal.

Eddie said, "She liked it. It doesn't matter that she was drunk. Next time I do it with her, I'll make sure she's sober."

Mr. Zuchowski laughed. "Be sure and take pictures." Turning to his son, Charlie, he said, "When you turn fifteen, I'll take you to Trina's. We'll take Buckley too. There's no point in taking Eddie since he's got so much experience already." Trina's was a whorehouse. Everybody in Galveston knew Trina's.

Without thinking, Buckley said, "Don't take me."

Mr. Zuchowski nodded. "Don't worry, Buckley. It'll be all right. We won't force you to go."

But why wouldn't he go? What was there to fear? There might be a girl at Trina's who looked like bubbly Barbi Benton. She'd fall in love with Buckley and leave Trina's behind. Buckley sipped his Coke. It was incredible that after a lifetime of worrying about his mother's health and safety, of worrying about the reverend humiliating him, of worrying about the bullies at school beating the shit out of him, of worrying that Winter would scream at him, *this* was now his biggest fear: embarrassing himself at a whorehouse. Life was good.

Some people, like Paddy John's son, Tide McGowan, get lost in the filthy crevices of life, and they never get found—at least not whole. Sitting across from him, Abigail Pitank recognized Tide's position, as if dog fur and dust clung to his very being, not just his clothes. As he talked incessantly about his mother, Abigail worried that he'd already suffered too much damage to recover. There was something in the way he spoke quickly, manically, as if at any second, this scene, the four of them sitting in the Sizzler, could implode. Tide said, "Judy from *The Jetsons* is just like my mom. Her name's Judy, like Judy Jetson. Judy. Have you ever seen *The Wizard of Oz*? Judy Garland stars in that as Dorothy." Tide's face was slick from buttered hush puppies.

Buckley sipped his Coke from a straw. Why were they at the Sizzler? Reverend Whitehouse had liked the Sizzler.

Padraig John put his arm around Abigail.

"Where's Judy now?" Buckley asked Tide.

Abigail shot him a disapproving look.

"On TV."

"What show's she on?" Buckley pressed.

Abigail said, "That's enough."

Tide stuffed a hush puppy in his pocket. Padraig John said, "I think she's still taking acting classes."

"That's right," Tide said, reaching over the table. To Abigail he said, "Are you going to eat your hush puppies?"

Buckley looked disgustedly at Tide.

"No, sweetheart."

Tide stuffed them and her packets of margarine in his pockets. "After my mom finishes her acting classes, she'll probably get a part on a soap opera like *Days of Our Lives*. She's always watched that show, and I've seen her practice the lines."

"Where does she take acting classes?" Buckley asked, knowing full well that Tide's mother was somewhere getting stoned or whatever it was junkies did. He wasn't sure if they used needles or snorted or what kind of drug they took, only that Tide's mom was a junkie.

Tide said, "She's close by. She hates for us to be far apart. When she moves to Hollywood, I'll go with her."

Paddy John said, "I'll get the check."

Abigail said to Buckley, "It's rude to pry into someone's business. You don't need to pester Tide with so many questions."

"Sorry, Tide," Buckley said. "Sorry, Mom."

Tide said, "It's okay. I like talking about my mom." He pulled a hush puppy from his pocket and took a bite before putting it back.

Since Judy McGowan, Paddy's former wife, had disappeared, leaving behind a few possessions, some tattered furniture, some black-and-white photographs, a thawed turkey on the kitchen floor, and Tide, her son, Tide had moved into Paddy John's home. It was a small one-bedroom apartment, but it was clean, which Tide appreciated. Afraid to sleep alone, he slept with Paddy John, insisting the door remain open, the hallway and bathroom lights lit. Tide was terrified of the dark. Paddy John had called social services, not to find a more suitable home for Tide, but because, having experienced the trauma of war, he could tell that his son had been traumatized in his former wife's care. On the phone, he explained, "The boy needs someone to talk to."

"We'll send a caseworker out as soon as one's available." Months passed. Still no social worker.

Tide hoarded food such as hush puppies, apples, American cheese, and bologna beneath his pillow. Every day, Paddy John threw the rancid food away, took the pillowcases to the laundromat, and tried reassuring his son: "There's plenty to eat. Hell, my girl-friend works at a restaurant, and if worse comes to worst, there's an ocean full of fish out there, and I'm a hell of a fisherman. Please don't worry."

In kindergarten, Tide volunteered to pick the other students' lunch trays up from their desks. He stuffed his pants with their discarded rolls and butter packets. He ate the rolls he'd saved after Padraig John was asleep, or he hid them beneath his pillow. Padraig John, unsure how to handle the situation, returned to the laundromat. It was pretty clear that Tide hadn't been well fed while he was in Judy's care. When Paddy John asked about life with Judy, Tide said, "It was fine." He wouldn't talk about whatever it was he'd endured. After consulting the school guidance counselor and Tide's teachers, Paddy John was told that it might be years before Tide was willing or capable of discussing his past. It wasn't much comfort to Paddy John, who wanted his son to be happy. When he asked Tide, "How are you feeling today?" Tide answered, "Fine."

He always claimed to be fine, despite his food hoarding, fear of the dark, and elevation of his junkie mother to famous Hollywood actress status.

Across town, on the waterfront in a dilapidated red-curtained house, Judy McGowan squirted baby oil into her palm. She massaged Charlie Zuchowski's dad, Mr. Zuchowski, starting with his shoulders. She said, "It feels good, doesn't it?"

It didn't. Mr. Zuchowski felt sorry for and simultaneously disgusted by Judy. They'd gone to high school together, and now she was seriously messed up—not even the kind of girl he wanted rubbing his back, let alone anything else. Her face was sallow. Her hands were bony and cold. The heater was on the fritz. He felt cold all over. "Just stop," he said, getting to his knees and taking a seat on the table.

"Do you want me to suck you off now?" she asked.

"I don't want you to touch me." He'd have to tell Trina that this was not the kind of trash he expected when he came to her establishment.

Judy said, "Didn't we go to high school together?"

"I don't think so. If you'll excuse me, I'd like some privacy, please."

"Sure thing."

Excerpt from
THE HANDBOOK FOR LIGHTNING STRIKE SURVIVORS

Galveston, Texas, suffered the Great
Storm of 1900, a massive hurricane that
killed 6,000 residents.
Surprising to most people:
Lightning kills more people each year
than hurricanes and tornadoes.

13

Fall fever, 1980

Colin Atwell was in Becca's reading, math, social studies, and art classes. He was still weird, but he liked art. Becca liked art. Her teacher, Mrs. Fairaday, said Becca's self-portrait was "the most compelling" she'd seen in her sixteen years as a middle school art teacher. In Becca's painting, red flames shot from her eyes, and the top of her head opened like a lid. Mrs. Fairaday even suggested Becca attend an artist's summer camp, to which Becca's mother said no. The first image that sprang to Mary's mind was from the sixties: flower children high on god knows what, smeared with psychedelic body paints. No, Becca would not attend an artist's summer camp. Becca knew that there was no point arguing with her mother, who was irrational and paranoid.

Despite no artist's camp, the summer passed quickly. Becca had a knapsack for her charcoals and sketchpad and spent most days drawing the beauty she saw everywhere in Chapel Hill. It seemed better to sketch and shade without instruction, which stifled the imagination.

Today, Colin Atwell was joining her. In the sunshine, her hair streaked gold, Becca waited for Colin on the green lawn of Polk Place. The sun was high in the October sky. She gnawed a pencil, the yellow flaking away. He was late. She knew he might not show at all. That's partly why she waited—to see if he would. She sat Indian-style and wrote his name, *Colin Atwell,* in her sketchbook. She was a sixth-grader now.

Colin flicked her in the back of the neck before dropping onto the lawn. Forever flicking her in the back of the neck and knocking the back of her knee with his knee so that she wobbled on the bleachers during chorus, he called her "Rebecca of Sunnybrook Farm." He shot rubber bands at her when Mrs. Creighton, the chorus teacher, wasn't looking, and he pretended to dislike Becca because he thought that was how boys got girls to like them. Basically, like many little boys, he was clueless.

She grabbed the back of her neck. "That hurt!"

"No it didn't." Grabbing Becca's sketchbook and rolling onto his back, he stretched one hand toward Becca.

"Don't do it."

"What?" With two fingers, he poked her in the waist.

"I'm not ticklish. I told you."

He mimicked, "I'm not ticklish. I told you," and rolled onto his stomach. "Are you going to the homecoming dance?"

"Maybe." Sometimes she went to Richmond with her dad when he had meetings with Atkins and Thames. Hardly teaching anymore, he said he was successful now. Becca couldn't tell a difference.

"Keep still," Colin said. "I'll draw you." He wanted to make her look the way she looked to him—bright, explosive, inviting, alluring—but he couldn't, so out of frustration he drew a snot-nosed monster.

Becca posed, squinting in the sunlight at the magnolias that blurred. The sun blazed in the viburnum and japonica, and she'd forgotten her sunglasses. This morning she'd applied two layers of pink lip gloss and her mom's blue eye shadow. She had this feeling that Colin was going to make a move and kiss her. He might ask, "Will you go with me?" and she might say yes because even though he was no Kevin Richfield, he genuinely liked her drawings and paintings. He said the right things, knowing what she meant, what she thought, what she felt when she made art; saying things like "The texture here is perfect," "You used the right shade of yellow. It makes it soft," "This is wonderful. It's my favorite painting because it's like you pieced yourself inside it." She probably would "go with him." She'd kiss him too—if he tried. They'd hold hands and walk the main hall at school. A boy who knew and loved art, even if he was weird—and Colin was weird—was good enough for her.

He passed back her sketchbook. "You like it?"

"No!"

"What's the matter, Rebecca of Sunnybrook Farm?"

"You're not funny." She got up, clutching the sketchbook to her chest.

"I was just kidding."

"You drew an ugly monster! Is that what you think I am?"

"Of course not."

"What was I thinking, meeting you here? You're an idiot."

"Wait."

"Don't bother me." With the pencil back between her teeth, she stepped blindly into the midday sun, hoping he'd follow, feeling suddenly mad at her father, but unsure why. Colin called again, "I was just kidding," but he didn't chase after her. Instead, he sat defeated, feeling stupid. Try as he might, he could never tell Becca how he felt. Why couldn't he say "I like you"? His best friend, Julian, said that if you tell a girl you like her, she won't like you back. And what if she never liked him back? He couldn't keep wobbling her knee for the rest of the year. Colin thought he was running out of options.

As she walked home, Becca felt feverish, unhappy, angry, frustrated, and desperate, all at the same time. Her hands in fists, she tromped. In the distance, she saw Kevin Richfield outside Pepper's Pizza with three eighth-grade girls. Becca was burning up. She hated those stupid eighth-grade girls. She never should've considered settling for Colin Atwell.

I'll skip Richmond this weekend. I'll go to the dance. Maybe

Kevin will be there. She was burning up, ravenous for *something*; an emptiness gnawed her gut.

Mary was dusting the coffee table. "How was your day?

"Fine." Becca took four Chips Ahoy cookies to her bedroom. She fed one to Whiskers. Her sheets gritty with crumbs, she fell into a deep sleep. She slept all afternoon and through the night.

Later in the week, she approached her father about their trip to Richmond. She didn't want to disappoint him, but she wanted to attend the dance. Rather than being disappointed, her father said, "I didn't think you were coming with me this weekend. No harm. I've got meetings back to back."

"All right." It would've been nice if he'd told her sooner.

Sadly, it rained the night of the dance. Downstairs, Becca searched for her hair clips on the sideboard, feeling insignificant in comparison to Mother Nature. She often compared herself to the weather. The back door swung open and she saw Grandma Edna, drenched, her white hair loose and matted to her face. She didn't see Bo. Before Becca could speak, the door slammed shut. The electricity went out for a second. Whiskers barked. She felt her own forehead. Again she was on fire. She pushed open the back door. "Grandma Edna, are you there? Where are you?" There was the warm rain and a gentle wind. She pulled the door shut and went upstairs to her mother's bedroom. "I don't think I should go to the dance."

"Why? Is it because you don't have a date? Big deal! It's a middle school dance. You'll have fun."

"That's not it, Mom." She hesitated. "When I was downstairs, the door blew open and I saw Grandma Edna. It was just before the electricity flickered. Maybe she's trying to tell me something."

Her mother said, "I hate when you do this. She was my mother, not yours. If anyone is going to see her, it would be me, and I don't see her. There's no such things as ghosts." She quaffed her drink. "Fix me another one," she said, handing Becca her glass. "Scotch, and two ice cubes."

Becca took the sticky glass.

"You're going to the dance, and you're going to have fun."

As Becca turned away, Mary grabbed her sleeve. "Just one ice cube." Becca's mother was unrecognizable: ruddy face, bulbous nose, gray skin under vacant, bloodshot eyes.

When Becca returned with the drink, her mother took a sip and said, "Sit down. I have something I want you to wear."

"Mom, I think I have a fever."

"Nonsense." Mary felt Becca's forehead with the back of her hand. "You're anxious. Now sit down."

Becca sat on the edge of the bed. Mary opened her large oak jewelry box, necklaces hanging in shimmering rows. Becca spotted emeralds, rubies, and diamonds. A long time ago, her father had spoiled her mother with jewels. Mary had once told Becca, "I felt like Elizabeth Taylor. I always had some new rock for everyone to admire."

"Here we go," Mary said. "This is going to go perfect with your dress." She pulled out the purple butterfly brooch. "This was my mother's, and before that, it was her mother's, and now it's mine. I want you to wear it tonight for your first formal dance. One day it will belong to you."

Becca knew the story, but she listened raptly, loving stories, loving history, loving the connections between people that can be sustained through the smallest trinket. "I love you, Mom."

Mary pinned the brooch on Becca's dress. "It looks beautiful." They admired it in the vanity, hearing the honk of Belinda Drinkwater's Pinto. Mary said, "You'd think she could ring the fucking bell."

"It's raining."

"It's only decent."

Becca left with her curly hair loose, frizzing in the humidity.

• • •

Belinda Drinkwater said, "Meet me here out front in this exact spot at nine-thirty sharp."

"I think we get it, Mom," Carrie said. Belinda waited for a hug, but this was middle school; she got a "See you later, Mom."

Carrie wore a snug blouse, a white miniskirt, and red and white striped tights. She looked, Becca thought, like a candy cane. Her blond hair was pulled tight in a clip. Becca wished she had worn a miniskirt, but she didn't own any.

Carrie had boobs—really big boobs, noticeably big in the red shirt she'd somehow stretched across her chest; and Carrie was taller than most of the boys, so their eyes were at her chest when she talked to them. Sometimes Carrie wore colored bras and light-colored tops, so Becca could see the pink or blue straps through Carrie's shirt. Sometimes Becca wanted to tell Carrie that she was starting to look like a slut, that people were talking about her, that boys were saying things about her (things Becca wished they'd say about her: exclamations like "Holy shit! Did you see her?").

Kevin Richfield approached the two girls, who swayed back and forth to the music, each with her cup of bland punch. Staring at Carrie's chest, he said, "Do you want to dance?"

Carrie gave Becca *that* look: *Is it okay? Let's be serious. It has to be okay. It's Kevin Richfield—eighth-grader.* Eyebrows raised. Hopefulness. *I might talk about you the whole time.* Becca reached for Carrie's cup of punch. "Have fun."

They danced to "Rock with You" while Becca leaned against the folded bleachers holding two cups of punch. Carrie's chest was pressed into Kevin's. It made Becca sick.

Looking at Kevin and Carrie, looking beyond them—at the lonely boys snapping their fingers, counting right foot, left foot, and the stupid girls applying lip gloss and checking their hair—Becca spotted Colin Atwell. He spotted her too. He turned with his back to her, yanking at the belt of his pants like he might moon her. He high-fived one of his friends. *He's a jerk.*

The rain picked up. Inside the gym, it sounded like a bag of marbles being dumped on the roof. Then it stopped. *Boom!* A loud clap of thunder, and Becca ducked, spilling the two cups of punch she'd held. Her stomach ached. She huddled there, red punch spreading across the gym floor. It wasn't supposed to thunderstorm. Just rain. She'd checked the forecast.

Mrs. Lewis, the school librarian, who very much looked the part of school librarian, with her hair in a bun, spectacles, and high-necked ruffled blouse, said, "What are you doing?" Looking at the spilled punch, she added, "This is why we shouldn't have these inane dances." The thunder boomed, and Becca heard a dog howling.

"Did you hear that?"

"It's raining, dear. The punch!" Mrs. Lewis pointed to the floor.

"Sorry," Becca said.

"Sorry is right!" Mrs. Lewis called out to one of the custodians.

Becca felt flushed. She shouldn't have come to the dance.

Becca headed for the door. On her way, Colin Atwell bobbed the back of her leg, tipping her backwards, catching her just in time. He was smiling. "You made it? Do you want to . . . you know?"

"I don't want to 'you know' anything with you. I'm leaving."

"Do you want to dance, Rebecca of Sunnybrook Farm?"

"Are you deaf?"

Becca made her way toward the gym doors, thinking, *Everything's going to be okay,* but feeling the opposite. She pushed the door's silver bar, and the force of her palms along with the fierce wind propelled the door to slam back against the brick. The frustration and anger that had been bubbling in her gut spread up into her esophagus. It wasn't just Carrie and Kevin. It was her mom too. She felt sick. It wasn't okay. Nothing was okay. *Fuck lightning. Fuck Carrie. Fuck Kevin, and fuck God! Fuck everybody.* She hated the *stupid* corduroy dress that clung to her *stupid* white tights. She made a fool of herself cowering on the gym floor. She was a flat-chested, *stupid*, punch-spilling idiot.

Becca ran into the rain that blew in sheets from the south. She heard the same dog howling in the distance. She had to go home. Maybe that howling dog was Bo trying to warn her that something was wrong. With the rain pelting her freckled cheeks, she looked up at the strange sky, a pale lavender in some spots, like it was far away, like the distant mountains at Grandma Edna's, like there was breathing room—dark and menacing in other spots, like a low ceiling pressing down on her. *Please don't let me get hit by lightning. Please, God. I didn't mean fuck you. I didn't mean it, really. I didn't mean fuck Carrie or anybody else. I'm sorry. Something's wrong with me.* Despite her parents' atheism, Becca believed in Grandma Edna's god. Grandma Edna was smart.

Colin Atwell followed Becca through the gym doors, across the parking lot.

He wasn't thinking about the storm. Becca was the only girl with whom he'd hoped to dance. She was the only girl he had ever liked in his entire twelve-year-old life. He recognized something in her that he'd never perceived in any other girl. He didn't want to flick her neck or wobble her knee. He wanted to hold her hand and touch her breasts. He wanted to kiss her on the mouth, but he didn't know how to do those things. He chased after her, yelling, "Wait up!" He'd say *I like you.* Even if it meant she wouldn't like him. Even if she wouldn't stand beside him in chorus, he would tell her how he felt. He would say *I like you.*

As Becca ran through Morgan's Woods for the shortcut to her house, Colin followed. The wet leaves soggy underfoot, the trees canopying the two of them from the storm, she couldn't believe she was actually out in the middle of a thunderstorm. She couldn't believe she was rushing home, and she didn't know what was compelling her to do so. Was it Carrie with Kevin? Was it the fire in her gut? Was it the sky pressing down, making it difficult to breathe? Was it the vision of Grandma Edna, dripping wet, just outside the den? Was it Whiskers cowering alone under her bed? She didn't know, but she ran.

The brightly colored leaves of autumn were muted blood red in the darkness, a few clinging to Becca's tights. Slugs squished between the treads of her brown leather Mary Janes. Colin kept calling "Wait up," and halfway through the woods as she approached Forest Theatre, the place where the yearly ballet recital was held, the purple butterfly brooch came unhinged, falling from her dress into wet maple leaves, an insignificant speck of amethyst. Becca kept running. A quarter of the way across the wide lawn of Mc-Corkle Place, she saw lightning strike the dome of the Old Well. White everywhere. Becca, beaded and dripping with rain, her knotted curls crowned with pine needles and twigs, vibrated from fall fever. She was dark and muted like the autumn leaves. She was speechless.

Colin took her hand. "Holy shit," he said. "Did you see that?"

She pulled her hand away.

"What's the matter? Why are you running?" Colin's father had warned him that girls, women—it makes no difference—are crazy. Colin's own mother was a runaway. Colin thought Becca especially crazy. Maybe that's why he liked her.

"I have to go," she said.

The house's back door was unlocked, the rooms dark. Colin tried to wipe his mud-caked Buster Browns on the straw welcome mat, but gave up, following Becca inside through the den, past the library, and into the kitchen, where Becca's mother was slumped on the floor, her back against a bottom cabinet, her head limp, her hair wild, a mountain of photographs between her bare legs. The cuffs of her robe, the tips of her red hair wet and putrid with bourbon. The empty bottle of Jim Beam touching her big toe. Red toenail polish. Freckled, milky legs. White robe. In her mother's right hand, the black-and-white photograph of Mary Wickle and Rowan Burke on a St. Patrick's Day parade float. She hadn't been lying. She was wearing a top hat and Rowan was kissing her. The girl in the photograph looked at the camera with confidence, so much confidence, that Mary hardly resembled her.

Had Becca's mother been conscious, she would've told her daughter, *Our picture almost made the newspaper.* She would've added, *You look positively terrible. You're soaking wet.* She would've then returned to the matter at hand: *Just look at how young I am in this picture.* Instead, Mary was unconscious, mute, with Becca imagining what her mother might say.

Colin backed away, knocking his head into the telephone. The receiver clacked to the floor. Becca looked to the window, at the unrelenting rain, at the puddle of water at her feet, at her white tights, at her own knees dropping to the linoleum. She could hear Whiskers upstairs, whining. Her world was slowing down. "Mom," she said. "Mom?" She wiped at the sticky crust around her mother's mouth, pulling her mother's robe tighter and cinching the waist. She lifted her mother's head, propping it upright against the cabinet. Earlier tonight, when she'd felt anxious about the dance, she'd wanted to be a little girl again. She'd wanted to nuzzle against her mother, to hear her mother say *I'm proud of you* or something encouraging. Now, Becca indulged in that missed opportunity, resting her head on her mother's lap, holding tight to her waist, pretending she was an innocent girl and her mother was proud and doting. Becca shut her eyes and waited for *whatever will be, will be; the future's not ours to see. Que sera, sera.* There was nothing else to do.

Becca was eleven when she found her mother slumped against the kitchen cabinet, when she lost her mother's favorite brooch racing through the woods, when Colin Atwell waited with her for the ambulance to arrive. When Colin said, "I'm sorry. I need to call my dad. I don't want him to worry." When the paramedics roused Mary from her stupor and insisted on taking her to the hospital. When the ambulance drove away and Colin left with his father, and Bob and his cheating whore wife stood in the drizzle, gawking at the red ambulance lights. When one of the paramedics suggested Becca wait with the neighbors across the street, and Becca waited in her bedroom instead for her dad to come home. She got out her sketchbook, composing a poem:

> *Do you think he's gonna go?*
> *Do you think he's gonna leave?*
> *Do you think if he goes*
> *I can still believe?*

Beside the poem Becca drew an imposing man with a thick head of black hair. She sketched an Austin Healey on his right and a strawberry on his left, then, staring at the sheet of paper, eventually scribbled over his face. Crying, she realized that no matter how hard she tried, it is nearly impossible to hate one's father.

She didn't know when he'd be home. She stared at the raindrops beading on the windowpane, pressing her cheek against Whiskers's cool, wet nose.

She was eleven the next day and for the rest of that year, when Mary promised to pull herself together, that things would get better; when Becca chucked her drawer full of useless watches and fed chocolate chip cookies to the mourning doves in the backyard. When Becca felt that she'd lost something more than her love of cookies, something more important, something irretrievable, but she didn't know exactly what it was. When her mother said, "I'm really sorry. I'm so embarrassed. I'm going to be a better mom, a better wife, a better everything."

When Mary asked Becca, "Where's the butterfly brooch?"

"I've got it. I'll get it."

When Colin Atwell found the brooch beneath a pile of leaves and remembered Becca wearing it at the dance.

He tried in vain to return the brooch to her. She wouldn't

speak to him, let alone look at him. It wasn't him. It was her. He was part of an event she wanted to forget.

Every few years, he found the brooch like new, remembering the downpour, the Old Well struck by lightning, and crazy, beautiful Becca Burke running for home.

Excerpt from
THE HANDBOOK FOR LIGHTNING STRIKE SURVIVORS

Recently, a small group of lightning strike survivors have connected with former electroshock patients, discovering that the volts of electricity, whether rendered by man or storm, have similar effects, including (some already mentioned) memory loss, numbness, tingling, poor circulation, difficulty concentrating, and inexplicable health problems like headaches, difficulty socializing in groups, and other forms of anxiety.

A few cases I researched indicated that the lightning strike victims, rather than gaining respect for Mother Nature, and rather than fearing storms, felt superhuman. Approximately 1 out of 200,000 people in the United States are struck each year.

You are far more likely to be struck by lightning than attacked by a shark. If you are at the beach and you see storm clouds approach, seek shelter immediately. It doesn't matter if it's not raining. A cloud can produce electricity without producing rain.

14

Adios, 1973

Joan Holt said, "We're neighbors with the Mexicans, but that doesn't mean our cultures are anything alike. Take, for instance, tacos. I don't go in for the soft kind, and I've never seen a real Mexican taco that wasn't soft. I like a crunchy shell, like the kind you get at Rio Grande downtown."

Buckley was pretending to listen, scheming how to get two dollars so he could buy Flamehead a hot fudge sundae.

Joan Holt said his mother was "getting all dolled up for Paddy John again."

Buckley said, "Paddy John's all right," adding, "Do you remember that girl Marty Bascott who was hanging out with us last week?"

"Flamehead? I've known her and her mama since Flamehead was a baby. What about her? Who the hell knows where she got that red hair?"

Buckley shrugged. "I was thinking . . ." he began, "that it would be nice if I could . . ."

"If you could what? Are you starting to stutter?"

"No," Buckley said. Sometimes Joan Holt was difficult to deal with. "I was thinking that maybe I could earn some money somehow, like two dollars, so that I could buy Flamehead a hot fudge sundae at the Dairy Queen."

"When you ask a favor, it's best to spit it out. There's no sense prolonging the discourse."

Buckley would've asked his mother for the money. She was making great tips, but if he asked her, she'd say, *If you can do me a favor and spend more time with Tide. That little boy needs a good influence like you. He admires you. In addition, you might be nicer to Paddy John. He's never been anything but kind to you.*

No, Buckley preferred asking Joan Holt—just so long as his mother didn't find out about it.

Joan said, "Get my purse. It's in the kitchen, and while you're out eating ice cream, I'll come up with a list of chores for you to do. I don't think there's any better way to learn the worth of a dollar than to work for it."

Buckley set Joan's purse on her lap.

"I'll give you five dollars and you can clean both of the bathrooms later this evening. I hate cleaning the bathroom."

Buckley brightened. "Are you serious?"

"That can be your weekly chore."

"Are you serious?!" He could take Flamehead to the movies. He could buy her a necklace or a ring or lip gloss or some other junk girls like.

"I'm not the one stuttering around here."

His mother had confided long ago, "Joan's a screwball." *No,* Buckley thought, *she's a dream.*

Flamehead ate her hot fudge sundae, even the maraschino cherry and the wafer cookies. She ran her finger along the bowl's interior for the last melted bit of ice cream. Buckley got a soft serve cone.

Setting down the glass dish, Flamehead said matter-of-factly, "My sister did it with her boyfriend."

"It?"

"In my parents' bed."

"How do you know?"

"I watched from the window."

"You're kidding!"

"Not one bit."

"What did you think?"

"I thought it was disgusting. Her boyfriend is so ugly, and he was all sweaty, and I could see his butt. It was enough to make me retch. Of course, I didn't actually retch."

"Of course." It dawned on Buckley that his mother and Paddy John might be doing *it*. The thought made him want to retch. He dismissed it immediately. They were both far too old to be doing it. He wondered if Flamehead really did go to second base. *What exactly is second base?* Buckley said, "Are you going to wait until you get married before you do it?"

"Are you kidding? Of course not. I'm going to wait until I'm in love."

"Me too." He liked Flamehead.

Sitting outside, she leaned in without warning and stuck her tongue, cold and sweet, between his lips. Unsure what to do, Buckley opened his mouth. She tasted like ice cream. Her tongue sat in his mouth. *Is this second base?* She retreated. "You're supposed to move your tongue around."

"I know that," he said.

She leaned in again. Buckley moved his tongue in rhythm with hers, following her cues. When she stopped, he stopped.

"You're a pretty good kisser," she said. "Do you have any gum?"

"Sure." He pulled a pack from his back pocket, remembering the reverend and his disdain for gum chewing. *Screw you, Reverend Whitehouse.*

"I like your T-shirt," Flamehead said.

"This thing?" Buckley looked down. It was a gift from Paddy John. By far the coolest shirt he owned: Jimmy Page playing guitar.

"Did you have a girlfriend in Arkansas?"

"Not really," he said.

"Do you want one now?"

Buckley leaned in, taking the initiative. He put his hand at the back of her neck, like he'd seen in the movies, and kissed her without even thinking about how he was doing.

As he released her head, she was breathless.

"Does that answer your question?"

Buckley R. Pitank was in heaven.

Buckley saw Paddy John at the laundromat.

Paddy John said, "It's a small world."

"I guess. Where's Tide?"

"With Sissy. Where's your mom?"

"You'd know better than me."

Buckley put his T-shirt and three pairs of jeans in the washer. Paddy John folded his pillowcases and sheets. Buckley spotted one of his mother's blouses among Paddy John's bedding. He said, "She'll never marry you."

"You don't think?"

"I'm just saying—if you were thinking of asking."

"I was going to ask your permission first, seeing as you're the man of the house."

"She can't marry you."

"Why is that?"

"She just can't." Abigail was still married to John Whitehouse. It was strange to think that he and his mother were missing persons. They might have been on milk cartons somewhere, if anyone had bothered to take their pictures ever.

"How come? Explain it to me. I love your mother. You know that, don't you?"

"I guess."

Paddy John's laundry was neatly sorted and folded. "You guess? Don't guess, son. Jesus Christ! Gusto requires certainty, and life ain't worth living without living it with gusto."

"Whatever you say." Buckley stuffed an Oreo in his mouth,

black crumbs tumbling down his chin. "Maybe you should write a book."

"Maybe you need your mouth washed out with soap."

He would've said *Fuck you* to Paddy John, but he knew that his mother would never forgive him. He never spoke disrespectfully to his elders, but he was changing. Simply put, he didn't care what Paddy John thought of him. It was wonderful not to care. For the first time in his life, he felt free from dread. He had two best friends and a girlfriend. He had long hair, a cool hangout, and the ocean. He had a surrogate grandmother—who was paying him five dollars a week to scrub the toilet. He had the May 1973 centerfold of Barbi Benton in his bedside drawer.

In July, a month shy of her and Buckley's one-year anniversary in Galveston, Abigail lit a candle in her bedroom on Sealy Street. She looked in the dresser mirror at herself and the flame. She wished for Buckley to grow up happy and good. She wished for Paddy John to always love her. She crossed her fingers and blew out the candle. Running a brush through her dark hair, she wondered if she could somehow send divorce papers to John Whitehouse without revealing her whereabouts. She didn't know how legal matters worked, but she couldn't face that man or her mother again. She liked to pretend that, except for Buckley, the past didn't exist.

Meanwhile, Paddy John made plans for their anniversary. He bought a secondhand picnic basket and a new (new to him) shirt at Harborside Thrift. He bought an eight-dollar bottle of sparkling wine and a dozen fudge brownies from Betty's Bakery on Nineteenth Street. He told his buddies Jake and Saul (and his feminist friend Sissy) that he loved Abigail more than anyone but his own son. "She's a spitfire, that one. I can see spending the rest of my life getting to know her." Maybe in another six months, he'd propose. She made him feel energized, which was good, because he was not an old man but he tended to act like one.

He and Abigail had been dating for eight months. This

anniversary was important to Paddy John, who'd never before kept track of such things. Having a kid at home had changed him. He told Abigail, "Bring Buckley tonight. He's your family so he's my family." Paddy never criticized Buckley in front of Abigail, but he worried that without a male influence or some level of discipline, Buckley would falter in this world. The boy seemed apart from the earth. Paddy John couldn't put his finger on it, not knowing how many years Buckley had spent with his face pinned to the red clay of the earth, not knowing how Buckley reveled in being apart from the earth.

Finding Abigail at the vanity, brushing her hair, Buckley said, "I don't want to go tonight. Paddy John is boring. You'll just make vomit eyes at each other."

"Vomit eyes?"

"All lovey-dovey."

"That's what you and Marty Bascott do."

"She's not a hundred years old."

"Neither am I."

Buckley sat on his mother's bed. "You lit a candle?"

"I said my prayers."

Buckley smiled. "Will Tide be there?"

"I'm sure of it."

"He's annoying."

"He's five years old."

"He had a birthday. He's six. But, it doesn't matter how old he is. I don't want to go." Buckley flung himself, arms overhead, back onto Abigail's comforter.

"Do this for me."

He got up. "Fine."

"And be nice to Tide."

"I'll be nice to Tide. I'm always nice to Tide. *Poor Tide. He's had such a bad time.*"

Abigail whipped around. "Don't be a smart aleck."

Buckley said, "I'm sorry, Mom."

"I expect more from you."

"I'm sorry." He left, closing the door behind him. He never wanted to upset or disappoint her. He was being a jerk, and he felt guilty.

For the past eight months, when Buckley wasn't with Charlie, Eddie, or Flamehead, he was keeping an eye on and entertaining Tide McGowan. At the drive-in, his mother said, "Take Tide to the swing set."

"I'll miss the ending."

At Brown's Lake, his mother said, "Take Tide to the concession."

"I'm playing with my friends."

"Let Tide play."

"Tide's too little."

"You were little once too." She whispered, "His mom didn't take good care of him."

Tide was not Buckley's responsibility, but he recognized that as he and his mom had run away, so had Tide's mother. It made him wonder if Paddy John was anywhere near as bad as the reverend, and they just hadn't seen that side to him yet. People, Buckley knew, have dark sides.

Paddy John opened Abigail's door. "I got some wine. I got some snacks for the boys. I got the radio and the cake, and check me out: I got all dressed up."

Abigail grinned. She wore a sleeveless bluebird-print dress. Her skin was tauter, her face youthful. "You look handsome," she said. "So what's the surprise?"

"Well, as you know, back in my wilder days, I was a sailor. I have connections." He beamed. "You, my sweet Abby, are having dinner on a thirty-six-foot fiberglass boat, top of the line, with yours truly at the wheel. There might even be champagne on board."

She grinned. "Seriously?" She'd seen the ocean. She'd walked through the waves as far out as her waist, but she'd never been *on* the ocean in water so deep she couldn't plant her feet on the sand.

Buckley, Tide, and Abigail followed Paddy John down the dock. Buckley, as instructed, carried the picnic basket, and Tide dragged the cooler. The sky was white: not gray, not blue. There were no thunderheads, no visible clouds, but at twelve seconds past 4:45, forty-eight seconds before 4:46, lightning struck Abigail Pitank. She had one leather sandal on the starboard side of the boat and one on the dock when she was hit directly, the lightning entering through her skull. She toppled and splashed into the water. Her one-hundred-thirty-pound body was pinned between the piling and the boat. Silver minnows, startled by the lightning and the dead weight, darted. Paddy John, blind from the lightning's strike, dropped into the water after Abigail. Rain fell: a drip, a drop, a downpour with gusts exceeding twenty miles an hour. Paddy John was wet and numb, oblivious to the rain and wind. Buckley was frozen, watching, knowing that Paddy John would save his mother.

Paddy John grabbed Abigail's arms and waist from the murky bottom, dislodged her chest from between the piling and fiberglass. He had trouble holding his breath, but he pulled until he had all of Abigail floating with him toward the surface. Lifting her head out of the water, needing a miracle, he saw her skull split open, charred black in spots. He held her body against his body. He was strong. He was muscular. He was a seaman, and he couldn't save the woman he loved. He kissed her parted lips, still warm but muddied. "I fucking love you." He punched the planks. She was gone. His raven-haired beauty had departed this world as quickly, shockingly, and mysteriously as she'd entered his life. He cried, but just a little. The time was not now. He said, "Buckley, I need help."

From the dock, down on his stomach, Buckley reached for his mother's arms. He was certain she'd be all right. He saw Tide standing there on the dock, the boy's bare knobby legs smudged with some kind of dirt, the boy's hands in fists. The boy doing nothing to help. Paddy John's working hands lifted Abigail at the hips, but her waist bent and her head and chest flopped forward. Buckley stopped her from landing face-first onto the dock.

Buckley pulled and Paddy pushed until she was out of the water.

Tide began to cry.

"Mom?" Buckley said. "Mom? It's me. I'm here." She wasn't allowed to leave him. She'd promised she'd never leave him. She'd said *never*. She'd promised! Padraig John, aware of the futile gesture, gave her mouth-to-mouth resuscitation. Buckley said, "She's going to be okay. Tell me she's going to be okay." Paddy John said nothing. Buckley took her cold hand; the rain pelting his neck and arms. Paddy John wrapped her head with a towel—like a turban—to cover the blood. Buckley seethed when Paddy John stopped mouth-to-mouth. "You're a piece of shit!" Buckley screamed. "I hate you." He started to run away, but a crowd had gathered. Paramedics pushed through. "She's my mom," Buckley said, standing helplessly on the wood planks. The crowd whispered. Some strangers cried. Some people said they'd seen the lightning hit. Buckley didn't remember much. He rode with his dead mother in the ambulance. At the small hospital, they called her DOA, dead on arrival. Buckley sat in a waiting room, waiting for nothing. She was dead. He covered his mouth, clasping his thumbs, his two hands like wings, fluttering. He sat for a long time, refusing to speak to anyone, until Joan Holt and Sissy came for him. Sissy was petite, but she picked him up, hoisting his thick legs around her waist. "It's all right," she said, knowing nothing was all right, but there are things a body needs to hear. "We love you," she added. "We love your mama."

Joan Holt said, "I am sadder today than when my Walrus died. He was old, and we had no children to miss." She coughed. "This is wrong. It's all wrong."

It is, isn't it? Buckley thought. When he woke up tomorrow, it might be different. If something is so wrong, can it be righted?

In the days that followed, Buckley was emotionally mute. He could not explain to Padraig John, Joan Holt, Sissy, or Jeanette that he didn't want to leave Galveston, that he didn't want to leave Charlie and Eddie and Flamehead or the ocean that his mother loved. He could not speak up. After the funeral service at Whitaker Memorial, he sat in Joan Holt's living room, his two hands in her hands, their four hands in her lap, his head at the bend in her waist, while his mother's friends whispered and ate food and tiptoed down the hall. Joan Holt said, "You can stay here, Buckley. With me. You're my grandson." He heard Padraig John in the kitchen. "Goddamn it." He heard Padraig John crying. He heard Sissy say, "Life isn't fair." He heard Tide laughing somewhere in the house. He wondered about Charlie and Eddie and why he hadn't heard from them. Did they know about his mom? They must know. It was in the newspaper. He heard Padraig John say, "I loved her."

Joan Holt stayed at Buckley's side, cradling his head. There were no words for mending.

Why hadn't Buckley's friends called? Why was his mother dead? For the last two nights, he'd hid beneath the covers, expecting that when the sun rose she would be standing over him. Hoping it was all a bad dream, but it wasn't. There was a funeral. There were carnations and angel food cake.

The night of her funeral, Buckley went to bed knowing she wouldn't be there ever again. She was dead. He got down on his knees, closed his eyes, clasped his hands, and prayed, "Dear God, you are Job's god and the reverend's god, and you did this to me. I guess it was wrong of me to try and be happy. I guess it was wrong of me to enjoy myself. I give up."

Three weeks later, he rode in the passenger's seat of the reverend's station wagon back to Mont Blanc, Arkansas. He thought about the last things he'd said to his mother. "I don't want to go." He hadn't. He'd been rude. She hadn't deserved it. He'd wanted to see Flamehead. He still hadn't gotten to second base (now that he knew what that was). He couldn't help but wonder: *If I hadn't complained so much, if I hadn't made her late to the dock, would she still be alive?*

It was Buckley's decision to confess to Joan Holt and Padraig John about his mother's husband, John Whitehouse. As much as he loved Galveston, he'd never be happy again, and he didn't deserve happiness. He deserved to suffer and pay for his sins. It was time to go home.

On the drive back to Mont Blanc, Buckley felt the breast pocket of his shirt. The folded Barbi Benton pinup was there. He reached into his duffel. The last candle his mother lit was there. That was all he needed.

The reverend said, "No good comes to those who run from the Lord."

"Sure," Buckley said. "That sounds about right."

I am originally from Mont Blanc, Arkansas, where most lightning injuries and fatalities occur between May and September.

It's hard to understand when lightning will strike. In order for it to travel from cloud to ground, it has to move through the air, which is a poor conductor. The reason lightning tends to hit tall objects is because lightning usually follows the shortest distance from cloud to ground. In the simplest terms, lightning is produced between the negative charge in a storm cloud and the positive charge on the ground. It's like a battery, a+ and a− connecting.

When I lived in Mont Blanc, eight cows fell dead when lightning struck the metal fence they were standing against. Still, I didn't take lightning seriously until it took my mom, who didn't deserve to die. I think I suffer survivor's guilt.

15

Go fish, 1981

Mary wanted a cigarette, but she planned to be good. Goodness was her theme. She made sandwiches for their trip, using Miracle Whip instead of mayonnaise because Rowan preferred it. This was an opportunity to work on her marriage. Her family. Her sanity. *Goodness* was her mantra. In the car, ankles crossed, she murmured, "Goodness."

Rowan drove toward the coast, thinking about his beautiful yacht, a real yawl, moored at Barnacle Bob's in Manteo. He hoped the captain he'd commissioned would be a decent sort. He thought about the open ocean, and Patricia—his Patty-Cake. His mother had been right. You don't go off and marry some girl from Podunk. He was too young when he'd married Mary. She was too hillbilly. Any woman in her right mind would've demanded a divorce by now, but Mary wasn't in her right mind.

"Should we go tomorrow?" asked Mary. *Goodness* playing in her head.

"Go where?"

"Sailing."

"We'll see."

Mary retrieved her leather cigarette case from the glove box and lit up.

"Do you have to do that? It makes the whole car smell." Rowan shut off the air-conditioning and rolled his window down.

"What does 'we'll see' mean?" The smoke from her cigarette

trailed into the backseat. Becca rolled down her window. Whiskers rested his chin on her knee.

"It means that we'll see. It doesn't mean anything. I have to call the marina and see if Paddy John's around."

"Who's he again?"

"The captain I hired."

"Why wouldn't he be around? You told him we'd be there." She should've taken a Valium. She puffed on her cigarette. Already she was blowing the goodness mantra. Better to be quiet. *Goodness.*

Rowan drove the longest route possible to Nags Head. It was one of his faults. He stopped in Bunyan, taking a picture of three old black men leaning against a cinder-block market. Inside the market, he snapped a photo of a heavyset woman manning a deep fryer. He pulled off the side of the road in Yeatesville, where a sandy-haired woman with clay-stained feet sold watermelon from a rusted pickup. Her two kids waved cardboard signs: WATERMELON FOR SALE! Cars sped past.

Rowan parked the Volvo in the gravel. "Over here, Becca. Right here." Taking her by the shoulders, his camera around his neck, he positioned his sunny daughter in front of the truck. The watermelon woman leaned with her back against the driver's side door, fingering her flip-flop for a rock.

Becca pushed her red sunglasses further up her nose.

"Say 'cheese,' Becca," he said. "Say 'I love watermelon.'"

"I love watermelon."

Rowan laughed. To the woman, he said, "Thanks! Thanks a lot," and handed her a dollar.

The woman said, "I don't need a dollar for you to take your kid's picture." She handed the bill back.

"Suit yourself."

The Burkes' first night at the beach, Mary unpacked. She put the sheets on the bed and drank from her silver-plated flask in the downstairs bathroom. She was thirty-four, but felt twenty-one sipping scotch, smiling at herself in the mirror. She gargled Listerine and listened to the wind whistling through the slatted gate. It was oceanfront country. She felt at home.

Becca walked Whiskers over the dune to a blanket of stars that reminded her of Grandma Edna's farm. Digging her bare heels into the sand, she watched Whiskers chase the surf. She felt beautiful. There was no other way to describe it. She hadn't lost the strange feeling that she was insignificant—but she felt beautiful in spite of it. The rock in her gut was gone, replaced by something warm and settling—like Thanksgiving dinner. She had substance.

Down the beach a good ways, she spotted a bonfire, the red flames leaping into the blackness. She wondered if this was what it was like to feel grown up—beautiful despite your smallness. She was a nobody when she looked up at the stars, but in their glory, nothingness was all she could hope for.

Whiskers settled beside her. He dug a trench with one paw, putting his nose there.

Give me a shooting star, Becca prayed. *Come on, Grandma, I need a shooting star.* Whiskers kicked sand in her hair. She waited. "Oh, come on! Tell her, Whiskers. Give us a shooting star." That instant, a star trailed across the sky, reviving Becca's belief in miracles. It didn't take much.

Later, at the Seamark grocery, Mary told Becca, "You're a very pretty girl. And talented."

"Thanks, Mom." Mary hadn't complimented Becca in a long time. "Is something wrong?"

"No," her mother said. "I just don't tell you enough how proud I am of you. It's not just how you look. It's your art. I should've let you go to that hippie art camp."

"There weren't any hippies there. There aren't hippies anywhere anymore."

"Well, Becca, I don't know. You young people . . . you just don't know."

"What don't we know?" Becca pursued.

"I don't know. I guess you know everything."

Becca rolled her eyes.

"But I love you. That's all I'm trying to say."

"Are you all right to drive, Mom?"

"Shut up. I'm fine. I'm just trying to be nice." *Goodness.*

"Got it."

Pushing the shopping cart, Mary said, "I love your dad."

"Me too. It's a given."

"We should buy junk," Mary said. "I mean, we should buy all the regular stuff too, but let's load up on ice cream and hot fudge and potato chips. I'm sick of watching my weight."

Becca said, "Awesome! I never watch mine anyway."

"You don't have to."

When they arrived back at the cottage, Mary sprayed Binaca into her mouth and practiced a smile in the rearview. "Your dad loves ice cream. I can't tell you how many banana splits we split." She was bright-eyed, nostalgic. "He used to say, 'It doesn't matter if you're fat—you'll never get rid of me.'" She laughed. "What a load of shit."

"Mom, are you okay?"

"Oh, honey, I'm fine. I'm better than fine."

"Thanks for saying that you think I'm a good artist."

"I mean it," Mary said. "I envy you. It's funny, but we all want better than what we had for ourselves. I don't know how that sounds." She cut the Volvo's headlights. Mary rested her forehead in her hand. Moths flitted around the driveway's light. Looking up, she asked, "Am I a good mom?"

It was the question Becca never wanted to hear, let alone answer. She could say, *No! To use Dad's word, you're a sot, and you spend too much time feeling sorry for yourself,* but instead, skirting the question, she said, "I love you."

"I love you too, sweetheart." They climbed the side steps to the cottage's back porch.

Rowan met them on the porch. He peeked into the bag. "Mint chocolate chip. My favorite."

Becca said, "You can't have any, Dad. Mom is going to eat the whole half gallon. It's some kind of world record."

"Good luck with that, Mary."

Mary said, "Wait until you see what I got." Setting her bags on the pine table, she pulled the current issue of *Yachting Today* from her grocery bag. "Pretty good, huh? I was thinking about you."

Rowan massaged his temples. "That was good of you, Mare, but"—he raised the current issue from his chair on the deck—"it came before we left."

"I thought you said it hadn't come."

"Well, it hadn't, but then it did. It came yesterday."

Great!

The ideal American family, they played Monopoly. Rowan owned Boardwalk and Park Place, and toward the end of the game, Mary, for no reason, moved his car to the jail square. He told her, "You know I have a get-out-of-jail-free card."

She shrugged. Neither he nor Becca said anything about Mary's smelly cocktails. Rowan sipped a single glass of white wine and they ate a bowl of potato chips in lieu of dinner. Becca drank her Coke through a straw, and watching her parents smiling at each other, she believed that the ocean was a magical place. She paid her father her last two fifty-dollar bills. "What about a loan?"

"Nothing doing." He played to win.

That night, Becca opened the bedroom window. With Whiskers curled at her waist, she listened to the waves sweep the shore. Before drifting to sleep, she thought that if any place in the world could bring her parents back together, this place could.

Later, she dreamed she took flight from the windowsill. Her arms were pelican's wings and she raised them slowly in the gusting wind. She glided out over the ocean until the soft light from the house disappeared. When the red sun crested the waves, she flew back. Whiskers was curled up on her bed, his head on her pillow. She hovered just outside. Someone had closed the screen. *Let me in.* She awoke in a sweat.

The next morning, they drove down Route 12. Mary's left hand rested on Rowan's thigh. Rowan pulled off on Pea Island. "I like this," he said. Theirs was the only car.

Mary and Becca climbed the dune. The beach was deserted. *Magnificent.*

Mary yelled to Rowan, "This is the spot."

As he unloaded the car, Becca ran toward the ocean, her flip-flops spraying hot sand onto the backs of her calves. Mary trailed.

Mary said, "The ocean is about youth, hatchlings and minnows, and it's about age, wounded seagulls, and dead fish."

Catching up, weighted with beach blankets and picnic baskets, Rowan said, "What the hell's gotten into you?"

"I was thinking about my mom. Once a year she brought me and Claire to this awful clapboard house five blocks from the beach. The plaster fell in patches from the ceiling. You had to jiggle the toilet handle and use the plunger if you went number two. The place had one bedroom, no air conditioning, and a screened porch riddled with holes. We'd get back to Prospect sunburned and covered in mosquito bites."

Becca dropped the beach bag and ran for the water.

Mary continued: "Funny. It was the time of my life. Dad never came. It was just us girls, and we always got along." Nostalgic, Mary spread her towel on the sand.

Rowan was no longer listening.

Meanwhile, Becca plunged through the breaking waves, shrieking as the water reached her waist. She knew her dad would say, "Dive under," and she did, emerging revitalized and no longer cold. She swam back and forth, waiting for her dad's diving entrance. Her mother never swam with them; instead, she waded just past where the waves broke. "Come on, Mom," Becca would plead.

"No chance in hell."

Today, Rowan dove into the water. Humming the theme song to *Jaws*, he chased Becca until she couldn't touch, grabbing her around the waist and tossing her into the air. She screamed.

Her dad said, "What if we never grow up?"

"What?" He didn't usually talk imaginatively.

"We'll never get old. Just like Peter Pan."

"I'm with you."

He bolstered her up, his hands forming a stirrup, tossing her into the waves where she couldn't touch. Again, he hummed the *Jaws* theme song. Becca swam for the shore. The harder she swam, the further she drifted from shore. She kicked and paddled, shouting, "Help!" There was no lifeguard here. The waves were big. She thought about sharks and octopi. "Help!" Where had her father gone?

Peering over the lapping waves, unable to touch and treading water, she saw her mother on shore waving, her face concerned. She saw her father there too, turning to see Becca drifting further out to sea. Becca wondered if they'd fight long enough for her to drown. She flailed her arms, and knowing how to float, lay back, eyes shut, thinking that if a shark ate her, a shark ate her. It's the fear of the thing—whatever the thing might be—that kills you. Becca could hardly see the sand over the lapping waves.

Lickety-split, her mother was past the breaking waves, paddling toward Becca. She secured one arm across Becca's chest and one under her armpit. "You're fine. Relax, and you'll be able to touch in no time." Her mother paddled and kicked. Becca floated. Her panicked breathing subsided. She said, "I'm scared."

"This isn't a big deal. It's the undertow. Next time, if you feel the waves pulling you out, swim parallel to the shore."

It's no big deal. It's just my life.

Around two o'clock, they ate their sandwiches. Miracle Whip again.

After his sandwich, Rowan slept. Mary read *People* magazine. Becca walked. She wasn't lonely like she thought she'd be without Carrie, just in awe of her surroundings. A salty foam on her calves, she watched as sanderlings diagonally chased the surf up and back. Becca thought about her parents, about today—how there might never be a better day. When she got back to Chapel Hill, using the Woolworth acrylics Grandma Edna had sent, she'd paint this scene—at least the memory of this scene. She'd keep the ocean, sand, and sky, and when fall arrived, and the school days with it, Becca would sit behind a desk, wishing she were elsewhere, and she'd have this day. She'd come back here in her mind. The pelicans skimmed the waves. The gulls fished the surf. Becca walked until her parents disappeared from view. In the distance, she spotted something shiny.

A blue fish. Not exactly blue: its scales a smattering of silver, green, and violet. The fish's gills puffed and its mouth, dime-sized, swelled and deflated in Becca's shadow. The fish was thirty feet from the tide, but it was alive. Without thinking, Becca lifted the fish with both hands, expecting it to flop about, but it was motionless.

She carried it across the sand, through the surf, to where she was waist-deep in the water. A school of tinny minnows swam in her path, or rather she in theirs, a few darting between her thighs. She lowered her fish into the calm green water. As if deciding what to do, where to go, her fish didn't move. She waited, and then he swam away.

For the rest of her life, Becca would try over and over to paint that fish, and she would fail. She didn't remember every detail of that Pea Island beach day as she had promised herself she would, because the details of that cloudless day were overshadowed by darker days, like the day the wind shifted and the flies came and they bit at the tourists' ankles and scores of puffer fish inexplicably washed ashore, and the flies buzzed around the rotting fish, and Becca threw up. She remembered *thinking* she had saved a fish. She remembered her mother's hand on her father's thigh, the salt dried on her face and back, her father lifting her into the air, and the sea spray speckling her cheeks, but she couldn't keep those memories close. She couldn't paint *that* fish. She couldn't gather that much hope or that much beauty because it hurt too much. Besides, there would be other fish to paint and other things to feel. At twelve years old, Becca had the rest of her life to feel.

The westerly wind blew the black biting flies from the Pamlico Sound across the swampy brush and clapboard houses, across the main highway and the beach road, over the dunes and sea oats to the beach. Along with the black flies that nibble on your ankles and calves, the westerly wind brought Patricia from Chapel Hill, Patty with two t's, not two d's. Patty who wrote a note to Rowan four years ago, a note that seemed insignificant, but to Becca and her mom, intuitively not. A note that was first in Becca's mother's palm, next in Becca's mother's jewelry box, and then stolen and stashed for four years in Becca's vanity drawer.

It was no coincidence that Patricia Heathrow—Patty—was in Barnacle Bob's.

Barnacle Bob's was a dark hole-in-the-wall with exposed oak beams and row upon row of black-and-white photographs of the old lifesavers—the Midgett family and other early inhabitants, who'd rowed wooden lifeboats through surf and stormy sea to rescue distressed seamen, from fishermen to sailors.

Rowan and Mary sat at a table with their captain-for-hire, Paddy John McGowan. They'd been on the water all day. Becca, due to sunburn, had remained behind at Barnacle Bob's with Paddy John's son—who was supposed to entertain her. He was fourteen, with acne and orange-crusted braces. Supposedly teaching her to shoot pool—when he wasn't very skilled himself—the boy bragged that he knew how to drive, that he'd smoked marijuana, that he came and went as he pleased, and Becca listened passively, checking the clock on the wall, wanting the day to end. Her shoulders itched; her face flushed from the sunburn. As soon as her parents returned from their sea adventure, Becca ditched the boy supposedly named Tide. *What kind of name is that?* She sat with her parents and their salty captain, Paddy John. He was a storyteller: "I was out in this squall. The water was up to my knees, and Harry was on deck trying to steer, but there was no use. The best we could hope for was staying afloat. We had no idea where we'd end up, and didn't much care. At that point, it was all about staying alive."

"Where did you end up?" Mary asked.

"When all was said and done, twenty-three miles off the coast of St. Augustine."

Mary was mesmerized. Becca sat with her chin in her palms, sometimes scratching at her shoulders. "What's a bilge pump?"

Rowan, suddenly distracted, said, "Excuse me. I'll be right back."

When he returned to their table, Patricia Heathrow was with him. She was tall and thin with bright blond hair, a pixie cut, and Becca noticed that her arms were too long, as were her legs, which were bronzed. She wore heeled sandals despite her height, and when she shook Mary's hand and said, "Hi. I'm Patricia Heathrow. I work with Rowan," Becca knew that this was Patty. She also knew that her mother knew. The Wickle women were remarkably savvy when it came to such matters.

Patty said, "What a coincidence!"

Mary said, "It certainly is."

"It's so nice to finally meet you."

"You as well. Can you sit?" Mary asked. She had a few questions for Patricia.

"My sister's at the bar, but it was nice meeting you. Small world."

"Same here." Mary gritted her teeth.

Paddy John said, "Pretty girl," and watched her walk away.

Rowan said, "I'll be right back," following Patty to the bar.

Paddy John said, "She's not nearly as pretty as you," reaching out and touching Mary's hand, which trembled ever so slightly under his.

Mary sat shoulder to shoulder with Paddy John, thinking, *This is the kind of man I was supposed to marry, but I wanted someone better. I wanted something better—the big house, the two point five children, the social clubs, the name. I didn't want a farm boy or a sailor or a blue-collar nobody.*

Paddy John said, "When I was in Galveston down on the docks, looking for some action, I see this fellow passed out in his undershorts. This little girl says to me, 'Don't worry,' but I worried. These women had taken everything the guy had. Not just his money but his goddamn boots. I knew I didn't want to drink there, and she says, 'Come on and have a drink. The first one's on the house.'"

"Oh my god," Mary said. She wondered if Paddy John cheated on his wife. She didn't even know if he had a wife. She could ask if he was married, but that might sound like a pickup line. No, of course it wouldn't. She was married.

"You wouldn't believe some of them ports. The shit that went on, that probably still goes on." He thought of Trina's whorehouse, his ex-wife there. Then of Abigail. He said, "I fell in love in Galveston."

"I've never been to Galveston." Mary wondered how Rowan could do this to her, how he could have one of his whores meet them on vacation. Maybe it wasn't planned. She'd almost believed there wasn't anyone else. Not right now, anyway. Not for some time. She'd been a laughingstock for so long. *Maybe he's over there right now telling her to leave.*

Paddy John slid the saltshaker toward Mary. "You should go to Galveston." Drumming his fingers on the table, he asked, "Your husband always work on vacation?"

"He works a lot."

"That's a shame. If I had a wife looked like you and enough money to buy that seafaring beauty, I'd quit my day job."

"Thank you." She knew that she'd been beautiful at one time in her life. That's how she'd caught Rowan in the first place, but lately she'd been feeling the difference between thirty-four and Patty's twenty-something. Feeling plain tired. Why hadn't her stomach ever lost its pooch after Becca? Why wasn't she born as tall as Patty Heathrow, as blond, as slim? She was Mary Wickle Burke. Mary the redhead. Rowan's wife. Former PTA member. Former Garden Club board member. Current cookie baker. She remembered part of a funny poem she wrote in college when she thought she was someone else: *I am not a woman. I am not a baby maker, I am not sweet smiles fetching his coffee and paper.* Something something. *I am not a cookie baker, an ordered homemaker.* Something something. She forgot. She *was* a cookie baker. She *was* a baby maker. She was a former member of the Historic Preservation Society. She was a laughingstock. A drunk. A former snob. She was Rowan Burke's wife, and he was never going to stop cheating.

Mary said, "I need a stronger drink." Like the topsy-turvy stone in Becca's gut, Mary had her stone, but it was a much larger, jagged rock, tipped with scotch and Valium to dull the points.

Becca studied the black-and-white photos lining the wall. Along with the lifesaver pictures, there was one of Orville and Wilbur Wright posing in front of their Kitty Hawk barracks. She was desperate for home. The rock in her gut flipped. She ran for the bathrooms in the corner of Barnacle Bob's, past the pinball machine Bounty Hunter, with its orange and blue lights spelling GAME OVER. The bathroom was marked by a pink and white anchor. She tried the doorknob but it was locked. She knocked. A voice from within said, "Hold your horses."

I can't, thought Becca, running into the men's room. She vomited with her hands on the rim of the toilet, her right palm in a spot of urine.

She felt better. Washing up with the powdered soap from the

dispenser, reminding herself that everything was going to be okay, a large man with muttonchop sideburns and a hairy gut hanging over his belt pushed open the door. Rather than saying "Excuse me," and stepping out, he said, "It says 'Gents' Head,' girlie."

Girlie? You've got to be kidding. "Sorry." She hadn't flushed yet.

He looked at the toilet and back at Becca. "You threw up? You had to throw up in here?"

"There was someone in the other bathroom."

"You didn't flush."

"And now I'm not going to." *Fuck you!* She'd had her palm on the rim of a man's toilet seat. Let him flush her vomit.

Becca went to the bar, grabbed her father's soft hand, and said, "Let's go. I don't feel good."

He pulled his hand free. "I need to talk business with Patty." He tossed his head back, a raw oyster sliding from its gray marble half shell into his mouth, reminding Becca of her mother when she took bourbon shots.

Patty smiled at Becca. "Rowe, you should go if Rebecca doesn't feel well."

Rowe?

"Hi, I'm Virginia." Patty's sister was an older, shorter Patty. "Are you having a good vacation?"

"I got sunburned." Becca tugged her dad's hand.

"All right, all right," he said. "In a minute. Go tell your mom we're leaving."

Becca went back to their table. Paddy John said, "Your mom's not feeling so great."

"Me either."

"I feel fine," Mary said. "Becca and I have no secrets. I was just telling Paddy John here that I'd make him a wager. I bet your dad and that woman are having sex, and I bet I can get one of them to confess."

"Mom, please don't."

"Don't what? What are you afraid I'll do? *I'm* not having sex with anybody." She tapped her chest with two fingers for emphasis. "Not me." Mary rose from her stool and headed toward the bar. Becca followed, urging, "Mom, don't. We're leaving. Dad said we're leaving. I got sick in the bathroom. I'm sick. I think it's the sunburn. Let's wait for Dad to finish talking and we'll go."

"Is that what they call it? 'Talking'? I think it's a little more than that."

Mary tapped Rowan on the shoulder but directed her question at Patty. "Are you having sex with my husband?" She tossed back a bourbon shot.

Patricia looked to her sister first and then to Rowan. She cleared her throat as if she hadn't understood Mary's question, as if Mary had made some mistake. "Excuse me?"

"You're not the first, so please don't play dumb with me." The bar was silent except for the splunks and sirens of the Bounty Hunter pinball machine.

Rowan said, "We're not doing this here."

"Why not? You do it in the garage. You do it in our bed."

Tide, approaching Becca from behind, put his hand on her shoulder. "Do you want to get out of here?" Becca didn't answer.

Mary said, "Own up. Are you having sex with my husband?"

"Don't do this." Rowan grabbed Mary's wrist. "Stop."

"Stop, Mom."

"That's good, Becca. Take your dad's side."

Tide said, "We should get out of here."

Mary yanked her wrist loose. "I want another shot." The bartender was drying glasses, pretending not to listen.

"I need another Jim Beam."

The bartender said, "I'm not serving you."

Paddy John shouted from the table where he still sat, "She's a friend of mine, and she needs that drink."

The bartender poured Mary's shot.

"We're leaving," said Rowan. "I'm sorry, Patty. I'm very sorry."

"I'm not going anywhere and neither is my daughter."

"We're leaving, Mary. Get your purse."

"I'm not going anywhere with you."

Someone in the bar clapped. Another person laughed.

A restrained look of anger on his face, Rowan extended his hand to Paddy John. "I wish I could say it was a pleasure."

"Our score is settled." Paddy John patted his front shirt pocket, where Rowan's check was folded. The two men shook hands.

"We'll be leaving now."

On his way to the door, Rowan took Becca's hand. He said, "I'm sorry about this, Piddle. Everything's going to be okay." She couldn't remember the last time he'd called her Piddle. She felt sick. Powerless. Mary grabbed on to Becca's other hand.

Even after this huge scene, they were leaving together as a family, Becca thought. Then her mother pulled Becca toward the bar. "She's not going anywhere with you."

Patty and Virginia placed a twenty on the bar. "Excuse us." They left Barnacle Bob's before the Burkes. Patricia Heathrow did not suffer indignities.

Rowan held Becca's left hand, Mary her right. Rowan pulled Becca toward the door. He said, "How can you do this, Mary?"

"She's *my* daughter."

Becca was being pulled apart.

"You're making a fool of yourself."

Mary reached for Becca's waist. "Come on, honey."

Rowan said, "She's not going anywhere with you. You're drunk."

Grandma Edna and Bo came to see me.

"You screwed the babysitter!"

Rowan let go of Becca's hand. He said, "We're leaving."

I killed Bo. I didn't mean it.

Mary let go of Becca's hand. "Let's go then."

The miracle fish in Becca's hand was gone. There was no such thing as a miracle fish. Somewhere in the room a stool over-turned, a glass shattered, and someone called, "Julianna, I need a stiff drink. I can't listen to this shit." Someone else laughed. Becca saw her miracle fish swarming with flies. She imagined the dead fish rotting in her hands.

Rowan left for Chapel Hill that night. Becca begged him, "Please take me with you."

He said no.

Becca had no idea that her mother wanted to beg the same thing of Rowan. As much as Becca wanted a caretaker, so did Mary. Age is but a number.

That same night in Chapel Hill, Colin Atwell took Becca's purple butterfly brooch from his sock drawer and studied each of the shimmering amethysts, snug in their platinum settings. He counted twenty-eight. Colin's dad called from their den, "Get in here! The game's on." Colin switched off his bedroom light. "Coming, Dad." Colin was always a good boy: the kind of boy Abigail Pitank Whitehouse had hoped Buckley R. Pitank would be.

In her beach house bedroom, Becca pulled the window shut. Even so, the ocean waves made themselves heard.

Pivotal events, occurrences that should be embedded, second by second, in your memory, are too immediate for reflection. Even years later, the seconds mix together like batter, the ingredients indistinguishable.

Mary lights a cigarette at the kitchen table. "He's moving in with that Patty person. He's putting his suitcase in the car."

There's the puffing on a green-ringed cigarette, the shuffle of slippered feet beneath the table, the cup at her mother's lips, the little dribble of coffee running down the side of the cup, the exhalation of smoke, Becca's hands on her hips, her bare feet, one foot crossing the other to scratch at a mosquito bite on her left calf; her voice, cracked and insistent: "It's Sunday," because she doesn't know what else to say. "It's Sunday," thinking, *Sunday is the day Dad and I go to breakfast at Sutton's. Today's Sunday. He would've said something. He wouldn't just leave.*

The screen door slams shut behind Becca. She manages, "It's Sunday," and he smiles. He shuts the Austin Healey's trunk. Certainly he couldn't have packed much in there. Certainly he's not leaving for good, and he meets her in the middle of the driveway halfway between the side door and his escape. He wipes his hands down the front of his khakis, smiling like everything's okay. Becca's hands are clasped together under her chin; unconsciously her fingers curl around one another like when she made the church with all the people and the steeple when she was very little. She feels small, not small how she felt on the beach with the ocean and sky; not small like she was part of something great and beautiful, but small insignificant, like an ant or slug squashed, unnoticed.

Becca thinks this is like acting, like playing a part in an after-school special where some girl, not her, is abandoned, and if someone were to play Becca right now in a movie, she'd pick young Hayley Mills because she always liked *The Parent Trap*. Needless to say, Cary Grant would play her dad.

Her father touches her arm. "Look," he says. "I need to leave. I can't stay here right now."

"Where are you going? Are you coming back?"

He shakes his head no.

"Were you going to say goodbye?"

"Of course."

She scratches at the bundle of curls at her neck. "Don't go."

"I'll see you later this week. Okay?"

It's not okay. She's already said "Don't go." He gets in the car, gripping the steering wheel, looking in the rearview mirror at his tan face, at that "fine jaw" he told Becca he got from his father, who got it from his father, who got it from his father—a Burke blessing—and adjusts his baseball cap. His arm hangs over the driver's door, the whiter side exposed, waxlike in the sun.

"I love you," he says.

Becca is not Hayley Mills and he is not Cary Grant. This is real. Unlike the Pea Island beach day and the magic fish, the bad feeling of this day remains. Details fade. For a couple years, she'll remember her mother's slippers brushing the kitchen tile. She'll remember the Carolina blue of her father's baseball cap. The rest is batter. It's all mixed up, and none of it tastes good.

An excerpt from
THE HANDBOOK FOR LIGHTNING STRIKE SURVIVORS

It happens so fast, it's hard to describe. I didn't get directly struck like my mother, but the electricity changed me forever.

I am depressed, reliving that awful day in flashbacks. As you read my book, keep in mind that the survivors quoted are real people.

Some quick facts to know:

Lightning can strike when the sun is shining.

Summer is when most strikes and fatalities occur in the United States.

Despite warnings, people don't usually heed thunder or dark clouds.

25% of strikes occur on or near the water.

California and the northwestern states have the least number of lightning strikes, injuries, and fatalities each year.

16

Clementine, 1975

His mother was dead. His life changed. The Mont Blanc landscape, the red clay roads, the Holy Redeemer Church, Grandma Winter, and the Reverend Whitehouse were the same. No one seemed to notice that he'd been away.

"What was she thinking, running off like that?" Winter asked.

When Buckley tried to answer, she stopped him. It was a rhetorical question. Winter and John Whitehouse suggested that Abigail's death was God's judgment.

After all, she'd had an illegitimate child. She'd run away, abandoning her husband and mother.

Winter complained, "I buried a husband. Now my only daughter is dead. God judges me too." Trying to make sense of things for Buckley, she said, "Your mother sometimes lived wild and wouldn't listen. It isn't fair for you to be a victim all your life." Then she sobbed. Was she really sad? he wondered. Buckley didn't understand Winter Pitank, and he didn't have the energy to try.

The reverend took Buckley to the barber on Main Street to remedy the boy's weird hippie look. He bought Buckley new Wrangler jeans at the Kmart in Sherrill City. The boys at school no longer said or did mean things to Buckley. Instead, they ignored him.

. . .

In 1975, Buckley met Clementine Wistar, quaalude addict and resident of Drop Out City, Arkansas (a wannabe commune in Mont Blanc).

Clementine ran through a field of crackling sun-snapped briars toward Drop Out City's perimeter, a rusty barbed-wire fence that bordered Buckley's backyard.

There, Winter hung laundry out to dry, and Buckley, sixteen and red-faced, a morose young man, sat on the back steps of his cinder-block house, drawing a peace symbol in the dirt with a twig. It was August and hot.

Clementine wore a man's striped dress shirt and a pair of green army boots. She waved from the barbed wire to Buckley, her hair dark and slick, even from that distance, just like his mother's.

"Where you going?" Winter asked.

"No place." Buckley walked toward the barbed wire that separated Winter's property from the hippies in Drop Out City, formerly Moss's Ranch and Stables. He carried his drawing twig and pretended to amble, all the time heading straight for Clementine. *Such a pretty girl,* he thought. *She could be a Barbi Benton if she weren't stick thin, if she weren't a drug addict.* He knew what she was. He knew she was weak. He wanted to know her weakness better. He wanted to save her, but there are some people who can't be saved. Who can't be lifted up and made into the people they were never born to be anyway. Buckley didn't know these things. He saw possibility in her dark eyes, and even on this day, when Buckley saw Clementine up close—her eyelids droopy, her face pale, spotted here and there with stray freckles like a blind man had dotted a white canvas—when she hid her face behind a freckled hand, the skin yellowed around her mouth, he still believed he could save her. He said, "How's it going?"

Clementine's lips were dull and cracked, like the clay under his feet.

Buckley squeezed between the bottom two wires, the barbs catching and tearing his shirt. "Did you go down to the free clinic?"

"No," she said, "I changed my mind." Clementine leaned against the barbed wire. "Shit," she said, sucking at a bead of blood on her forearm.

"What'd you do that for?" he asked.

"What?"

"Never mind."

"Guess I'm klutzy."

She wiped at the cut on her arm.

"You should go to the clinic. It's free. You can get a checkup."

"I'm not much for charity. They'll treat me like dirt."

"No they won't. You have to give people a chance."

She said, "I love you."

"You don't even know me." He stiffened, sliding his hands deep into his pockets.

"Sure I do. I know you, silly."

It seemed to Buckley that her eyes were barely open. He looked toward Winter, who was oblivious (she needed glasses), hanging his underwear in the August heat. Winter complained about Drop Out City all the time. "Bunch of hippies is what they are. Peace and love, my foot. I think the lot of them ought to move to Mexico or Canada if they don't like how real Americans live."

Clementine grabbed Buckley's wrist, the drop of blood beading down her arm onto his hand—which he kept in a fist because his fingernails were crusted black. Clementine guided him back the way she'd come, toward Drop Out City. Then, halfway through the brambles, Clementine stopped and said, "Touch my neck. Touch my back." She let go of Buckley's wrist and settled on the scorched earth, the briars pricking her calves and knees. Buckley knew she felt nothing. Down on the ground, he rubbed her neck, his hand inside the man's shirt that bunched at her knees. He rubbed her shoulders and her back, and Buckley thought, *She's such a small thing. Five feet, maybe, and not more than one hundred ten pounds wet.*

"Do you remember when we met?" she asked.

"Last week."

"Do you remember what you said?" she asked.

"I said hi, and I asked you what it was like living in a hippie commune."

"And what did I say?" Clementine tilted her head to the right.

"You said it's like living anywhere else."

She laughed again. "Do you want to drink some beer? My old man is split." She put Buckley's palm on top of her head as if he were measuring her height, marking it on an imaginary wall. "I feel good."

She did feel good. *So very, very good*, Buckley thought. "All right," he said—about the beer. Buckley knew her old man, as Clementine called him, had split. That's mostly what she talked about when she did talk: about how her old man was supposed to make a big score and they (she and the old man) were getting the hell out of Drop Out Shitty, Arkansas; about how she was going to New York City to get herself together and be a superstar or some kind of star. She said, "I'm not kidding, Buckley," and when he didn't say anything, like *Of course you're going to be a superstar, I know you are, you'll be a big star*, she said, "Fuck you. You don't believe me." She slapped him on the arm. It didn't hurt because she moved in slow motion. He'd known Clementine Wistar a week, but it seemed years.

As they sat on the hot earth, Buckley held Clementine's hand. It was soft and tiny in his. He listened to the sound of her breath. This was how it was with them: quiet a lot of the time. A while later, Clementine got up and they climbed the steep orange cliff dug out by a bulldozer. Moss, the former owner of the ranch, had years ago begun a housing development on the property. Unfortunately, the backers pulled their money out, and now there was a steep clay hill where a few of the remaining kids from Drop Out City rode flattened cardboard boxes down the slopes.

Drop Out City, like the rest of Mont Blanc, had endured a six-year drought. The idea of subsisting off the land had failed. The end result was a barren landscape littered with trash. Buckley spotted a Roger's Gourmet Pork 'n' Beans can and kicked it.

Today, Clementine and Buckley walked past the garden. It was a forty-by-forty-foot plot of inedible, sun-scorched vegetables and fruits. Nothing ever grew big or juicy enough to consume. The tomatoes, peppers, squashes, and beans shriveled and dropped desiccated onto the dirt. The garden was intended to be the center of the community, and in a sense it was. As the food source diminished, so did the dropouts. Those who remained in Drop Out City like Clementine lived off the scarce charity of Mont Blanc's residents—most of whom hated the people they termed "deadbeat hippies."

The Vietnam War, which was never *officially* a war, had ended unofficially this year. After fourteen years of fighting and 56,559 Americans dead, the unofficial war, the "minor skirmish," was over. This same year, the dream of communal living died forever in Arkansas. This dream of brotherhood and sisterhood and peace had disintegrated into a circle of tin shacks inhabited by drug addicts, fed by a dwindling few drug dealers—like Clementine's old man, Scott.

Most of the deadbeat hippies had left by August 1975, when Buckley went to Clementine's tin-roof shack for the first time. The dropouts had dropped back in, going home to their suburban parents to endure the "I told you so" speeches. They were the lucky ones. Not Clementine. She was unlucky. She didn't know the way home anymore.

As they sat on a sleeping bag, dirty clothes strewn and heaped around them, flies buzzing at the doorway, Clementine said, "I'm going to New York City. That's where the action is. I just gotta get some money saved."

Buckley knew what to say by now. "You'll be a big star on Broadway."

"In movies too," she said. Clementine sang a version of "Tomorrow" from the musical *Annie*. Her voice was scratchy, but charming nonetheless, Buckley thought. Clementine crawled around, digging under her clothes until she found the stash of beer. "They're warm." She dug into a paper bag and popped a pill.

"What are you taking?"

"You know."

"Can I have one?" Buckley wanted to feel good.

"I only got three left. If I get some more, I'll share. You understand. Have a beer." Buckley knew that Clementine was lonely. Anyone who chose to hang out with him was lonely. He wasn't the best company, he imagined. He didn't have much to say.

"When I get to New York, I'm going to get my own apartment and a good job in a skyscraper, and I'll look out at the world." She fell back on the sleeping bag. "The world is so big. Drop Out Shitty is so small." Buckley drank his hot beer. It tasted terrible, but he drank the three beers she gave him as fast as he could. Otherwise she'd say, *What's wrong with you? Get out! Get the fuck out.* She'd said these things previously. The first time he refused her offer of a warm beer, she said she didn't have time to waste on squares. He drank quickly now, smiling and burping.

The last two times they chilled in her shack, the flies had buzzed too. She'd said, "I'm seventeen." He'd lied and said, "Me too." It was only a year's difference from the truth. She asked about his family and he lied some more, saying, "My dad's a sea captain." She didn't care what he said. She never pressed him for the truth. He told her that his mother was dead, but he left it there. He still couldn't talk about her death. It was two years ago, but it was like yesterday.

Today, Buckley thought about how Clementine was so small and pale despite the Arkansas sun, so pretty, even with the yellow stains around her mouth—and then she touched him. She pressed her head, that silky, oily head of hair, onto his stomach and slid her hand under his belt into his jeans. He said, "Stop. You don't have to do that," and he tried to scoot away. Or maybe he only considered scooting away. It's what he should've done. He should've stopped her, but she made him feel so good, and it was better with her small hand, better than using his own. Those black fingernails he couldn't scrub clean for all the soap in the world. And then, after he made a mess on her sleeping bag, she said, "Get out."

Before he left, she was sound asleep on a pile of clothes.

The next day she was at the barbed-wire fence again, explaining that her old man, Scott, would be back any day. "Then, this won't be cool," she said, tucking her hair behind her ears. She scratched at her neck, which was red from a mosquito bite. "Anyway," she said. "You know. I don't know. What are you doing?"

Buckley and Clementine made for the clay hill again and went to her shack. The few people meandering through the commune, even the little girl not more than six, a sickly-looking barefoot waif, didn't say hello or anything to either Buckley or Clementine. Like all of Mont Blanc, Drop Out City was not a friendly place, but it didn't matter because today Clementine was in a bright mood, her eyes open wide. Buckley suspected she was running out of pills, and he asked as much.

She said, "The fuckers won't share." She scratched again at the mosquito bite on her neck. "It's cool though. Scott's gonna be back anytime. Maybe today. So it's cool."

Buckley had brought her a Baby Ruth candy bar. She ate it, licking the bits of chocolate and caramel from the wrapper. She said she might bleach her hair blond in New York. She thought she'd look good with blond hair. "What do you think, Buckley?"

This time *he* touched *her*. He held both of her breasts, one in each of his hands, which he'd struggled to scrub clean the night before. He'd used an old brush with black bristles, and the tips of his fingers were raw from scrubbing, but his nails were clean. His hands were clean, and as he knelt beside her, kissing her stomach, noticing her unshaven legs, the dark hairs and the orange dirt caked on her shins above her black boots, he wanted to give her a bath.

She said, "I think if I plucked my eyebrows, I'd make a good blonde."

Buckley thought, *I could be anybody*. He pressed his nose into the dip beneath her collarbone, and she said, "I don't like red hair. I don't know what it is. Definitely blond."

"I like your hair how it is now."

When Buckley said, "I better go," she said, "Please don't. I can't be alone." She looked around the shack. Buckley looked too. There was nothing to see but the grooved tin roof, the light streaming through the spaces where the walls failed to meet it. She said, "Scott said he'd be back before I ran out. I don't know what to do. I mean, no one will share. What am I going to do? How am I going to fucking sleep?"

"I don't know."

"Just go," she said. "It's cool. Go on."

"I'll come back."

"Can you get me something? Can you get me something that might help me sleep? I'm wigging. I can't stand being this awake. It's not right for a body to be this way, man."

After Buckley left, Clementine wrote in her diary.

August 18, 1975

Dear Clementine,

You're a stupid fucking bitch. Scott isn't coming back. No, no, no, no. Don't do this again. Scott left you for Diana what's-her-face, eggplant lady, and you'll never sleep again. You'll never make it to New York. You'll wind up married to some Arkansas hick and Scott will never come back. Yes, he will. He'll come back. He loves you. Why do you have to be this way, stupid? You know he loves you. He said "I love you," didn't he? He said he'd always take care of you. Please help me be all right again. Please let me be okay. You'll be okay. You'll be okay. He said you were pretty. He said "I love you." He said "I love you." "I love you, Clementine." Why can't you tell yourself the truth? What's wrong with you? You'll never sleep this way. You'll never sleep again. Dad, I'm so sorry for everything, but I think it's too late for us. I think it's too late for me.

Clementine

She shut her diary and, watching the light fade through the cracks, waited for Buckley.

Two hours later, Buckley returned with a plastic grocery bag full of canned green beans, corn, succotash, and a box of half-eaten Cheerios. She didn't want the food, and he knew she wouldn't. She wanted something to make her feel numb. Something to let her sleep again. Stealing two of his grandmother's Nembutal sleeping pills, Buckley had come through for her.

Clementine said, "Red devils. You're a lifesaver."

Buckley shrugged. He didn't know what a red devil was.

She swallowed them with the last remnants of a day-old beer. "Thank you."

In September, Buckley skipped school to be with Clementine. Neither of them did much talking, but it was comforting because he could be quiet with her. Every day, they went to the post office to see if her old man, Scott, had sent word. Finally, there was a postcard addressed to Clementine Wistar, Drop Out Shitty, Arkansas. She was jubilant.

"It says he's coming back. It says he's just got to raise the bus fare. He's coming back." Her eyes glazed over with glee or tears or sedatives.

Buckley smiled and said, "Great," even though he doubted Scott would return from California. There was some woman—Diana—he was seeing, and she had cash, Buckley knew, because sometimes Clementine went into a rage talking about Miss Moneybags. "Fucking bitch." "She's old as shit." "I hate her!" "Scott's just after the money." "He needs the money so he can come and get me. It makes perfect sense."

"Definitely," Buckley agreed.

Clementine stole six-packs of beer from the Safeway. Buckley drank with her.

Buckley stole his grandmother's sleeping pills, wondering what he'd do when there were no more left, when Winter discovered they were gone. He wouldn't think about that right now. Right now, he was in love. It was a good thing to be.

Excerpt from
THE HANDBOOK FOR LIGHTNING STRIKE SURVIVORS

Lightning strike victims may have trouble wearing a watch that keeps time due to their altered electromagnetic fields interfering with the watch's battery. This effect hasn't been proven, but those victims who report it say the effect is temporary, lasting sometimes for months, sometimes for years.

Researchers contend that lightning strike victims are more likely than the general population to become alcohol and drug dependent, seeking an escape from physical and mental side effects.

17

Kiss me, Kiss me, Kiss me, 1981

On her way home from Carrie's, Becca spots Kevin Richfield, fourteen now, standing in Bart Carlson's yard. Bart too is fourteen, but he's not good-looking like Kevin. He's a fat bully.

Kevin calls, "Hey! What are you doing?" It's mid-October, but eighty-plus degrees. Shielding her eyes, Becca approaches Kevin. The sun is going down.

"What are you doing?" he asks again.

"Going home."

Kevin's wearing shorts and a T-shirt that brings out the blue in his eyes. When Becca is nineteen, she'll see Kevin's eyes again in the eyes of her art professor, Christopher Lord, a.k.a. Apple Pie.

"We're playing hide-and-seek."

"You and Bart?" Becca looks at the two-man tent Bart keeps set up in his backyard for hide-and-seek, which isn't really hide-and-seek anymore, now that Bart and Kevin are freshmen in high school; rather, it's some deranged kissing version of the children's game—or so she's heard.

"You and me could play?"

Bart, holding the water hose, approaches and points the nozzle at Becca.

"Grow up," Kevin says, shielding Becca, and Bart shoots the water spray beside them instead of at them.

"I'm just fooling, man."

"Stop fooling."

"I'm going home," Becca interrupts.

"Have you seen the inside of Bart's tent?"

"It's a tent. I've seen a tent."

"Not with me." Kevin smiles. His eyes are so bright. His arms, strong and tan.

"I'm going to get something to eat," Bart says.

Kevin unzips the green tent door and pulls the two nylon flaps back. Becca ducks to avoid the top zipper. Inside the tent, Kevin crouches over her because it's a low dome tent. Becca sits Indian-style on the slick nylon bottom, feeling the pointy twigs and rocks of Bart's yard under her thighs. She has always wanted to talk, *really* talk, to Kevin Richfield, the boy who rode his bike past her house for three years, the boy she thought was her destiny.

While she thinks dreamily, Kevin Richfield thrusts his tongue into her mouth. He slobbers on her face, and she feels the metal of his braces on her lips. He moves his tongue around hers. She tries to keep up with him. She doesn't know what she's doing. Then he stops. Unzips the tent door. He's leaving.

She says, "Do you want to kiss again?"

"Not really."

"That was a good kiss." What is she supposed to say?

He says, "Thanks." The tent flaps blow in the evening breeze.

Kevin Richfield has crawled out of Bart Carlson's tent, and Bart Carlson tries to crawl inside. Becca pushes her way past him. She's twelve years old, being passed off to fat Bart Carlson. This is her first kiss.

She runs home to nothing. Her mother is in bed—maybe sleeping, maybe passed out. Becca and Whiskers watch *The Love Boat* and *Fantasy Island*. Barbi Benton is guest-starring on *The Love Boat*. Becca wants to be Barbi Benton. Not for the big hair, the big teeth, or the big boobs, but for the earnest smile. *No one*, Becca thinks, *is that great an actress. Barbi Benton must be the happiest girl in the world.*

. . .

Six months later, shortly after her thirteenth birthday, Becca meets Irvin, Carrie's bad-boy cousin from California. He's staying with the Drinkwaters for a few months while his own parents try to figure out what to do with him, where to put him permanently. He's trouble.

Everything at Carrie's house is different from Becca's own home, which is now half empty. The Drinkwaters throw nothing away. Like Becca's dad, they're collectors, but rather than collecting coins and vintage sports cars, they collect dust, spilled salt, sponges soaked in bleach, dryer sheets, coffee cups, *National Geographic*s, yarn, and bobby pins. There is never a clean surface.

Laundry sits folded and piled on the kitchen chairs for weeks because the dressers and closets are full, and the furniture throughout their home is torn and scratched from the once stray cats Belinda has lured into the house with tuna fish and milk.

Belinda says she can't help loving the animals, and Carrie's dad, Pete, shouts, "Goddamn it!" and says she'd better help it. The heavy shag carpets are flat and browned and smell sickly sweet like cat piss. The cats stretch and purr, drinking their milk on the kitchen counter as Belinda strokes their backs.

Becca spends as much time as possible at the Drinkwaters', and Pete says she's his second daughter.

It's Friday night. They all watch TV. Carrie's parents sit on the bigger, newer sofa in the den, and Irvin sits on the floor with his back against a small brown ottoman. Belinda yawns, her cross-stitch on her lap, glancing at the TV every few minutes. Becca watches her stitch.

Irvin, who's tall and rail thin, has a shaggy mop of black hair. He glances at Becca. He's already told her that he thinks she's mature for her age, that she's pretty. Already he's pressed his thigh against hers in the kitchen when no one was looking, and his thigh, that pressing of muscle against flesh, sent shivers through her body.

Belinda says, "Do you want to see the pattern?"

Becca scoots closer.

"This is an easy one. The sill will be . . ." Belinda looks down at the plastic package in her lap. "Green. This green." She pulls the color out.

Pete shushes them and says, "Irvin, turn up the TV. I can't hear shit with all this jabbering." Pete lights a cigarette and puts his feet on the coffee table. He is a small but gruff man, and Becca is sometimes afraid of him despite his "second daughter" talk. "Now get the hell out of the way," he says to Irvin. "Move." Irvin, smiling at Becca, backs up to his place by the ottoman.

At two in the morning, Irvin taps on the doorjamb of Carrie's room, whispering, "Becca." In the darkness, he strokes his chest.

Becca recalls what he's said: She's pretty, mature for her age. So she is. So she wants to be.

Careful not to wake Carrie, she follows Irvin down the hallway to the den. They sit on the shag together. Irvin picks up a *National Geographic* from the coffee table and flips through it in the darkness. Very little is said. Becca says, "I've never been to California," and Irvin says, "You told me that already. It sucks anyway."

Irvin says, "I'm going to start my own band," and Becca says, "That's really cool. I like music."

Irvin says, "I'll get you backstage passes when we play." Becca says, "Cool." How can she match backstage passes? She's got it: "The same year I met Carrie, I got struck by lightning."

"Very cool."

She never thought of it that way. She's very cool.

Irvin leans in and kisses barely thirteen-year-old Rebecca Burke. He pokes his tongue between her lips. She thinks, *I'm pretty good at this kissing thing*, and feels Irvin's fingers at her waist, slipping under the elastic of her pajama pants. She whispers, "What are you doing?" and he kisses her again, pulling at the springy waist of her pants. "No."

He sits beside her, his fingertips brushing the edge of her

underwear below her hip bone. "Come on." He pulls again at the elastic band.

"You," she says, sitting up, her forearms folded at her waist. "You first."

Irvin grins. "I like you." On his knees, he pushes his sweat-pants down.

"You're not wearing any underwear."

"Touch it. Do it."

Becca has never seen a penis standing up before. She saw her dad's a couple of times by accident when he'd just gotten out of the shower. She's never seen anything like what is in front of her, attached to Irvin. Like a fat wrinkled finger. A pink snake. A gearshift in her dad's '61 Austin Healey. She holds on to it.

Irvin says, "What are you doing? Rub it."

Then, as she's rubbing up and down and up and down, he says, "Ouch." On the carpet now, his pants around his ankles, Irvin lurches off the floor. "Be gentle." With one hand on his forehead, hiding his eyes, he says, "Take it easy. It's not a gearshift." Funny, that's just what she'd been thinking about. He moans when she gets it right. Becca is on her knees, concentrating. He says, "Ah," and "ah" again. Then Becca puts her mouth around it. No prompting from Irvin. She's heard about blow jobs before, and Irvin says, "Oh yes, oh yes," and then he's vibrating. His thighs shake.

Wrapping his arms first around her neck, then around her waist, squeezing hard, he says, "I love you."

Since her dad left, she hasn't felt anything close to happiness. Until now, that is. Until she made someone happy. Until Irvin said "I love you." It was so easy to make him love her. This was her second kiss.

If you want to dislike Irvin for taking advantage of Becca, don't. Irvin Drinkwater genuinely loved Rebecca Burke when she was on her knees with his penis in her mouth. Love is sometimes fleeting.

Excerpt from
THE HANDBOOK FOR LIGHTNING STRIKE SURVIVORS

Victims who feel their trauma has gone unrecognized may act out, seeking attention through outlandish behavior, including violent and sexual acts. There is the other extreme: where the victim withdraws completely from society, refusing to leave his home. Both extreme behaviors are considered "attention getting."

18

Kill me, Kill me, Kill me, 1975

Clementine told Buckley that in June she'd overdosed on pills. "Yellow jackets," she said, "but the nurse called them Seconal." The nurse at the clinic held her hand, brushed Clementine's hair back from her face and asked if she was comfortable. " 'How you doing, sweetie?' is what she said. Sweetie. It made me want to be a nurse or something. She was so nice; I can't explain." She didn't have to explain: Buckley knew about the kindness of strangers. Clementine continued, "The nurse told me I was too precious to kill myself, and I told her I'm not trying to die. I don't want to feel pain anymore. That's not the same as wanting to die."

Buckley thought, *Yellow jackets and red devils—Winter's sleeping pills. The devil with his pitchfork. The yellow jackets circling. Things that sting and prick.*

He massaged Clementine's shoulders and looked through the front door of the shack at a boy sitting in the dirt. Buckley felt sad for Clementine. He felt sad for the boy crouched in the dirt. He felt sad for the whole world, what a waste it all was, but he felt glad too that Clementine had confided in him. He was glad that someone was finally being honest with him—the way his mother had been. He was determined to help Clementine. She blew her nose into a dirty tube top. "And then Scott came and got me, and the nurse said, 'Don't go, sweetie. Don't go with him. You need to go home.' She said, 'You're just a girl.' Isn't that sweet?" Clementine blew her nose into the tube top again.

Chuck, Clementine's new supplier and old man, ducked his head into the shack. "My turn," he said. He shook a brown lunch bag and Buckley heard the loose pills dance inside the paper. "What did I say, Buckley? We're a community. We share."

"See you later, Buckley." Clementine's face was anxious, but she smiled up at Chuck. "I'll see you, Buckley."

The Reverend Whitehouse flung a mud-crusted boot at Buckley when he walked into the kitchen. "That girl's a whore, boy."

"Who?"

"You're coming to church Saturday *and* Sunday. Do you hear me?"

The reverend wasn't a particularly mean man, just a cold man. A serious man making ridiculous demands with one thing in mind—his dwindling congregation.

There were only thirty people in the reverend's whole congregation, so if someone was missing, the Reverend John Whitehouse and Winter Pitank took notice. The missing someone, the lax congregant, got a Christian visit to remind the offender about the importance of his soul; to remind the ailing someone that this was not the end of the journey but only a stepping-stone to a better place; to remind the lost sheep that it wasn't too late for him to give to the Lord, to return to the flock, to share the wealth the Lord bestowed—every last cent.

After all, the reverend was a man who liked to eat. His girth showed that, and he couldn't eat very well without money in his pocket and food on his table. He might've married his dead wife's mother, the way she took care of him, if it weren't inappropriate—the age difference. This was how the reverend thought.

Buckley didn't know what went on in the reverend's mind; nor did he want to know. Once free of Mont Blanc, en route to the University of Arkansas, Buckley would never have to see his fat zucchini-nosed stepfather again. He might've hated him, but he couldn't waste that much energy on the man.

Buckley tossed the reverend's boot back over toward the kitchen table. The reverend whispered, "How is she, anyway?"

"Who?"

"Your little girlfriend. How is she?" The reverend glanced through the window at Winter out front, parking the truck. "Come on, Buck."

As Buckley walked toward the bathroom, shaking his head in disgust at what the reverend suggested, the reverend called, "You're a weird boy."

Sitting on the toilet, his shorts around his ankles, Buckley thought of Clementine's story. She had said her dad called her a whore and a freak and told her to get out of his house. He'd said, "You're dead to me." Maybe it was better not to know his father than to have a father like Clementine's.

Clementine told Buckley, "He's a bastard." Buckley knew she was never going home. She said, "If I'm dead to him, he's dead to me."

Buckley told Clementine his mother *really* was dead. He broke down and told Clementine that after the lightning hit, when they were trying to lift her to the dock, he could see her brain. The lightning had burned her and split her head open, and he knew she was dead. He told Clementine that if there was a god, which he seriously doubted, then that god was unjust. She agreed, adding, "God's a bastard too."

Taking his hands in hers, she said, "You can touch me."

"That's okay." He didn't feel right about it anymore, now that Chuck was around. Chuck could give her the drugs she craved. Buckley brought canned food and candy bars. Chuck delivered pacification in paper bags.

The bathroom was small like the rest of the house, and Buckley propped his feet on the bathtub. He remembered wanting to feel good like Clementine, wanting to feel numb, and Clementine said the world was unbearable without the pills. She said she wanted to feel nothing all the time. She loved being numb. Buckley, on the other hand, felt he deserved to live in pain.

He remembered the day after his mother's funeral, telling Joan Holt and Padraig John that he needed to call his grandmother and the reverend. He remembered feeling no allegiance to his stepfather or his grandmother, but feeling he deserved Mont Blanc. He deserved misery. It was *his* fault that his mother was dead, even though Padraig John said, "It's nobody's fault, Buckley." Even though Joan Holt said, "You can stay here with me. I'm your surrogate grandmother." Buckley felt that he didn't deserve to be happy when his mother was dead.

At sixteen, Buckley had received letters from both Paddy John and Joan Holt. Each of them wrote to Buckley to ask about school. To ask when he might visit Galveston. To see how he was making out in Arkansas. To tell him that they still mourned the loss of his mother—recalling daily the funny things she'd say and the way she was entranced by the ocean. They missed her. They missed him. Padraig John, two months after Abigail's death, wrote:

September 16, 1973

Dear Buckley,

I hope all is good for you back home. We sure miss you here. Tide keeps asking when you're coming back. He took to you like a brother. I know it's not fair of me to ask anything of you, but I need to ask this question, and if you can't or don't want to answer it or don't know the answer, I understand, and maybe I already know the answer. I hope I do, but did your mother love John Whitehouse? How come she run away from there? Do you think she loved me? I loved her very much, and even with the days passing, my feelings for your mother remain.

I hope that you are doing good in Arkansas. Your mother loved you so much. She always said you were a good boy. I hope that we can keep in touch, and that you know me and Tide are here for you if you need anything.
     Your friend,
     Padraig John

Buckley drafted multiple responses to Padraig John (as he did to Joan Holt) but didn't send one letter. He couldn't. It was too painful. Nonetheless, the letters from Joan Holt and Padraig John kept coming, and when Buckley was with Clementine, swallowed up in a junk food, warm beer, dirt-encrusted haze, he remembered his old life and knew he'd made a mistake leaving Galveston. Then he reminded himself that he couldn't have stayed and lived his life there with his mother dead in the ground.

He didn't deserve to be happy, but it was with Clementine when he sometimes forgot that he didn't deserve happiness. It was Clementine who poked at his ribs to make him laugh. Who asked Buckley to keep talking when the walls were closing in, when the sleeping bag, damp under her warm hands, felt like taffy, like it would suck her in and choke her.

The reverend shouted, "Did you fall in?"

Buckley flushed the toilet. He thought, *I'll be getting out of here soon. Maybe I'll go back to Galveston. Maybe I'll go to New York with Clementine. You never know.*

Clementine spent Thanksgiving 1975 with Buckley and his "family" at the Holy Redeemer Church. She ate a few scraps of dark meat and some canned cranberry. After supper, she and Buckley sat in one of the back pews, listening to the reverend's booming voice. He was trying to convince one of the parishioners to invest in some riverfront property. "A no-lose situation. Win! Win! You can't let this opportunity pass you by. You'll kick yourself." He slugged his punch. "I'm not kidding you."

Clementine laughed. Turning to Buckley, she said, "He's so full of shit."

The doors to the church stood open, the November air cool. It was dusk. Clementine looked stunning to Buckley in the waning light. Her hair was clean and pulled back in a ponytail. She had rubbed Vaseline on her lips and eyelids, and she glistened in the soft light.

Buckley said, "He's selling Amway products now."

"What's that?"

"It's like aerosol cans and cleaners and empty bottles. He says he can make a million dollars. He's got all these boxes of cleaning supplies in the shed. I don't know, but I'll tell you, there's not going to be anybody left at Holy Redeemer if he keeps taking everybody's money."

"The good Lord will provide, Buck," she mocked.

Buckley smiled. He loved Clementine. He worried about her.

Chuck had grown tired of her blow jobs. She was no longer worth his dwindling stash, and Scott had not come back. To her own father she was dead (sometimes people don't think what their words can do), and Clementine was beat from trying to live in this world. She was putting on a good show today and congratulated herself for the clean hair and plaid skirt, the white tube socks Buckley had loaned her, which she folded down like bobby socks, and the baby blue polyester blouse she'd hand-washed and hung to dry. Genuinely, she could say, "I look pretty."

When Buckley was in the bathroom, Clementine left the Holy Redeemer. She waved goodbye to Winter and Buckley's stepfather, but they didn't see. Church sucks. She hated thinking about God, this asshole who crucified his own son so that people like her, pathetic people, could have eternal life. What about this life? Face the facts: If you can't live here and now with any level of enthusiasm, you might as well forget about some Nirvana afterlife. If you can't get this one right, what makes you think you'll do better in the next place? She was never getting to New York. She was never getting Scott back. She would never be able to live without her drugs. The world was too much.

Crossing the parking lot, she passed the reverend's unlocked pickup, spotted his hand-carved gun rack, the shotgun, the floor mat scattered with shells. Maybe the asshole upstairs was trying to tell her something. She'd borrow the gun. He'd get it back later. This was the same gun Abigail Pitank had worried would ruin her son.

Clementine carried the gun, barrel in hand, on down the road toward Drop Out City. A few cars passed, the drivers doing double takes, but no one stopped. A trucker honked his horn and waved. A station wagon passed, two children pressing their noses to the back window. Walking down that road, she made a deal with this shit god that if someone stopped, if someone came after her and said, *Don't do it,* she wouldn't do it. She'd keep living. She'd know it was a sign that the world wasn't as cruel as she suspected.

When Buckley exited the bathroom, he expected to find Clementine beside the church ladies, eating pie. She wasn't there. He thought she might've dozed off in one of the pews. No Clementine. "Have you seen Clementine?" he asked the reverend, who said, "Girls need space. Don't smother her. Have some pie. Relax." The reverend introduced Buckley to a circle of men. "This here's my boy." He put his arm around Buckley's shoulder. "I was just telling Joey and Dan about that cleaner we've been using on the truck. It's like magic, and you don't ever run out. Isn't that right, Buck?"

Buckley didn't answer.

Winter handed the reverend a slice of pie on a Styrofoam plate.

The reverend said, "You are one fine cook, Ms. Pitank." Introducing her, he said, "This here's my mother-in-law. Best one in the world." To Buckley, he said, "Go on. Tell these gentlemen how that spray made the hubcaps shine. It's safe to use in the kitchen too, so it's an ideal gift for the wife."

"It's great," Buckley said. "I have to go."

The reverend said, "Where do you think you're going?"

"I need to find Clementine."

"She's probably in the ladies' room. Buck, tell Mr. Jones about how those windows shined."

"They shined."

"See, I told you, and no elbow grease either. Isn't that right?"

Buckley didn't answer. He trotted to the ladies' room. Pushing the door open an inch, he called out Clementine's name.

Mrs. Jones exited the bathroom.

"Is Clementine in there?"

"There are no young women in the bathroom. Only old women." She laughed.

As Buckley left the church, the reverend calling after him to wait, the sun having set, Clementine Wistar climbed the clay hill to her lonely shack. Buckley drove to Barry's Pool Palace where Chuck hung out, thinking he'd find Clementine there.

Clementine sat on her sleeping bag, her Drop Out City shack now clean. Her clothes folded. The darkness in the room like a blanket warming her, she took off her shoe and fumbled, her toe on the trigger of John Whitehouse's shotgun, the barrel just below her nose. Ironically, as Buckley drove his stepfather's truck toward the old dirt hill, as Buckley parked and climbed the hill, hopeful that Clementine could come and stay with him in his grandmother's house, could maybe move in with them and get a job, Clementine had a second thought. She thought maybe she didn't want to die. *Maybe I want to live. I'm only seventeen.* The gun went off just the same. Buckley heard the shot, the sound of the gun like thunder smothering him.

Before he reached the shack where light had seeped in during the warm Arkansas fall he'd spent with her, he knew that Clementine Wistar was dead. She was not recognizable when he found her, legs washed clean for church and Thanksgiving dinner. He recognized her legs and glanced at the folded clothes.

When he carried her down the hill, blood soaking his shirt, he dropped her twice. He struggled to get her to the truck, saying again and again—as he'd done with his mother—"Don't do this to me." Struggling to put Clementine in the passenger's seat, he dropped her one final time outside the truck, her limp arm knocking the door.

As he slammed the door, her head, what was left of it, slumped onto the metal glove compartment.

"Don't die on me." But he knew she was already dead.

He drove twenty miles to the emergency room, repeating his mantra, "Don't do this to me." The emergency room nurse, earning time and a half—it being a holiday—remembered Clementine: the girl who tried to kill herself with Seconal. She'd come to the clinic in Mont Blanc. This time there was a boy with her, an innocent-looking boy, who was not crying. He was numb now, finally. He had achieved what Clementine had so desired. He sat with a clipboard, paperwork, all blood-soaked, a dead girl in his lap.

Three years later in Farmville, Virginia, the nurse told Clementine's story as Claire Burke's stomach was pumped and she vomited. Claire Burke was saved from death, and a little girl, believing herself invisible and invincible, stood in the Farmville General Hospital corridor, overhearing the sad tale of one Clementine Wistar.

Buckley stood in the hospital emergency room as Clementine Wistar was taken from him, lifted onto a gurney, and rolled away. Never seen again. The nurse said, "I'm sorry." Buckley didn't hear her.

He drove home that Thanksgiving night to Winter and the reverend. The reverend was already asleep in his bed, while Winter, not looking at Buckley, not seeing the dried blood crisp on his collared shirt, said, "Your little friend's nice, but next time ask before you take the truck. We had to get a ride with the Willises. You know I don't like them."

"It sounded like a gun exploding in my ear. I wanted to run, but I was paralyzed from the neck down. I wanted to scream, but my voice was gone. I remember thinking, <u>Why, God? Why did you do this to me?</u>

Afterward, I stopped going to church. My wife is upset, but I told her, 'Going to church isn't going to help me, and it's not going to help you either. The universe is random.'"

Account by Gene Redberry,
struck on a golf course in Miami,
Florida.

19

Patty-Cake: A brief history, 1977-81

In February 1977, Rowan Burke met Patricia Heathrow. Jimmy Carter was president and Becca was seven years old. In another two months, she'd turn eight. In August, she'd be struck by lightning.

With barely a tap at the doorjamb, Patricia Heathrow bustled into Rowan's cramped office in Venable Hall. She was brusque, reminding him on that February day of his wife, Mary, when they'd first met at UNC. She was beautiful, as Mary had been, as Mary still was, but this was a trait Rowan now rarely recognized in his wife.

Sitting across from Rowan, Patricia dug into her briefcase, muttering to herself about the ridiculous drive, the traffic on I-85, how they ought to double her salary. She plucked a handful of folders from the case and centered them on his desk, on top of the stack of tests he needed to grade.

Without introducing herself, she said, "Mr. Jones is interested in the formula *on paper*. Very interested, but we'll need you to meet with the chemistry board." She leaned back in the chair and, stretching her arms above her head, said, "Is there a good place to eat around here?"

He'd spoken to this woman on the phone. They'd arranged to meet at two o'clock. It was now twelve-fifty. He said, "You're Patricia." Extending his hand across the desk, he said, "Rowan Burke. It's a pleasure."

"Patty," she said. "That's not a contract." She pointed to the stack of colored folders. "It's a proposal. Something to consider and what we'll expect in your presentation to the board." Rising from the chair, she said, "I'm famished. Have you eaten?"

He had in fact eaten in the cafeteria across from Venable, but he lied. This was important.

He told her that they could walk, but she insisted on driving because of the cold. When they reached her car, she plucked a parking ticket from the windshield, then unlocked the Cadillac El Dorado and flung the blue ticket into the backseat, where it settled on a stack of multicolored folders—much like the stack left on his desk.

On that first meeting, Rowan thought mostly of the fortune he could make if Atkins and Thames bought his additive, if they hired him as a consultant. He thought about the cars he would buy, the yacht, the vacations, the life that he deserved. He thought about Dean Thompson, that pompous bore; about Mark Cusemeo, Texas hick. Rowan's family was a founding family. The Burkes built the school, the town, the history that was packaged and sold in Carolina blue sweatshirts and flags, and he was passed up for tenure. He was snubbed by the lot of them. His mother had shaken her head at his marriage, at his career choice, at his untenured position, at his disregard for and lack of wealth. "What do you expect?" she'd said. "You were given every opportunity. All that you could want, and look what you did with it!" His mother was dead now for two years, yet he could see her pointing that bony finger—her manicured nails. She'd been right on every count.

At the red light Patty asked which way and Rowan told her to take a right. Since they were driving, he'd take her out to Lucia's on Airport Road. It was a new restaurant in a new strip mall where Rowan still remembered the Matteo Farm: horses and cattle grazing. He remembered frozen days like today, riding his bicycle past the farm to school, the patches of grass crunching beneath his tires. Now the farm was a paved strip mall with a dry cleaner, a pet store, a doctor's office, and Lucia's, a mediocre Italian restaurant run by Germans, and here, in this dive where he felt certain the food would be undercooked or overcooked or just plain bad, he wouldn't have to worry about running into Dean Thompson, Caleb Smook, Mark Cusemeo, or anyone else from the department who'd ask questions.

Inside Lucia's, after squinting at her plastic water glass with its scratched Coca-Cola logo and pushing it to the far edge of the table, Patty ordered a Greek salad, no olives, extra onion, dressing on the side, and a plate of spaghetti. "I want it al dente," she said, "extra mushroom, light on the marinara."

"Mushroom?" the waiter asked.

"Lots."

Sitting across from her, Rowan thought briefly of what it might be like to sleep with Patricia Heathrow. *Patty.* The waiter reached for her menu, and she said, "I'll keep it." A pimply-faced twenty-something, he rolled his eyes and tucked Rowan's menu under his arm. Patty studied her menu. "Maybe I should have ordered garlic bread. Have you had their veal?"

"It comes with it," Rowan said.

"Veal?"

"No." He stifled a laugh. "Garlic bread."

There were few women he met who didn't cause sex to cross his mind. He didn't like fat women (not that Patricia was fat); he never had, but even with the fat ones, he sometimes imagined what it would be like. Had Patty not been his ticket to Atkins and Thames, he might have thought more about a tryst, a one-nighter or a two-weeker, but he would not risk this opportunity.

She drummed her red nails on the table. "I like Chapel Hill. I don't like this song." The jukebox played Kiss's "I want to rock and roll all night and party everyday."

Rowan laughed. "My daughter does."

"How old?"

"Seven and a half."

"You've got to be kidding. How old are you?"

"Guess." He twirled the saltshaker in a circle beneath his pointer finger.

"Forty-five."

"You're funny."

"Thirty?"

"Close. Thirty-two."

Patty told him that she was twenty-three, that she'd graduated top of her class from Vanderbilt. She was a goal setter. A go-getter. A success. She planned to retire by forty. Rowan sipped his Pepsi and decided he had no sexual interest in this woman. She tried too hard. She talked too much about herself. She was too determined and too arrogant. She dug back into her briefcase and retrieved a compact. "I'm fucking exhausted," she said, pressing at the skin beneath her eyes. "The price we pay for success."

Smiling across the table at her, at her sheer arrogance, at the price he had to pay if he wanted a contract with Atkins and Thames, Rowan thought, *You are a baby. You're twenty-three. You don't know anything.* He couldn't know then that she was just as determined in her romantic endeavors as she was in her corporate pursuits. He couldn't know then that she would follow him to the Outer Banks of North Carolina in another four years to meet his wife and daughter.

At lunch during their first meeting, only one decision was made: they would never eat at Lucia's again. Patty poked at a mushroom with her fork. She twirled a knot of fat white noodles onto the tines and then dropped the fork, pushing the half-eaten plate of pasta to where the dirty water glass had been. "It's like Franco-American spaghetti."

"You liked the garlic bread."

"I was starving."

He picked up the marinara-blotted check. "So when exactly will I present the additive to the board?"

She shrugged and said, "Things are still up in the air. Read the proposal. That's why I brought it. That's why Dottie Jackson typed it up and put it in the pretty colored folders." She drummed her nails again.

After their mediocre lunch, Patricia Heathrow drove Rowan back to Venable Hall. In the car, he stewed. He didn't like anyone condescending to him; he didn't want to work with this woman, but he said, "I'm sorry lunch wasn't so good."

"No, it wasn't so good." She pulled up to the curb. "Call me after you read the proposal. I'm at the Carolina Inn. The number's in the red folder."

Walking down the cobblestone path to the side door leading upstairs to his closet of an office, Rowan felt disappointed. For the first time since he'd spoken with Dr. Glover at Atkins and Thames six months earlier, he thought, *This isn't going to work. That woman is a bitch.* He pulled his wool coat tighter across his chest, stuffed one gloved hand into his pocket, and thought, *They aren't going to give a shit about my additive. There won't be a patent. It won't work.* He turned and waved goodbye to Patricia Heathrow, who hadn't driven away, who appeared to be rifling through her oversized briefcase in her overpriced American car. She didn't wave back. He pushed the side door open and trudged up the back steps. *There won't be a contract. There won't be anything.* He had a feeling. He had a department meeting at four-thirty. He sat at his desk and picked up a few of the "pretty" colored folders. He never again wanted to grade another freshman chemistry exam or attend another faculty meeting. He opened his desk drawer and pulled out a palm-sized mirror—checking his own eyes for wrinkles. Who did that woman think she was? *She* planned to retire by age forty? He had eight more years until he'd turn forty, and he planned to retire by then too. He pushed the desk drawer shut, tucked the pretty colored folders under his arm, and carried them home. He didn't have time for department meetings. Maybe he was sick.

Two days later, Rowan met Patricia at the bar of the Carolina

Inn on Franklin Street to discuss his upcoming presentation to the board. He phoned her that morning, and she said things were no longer so "up in the air." She said, "This is such a done deal, Rowan. It's entirely win-win."

They met at a back table closest to the veranda. Rowan ordered a martini and said, "Did you know the university actually owns this inn? My grandfather went to school with the man who built it." He looked around admiringly, proud of his heritage.

"I didn't know that." She rifled through a small sequined handbag. "Be back. Bathroom." She was always rifling. Rowan watched her speak to one of the waiters. She was sleek and long. As she laughed, he noticed her wide-collared blouse open at the neck, her olive skin glistening where her collarbone protruded. Her silk pants sweeping the tops of her feet. Swishing back and forth. When she sat back down, he said, "This is a beautiful hotel."

Patty sipped her martini. "So, your grandfather built this place?"

"He knew John Sprunt Hill, the man who built it. They went to UNC together. In 1935, John gave it to the university."

"Big gift."

After her third martini, after flirting with their waiter (who was barely twenty-one), Patty condescended to Rowan. She told him the particulars of the presentation, adding, "Don't slouch. Don't talk money," as if he would, and then, clutching the edge of the white tablecloth with her long nails, like eight perfect drops of strawberry candies, she said, "Upstairs. I have to show you something."

On the way to her suite, she leaned against him in the elevator. "Once we get the patent it'll revolutionize sales." Dropping her head back onto his shoulder, she smiled.

What should he think? What was she doing? *She's flirting with me, and I like it. I like her mouth. I like her mouth when it's shut.*

Walking down the corridor, Rowan's feet sank into the deep red carpeting. But he had a conscience. He had a sense that he shouldn't be doing this. He thought about sweet innocent Millie—only two years younger than Patty. He thought about Mary. He'd lost all zest for that woman.

Once inside the suite, Patricia picked up two brown-wrapped chocolate chip cookies from the chest of drawers. "Complimentary cookies." She dropped onto the queen-sized bed with her cookie.

Patty's suite was elegant. Atkins and Thames had spared no expense. Rowan loved this place. He always had. If he could, he'd take up permanent residence in the Carolina Inn, with its antebellum plantation house decorum, the antiques, the intricately patterned wallpaper in deep reds, beiges, and forest greens. He walked toward the window, his eyes fixed on the moss green drapes. The moon full through the upper-right pane.

"Is that it?" he asked.

"Is what what?"

"Is that what you had to show me? A cookie?"

She stood and kissed his cheek, her breath smelling of dark chocolate, and handed him the other unwrapped cookie. She said, "Don't you like cookies?" She put his hands on her hips. "Come on—you like cookies."

He said, "I'm married," and thought of Millie. Those pink lips. How her thighs gripped like a vise around his waist.

"I didn't ask if you were married. I asked about the cookie." He walked backward away from the window and she walked toward him. Catching up, she pinned the backs of his knees to the bed's edge, giving him a small kiss—a taste of chocolate. He kissed back. In addition to chocolate, she smelled like jasmine. If he let go, if his knees wobbled, if he fell back—and all it would take was a nudge—then he'd surrender. He liked cookies. She put her right hand on the back of his thigh and he dropped to the bed. It was quiet now. Rowan metaphorically waved his white flag.

Perched on his elbows, he watched her untie one of his shoes and then the other. Those strawberry-candied hands. He watched the way she intentionally swung her hair from shoulder to shoulder, the way she licked her lips. She pulled off his socks and draped them over his shoes, which she'd set side by side, laces tucked. Everything this woman did was deliberate.

She straddled him on the bed. A strand of her blond hair stuck to his bottom lip. He said again, "I'm married."

She said, "I like that."

It turned out that Patty was right about Rowan's additive, about his contribution to Atkins and Thames. (Patty was seldom wrong.) Within three months, papers were signed. Their deal was legal. Rowan sat across from Franklin Thames himself, the old white-haired man smoking a cigar, offering Rowan a menthol smoke from his gold-plated cigarette case—an antique from the 1930s.

"I don't smoke cigarettes."

The old man laughed. He leaned forward and pulled a cigar from his shirt pocket.

Rowan slipped the cigar into his jacket. "I'll save it for later."

The two men were alone, Thames having excused the other members of the board. He said, "Just between you and me and Rick and the other chemists . . ." He laughed again. *A jolly old man. A rich old man.* ". . . your additive is going to double our sales. Rick says it's entirely tasteless. No one will know the formula's changed. Hell, no one knows the formula." The old man puffed his cigar and leaned back. "No one will ever again be a 'part-time sometimes' smoker."

"Good news for us."

"You have no idea how good."

But Rowan knew. The zeroes on the first check issued to him by Franklin Thames were evidence of his additive's contribution. No more *sometimes* smokers, those smokers the board of Atkins and Thames dubbed "dabblers." Those smokers unwilling to commit. With Rowan's additive, no more dabblers.

Rowan never smoked cigarettes. He found them vile. Sitting in the board room that warm May day across from Franklin Thames, Rowan convinced himself that he was doing nothing wrong. People had always smoked and would always smoke. The fact that his additive, the QR66 formula, tripled the effects of the already addictive chemicals in the Atkins and Thames cigarette, all twelve flavor combinations, was irrelevant. No one put a gun to anyone's head and forced him or her to smoke. Besides, Atkins and Thames funded elementary school reading initiatives, after-school and preschool programs for at-risk children, Santa Families, cancer research, and canned-food drives for church-sponsored homeless shelters. Atkins and Thames did more good than harm.

Three months later, in August, the same month that Becca was struck by lightning, Patty Heathrow left a note on Rowan's desk:

> *Rowe,*
> > *I'll be a half hour late.*
> *Patty*

`Rowan slipped` it into the front pocket of his denim jacket, which he tossed on the ottoman before hurrying upstairs to dress for dinner.

There was nothing incriminating in those lines, so he would forget the note that his wife would find two days later, that she would stash in her jewelry box because she'd never heard of this Patty and this Patty had addressed this note to "Rowe," not Professor Burke or Mr. Burke or Rowan.

By the time tall, lean Patty with the golden pixie hair extended her hand to Mary in Barnacle Bob's, Rowan's musings of a one-nighter or a two-weeker, these trysts that were an impossibility in his mind four years ago, had grown into a full-blown affair, a perfect affair because to his thinking there was no risk.

When he and Patty met over the years, whether it was in

Chapel Hill or in Richmond, she showed no interest in clinging to him or belonging to him. She wanted nothing from him. When he suggested more time together to appease her, and because he felt guilty about the affair with Millie, she said, "We spend enough time together. Do you want me to stop liking you?"

In February 1979, two years after the affair with Patty began, as Becca finished her first successfully landed round-off cartwheel in gymnastics, Rowan sat across from Patty in the Paris Steakhouse in Richmond, Virginia. His mother-in-law was dead a week then. Outside the restaurant, a mean February wind blew, and through their booth window Rowan watched the wind sweep and swirl a cellophane cigarette wrapper. Even inside, where a fire roared, the wind chilled Rowan. He didn't like death. No one did, he knew, but he didn't like the three days he'd endured listening to his daughter question the existence of God and spirits, listening to his wife rant about apologies she was owed from the dead. It made him uncomfortable. He raised his coffee cup. "It's been two years this month."

Patty shrugged and looked back at the newspaper in front of her. "Let's not make it a big deal." He'd bought her a gold locket for their anniversary, and he felt for the jewelry box in his pocket.

She said, "If you bought me something, I don't want it. I like to pick things out myself."

"Got it." He left the locket in his pocket and felt stupid thinking that this affair between them required such gestures. He looked out the window again, at the dark expanse of parking lot and the tiny white cigarette butts dotting the paved landscape. Cigarette butts were now his bread and butter.

Against his better judgment, Rowan was falling hard for Patty, because she asked nothing of him.

Two months later, after Mary caught him in bed with Millie, he told Patty what happened.

"You're screwing the babysitter in your wife's bed!"

"Normally we meet in the garage."

"That's sick, Rowe. Something's wrong with you." They were in bed at the Madison Hotel, and Patty pulled the comforter up under her arms. "Is Mary going to divorce you?" She didn't wait for him to respond. "Your wife's either stupid or insane." Patty fluffed her pillow and rolled onto her side, facing away from him. "Or both."

"I'm sleeping in the garage."

She rolled over and faced him. "Alone, I hope."

He laughed.

"Does Rebecca know?"

"I don't think so."

They lay in silence that morning, Patty staring down at the bunched-up comforter tucked around Rowan's waist. Rowan stared at her draped figure. He said, "Mary's stupid and insane."

"You like them young."

"Are you jealous?" He kissed her forehead. "I like you, Patty-Cake."

"I feel bad for your daughter."

"Becca's fine. Don't talk about my kid."

Despite his initial feelings about Patricia Heathrow—mainly that she was a bitch—he never perceived her as a threat to his family or his career. She seemed unmoved, unaffected by his affairs. Her only concern regarding his family (when she showed any concern at all) was for his daughter, the "odd" girl she saw haloed in snapshots. She occasionally joked, "You could sell Rebecca to the circus." In her announcer's voice she said, "Introducing . . . Lightning Girl."

They were lovers and nothing more. In Rowan's mind, they had an understanding. Without expectation, there would be no scene. No tears. No disappointment, but on one occasion, when they'd planned to meet at Poe's Pub on a Saturday night before he drove back to Chapel Hill, this understanding was blurred for Rowan.

Patty didn't show up.

She didn't telephone the pub with an explanation, and he imagined the worst, the most dramatic tragedy. He sat at the bar until well past eleven, with the regulars crowding him in their coarse denim and greasy leather, the smoke from their cigarettes coating his new Ralph Lauren sweater, and he pictured Patty dead on a road somewhere. He saw her tumbling across the pavement like Jessica Lange in *The Postman Always Rings Twice*, her blond hair pink with blood, her lean arms and legs splayed across the double white lines. He was worried and told himself to stop imagining the worst. He phoned her six times that night, but because of their understanding, their no-strings-attached rule, he didn't go to her apartment.

Patty called his hotel the next morning to say she'd had a bad headache. Maybe it was her tooth, but she hadn't felt well. She was sorry.

He said, "I called you. Why didn't you call Poe's?"

"I had a headache."

"I was worried."

Again with the headache story.

Patty was no ditzy blonde. She never missed a beat. She was the epitome of common sense and organization. Headache or not, she would have had the wherewithal to phone, but he let it go. He'd see her again, but not for a while. He'd let things cool down. He'd spend some time with Becca. Maybe she'd like to come to Richmond with him: a father-daughter getaway. He'd ask.

For four years, Rowan didn't know he was being played like the snare drum that Patty Heathrow had played in high school. He didn't know that by the time she was in the eleventh grade, Patty rarely missed a beat or dropped a drumstick. Not her. Not his Patty-Cake. She won first place in regionals with her flam paradiddle-diddle and her perfect fifteen-stroke roll. She learned to play the snare in the sixth grade. She played thumbs down, and it took four years before she won her first competition. She

had practiced her sixteenth notes on a pillow to build up speed in
her left hand before switching to wood, before touching the sticks
to the drum. She was meticulous and disciplined. She knew how
to play to win. *You don't rush things*. Rowan didn't even know she
was a percussionist, let alone that he was being brilliantly played.

Sitting in Barnacle Bob's, watching Patty shake his wife's hand,
he was anxious to talk to Patty alone. Rowan knew this was no coincidence. He thought he knew what Patty was doing, what she
was trying to do, but then he thought that he never knew what
Patty-Cake was doing, and that made him want her all the more.

"I've worked outdoors my whole life and I've never been struck, and then one day, the sky so blue, not a cloud anywhere, and my wife, Darlene, brings me a glass of water. The lightning hits her. I saw it. It entered through her back and out her left heel. She survived, but she can hardly remember my name, and we've been married twenty-four years. She walks with a limp, and sometimes calls me by another man's name. The other thing is, she's got this awful scar on her back where the lightning entered, and we know when it's going to storm now because her back will start to hurt real bad and she'll take to her bed.

I am glad Darlene survived. I only wish that I was the one who got struck."

Account by Patrick Fitzgerald, rancher

Merry Weather, 1978

Buckley sits alone in the common area of Hawthorne Dormitory at the University of Arkansas, thinking about the past—his mother and Clementine, and sometimes the reverend and his grandmother. He remembers his mother, half the woman she had been, her skin fatless and sagging in yellowed pouches off her bones. Clementine giggling and drunk, calling him Scott. Clementine saying "Ah." How she would "Ah" and "Ah" and "Ah," and how she would say it softly, like she was in ecstasy and she was the happiest person he'd ever known, and how she would say "You need to relax. You're just a kid, for Christ's sake." Buckley's stepfather, the Reverend John Whitehouse, said, "No man nor woman should be loved more than the Lord." Buckley's mother's breathing fainter, the skin swinging from her arms and drooping from her knees. How he loved his mother more than any lord. How he loved Clementine more than any lord. How the nitrates in Vienna sausages and pork rinds will make you mean, and he sees the summer squash nose of the reverend, puffy and bumpy and red, and he imagines he's pulling that nose out of one of those big jars, his hand in the cold liquid, digging for it like it's a red-hot sausage, and someone shouts, "Loser," and he sits up on the tattered sofa and the past is gone. His dorm-mate Cliff plops down beside him.

"Have you got it?"

"What?"

"The questions for the exam. Shit, man! The questions. Are you jerking off?"

"Yeah, man, right here." Buckley shuffles through the papers, which are damp and crinkled on the sofa.

"You made my fucking day."

Buckley stole the questions from Dr. Cooper's desk, mimeographed the two sheets, and replaced them within the same hour. Though he knows he'll be expelled—if caught—he doesn't care. To tell the truth, he's got nothing to lose.

At three o'clock he waits in the dark, windowless corridor outside Dr. Jack's office. His appointment's for three-fifteen, but he's not supposed to be late again. He's been warned. He's lucky he wasn't expelled already, but there's no precedent for such behavior, nothing in the code of conduct about standing on top of a university dorm with a TV antenna during a thunderstorm. Buckley apologized. How many times? A hundred, and yet he's here waiting for Dr. Jack to once again ask him about his classes, about his family, about the antenna and the rubber gloves and Martin Merriwether. Does he feel responsible for what happened to Martin? It's implied that he should feel responsible.

Buckley rooms alone now. He's still in the dormitory because that's part of his scholarship, but he has a private room, and Tad, Martin Merriwether's replacement, is always dropping by, poking his head in, forcing his way into Buckley's corner of the world to make sure everything's "on the up-and-up," because ultimately, the new resident assistant explains, he's responsible for the safety of the residents. Doesn't Buckley understand these things? And Tad has no intention of putting his life at risk to help Buckley. According to Tad and the rest of them, Buckley is a problem. He's to be watched.

Buckley explains to Dr. Jack, "It's impossible to make someone get struck by lightning." Sure, thinks Buckley, there are models and drawings and diagrams and pictures of lightning strikes, but there's never been a case where someone made lightning strike somebody. Or somebody else, he should say. Buckley imagines some poor sap with an electrical rod duct-taped to his torso on top of the Empire State Building or the Eiffel Tower and chuckles inwardly. It's ludicrous. "It wasn't my fault."

"Of course not," agrees Dr. Jack, who sits across from Buckley in a squeaking leather chair. There's no sofa, just Dr. Jack and his junky old wooden desk, his steno notepad, and beyond that, a filthy window beaded and streaked with late-summer rain. "Not directly."

Buckley tries to think of something else to say, because he's always wanted to be a team player and he's supposed to talk, to tell how he feels. That's why he's required to be here. To get it all out in the open. He retrieves a dusty paperback from his satchel. He licks his pointer finger and opens the book to page three. "According to Dr. Schwartz, only twenty percent of people struck by lightning actually die." He holds the book *Lightning Statistics* open for Dr. Jack.

Dr. Jack takes the book.

Buckley says, "Dr. Schwartz has studied Florida storms for the past twenty-five years, and he writes that no one has systematically compiled statistics in terms of counting how many people have survived being struck. There are just case studies. See. Look." Buckley points. "Right there." He's invading Dr. Jack's space again. "Dr. Schwartz guesses, based on his own compiling of case studies, that almost eighty percent of people struck survive, like Martin, but then they have burns, paralysis, sometimes amnesia." Buckley folds his arms across his chest and leans back in the chair. "Like Martin."

Dr. Jack turns the page. "So?"

"Can I have that back, please?" Buckley reaches across Dr. Jack's desk. "Please."

"What does all this mean, Buckley?"

"It probably means that whether or not you survive depends on the power of the storm, and from what I can tell, most people who die are struck in the head. They die from brain injury or heart attacks. But, let's face it, Dr. Jack. It means that if you hear thunder, you ought to take cover." Buckley snatches the dusty book and slips it in his backpack. "It means that the hair on your head and your arms will really stand up if you get hit or if you're about to be hit." Buckley brushes his own black arm hair with his fingers. He's felt it.

"And Martin?"

"I told you. It was a mistake. I'm sorry." He is, he truly is, but he didn't know Martin was going to spy on him. He didn't intend for the lightning to hit Martin. It was supposed to strike him—Buckley. All logic would dictate that the lightning hit Buckley, not Martin, and it might have, if Martin hadn't fouled everything up by nosing into Buckley's business and following him onto the roof.

"Why," Dr. Jack begs, "would anyone want to get struck by lightning?"

Buckley has explained the experiment before—the reasoning behind it. After years of sitting in dusty libraries reading about lightning experiments, from Benjamin Franklin to C. T. R. Wilson to NASA, it was Buckley's turn. He knew what he was doing, or he thought he knew what he was doing, and standing in dead brown fields during thunderstorms had accomplished nothing but sopping shirts that were still wet the next morning, when the reverend forced him to wear those same damp clothes to school. He wasn't looking to die when he went up on the dormitory roof, but he was hoping and wishing and strategically prepared to get struck. After Martin was hit instead of him, when Buckley had first thought Martin was dead, he thought of the physicist Richmann, the ball lightning reportedly a fiery blue, the mark they found on the dead physicist's forehead the size of a baseball, the two holes burned in one of his shoes. But Martin sustained finger burns. Charred fingertips. Martin wasn't a very good resident assistant anyway. He was always smoking somebody's reefer, hitting on somebody's girlfriend. Buckley never liked him, but now he envies him. Martin got what Buckley wants. He's been struck by lightning and survived. Of course, Martin doesn't remember being hit. He doesn't know his own name. He has burned fingertips, singed blond hair, and amnesia.

Martin was the captain of the swim team, a finalist in the Arkansas state championships, king of the butterfly stroke, but now he can't swim. It's one of the things he's forgotten how to do. It's one of the reasons Buckley is in counseling twice a week. The other boys say Buckley is plain lucky, because if and when Martin Merriwether remembers who Buckley is, Martin will kill him.

Buckley has been to the hospital once as part of his penance and to discover what effects the lightning had on Martin.

The nurses whispered as he made his way down the newly painted avocado green corridor. Buckley thought it was an ugly color and the nurses thought he was an ugly boy. He knows what they thought. A nurse blocked his way into Martin's room. "Are you family?" she asked.

Buckley didn't respond. The idea that he and Martin Merriwether, so handsome and popular, could be related was preposterous.

People are leery of Buckley, and here he sits once again trying to convince his psychiatrist (Dr. Jack's degree is in social work, but Buckley hasn't bothered to read the degrees that hang crookedly on the wall) that he isn't crazy. That someone has to find out the effects of lightning on those who survive. Somebody has to find out why some people die and others live. Why did Martin Merriwether live?

Dr. Jack notices Buckley's brown corduroy pants, his green shirt with white lettering, ARCHIE'S PIZZERIA. Dr. Jack thinks he remembers Buckley working there last year. He thinks Buckley is an odd young man. And funny-looking.

It's only three-thirty. There's still time for the mother talk, which Buckley has hoped to avoid by bringing *Lightning Statistics* by Dr. Herman Schwartz.

"How are your classes going?" Dr. Jack asks.

Buckley thinks, *It's like he's checking questions off a list.*

Dr. Jack marks his steno pad with a check.

"Good," Buckley says. "I have a B in American literature." He does it for his mother. Reads the books, memorizes the passages, tries to figure out what these novelists are saying but won't just say outright. It's hard. He hates literature, but his mother loved it. He hates art history too but had to choose between art history and music appreciation. His mother loved the arts. If it weren't for her, he wouldn't even be in college, but this is what she wanted, and he owes her his life.

"Is that with Dr. Cooper?"

"Yes."

"I had a class with him. God, how many years ago?"

"I don't know."

That was a rhetorical question, thinks Dr. Jack. "So, how are things going? How are you feeling?"

"I'm fine."

"What have you been doing other than your classes? Any more experiments?"

Buckley rolls his eyes and thinks to tell Dr. Jack, *I've been stealing exam questions so the other boys will like me or at least tolerate me. I've been following Marjorie Danato around campus because she looks like Clementine Wistar, a girl I once loved. I'm an upstanding young man waiting to graduate. Working as hard as I can so I don't ever have to see my stepfather again.* Buckley squirms in his chair. "I'm not allowed to do any more experiments." Besides, it hasn't thunderstormed since the night Martin loused everything up. Now it just rains.

"You can tell me the truth, Buckley."

It's three thirty-five. He might as well get it over with. "I've been thinking a lot about my mom."

"You'll never forget what happened. You'll never forget her, and you shouldn't."

"Are your parents alive?" Buckley asks.

"Happily, yes."

"I miss my mom." Buckley leans forward and rocks, both hands on his knees, his knuckles white. "She was my best friend."

A week earlier, the night of the infamous Martin Merriwether incident, Buckley sits on his bed, clutching his transistor radio listening to the National Weather Service. Dangerous lightning. Possible hail. He opens his dorm window. The sky outside is a deep purple and the normally bustling quad, bare but for a few stragglers rushing to Parson's dining hall for dinner. The starlings usually perched in the birch tree dot the darkening sky, taking flight. A handful of leaves drops to Buckley's window and he pins one to the sill with his palm. The air is thick with wet heat, and Buckley wipes the perspiration from the stubble above his lip before trailing a leaf to his bed. Buckley is prepared.

He pulls the blue rubber mat he stole from the school gymnasium out of his closet. A month ago, he bound it into a roll with two pieces of rope and propped the mat against his few good shirts. When his roommate, Jeremy, first saw the mat bulging out of Buckley's half of the closet, he joked, "For your own rubber room."

Ha. Ha. You're so funny, thought Buckley.

Buckley retrieves the rubber-duck yellow dishwashing gloves he bought at Collier Drugs from his top drawer and stuffs them in his back pocket. Lastly, he ties on his new rubber-soled canvas tennis shoes with the price tag still attached. (He can be absent-minded.)

He's got everything but the 1963 TV antenna he bought secondhand at Michael's Antiques downtown. It was the biggest one he could find, and the cheapest, but there was no way he could fit that thing in the dorm room. He imagines his roommate Jeremy's face if he'd seen the antenna, and he laughs. He's giddy with anticipation. Darkness falls and the wind picks up, tossing stray leaves onto the dorm room floor. Buckley forgets to shut the window but shuts his door and awkwardly lugs the gym mat down the stairs. On the first floor, he sees his resident assistant, Martin Merriwether, sitting in the common area, reading a book. Buckley smiles and tries to act normal (but he doesn't actually smile that much). "Hi," he says, holding the gym mat at his chest. Every few feet, Buckley has to set the mat down.

"Somersaults?" Martin rests his book on his thigh and watches Buckley.

"Yeah. Gymnastics." That was a dumb thing to say.

Buckley pushes the door open with his back, and once free of Martin's glare, pulls the mat across the quad toward the girls' dorm and cafeteria, Hopewell Hall, the tallest dormitory and hippest dining hall on campus, where he's stashed his antenna in the corner of the service stairs. He asked Mr. Schumacher, the cafeteria manager, if he could keep it there. "Not for long," Buckley explained. "Only a couple weeks. It's for an experiment for class." Mr. Schumacher grumbled and mumbled as he did with everyone about anything. He smelled of cabbage and gravy, his cafeteria smock browned with grease, his white chef's hat adorned with an angel pin, the hat wilting like a flattened soufflé from the kitchen heat. "A birthday present from the wife," Mr. Schumacher explained, pointing to the gold pin centered above his forehead.

Buckley remembers saying, "It's really nice."

Buckley now makes his way stealthily, as stealthily as possible with a thirty-pound rubber mat, through the back service entrance, where his great antenna waits, and he trudges past it, pulling the mat from stair to stair. He has to get the mat up on the roof first. He isn't going to stand up there in the thunderstorm with his antenna and no mat. There isn't much lightning research, not that Buckley's been able to find anyway, but he figures that his chances of surviving a strike are better if he's standing on a rubber mat. This way, the lightning can travel through him but the mat will stop the return charge. Or so he thinks. He doesn't really know, because this isn't the kind of thing you plan or implement on any old day.

On top of the roof, Buckley hears the tree limbs creaking around him, the leaves' loud rattling like pennies in a can. He unrolls the mat and rushes back downstairs for the antenna. It takes him a good twenty minutes to carry the metal contraption up the eight flights of stairs, and he wonders why he didn't just store the antenna on the roof to begin with. He has to stop five times to catch his breath, and the backs of his thighs ache. The new tennis shoes pinch his pinky toes.

It's dark outside now, and lightning flashes in the distance. It zigzags, splitting the sky in two, revealing cookie-cutter townhouses and the downtown Fayetteville mall. Like daylight. Buckley carries the antenna to the mat, which is centered on the roof, and there are more mini-explosions where the charge touches down, streaking the sky with gold. The first drop of rain strikes the back of his neck. He checks his antenna, bends the rod vertically, and remembers reading that George III insisted that the best lightning rods had round tips because Benjamin Franklin was a traitor and Benjamin Franklin said pointed rods worked best. *What an imbecile George was.* Buckley laughs. More raindrops fall, and they feel like needles on his exposed neck. Thunder claps in the distance. He sings, "Raindrops on roses and whiskers on kittens, bright copper kettles and warm woolen mittens." Rain pours off the bridge of his nose. *She loved that song. She loved Julie Andrews.* He is already drenched. *The gods are here.* He positions himself on the mat, duct-taping his rubber gloves to his forearms for good measure, cutting away the sticky tape with his incisors, pulling and struggling, the fat silver roll of tape hanging from his right arm and bottom lip. He forgot scissors. He manages to pull the tape free, and with it a wide patch of arm hair. He drops the tape to the mat and it rolls away, propelled by the wind. Buckley lifts the antenna. *Here it comes. Zeus.*

Thunder bursts, and lightning strikes a two-hundred-year-old maple not four hundred feet away. Buckley watches half the tree fall, the wood splintering, the tree crashing down on top of a Volkswagen van. It's Buckley's turn. He thinks, *Come and get me. I'm ready. Come on! Come on, you fucker.* Buckley's never been one to use profanity, but he thinks it, and the word explodes gutturally: "Fucker!" Sissy always said "Jesus God." Buckley digs his two front teeth into his bottom lip, and Martin Merriwether busts through the roof door, shouting, "What the hell are you doing? Get off the roof!" Martin, clearly exasperated, runs toward Buckley. The roof turns white, everything white. Buckley sees a blinding, glittery, sparkling split second of white, and Martin lying on the roof in the pouring rain. Buckley doesn't know what Martin saw. All he knows is that the lightning chose someone else. Not him.

Buckley drops the antenna on the mat and rushes over. Lightning continues to touch down all around them, striking Old Main, Hunt Hall, and the dusty Mullins Library. It is the most powerful, awesome storm Buckley has ever seen. He puts his ear to Martin's chest and checks for a pulse. Martin's hands are limp, his fingertips charred. Buckley wonders if Martin's shoes are burned and begins CPR. There isn't time to check the shoes. With each compression of Martin's chest, Buckley weeps a little more. With each breath of air, Buckley's teardrops fall to Martin's cheek. When the others arrive, they either don't notice Buckley's tears or think he's crying *for* Martin Merriwether. But really, he cries for himself. *What else did she like?* If the memories are ever gone, he'll kill himself. *She talked about this key lime skirt her dad bought. His name was Joe. He died. She loved macaroni and cheese.* Someone says, "You saved his life, Buckley." The rain continues, but the lightning has gone. The storm is over. Billy Joel is right: Only the good die young.

Martin was struck by lightning and is riding in an ambulance on his way to Fayetteville West Hospital. Buckley is in trouble for having a TV antenna and a stolen gymnasium mat on the roof of the girls' dormitory—for getting Martin Merriwether struck by lightning in the first place.

Later that night, Buckley flips on the light switch in his dorm room. His new shoes make a squishing noise on the cheap carpet—where a pile of leaves sits as if raked there on the third floor intentionally. Buckley shuts the window and sits on the bed, hating Martin Merriwether for stealing his thunder.

Excerpt from
THE HANDBOOK FOR LIGHTNING STRIKE SURVIVORS

Martin Merriwether, a classmate of
mine in Fayetteville, was struck by
lightning. I was trying to attract the
lightning to myself, to feel what my
mother felt. I didn't want to die, and
I didn't want anyone to get hurt, but
the lightning chose Martin, not me.

I am happy to report that Mr.
Merriwether is in good health, living in
an undisclosed location today. He never
remembered coming onto the roof to find
me, and he never remembered being
struck. He took a semester off from
school before resuming his studies and
graduating at the top of his class.
Martin Merriwether declined being
interviewed.

21

What are the odds? 1985

Between the ages of thirteen and sixteen, Becca forgot that she was a lightning strike survivor. She forgot to fear thunderstorms. She forgot the haloed photographs, the fireflies, and the watch hands losing time. Remembering, she felt loss; forgetting made growing up doable.

In high school, she managed to snag Kevin Richfield. A quick study with books and art, Becca was also a quick study with boys, using sex—withholding or granting—to her favor. With some boys, she played hard to get. With the ones who expected her to say no, she was easy to snag. It didn't matter too much to Becca because every boy prior to Kevin Richfield was a stepping-stone: a warm-up.

With sex-sex, Kevin lasted two minutes. Eyes closed, he grunted on top of her. It was always the same: her blouse unbuttoned or stuffed under her chin, her jeans in a heap, Kevin on top. Sometimes he shushed her because he couldn't concentrate if she made noise. Because he refused to wear a condom, Becca went to the health department for birth control pills. She wasn't getting pregnant.

As far as boyfriends went, she guessed he was all right.

He forgot her birthday despite subtle reminders like "I wonder what Carrie's going to get me? My mom will probably buy me something 'encouraging.' That's her thing now: canvas and paints or inspirational plaques with dumb sayings like 'Hang in there' and a picture of a kid hanging from some monkey bars."

When Kevin showed up empty-handed on her birthday, she didn't cry. They ate cake. Kevin said, "Birthdays are lame. It's another way for Hallmark to make a buck."

Carrie was there. She said, "I made Becca's card." She showed it to Kevin. It was folded black construction paper and read in bright cutout letters: *HOPE YOUR BIRTHDAY IS PUNK ROCK.*

Kevin handed the card back to Carrie. "How affordable."

Becca's mother said, "Who wants ice cream?"

Rowan couldn't be there, but he purchased a Datsun 280ZX for Becca, having a salesman from the dealership deliver it. Becca was less than enthused. "Big spender," she said.

Carrie's gift—Pat Benatar's album *Get Nervous*—was a bigger hit than the car. "I really wanted this," Becca said.

The Datsun was visible through the kitchen window. Kevin repeated, "Holy shit! Look at that car." He was fixated, practically drooling, while Becca opened her gifts. Her mother, as Becca had expected, bought paints and pre-stretched canvases. "I'm trying to be supportive of your art. I respect your talent." Becca's mother was reading mind-numbing books on how to be a better, happier person.

After the cake and ice cream, Kevin said, "Can we take her for a spin?"

"I guess so," Becca said.

"Can I drive?"

"I don't care." The keys were in the ignition. It was more like Kevin's birthday than Becca's. As the couple sped away, Carrie looked at Becca's mom. "He's sort of a jerk."

In May, Becca went to prom with Kevin. It was everything she'd imagined. Silk gown, rose corsage.

Later that night at the Holiday Inn after the sex-sex was over, Becca said what she'd been thinking all night: "Do you want to still be together when you leave for college?"

"What?" Kevin lit a cigarette and clicked on the TV.

"When you go to college, do you still want to stay together?"

"Don't be stupid. Yeah, I want to be with you. Florida isn't California." He squeezed her shoulder and blew a smoke ring.

They dated into the summer, disappointing the Whitby boys, private academy students Becca had entertained before snagging Kevin. The Whitby boys missed Becca's ability to roll a quarter off the bridge of her nose into a shot glass. They missed her fair skin, her no-nonsense way of speaking. She said, "Sex is sex. People fuck it up, thinking it's all tied up with love. It's just sex."

Becca told Carrie the same things. Their views sharply differed. Although Carrie had sex with her boyfriend, Mike, she was never going to be with another man. She thought sex had everything to do with love and guilt and all sorts of emotions. She said, "It's about your soul. You're giving a small part of your soul to someone else."

"You should write greeting cards."

"I've been with Mike since eighth grade. He's part of me. We'll get married. We'll be together forever. We'll share our lives. It's a gift."

"Seriously, you should write greeting cards."

"I guess you're only screwing Kevin now," Carrie said. "You're not fucking those Whitby boys?"

"Kevin's not exactly into the free-love thing."

"Go figure."

Becca laughed.

The two friends spent less and less time together. Becca was always with Kevin, and Carrie was always with Mike.

The summer wore on, and Kevin prepared to leave for college. Becca started asking, "Is everything okay? Are you mad at me?" because the scribbled love notes he'd once written to her had stopped.

"If you'd stop asking me that question, I wouldn't get so pissed."

With three weeks until Kevin's departure for the university, he pulled up in his Camaro. "I just waxed her."

"She looks good. Do you want to drive the Z?"

"What did I just say? I just waxed my Camaro. We'll go to the mall in my car. I hate it when you act like you're better than me just because your dad has money."

"I don't do that."

"Sure you do."

Becca waited for him to unlock her car door so they could go to the mall. He needed new jeans for school.

She slung her canvas bag over her shoulder. In a new summer dress—orange and yellow daffodil print—Becca rocked heel to toe in her flip-flops. "Is everything okay?" she asked.

"What do you think?"

"I don't know. You seem mad."

"I'm not fucking mad."

Becca plotted what to say next, how to make peace, when her right arm began to ache. The hairs on her left arm stood up. She thought that she knew what was coming, but she didn't have time to react. There hadn't been any other warnings, no rain, no black clouds, but it didn't matter. The world exploded. Blinded by whiteness, Becca fell into a thundering, furious abyss. The boom was deafening. The insides of her eyelids were white. The rest of her body disappeared inside the sparks.

Only after feeling gravel in her back and a prickling sensation in her toes did she understand that she hadn't died. Her fingers tingled. Her head throbbed. She felt her heart beating erratically inside her chest. She was on the ground five feet from where she'd been standing before the strike. Kevin looked like an umpire standing over her. He said, "You're bleeding."

He pulled her up, brushing the gravel from her sundress and retrieving her blackened flip-flop. He handed it to her. He didn't speak, and neither did she. In the strike, her dress straps had fallen off her shoulders. She put them in place. She smoothed the daffodil print across her chest and stomach. Her hands felt strange, like they were disconnected from the rest of her. Picking bits of gravel from her arms and thighs, she turned from Kevin and opened the side door to her house. She left it open.

In the bathroom, she saw bright blood streaming from her left nostril onto her lip. It tasted warm and salty. Outside, a light rain fell.

Mary appeared in the mirror. She stood behind Becca, holding on to a charred flip-flop. "What happened?"

"I got struck by lightning again."

"Are you sure?"

"I guess."

"I'll take you to the hospital."

"Where's Kevin?"

"He left."

"He left?"

"He said something about going shopping." Mary took Becca's head into her hands. "You're bleeding."

Blood trickled from both nostrils now. "It's just my nose, but I don't feel good."

"It's not just your nose. It looks like you hit your head."

Becca pulsated, feeling every beat of her heart. It was like she could feel the electric current traveling through her bloodstream.

Unlike the last time, she felt heavy, her feet like bricks. It was too difficult to move. She just stood there, feeling a sudden familiarity with death, like she'd died, feeling what Bo must have felt as the fire shot through his brain.

Becca's mother drove the 280ZX to the emergency room. Becca did not remember the drive; nor did she remember the triage nurse who checked her pulse and blood pressure. Both were low. "Did you see the lightning strike her?" they asked Becca's mom.

"No."

"Was anyone with her?"

"A boy."

The nurse examined a burn on Becca's heel. "Maybe this is where the lightning exited." She slipped her pink stethoscope into her pocket. "Or maybe she wasn't struck by lightning. Could the boy have done something violent to her?"

"No!" Mary said. "You think he knocked her in the head and burned her foot?"

The nurse asked Becca, "How do you feel?"

Becca couldn't talk. This time, unlike last time, the lightning stayed with her, pulsing and circling through her body. She felt confused, like if she tried to put words together, they'd be in the wrong order. *Was Kevin going shopping?*

"Do you know what day it is?" the nurse asked Becca.

No response.

"We'll take her back now. We'll get an IV started, and we'll get that blood pressure up. She's going to be fine. She's probably just in shock."

From her spot on the gurney, Becca recalled Claire's trip to Farmville General. No one held Claire's hand, but Claire had wanted to die. Becca's mother held on to Becca's hand. Becca suspected that she was squeezing her hand for reassurance, but Becca couldn't feel the hand so good. Her hands were still disconnected from her brain.

There was a new nurse now. She was bubblier than the triage nurse. "We're going to start her on some atropine. It should help her come around."

"She could talk earlier," Mary said, "right after it happened."

"If she was struck by lightning, there's no telling how the electricity is going to affect her."

They put blood pressure cuffs on both of Becca's arms. "Once we get her heart rate and blood pressure stabilized, we'll run some tests."

"What kinds of tests?" Mary asked. She stood in a white-walled room. Becca thought, *There are no windows, no lightning, no thunder, no rain.*

"The doctor will be in shortly."

Mary blurted, "She was struck once before."

The nurse turned around. "When?"

"I can't remember. When she was little."

Becca managed, "Time went backwards."

The nurse left. This was the nurse's first lightning strike. It was unexpected, difficult to decipher, and hard to treat—except for immediate symptoms like low blood pressure.

Mary sat in a chair at Becca's side. There was a telephone on the wall, and she tried calling Rowan. No answer. Next she tried phoning Kevin Richfield to get a better account of what had happened to Becca, but he was apparently out clothes shopping.

Time passed slowly. Later that night, the doctor entered. He shook hands with Mary. Becca slept. "How does she seem?" he asked.

"Okay, I think. She's talking some. She says she feels heavy, like a sack of flour. That's what she said."

He smiled. "You'd think we'd know something about lightning, but we don't. I'm not going to lie to you. Mother Nature is our greatest mystery. There's this surge of electricity entering and exiting the body, possibly affecting circulation, major organs, brain synapses . . . We don't know. What we're going to do is start with some tests."

"What about her blood pressure?"

"That's right where we want it to be."

"What tests?"

"A blood panel, one tonight and one tomorrow, a CAT scan, X-rays, and an EKG. We'll want to monitor her heart for the next twenty-four hours to make sure there's no late onset of arrhythmia. Millions of volts of electricity have passed through your daughter's body. We need to find out what kind of damage has occurred." He lifted the sheet covering Becca's feet, glancing at her heel, glossy with salve. "Most likely the exit wound."

"That's what they said."

"You can wait in here while they start the tests, or you can go home. It's up to you."

"I'll wait." Mary tried to tell him about the other strike, the one when Becca was little, when they'd done nothing but laughed it off because "if you'd been struck by lightning, you'd be dead." Apparently, that's not the case.

"I didn't formally introduce myself. I'm Dan—Dr. Dan Oberman."

"Is she going to be okay?"

"The best I can say is 'I hope. I think.' Everything looks good so far. She's stabilized. Like I said, lightning is not science for us, at least not yet: It's a guessing game. Rebecca's young. She's resilient. No allergies or health issues to speak of?"

"No," Mary said. This would have been a good opportunity to mention the former strike, but she didn't. She was embarrassed that they hadn't taken her to the emergency room then, but Becca had seemed fine. She hadn't been bleeding or anything.

Dr. Dan said, "One thing I can tell you: She got the initial bolt. Had it entered and exited her body through the same path, she wouldn't be here now. She'd be dead or brain-dead. She's fortunate. The return surge of electricity is the more powerful charge. Why it didn't exit the way it entered, I don't know. That was the path of least resistance."

Mary said, "My mother's dog died."

Dr. Dan said, "Nurse April will come for Becca. She'll draw blood in here—hopefully without waking her. The rest of the tests will be performed upstairs, and depending on her status, she'll be placed in the cardiac unit. That's our biggest concern right now, not knowing how her heart and vital organs were affected."

After he left, Mary called Claire. She dialed long distance even though there was a note taped to the phone reading NO OUTGOING LONG DISTANCE CALLS. She didn't even say "Claire" when Claire answered; she said, "Claire Bear." She said, "I need you."

Nurse April entered. "I'll make sure they get you a cot once we've got her in a room."

The next morning, Claire Bear arrived with the sun. Stick thin, she took three-minute smoke breaks. She seemed manic, which was no help to Mary, who felt downtrodden and sad. Mary explained, "Her boyfriend went clothes shopping while Becca underwent a battery of tests, while Becca almost died."

They went outside to smoke.

Claire said, "I'm glad you called. I miss you."

"Thanks for coming. I ought to call Carrie Drinkwater. She'll want to be here."

Within twenty-four hours, Becca's IV was removed. Her pulse and blood pressure were normal. The tests revealed no damage to her internal organs, and after thirty-six hours in a foglike state, she began speaking lucidly, even enthusiastically.

There were flowers in her hospital room. She wanted to know if Kevin had sent them, but then she remembered his position on Hallmark and the gift-giving racket. Carrie had brought the flowers. She came every day to visit Becca, as did Becca's father, who still doubted that she'd been struck by lightning. "I just find that hard to believe," he said. "Maybe there was something wrong with Kevin's car, some spark or something, and you got electrocuted." Becca didn't care what he said. She was glad that he had come.

Kevin telephoned, but he did not visit. He said, "Don't take it personally, but hospitals give me the heebie-jeebies. There's all those sick people." He didn't send a card, but she didn't expect one. She was anxious to go home and get back to a normal life. Soon, Kevin would be gone and she wouldn't see him until his fall break in October.

Because Becca suffered headaches requiring pain medication, Dr. Dan kept her in the hospital for a week. He wanted to make sure the headaches—which he felt confident were a result of her fall—subsided.

Just shy of her sixth day in the cardiac unit, her head stopped aching. She took a walk down the hall, visiting with the nurses and rushing back to her room when she heard machines beeping, paddles rubbed together. Jolts of electricity administered to someone's chest. A heart had stopped beating. She felt closer to death than ever before, and it was terrifying.

Lightning, like many things, is beyond our control. We can't predict or prevent a strike.

Thunder is lightning's hello.

Acoustically shocking, it can deafen you. The rise in temperature and air pressure creates expanding air inside a lightning strike, thus producing a sonic shock wave: thunder.

If stuck outside during a storm, crouch close to the ground, using your arms or hands to protect the ears.

22

Treat the apparently dead first

In 1981, Buckley dropped out of the University of Arkansas, not because his grades were poor, but because he didn't fit in there. He couldn't talk to anyone, and after the Martin Merriwether incident, the student body treated him as if he were a sideshow freak. The only people he actually spoke to were Dr. Jack (who was paid to listen) and the cafeteria cook, Mr. Schumacher, who—after the Martin Merriwether incident—said, "Boy, you is troubled. I'd get to a church or find a good woman or both." Based on past experience, Buckley ignored Mr. Schumacher's advice, leaving Arkansas forever.

He left his courses, the dull professors, the chipper cheerleaders, the jocks, the social workers, the psychiatrist, and his lightning experiments. He left poor Martin Merriwether still suffering amnesia.

He wrote to Joan Holt, who passed the news on to Paddy John, who was doing well with his own charter fishing business in Wanchese, North Carolina, and Paddy John sent Buckley five hundred dollars to get him started.

Paddy John wrote,

February 4, 1981

Dear Buckley,

I was surprised to hear from Joan and Sissy that you are dropping out of college especially since you are almost finished,

*but I'm not one to judge. Joan wrote to say that you might try
Manhattan.*

    *I have never been fond of big cities, but I've heard stories
about the ports in New York. I suggest you stay clear.*

    *I hope this check (enclosed) will help you get on your feet.
Not everybody is meant to go to college or finish.*

    *I know that your mother wanted more than anything for
you to be happy. Education isn't school. You can be dumb and
be president of our country. That's been proven time enough.*

    *If you ever need a job, we could use an extra hand with the
business in Wanchese. It is unspoiled and beautiful here. Remember to keep in touch.*

    Sincerely,

    Padraig John

His first day in New York, Buckley got a job working as a
dishwasher for an Italian restaurant, Damici's. During the inter-
view, Frank Damici, the owner, asked Buckley if he had family in
New York. "No, sir," Buckley said.

"What brings you here?"

Buckley shrugged. "Seemed as good a place as any."

"Do you want to be an actor?" This was a question Buckley
would repeatedly be asked.

"No, sir. I want to work. I want to wash dishes."

"Where's your family?"

"Galveston."

"Why don't you go there?"

"I've been there."

Frank Damici could no more understand how a person could
live in a city, or anywhere for that matter, without family than he
could understand this crap with people not believing in God or
Pope John Paul II's infallibility, or these lesbo women's-libbers
moaning about their failing Equal Rights Amendment.

He had thirty-six grandchildren, all of whom crowded the

Damici restaurant at some point during the week. "Family is everything," he said to Buckley, who once more shrugged.

Right away, Frank Damici suspected Buckley was some kind of atheist because he never mentioned church. Then he suspected Buckley was Baptist or Pentecostal because he said he was from Arkansas. Then he suspected Buckley was homosexual because he was never with a woman and he kept the kitchen immaculate. But Frank Damici knew that Buckley couldn't be a Baptist or Pentecostal or any type of Christian and be a homosexual, so he figured Buckley was just strange. At least the boy was a hard worker.

Smelling of grease and garlic, Buckley was tired from a ten-hour shift washing dishes and working the grill. The sidewalk outside his walk-up on 172nd Street smelled like sweet-and-sour sauce.

He'd recently begun researching lightning at the midtown branch library, and he had an idea for an introductory section of his work-in-progress, The Handbook for Lightning Strike Survivors. It was a project Buckley initiated to match the aspirations of the waiters and waitresses, the would-be actors and actresses, he worked with at Damici's. He was a writer. In 1981, he kept a spiral notebook scribbled with lightning victims' stories and statistics.

He started the project after one of the prettier waitresses, Carol, asked Buckley, "Are you an actor or a singer?"

"Neither."

"What do you do?"

"I wash dishes."

"Be serious. Are you an artist?"

Buckley didn't say anything. He thought of Clementine. Carol could be Clementine if Clementine had lived. Buckley dunked another plate in the soapy water.

Two weeks later, having not spoken to Carol since their initial conversation, he stopped her, her hands full, carrying a tray of outgoing orders, and Buckley blurted, "I'm a writer. I'm writing a book about lightning."

"I'm kind of busy right now, but good for you."

Buckley could sense when people thought he was retarded. Carol probably thought that about him. In his head, he rehearsed, *I'm a writer. I'm writing a book about lightning strikes. About people who survive. It'll be a handbook for them. Something easy to understand.*

Buckley, remembering his first weeks at Damici's, dug for his keys. Carol didn't work there anymore. She actually landed some off-Broadway role playing a woman named Purple. He'd been to see the show, leaving during intermission. It was a strange sort of performance piece lacking a story line.

Buckley carried a large ring of keys. Oftentimes he was in charge of locking up the restaurant and the walk-in freezer where Damici kept his meats. Flipping through the ring, Buckley came up with a line for his book: *When lightning strikes, treat the apparently dead first.* He'd always believed that his mother could've survived, if she hadn't been directly struck, if she hadn't fallen off the dock, if she hadn't been burned. Too many *ifs*. In Arkansas, Dr. Jack had said, "You said that her brain was showing." Buckley remembered Dr. Jack pointing at him, his face stern. "There was nothing you could do. Nothing." Buckley knew from research that others had survived. The majority of people struck *survived*, even after "appearing" dead, even after their hearts had stopped. He couldn't save his mother, but maybe his book could save someone else. It was possible. *Treat the apparently dead first.*

Treat the apparently dead first. Write that down.

Finding his key, he raced upstairs to his apartment. He felt fortunate that most of the other tenants were quiet, keeping to themselves. He unlocked his door, dropped his knapsack on the floor, and finding a grease-stained paper bag, wrote in red marker, *Treat the apparently dead first.* It was important. His book would be important.

TREAT THE APPARENTLY DEAD FIRST

Most lightning strike fatalities are caused by cardiac arrest. Begin CPR immediately!!!

23

Time to fly, 1987

Before Becca takes an Amtrak one way from Chapel Hill to Penn Station, by way of Greensboro, Charlottesville, and Washington, D.C., she writes a letter to Buckley Pitank.

> *Dear Mr. Pitank,*
> *Thank you for your book! I've been struck twice. I didn't know (until your book) there were other survivors out there like me. I'm sorry your mom died. I really am.*
> *Sincerely,*
> *Becca Burke*

It's short, to the point. She doesn't tell him that she once believed the lightning gave her special powers: the watch hands, the fireflies, the halos. She had a wild imagination as a child. Believing the dead walked the earth. Believing she saw Grandma Edna and Bo after they died. Believing she saved that fish.

The past is gone.

Her mother teaches poetry to old people now. Her father lives on Cedar Island. He takes photographs. The Yeatesville picture of her standing beside the watermelon truck is on display at the Belle Tara Gallery in downtown Chapel Hill. She doesn't want to see it. It reminds her of that trip to the beach—when she still had hope. Her father's photographs have been widely and enthusiastically critiqued. He claims to only "dabble" in photography. *He's a liar.*

It strikes Becca as strange that someone who seems heartless can take an emotionally compelling picture.

Her latest painting received an honorable mention at the Carrboro County Fair. No one cares.

Carrie no longer speaks to Becca.

The tone has changed. The colors are brighter. The windows are open. The curtains are red. The rain has ceased. The landscape altered.

Becca's life is no longer a still life—a bowl of fruit, static and boring, making turkey and bologna sandwiches for her mother, spraying Pledge, rubbing at the furniture that won't come clean, licking dust from her fingertips—but it's a life, still.

Many of the train's passengers disembark in Baltimore. Becca hopes to make friends at the School of Visual Arts. Her dad has arranged for a loft in the Village. Her possessions are already there. She's excited. She's sad. She's leaving Whiskers behind. Mary said, "He's not a city dog."

"But he's my dog."

"He won't be happy."

Becca wants him to be happy.

She's not happy.

There is a reason that Carrie no longer speaks to Becca. It has to do with lies. Becca is all too familiar not only with death but with liars. Her father lied. Kevin lied. Carrie's boyfriend, Mike, lied.

Carrie was in Texas visiting her grandmother.

Becca telephoned Mike. She needed an ear.

They met on the lawn of Coker Arboretum just shy of midnight. "How can I get Kevin to like me again?"

"You can't." Mike yanked a patch of grass from the ground, dropping the blades on his jeans. "Plus, you can do a lot better than him. You're so pretty."

"I thought we were meant to be—you know, like with you and Carrie."

Mike was blond, like Kevin, but with a wider nose and his face pocked with acne. He dropped a few blades of grass on Becca's calf.

Mike said, "I like you."

"I like you too. You make Carrie happy."

"No, I *really* like you." Mike leaned in, attempting to kiss Becca, the blades of grass on his jeans spilling to the dirt.

"What are you doing?"

He climbed on top of Becca.

"Stop it!" She pushed him off—which wasn't easy.

"We could do it. Carrie won't find out. What's the harm?"

Becca ran from the arboretum.

That same night, Mike called Carrie in Texas: "Becca hit on me. I guess she's so upset about this Kevin thing, she'll try and do anybody."

Carrie planned to marry Mike.

Carrie knew Becca's history with and feelings about sex.

Becca and Carrie Drinkwater, best friends since third grade, no longer.

On her way to New York, *The Handbook for Lightning Strike Survivors* open on her lap, Becca reads that victims often suffer sleeplessness, listlessness, and pain in different regions, depending on where the lightning entered the body. Becca thinks, *I have every one of these symptoms. Even my soul hurts.*

Before she left Chapel Hill, Buckley Pitank responded to Becca's letter. She keeps the letter nearby, rereading it now:

August 1, 1987

Dear Ms. Burke,

Thank you for buying my book. Thank you also for your condolences. I am glad to know that you feel less alone as a result of my book. That was one of my goals when I started the project. I wanted people to know they weren't alone. I also hope that The Handbook will help prevent future lightning deaths. As you've read, most lightning deaths are preventable. Please do your part.

Thank you again for your interest and personal story.

Sincerely,

Buckley R. Pitank

Becca muses on "Do your part." Buckley R. Pitank sounds like Smokey the Bear.

The loft is on the southwest corner of Washington Square Park. There are high ceilings and exposed brick. It's more than she needs. The four windows that face the park are thick-paned, long, and full of light before noon. She takes morning classes and paints late into the night. She doesn't know what she's doing at four in the morning, her hands permanently stained, a palette of browns and reds slopped onto another layer of paint not fully dry, but she can't stop. Before dawn, she remembers Grandma Edna asking, "Can I keep it? Can I keep the sketch?" It had meant so much to Becca. Going to the kitchen for coffee, she sees Grandma Edna leaning against the counter, those long freckled arms crossed, smiling at Becca. Becca rubs her eyes, and Grandma Edna is gone.

Paintings that aren't good enough (and none of them is good enough) are mishandled and chucked into the unused pantry. She thinks the second-year professor Christopher Lord is talented and cute. Some of his paintings have been on display in the main hall. His eyes remind her of Kevin Richfield's.

Excerpt from
THE HANDBOOK FOR LIGHTNING STRIKE SURVIVORS

In one study, young and old victims of
lightning and electric shock were given
the task of drawing what the electricity
felt like. Because victims have difficulty
verbalizing electric shock, art can help
survivors remember (and hopefully heal).

In this particular study by
S. Razzleford, the pictures produced had
one similarity: jagged, sharp, or
pointed edges appearing somewhere in
the picture.

24

Publication, 1984

It took Buckley five years to write *The Handbook for Lightning Strike Survivors.* He did most of his research at the midtown library. He took the 6-train before and after work. When he forgot his legal pad, he jotted notes on Damici's take-out menus, paper bags, anything at hand. He spent his days off reading NASA publications at the library. Arriving home late, he typed his notes on a Remington portable he bought secondhand in Chelsea.

Engrossed in research, Buckley quickly learned that NASA knew more about lightning than any person or organization, because the space program, from its inception, was plagued by lightning hazards. NASA needed their meteorologists to accurately forecast and predict strikes. During *Apollo 12*'s 1969 launch, lightning briefly knocked out vital electronics. Fortunately, the astronauts were able to regain control of their ship.

At Damici's, Buckley talked about his research. He talked more than ever. The waitresses told him that his next book should be about something less technical. "Write a romance, or if you really like nonfiction, write about abortion. That's really controversial. Or you could write about the Reagans' astrologer. It's good to know that even stiffs like those two believe in astrology."

If Buckley had decided to write a book about the Reagans, he might've discovered that his biological father currently worked for the Reagan administration, meeting on several occasions with

Panamanian leader Manuel Noriega. His father's official title was hospitality liaison.

Because of Buckley's organizational failings, the book was taking a long time to complete. Each time he read about another survivor, he revised the book. *I wish my mom had survived.*

To feel the weight of the typed pages excited him. It was incredible to produce something of substance. As the pages grew, he took to carrying the manuscript everywhere. On the subway, holding his green knapsack, the pages inside, he knew that his mother would be proud of his accomplishment.

Buckley wrote to Paddy John, confessing, *I might never finish* The Handbook for Lightning Strike Survivors. *Reading all the survivors' stories makes me feel close to my mom.*

Paddy John wrote back, *You once wrote to me that your book could save someone's life. I say finish it. Publish it. Stop dicking around, and put it out there.* He also wrote: *Tide is a mess. His grades are poor. I caught him smoking marijuana IN MY HOUSE.* Tide was nearly seventeen now—which was hard for Buckley to imagine.

Early mornings, before the clanking pipes and noisy radiators distracted him, Buckley worked on *The Handbook* or wrote letters to his friends in Galveston—Sissy and Joan, or Paddy in Wanchese. Even though Buckley had never liked the kid, he'd been a kid himself then, so he hated to hear that Tide was doing poorly.

With each letter from Paddy John, the news concerning Tide got worse: he was skipping school and drinking beer. Buckley didn't pray, but he wished really hard that Tide would straighten up.

On Friday night after working the dinner shift, Buckley watched *The New York Nighttime Music Hour,* a public-access variety show featuring Kate Lovely, a Forty-second Street favorite, stripping to bagpipes. He sat there laughing, thinking, *Paddy John is right. Soon, very soon, I'll give the book up. I'll put it out there.* He leaned across the couch, reaching for his knapsack. Pulling the pages out, he held them to his chest. *Soon.*

Two years later, in March 1986, Sycamore Press published one hundred copies of *The Handbook for Lightning Strike Survivors.* Buckley dedicated the book to his mother.

Excerpt from
THE HANDBOOK FOR LIGHTNING STRIKE SURVIVORS

What you need to know:
Each year, thunderstorms in the United States produce an estimated 20 million lightning strikes. The most cloud-to-ground strikes occur in southern Florida, Texas, and parts of Louisiana. 30% of the time, the lightning forks, touching down in two or more spots.

Never wait to see lightning strike! If the wind picks up and clouds form overhead, seek shelter immediately!

If indoors, don't use the telephone. Don't shower or bathe. Stay away from doors, patios, and windows.

25

You're the reason men break down, 1987

Mary sang. The house was empty except for her and the dog.

"I think I saw you in an ice cream parlour, drinking milk shakes cold and long, smiling and waving and looking so fine, don't think you knew you were in this song . . ." In the kitchen she twirled, her red A-line dress opening like a flower. She tapped her heels against the floor tiles. She loved her job.

She did not have to work. Rowan was incredibly wealthy, having developed fourteen different cigarette additives for Atkins and Thames, none of them as lucrative as his first additive, QR66, but he was financially set for life, and John Saltz, Mary's lawyer, made sure that she and Becca saw a large chunk of Rowan's fortune. There was no disputing his extramarital affairs. Mary had known from the onset that Rowan wouldn't raise the issue of fidelity in a public courtroom. He wouldn't have his name dragged through the mud. The settlement was weighty and quick.

Slipping her heels off, Mary settled in an old recliner. She tapped the points of her shoes together. She'd found her niche: It was teaching poetry—her first love. It was Browning, Keats, Byron, and Ginsberg! It was Auden and Ashberry! It was wonderful. Leaving her shoes in the den, she sashayed to the garage. Digging through cardboard boxes of college textbooks, dusty paperbacks, and literary essays, she remembered Dr. Carver telling her, "You know your stuff, no doubt about it" and "Even if you sometimes come across as ditzy, it doesn't matter because you're smart. You're the reason men break down." She remembered liking herself, telling her father she was leaving Prospect and she never wanted to see him again. Late at night, she'd applied to one college after another, paying the application fee with money she'd saved and stashed beneath her bed. She remembered, having earned a full scholarship, taking the bus from Farmville to Chapel Hill. She was seventeen.

Among her books, Mary found her first publication, an essay on Kate Chopin's *The Awakening*. She'd been so proud, fruitlessly sending copies to her parents—who didn't call or respond. What had she expected?

Dr. Carver had commented, "You don't go home for holidays."

"My parents died."

Dr. Carver was three times her age, and she loved him. There is solace in poetry. There is solace in art. Mary was nostalgic. She felt happy—an unusual and wonderful thing to be.

Then she found an old notebook, the pages yellowed and scrawled with black ink. She had her father's handwriting.

She was sixteen, attending Prince Edward Academy. (There was no public school, as to avoid integration.) She'd been to see the movie *It Happened One Night* at the drive-in. She'd gone alone. She loved Clark Gable.

When she got home, her father was waiting with his belt. Mary felt for the buckle scar on her lower back.

She turned the pages in the old notebook, remembering the poem she'd written that night, wanting to read it again but not wanting to remember the rest—her father in pursuit, shouting, "You broke curfew!"; hearing the leather slip from his belt loops and the clack of buckle against the plaster wall; feeling the buckle strike her back, the burn of blood rising to the surface. Her room wasn't close enough. She wasn't going to make it. She fell, and the buckle had come down again, but the first hit had been the charm.

She turned the pages. There was nothing to fear. Not anymore.

THE SPACE BETWEEN YOU AND ME

The space between you and me grows with each door
    slamming shut,
with each boot hurled. With that fork you threw at me.
The space between you and me is greater than the universe,
and I think to pounce when you sleep
when you first wake
when your feet are bare and
your hands are empty.

She smiled, remembering how she nightly wished him dead. He never got the best of her.

Mary's mother lived in that space between Mary and her dad. Her hands had smelled like baked pears and Mary swore she could smell those hands now—just a whiff.

Mary remembered her dad pressing one boot on the back of her thigh, pressing her chin into the floor with his left hand. She'd stifled the tears. Without her permission, some fell anyway—a response to pain, but she wouldn't give him the satisfaction of seeing her cry.

He said, "This is my house. My rules. You break curfew, you pay."

There was no point in trying to explain that she couldn't miss the movie's happy ending. She adored Clark Gable: so charming and suave.

An hour later, her mother had knocked at her bedroom door. It was late. Mary's father was asleep. Her mother brought baked pears and warm milk.

"I'm not hungry," Mary had said.

"He doesn't mean it."

Mary took her notebook into the kitchen, the pear aroma staying with her. She fixed a Jim Beam and Coke. Her hands were aged now; brown spots mingled with freckles. It was funny to see them this way, reminding her of her mother.

My mother loved me. Mary sipped from the sweating glass and cried.

Her mother would say, "There's no sense crying over spilled milk or bourbon and Coke."

Craving a jar of her mother's pear preserves, Mary fixed a grape jelly sandwich. A lot of the women at the Dogwood Estates retirement center, where she now taught poetry, were like her mother—*stubborn and ornery, remembering their lives as well lived, as good, and hell,* Mary thought, *they ought to remember them that way.* She sipped from her glass. *Who wants to be old and full of regret? Who wants to be old and sorry for the life she's lived? Who wants to be eighty and thinking "I shouldn't have done that. I wish I could take that back."* Her mother would say, "Regret the things you haven't done, not the things you have. Learn from life. Live every day as though it's your last." *God,* she thought, *my mother was full of clichés.* Mary finished her drink. Smoothing a page in the old notebook, she wrote: *It's never too late to make peace with the world.*

Excerpt from
THE HANDBOOK FOR LIGHTNING STRIKE SURVIVORS

Education is your best defense.

Brigitte McCray, survivor from Chilhowie, Virginia, said, "When I was sixteen, I thought I was invincible. A few thunder booms didn't scare me. When I got struck, I saw God. I was too young to see God. Now at the first sign of a storm I go inside. I stay away from the phone, the plumbing, and the windows."

A poet and artist, Brigitte also travels to schools in southwestern Virginia to educate teenagers about the dangers of lightning.

26

Emphysema and Apple Pie, 1988

After one year, the pantry was piled with warped canvases of unfinished nudes and still lifes and oils never left to dry.

Christopher Lord, Becca's professor, met her for pizza on Bleecker Street. Becca called him Apple Pie in spite of his steel-studded leather jacket and his get-in-free card at CBGB's. She called him Apple Pie because of his wife and two kids on Long Island. Because of his board memberships and tenure—something her father had never managed.

Across the table, he squeezed her hand.

She said, "This is the sketchbook I was telling you about." She called it "*Mon Histoire,* My History." She felt the need to share it with him, wanting his approval. There were charcoal and oil pastel depictions of Grandma Edna, pen-and-inks of the woman selling watermelon in Yeatesville, of her dad in Barnacle Bob's, of her mom on the kitchen floor. There was a pencil drawing of Kevin Richfield.

He flipped quickly through the pages. "When did you do these?"

"Last year, when I first got to SVA."

"Don't show them to anyone. They'll think you shouldn't be here."

It was cruel.

"Who's the old lady?"

"My grandmother."

"It's so commonplace, Becca." He was disappointed.

Becca didn't eat anything. After Apple Pie finished his third slice of pizza, they went back to her place. They drank the wine he'd brought. They had sex-sex. Apple Pie could last until he was sure she'd climaxed. He liked to yank her red curls, pressing her naked against the exposed bricks. She liked it too. She was falling hard for him.

Every Friday after Apple Pie's two o'clock studio class, he went to Becca's loft. She promised not to tell anyone about the affair, although she did tell Jack and Lucy—her neighbors and closest friends in New York, and for some reason, though she felt compelled to confide in her mom, she didn't.

In Chapel Hill, Mary quit smoking.

Despite profiting from Rowan's work for Atkins and Thames, she didn't want to line his or his whore wife's pockets with any more cigarette money. She quit cold turkey by pretending (to herself) that she had emphysema. (She also pretended to have emphysema with the boy who bagged her groceries and a cashier at the Rite-Aid.) Claire said on the telephone, "That's a strange, deceitful way to quit," but, thrilled that Mary did so, she added, "Whatever works."

Carrie majored in economics at UNC Chapel Hill, and Mike worked construction for his dad's company. They got engaged. Mike's mother, twice divorced, gave him one of her old wedding rings.

As for Whiskers, he waited for Becca's return. She'd spent the night away before. He knew she'd be back. He waited on her bed.

Months passed. He waited. Every time the front door opened, he ran to meet her. He paced the purple flower rug, and Mary didn't have the heart to tell her daughter (who was finally free of Chapel Hill) that the dog's heart was broken—that he was waiting for a ghost of a girl, a girl who would never return.

Mary tried cheering him up. She took Whiskers for morning walks, and she took him to work. He wagged his tail, seeming to perk up, but every time Mary took him home again, he went to Becca's bed and waited. Finally, Mary shut him out of Becca's room and he lay with his salt-and-pepper back pressed against her door. Mary tried to coax him into her own bed, but nothing doing. He was waiting on Becca.

Fourteen months after Becca's departure, Mary found Whiskers, his salt-and-pepper back pressed against Becca's bedroom door, dead.

The vet ruled Whiskers' death congestive heart failure, but Mary knew the truth: a broken heart.

Becca was in the throes of Apple Pie then. She hadn't called home in a good while, and when Mary telephoned New York with the sad news, Becca wept.

She met Apple Pie outside his office door. He was with colleagues. She said, "I need to talk to you." It was obvious she'd been crying.

He said to his colleagues, "She's upset about her grade."

"Please, can I talk to you?"

"I don't budge on grades. I've explained this. Art is subjective. Consider me the audience for *all* work while you're enrolled in my class."

One of Apple Pie's colleagues patted him on the back before they left Becca crying in the hallway.

You might think Becca would toss Apple Pie aside, but she'd grown accustomed to the men she most revered discarding her like garbage. She was a smart girl, but some lessons are hard, taking years to learn, and even more years to master.

A lightning strike is not contagious. Don't hesitate to administer CPR. Don't think twice that you will be electrified by touching a victim. The human body does not hold an electrical charge: This fact is disputed by one victim, Sarah X., who reported, "I got struck when I was fifteen years old and ever since then, every time I touch someone, they get zapped." Sarah wouldn't meet with me to prove her claim, but I thought her story worth mentioning. One thing is certain: Electricity, lightning included, affects people differently. Sarah X said, "I'm cursed. I don't feel like I can touch my own grandbabies without suffering them some little bit of harm." (Sarah X.'s claims have not been substantiated by doctors, but that doesn't mean they aren't true.)

27

Mamma Mia, 1989

After The Handbook was complete and out there in the world, Buckley's only escape from loneliness was work. He worked longer shifts. He worked doubles and triples. He stayed at Damici's when he was off the clock. He sat at the bar, eavesdropping—anything to avoid being alone with his thoughts. Unfortunately or fortunately for Buckley, his new neighbor, Mia, didn't abide sulking or introverts. She also wore heavy black boots, which she used to kick at his door. "Wake the fuck up!"

When she first moved in across the hall, she introduced herself, saying, "I'm punk rock." Her boyfriend, wearing studs through his nose and eyebrow, said, "She's hell on wheels."

Buckley said, "She doesn't have wheels." He was trying to be funny.

"It's an expression," the boyfriend said.

Mia wore black eyeliner and black lipstick. Younger than Buckley, she said, "We'll hang out together. We'll be pals. When I'm out of beer, you share, and when you're out of beer, I'll share."

He said, "I work a lot. I don't drink."

This morning, as she kicked his door repeatedly, a neighbor shouted, "What's wrong with you? Stop that!"

Mia said, "Screw off."

The neighbor said, "I'm calling the landlord," and pulled her door shut.

Mia kept kicking. "You're getting me in trouble," she shouted at Buckley's door. "Don't get me in trouble." She kicked some more. Her boots were good for more than moshing. "Open up!"

Buckley said, "Go away."

"No." She kicked some more. "Open up!"

"Please stop."

She kept kicking. She was relentless. Buckley was not. It required too much energy.

They sat side by side on Buckley's sofa, Buckley's hands between his knees, his eyes to the floor.

"I want you to come over Friday. I'm having a party."

"I have to work."

"Then after work. I won't take no for an answer."

"I'll smell bad—like grease and garlic."

"I don't care. If you don't come, I'm bringing the party to you."

"I really just want to be left alone, Mia."

"I know. That's why I'm here. I revel in torture. See you Friday!"

It was after midnight on Friday when he got home, but he could hear the party still going strong. He showered. He didn't want to go. *The New York Nighttime Music Hour* was on TV. He sat on his bed and stared at a nail in the wall, wondering why when he felt sad he couldn't cry like a normal person. He showered and dressed.

Mia served cheap beer and vodka punch. There were potato chips and French onion dip—the kind you make with Lipton dried soup. The food reminded Buckley of the reverend. Maybe he should go back to Arkansas. He could rot away there. No, he'd rather rot in the Bronx. Mia got Buckley some punch. It smelled disgusting, but he drank it.

In the morning, he woke up bare-chested on Mia's floor, his shirt tied around his head. He vaguely remembered dancing on Mia's coffee table. (And he didn't know how to dance!)

Mia was in a burgundy robe, her dark hair draped over one shoulder. "I told you you'd have fun."

"What happened?"

"Nothing happened. You had some fun."

"I don't remember. Tell me."

"Do you want coffee?"

"No."

She sipped her coffee. "You want to hear the worst of it or the best of it?"

"Whichever."

"You were cute. Everyone loved you. When Sheila said her uncle died last week, you started crying. You took off your shirt to dry your tears, and then you got up on the coffee table, got everyone's attention, and told us how your mom got struck by lightning and how your girlfriend got shot in the face. That part was heartbreaking. And then everyone hugged you and said you should write songs because you had the bluest life they'd ever heard. You said, 'I never cry. I'm crying!' And then you tied your shirt around your waist and passed out."

"This is why I don't drink."

Mia made a pouty face. "You were adorable."

On Sunday, Mia took Buckley a paper plate piled with chocolate chip cookies. She said, "I didn't make them or anything, but I think when you take them out of the blue wrapper and put them on a plate, they taste better. It's the power of suggestion."

Buckley poured two glasses of milk. He said, "I'm not a mean guy, but I'm cursed. Everyone I love dies. I don't want to be friends with you or anyone. Just leave me alone."

Mia dunked a cookie in a glass of milk, ignoring his short speech. "So I must tell you that on Friday night, after you told us all about your mom and stuff, and before you passed out, you and my friend Sheila made out. She told you that you could call her Clementine. I think she totally likes you. Be-ware! She's a psycho when it comes to men."

"Please tell me that you're joking."

"Afraid not."

"I'm never drinking again."

If you are a lightning strike survivor,
understand that you are not alone.

If you were struck when the sun was
shining, you were still struck. If you
were struck without one drop of rain,
you were still struck.

Lightning can strike as much as ten
miles from rainfall, and there is no way
to predict the first strike.

Don't be afraid to tell your story.
Although an estimated 400 people are
struck each year, this is a low
estimate. Not everyone seeks medical
help. The heart may or may not stop. It
may or may not beat erratically. You are
in shock, both literally and figuratively.
Your thinking is changed, affected by
the voltage that's traveled through your
body. You might or might not lose
consciousness. You might or might not
cry.

28

Men, 1989

I'm <u>not</u> <u>an</u> *idiot. I have feelings. I deserve to be treated with kindness and respect. "She's upset about her grade." Who does he think he is?*

She called Apple Pie at home. She took the Valium and drank the beers and waited for him to rush over or call a fucking ambulance.

Instead, he said, "Don't call here again."

The next night, she was desperate and messy, complicated and bursting with apologies about why she kept calling. It was her dog. Whiskers died. He was gone. She didn't get to say goodbye. Was that too pathetic? She'd had too much to drink. She'd never call him at home again.

She waited outside his office at ten o'clock. He always stopped there after his studio class. She'd win him back. She'd make him desperate for her. She'd done it before. She was special. She didn't realize that there were four special students before her.

She leaned against the wall of the narrow hallway facing his office door. Maybe she should hide, but there was no place to hide. So she waited. She stared at a white knot of wood, like a bleach stain, just below the doorknob. It spiraled outward, growing darker and darker with each spiral, but the center was completely white. She was naked beneath a raincoat and army boots. She'd become desperate the way Aunt Claire had been for Tom—not fat like Aunt Claire, but the other extreme: waiflike, subsisting on cheap wine, Cheerios, and Fig Newtons.

Who the hell does he think he is? "Don't call me"?! "Don't call me"!?

She was drunk. She was mad. It was ten-thirty. She was sorry. She was seething. Floyd, the custodian, walked past, pretending not to see her. She fingered the white spot below the doorknob, hearing the *tick-tock* of the clock down the hall. She sat with her back against the door, her freckled white legs poking out from under her coat, bouncing the back of her head off the white spirals, pressing the rubber soles of her boots onto the opposite wall. At midnight, she kicked Apple Pie's locked office door and hurt her big toe despite the heavy boots. She hopped on one foot in the tiny hallway, cursing his name.

Apple Pie had messed with the wrong woman. She wasn't going to let him get away with it. He said he loved her. He said he only stayed with his wife "for the children." He was a liar. *All men are liars.*

After Apple Pie, there were one-night stands. There was Chris-with-no-last-name. There was a Joseph, a Danny, and a Richard. They came and went. Some of them were artists or musicians, but a lot of them were professionals with nine-to-five jobs. In a few years, they'd be nine-to-six jobs, eventually eight-to-six. "If you want to be successful and if you want to get ahead, you work: longer and longer hours."

It was 1989. AIDS and Republicans ran amok.

Lucy told Becca, "You'd better get tested."

"I use protection."

"It doesn't matter. You should get tested."

In Panama, U.S. troops captured General Manuel Noriega in Operation Just Cause. Richard Martin, Buckley's biological father, hid in a Panama City hotel, while nearby, his longtime girlfriend, Gabriela, fled her house with another of Richard's sons—Hector.

Her house, her whole village, caught fire and burned to the ground. She saw people fleeing. She saw people shot. She wondered if Richard would really take her and Hector to Miami. There was nothing left in Panama for them.

The CIA found Richard in his hotel room three days after U.S. forces took Noriega into custody. They also found six kilos of cocaine and *one* plane ticket to Miami. Richard had a penchant for ditching women.

He was flown to Miami first, next to Washington, D.C., where he was charged with treason and international drug trafficking. He claimed repeatedly that Noriega had set him up. Buckley's biological father, Richard Martin, was a liar.

Gabriela met a U.S. Marine named Claiborne Dodge, who gave her his rations. She gave him a photograph of herself that she'd saved from the ashes.

In New York, Becca took Lucy's advice. She got an HIV test. Two weeks later, she waited on a cushioned white table, kicking her feet back and forth, for the results. The nurse practitioner opened Becca's folder and said, "This test is confidential. Do you understand?" She said a number of other things, all implying to Becca that there was bad news. She kept asking, "Do you understand?"

Becca thought she might vomit. "Yes, I understand."

"The test is negative for HIV."

Becca was fortunate, and she knew it.

After I was struck, I lived danger-
ously. I couldn't sleep, so I went out
to bars. I cheated on my girlfriend. I
did things I wouldn't have thought about
doing before the strike.

I was a lifeguard. It was thundering,
but way off in the distance, so I didn't
think to tell the kids to get out of the
pool. I could've blown the whistle.
Instead, my whistle melted into my
chest. My head and neck were wet and
burned. The current traveled through the
lifeguard stand and me. No one died, but
one boy has permanent brain damage. I
have guilt. I should've gotten all of
them out of the pool.

I don't sleep. I take tranquilizers,
but still at night I feel awake. I feel
that whistle burned into my chest. In a
semi-dream state, I think my heart might
stop any second. Everyone thinks I
should be better. It's been two years,
but I'm not close to better, and it
seems like yesterday.

Account by Shankleford J., Austin, Texas

29

Double, double, toil and trouble, 1987, 1990

The Belle Tara Gallery sits back from Washington Street. In front of the building there's a small seasonal garden. Today there are daffodils, hyacinths, and tulips. The smell of hyacinth sticks to his clothes. It's 1987. Colin Atwell is eighteen. He didn't go to college in the fall like the rest of them. Instead, he's helping his dad build a tree house for their neighbor's six-year-old son. He's helping his dad clean out the basement. He's reading Gardner's *Art Through the Ages* and researching the children's drawings saved from the Nazi camp and ghetto Terezín in Czechoslovakia. His heart breaks again and again at the hope the children kept.

To date, he's written twenty-seven letters to his mother: it's his own little bit of hope. He doesn't know where she is, so he hasn't sent one letter. He keeps them in his underwear drawer beside Becca Burke's butterfly brooch. If he ever has a girlfriend, maybe he'll give the brooch to her.

His dad is teaching him economics and civics by letting him play the stock market. He's bought shares in Trojan, the condom maker. He's taking a cooking class at the community college and teaching one of his cousins to skateboard.

Last year, after working at Big John's Burger for four years, he hired a private detective to locate his mom. The dick, Nathan Lantree, part-time cabbie, part-time private eye, said, "I tried. I just can't find her." Still, he charged Colin for expenses.

Colin has no future plans, only immediate ones: He's going to see Rowan Burke's photographs at the gallery. There's also an artist, Kate Mammet, he wants to see. He's getting a haircut. He's going to take a walk around the university. He's going to read "Do Not Go Gentle into That Good Night" by Dylan Thomas for the fourteenth time in two days—to learn it by heart—a practice he has. On his way into Belle Tara, he recites, "Though wise men at their end know dark is right/ Because their words had forked no lightning they/ Do not go gentle into that good night." He thinks about the children in Terezín and how they raged through their art. *Do not go gentle. Never.*

If Paddy John knew Colin Atwell, he'd describe him as "a bleeding heart." As was Abigail—all the better still. The world has too many soldiers and too few peacekeepers.

Colin Atwell is adept at playing the stock market. Investing in safe sex was a good idea. Within three years, he makes his first million.

At twenty-one, he married Brittany Smith. She wore her hair in ringlets. She wore low-cut blouses. Sometimes skirts with jingling bells, like a Dead Head, except she didn't listen to the Grateful Dead. She bubbled. She sucked on Ecstasy like hard candy. She told Colin, "I'm almost always happy or I'm out of my mind." Wearing brown tights, her legs were made of chocolate. When she wore yellow, she tasted like lemon or sunshine. She said, "I smell like the beach."

Colin's dad said, "When I said all women were crazy, I didn't mean *that* crazy."

Colin insisted, "I love her. She's a free spirit."

"A little too free, if you ask me."

They bought a house on the shore. She wanted her own studio. "If that's all right?" She wanted nine hours a day to herself. "If that's okay? For meditation and work." Twice he found her naked, laced with red seaweed, lying on the sand.

He said, "Get up. Come on." She bubbled like fluorescent froth. He said, "I'm worried about you."

She snapped, "Get off my back!"

Colin was lonely.

They had a grand house. He had an expensive car and a big boat and he wanted a partner for life. He wanted to know what happened to his mother. His millions of dollars failed to buy him either of those things. He still thought about Becca Burke. Holding her brooch in his palm, he noticed that the pin was slightly loose. He'd fix it. He wondered how Becca was doing.

It was pathetic: thinking about a girl from middle school. Depressed, he telephoned his father, asking him to come for an indefinite visit. Colin and Brittany had already toured Europe. They'd been to Mexico, and Colin knew there was no place in the world that could heal him. He couldn't keep babysitting Brittany alone. Sometimes he imagined kicking her in the nose.

Last week, she'd seen him with Becca's brooch and commented, "That's pretty. I really like it."

He said, "It belonged to this girl I knew a long time ago."

"It's beautiful. I bet it's antique."

"It is."

"I like it."

What did Brittany think? That he'd give it to her? Colin would never let Brittany touch, let alone wear, Becca Burke's brooch.

THE EMPIRE STATE BUILDING

One of my favorite things about Manhattan is the Empire State Building. When I was a kid, I saw that movie <u>An Affair to Remember</u> with my mom. She loved when Deborah Kerr was running for the building, and her character, Terry, said, "Oh, it's nobody's fault but my own! I was looking up . . . it was the nearest thing to heaven! You were there . . ." My mom cried.

She never got to see the Empire State Building, which, for our purposes, is hit an average of 25 times a year!

Once used as a lightning laboratory, it's not where you want to be during a thunderstorm.

On another personal note, I've been to the top. If you're ever in New York, and the line isn't too long, you should take in the view.

30

Stoned, 1989

Buckley sat on Mia's floor, taking bong hits with Mia and her friend Paulo. His back against the sofa, he felt like he was melting into it. "I don't like this," he said.

Paulo said, "You don't like what?"

"Feeling weird."

"But you are weird. We're all weird." Paulo was twenty-nine, Buckley's age. "If you want to feel something different, get up and drink a soda or have a beer or turn on the TV. If you want to stop feeling stoned, go to sleep."

"Clementine," Buckley said, "did a lot of drugs, but I don't think she smoked marijuana."

Mia said, "What kind of drugs?"

"She liked pills," Buckley said, remembering her legs, how they looked scrubbed clean the day she died. He glanced at Mia's legs. Her calves and knees were exposed between her plaid skirt and black boots.

Paulo said, "Buckley's checking you out."

Buckley averted his eyes.

Mia straightened her legs. "Stop it, Paulo. You're such a fucking pervert. Buckley and I are good friends."

Buckley got up. "Maybe I'll have a beer."

Mia said, "Then you better split."

"How come?" Buckley opened the refrigerator. It was empty

except for a twelve-pack of Black Label beer, two sticks of butter, and a plastic pitcher of tap water.

"Sheila's coming over when she gets off work. She wants to play Clementine with you."

Buckley felt sick to his stomach. "Clementine isn't a joke."

"I know that, and you know that, but Sheila is seriously psycho—like, she's been diagnosed with every kind of mental disorder currently known to the psychiatric community."

Buckley popped the beer open. "What should I do?"

Mia said, "I'll take care of it. Just go home."

Paulo said, "What are you going to do?"

"I have a plan."

Buckley took his beer and went across the hall to his apartment. He locked the door. He wanted to watch television, but afraid Sheila might hear, he sat reading *The Catcher in the Rye*, a gift from Mia.

He heard Sheila banging on Mia's door, asking "Where's Buckley?" The apartment walls were paper thin. He heard Mia say, "Come on in," and he heard Mia's door shut.

Inside Mia's apartment, the bong water had been dumped, the bong had been stashed under the sofa, and Paulo sat in Mia's kitchen bathtub, pretending to read *Newsweek*.

Sheila said, "Where's Buckley? When I called, I thought I heard his voice."

Mia said, "He hasn't been here. Not since last night."

"What are you guys doing?"

Paulo said, "We're getting ready to take a bath."

"We're going to take off for Central Park. Get some fresh air."

Paulo dropped the *Newsweek* on the kitchen floor. "Do you have a hat I can borrow? The sun is terrible for my complexion."

"I'll find something."

"Well, let's get Buckley."

"That's not a good idea," Mia said.

"Why not?"

"I hate to tell you this, Sheila, but last night Buckley and I had sex."

"What about Luke?"

Mia said, "Please don't tell him."

Sheila said, "You and Buckley?"

"Yeah. He's madly in love with me—like, obsessed with me. You show some guys a little kindness and they go overboard."

"You're kidding."

Mia shook her head that she was not.

"But what about Luke?"

"I don't know. I might break up with him. I just don't know."

"Goddamn it, Mia. You knew I liked Buckley."

"But I might like him," Mia countered, "and I always get what I want."

"You can be such a bitch."

"That's what they tell me."

Paulo, climbing out of the bathtub, said, "She really can be a major bitch. It's a fact."

"I want to talk to Buckley." Sheila was petite, with thin lips and blue eyes. She repeated, "Let's talk to Buckley."

Mia said, "It'll be awkward."

Mia kicked Buckley's door. Even though she could've knocked and he would've opened up, she never did. "It's me," she said.

Buckley assumed that she'd gotten rid of Sheila. He opened his door to see Mia, Sheila, and Paulo standing in the hallway. He was still stoned and lacking words. Fortunately, he didn't have to say anything. Mia pressed her chest against his, draping her white hand with black fingernails over his head, and kissed him, tongue and everything. Feeling her hip against his, Buckley tingled. It was a long kiss. Buckley was melting into black-clad Mia.

Mia said, "I told Sheila that you belong to me now."

Buckley had black lipstick on his face. He nodded.

Sheila said, "Fuck both of you," and ran down the hall.

Mia and Paulo laughed. Buckley smiled. He was grateful for the ruse. He was grateful for the kiss.

An excerpt from
THE HANDBOOK FOR LIGHTNING STRIKE SURVIVORS

With yearly cloud-to-ground lightning strikes, injuries, and fatalities on the rise, I have written to the National Weather Service asking them to do more to educate people about the risks of lightning.

I received a prompt and concerned letter back, indicating that they have plans to increase lightning education, thus preventing injuries and fatalities.

On a personal note, I am pleased to know that there are individuals and organizations like me who comprehend lightning's impact. Together, I know we can prevent injuries and death.

31

This Artist's Life, 1989

Apple Pie screwed up.

He said, "Christ, Becca, you knew I was fucking married." He stood in her loft.

She said, "The married part is why you're Apple Pie and not Professor Lord. Your wife's Betty Crocker. You drive an Alfa. I hate you!" He was Kevin Richfield all grown up, with artistic talent. If she could call it that—talent. "I fell in love with you!"

"We can still be together, but you have to calm down."

"How will we be together?"

"Like before."

She said, "I'll lay it out for you. You're going to help me."

He laughed.

"You're going to help me become a successful artist."

"Private lessons?"

"Patrons."

"This isn't the seventeenth century."

"I'll call your wife. I'm not stupid." She wasn't. She knew better than to make threats to tell the university. Like they'd do anything. They'd discredit her. She'd talk to Mrs. Apple Pie instead.

He said, "You wouldn't!"

He didn't know her.

"Let's work it out."

She said, "I'll tell you how it's going to work. You're going to bring wealthy art-loving buyers to see my paintings, and you're going to tell the truth or lie . . . I don't care which . . . but you're going to say that I am the most talented upcoming artist you've ever had the pleasure to teach." She said, "Go home now and make some phone calls."

Apple Pie delivered Roderick Dweizer—art lover, philanthropist—to the student gallery on Twenty-third Street.

Becca had six paintings hanging up, *Fish, Number One* through *Fish, Number Six.* None of them was exactly right, but she was too attached to each one to throw any of them away. There was something good in each.

Roderick Dweizer looked at *Fish, Number Six.* "What is it? Oils and what else?"

"Graphite," Becca said. "*Fish, Number Four's* my favorite."

"*Six* is tremendous. The light right here." He pointed to the upper right corner of the *Fish, Number Six* canvas.

Apple Pie checked his watch, pacing the floor. "Roderick, we'll be late for lunch."

"Nonsense. You're the one who brought me here." To Becca, Roderick said, "He thinks you're quite good, you know? He's never asked me to look at a student's work before." Apple Pie struggled to smile.

Roderick Dweizer said, "I'm quite taken with this one." *Fish, Number Six* still. "What do you think, Chris?"

"I don't know."

"You're never short on criticism."

"I think it's simple."

Dweizer said, "I like the simplicity."

"It doesn't say anything. It's immature."

Becca shook her head. He wasn't following her rules. She asked Mr. Dweizer, "Do you know Mrs. Lord?"

"Quite well. She's a wonderful woman."

Becca said, "She must be."

Looking at her painting, Roderick Dweizer said, "The fish is dying."

Apple Pie said, "It's death-obsessed, envisioned by a morose, pouting teenager."

Dweizer said, "I don't think so. Note the contrasts here. There's all this darkness and death, and over here, we're blinded with light. The light's almost barren in contrast to the complexity of color here."

Becca's work spoke for itself. No matter what Apple Pie said.

No stranger had ever complimented her work. She smiled and stepped back behind Roderick Dweizer, folding her arms at her waist. She did what an artist is supposed to do: step back and wait, answer questions, seem confident. She didn't care if this man bought *Fish, Number Six*. It was enough to know that he liked it. It was enough to know that he gained something from it. That he appreciated it. That he could enjoy it. Apple Pie had taught her well. She was nineteen. She knew that Apple Pie expected Dweizer to tear her paintings apart, and he hadn't.

"Why did you do this?" Dweizer asked Becca, pointing to the red spot of paint, so thick and potent, it rose off the canvas.

"Because I felt like it." Not what Apple Pie had taught her to say about her art.

"I like it." He paced the canvas. "I would like to buy this *Fish, Number Six* for my daughter if it's for sale. Do you have a price sheet?"

"Do you see the light?" Becca asked.

"The light is why I want to buy it. And the darkness."

"I'm giving it to you."

"You don't give art away."

Apple Pie said, "I would give it away."

Dweizer shot him a look of contempt.

Becca said to Dweizer, "It's yours."

"Let me write you a check."

"It's yours."

Apple Pie felt sick. *Why did you ask me to bring him here? You can stand on the street corner and give your paintings away.* "Becca," he said, "Roderick came to see your work. If he likes something, you don't have to give it to him."

"It's a gift from me to you."

"Thank you." Dweizer added, "We should all go to lunch to celebrate your fine student and my fine gift. I'm famished."

"I am too."

At lunch, she told Roderick Dweizer the story of the fish on the beach and how during that same vacation her father's mistress came to the restaurant where they happened to be. She told him that for now she was painting fish exclusively, but one day, when she felt ready, she'd paint something else.

"I have a friend who owns and manages a small gallery in Soho. I want you to go see her. She's always looking for young talent. I'll give her a call. Her name's Sue."

Apple Pie had three vodka tonics at lunch. How had Becca managed to charm Roderick Dweizer? Then she realized: easily. She had charmed him, and she was the first of Apple Pie's bevy of special students to get the better of him.

Becca walked home from Randy Lee's fish market on Bayard Street at five-thirty in the morning, carrying a dead fish wrapped in newspaper. Later that morning, her fingers smattered and sparkling with fish scales in the first light of day, she dotted *Fish, Number Fourteen* with red snapper scales and cerulean blue oil paint. Her apartment reeked of dead fish and turpentine. Rolling her jeans' pant legs up and slipping off her sandals, she dirtied her calves with oil paints and fish scales, but like most artists, if she noticed the filth, she didn't care. She took off the lemon yellow blouse she'd worn out to Blondie's Bar and Grill the night before and pulled on one of her painting T-shirts.

She didn't sleep anymore at night. She hardly slept at all. She'd read in *The Handbook for Lightning Strike Survivors* that insomnia was a typical side effect for lightning strike victims. How could there be anything typical about being struck by lightning? She soaked a rag with linseed oil and wiped at the canvas's edge. She thought about Chris, a no-last-namer (she didn't want to know his last name) she'd met at Blondie's Bar and Grill last night. She remembered he kept pushing down on the top of her head in his bathroom on Broome Street in Soho, and her knee dug into the edges of the small white tiles until it bled, but she kept going because she wasn't letting him off that easy. When he took his hands from her head, she grabbed the backs of his knees and he almost fell on top of her. He said, "I want to see you again," and she said, "I can't do that."

They had sat on his bed, and he brushed the underside of her forearm with his fingertips and she felt this warmth, this tingling heat, spread up her spine and through her gut. She pulled her arm away. She had to leave him wanting more. Always leave them wanting more. Always leave when you're in control.

Now she was out of control, her red hair bristly and curled in the rising humidity and sunlight. The back of her neck and her thighs sweating. Her fingers were Prussian blue and cerulean blue, smelly and sticky with fish and linseed oil. The balls and heels of her bare feet stomped the drops of paint splotching the polished oak floor as she moved from palette to canvas to palette to canvas to oil to rag. *Fish, Number Twenty-two. Fish, Number Eighteen.*

She dipped her brush in turpentine, which she kept in an old Maxwell House coffee can, and then into the cadmium red. She kept her palette on a cherry table she bought secondhand in the Bowery. The table was the perfect size because she could fit two Maxwell House coffee cans, one filled with turpentine, the other filled with linseed oil, her tubes of paint, her palette, and her graphite pencils, and there was still room for her sketchbook, which she sometimes needed when she was uncertain what to do next, what color to use—or some new idea.

That morning at five a.m., she'd walked from Chris's to Randy Lee's fish market in sandals and blue jeans, her mascara smudged black under her green eyes, thinking, *It isn't so bad not to sleep.* Thinking, *I'll try and finish number fourteen.* Thinking, *I need to buy another tube of titanium white. It's not so bad not to sleep.* The sun wasn't yet up, but the shopkeepers were busy with the rattle and clamor of opening their front gates and shutters and hanging their scales. The street cleaners droned past, churning water that spilled into the gutters. Becca yawned. She didn't understand Randy Lee and he didn't understand her. She didn't speak Chinese and he didn't speak English. It was always the same. She said, "I want *this* fish." She picked the fish for their colors, for their scales, for their eyes and their fins, not for their taste. Sometimes the fish were still barely alive and flopped at her sandaled feet. "Not that fish. No. No. This one." Becca didn't want a fish that was alive. She'd have to walk to the river to set it free.

"Tuna? Tuna?" he asked. "Tuna?" and held the fish that was clearly not a tuna in front of her before dropping the barely dead fish onto the scale.

Every fish at Randy Lee's, from snapper to grouper to dolphin, was a tuna if you didn't speak Chinese.

As she started painting that morning, she thought about her father and his photographs. She couldn't believe he was having such success. She wiped her hands on her jeans before wiping the sweat from her nose. "It's just a hobby," he'd said on the telephone last month.

"You should be really proud, Dad."

"It's just a hobby, Becca. I take pictures. That's all. Don't make it a big deal."

But it was a big deal. Becca envied her father's success. She thought, *I could be happy for him if he appreciated—even a little— what he has.* Here she was living this artist's life, unable to sleep, unable to concentrate, frustrated with her painting workshops, feeling overwhelmed, and her father, the millionaire tobacco chemist, took a few pictures and showed them to a few of the right people.

He doesn't need the money, she thought, dabbing the canvas with her blue finger. *He's no artist. He doesn't care.* She rattled her brush in the can of turpentine. *Yet he's had a show in Boston and three in North Carolina. Four exhibitions. I should probably try and finish* Fish, Number Fourteen *or maybe* Fish, Number Twenty. *It's your first solo show,* she thought. *It's important. Just keep working. May, June, July—the oils never dry. May, June, July—the oils never dry.* Roderick Dweizer's friend Sue of Sue's Gallery telephoned in May. They met briefly. Sue scheduled Becca's first solo show. It was unheard of. Becca was excited, but sick. What if she failed? *I should think less about things. People. My dad. He sold the Yeatesville picture of me for two hundred and fifty dollars and he wouldn't buy a fucking watermelon from that woman. My show is going to suck. I'll be washed up at twenty.*

Becca remembered the Yeatesville picture. Her head lit up by the sun, by the lightning—kind of how she was all lit up now. She mixed the Prussian and cerulean blues with the cadmium yellows, stroking the canvas with her sable brush—a beautiful oily green. Remembering patience. She couldn't rush it.

She remembered Jacob Lawrence telling the rapt audience at the Museum of Modern Art that he painted each of his series, all forty paintings, simultaneously, one color at a time, moving from canvas to canvas.

Becca worked in much the same way. Not because she worked with bright acrylics, not because she worked for uniformity like Lawrence, but because she couldn't wait for the oils to dry. She couldn't wait to wash the burnt umbers and Naples yellow onto the gesso. The cobalt blues and cadmium reds mixed with linseed oil onto the Mars black. She couldn't wait for the layers to dry. She couldn't wait to finish the ocean struck by lightning and the beach strewn with thousands of fish all waiting for some miracle. For some god to save them. The whole world, every canvas, lit up with blasts of titanium white and ringed hard with graphite, then smudged.

Becca's calloused thumbs and index fingers dotted the canvases with fish scales and fins. Two months ago, her friend Paulo, a guy she'd met through Jack, had said, "You're mad with the paint."

Becca pretended innocence. "Is that a good thing?"

"That is the best thing."

Today she moved from one canvas to the next, the sun rising higher in the sky, flooding the loft. A light breeze blew through the open windows. Her warehouse fan whirred. She sprayed the quickly rotting fish with water to keep the scales bright. The eyes had already begun to sink, cavernous, into the fish's head. She rattled her brush in the linseed oil can and then it came. The quiet. She was on the beach with the fish in her hands. The rattle of brush in coffee can, the whisper of brush on canvas. The summer blue sky. The sound of the ocean. The sun on her back.

In the Bronx, Mia chain-smoked Marlboro 100s and felt sick to her stomach. Paulo told Mia about this painter with a lot of money who paints little fishes with scales. Real scales. "She is mad with the paint. She paints lightning too. You should see it. You would like it. You would hate her."

"Why would I hate her?" Mia asked.

"You hate everyone who is pretty and talented. She is both."

"And she's rich?"

"We all hate the rich."

Becca got lost in *Fish, Number Fourteen*, painting until she collapsed on the hardwood floor, both hands smeared with fish scales and yellow ochre, her forearms and face smudged with graphite. Despite what Apple Pie thought, Becca was the real thing: an artist. She painted because she liked the buttery texture of the oils between her fingers. Because she liked the smell of turpentine, and the sound the brush made tapping the edge of the coffee can. Because she went somewhere else when she painted and she forgot who she was, sometimes for half an hour, sometimes for hours. Once, for a whole day. Becca painted because she needed to paint. She had to paint. Becca was an artist.

The loft smelled of rotten fish, linseed oil, and turpentine, and as Becca slept into the evening, she felt Chris-with-no-last-name, who could be anybody, kiss her neck. At first she tried to crawl away but then sank into the nuzzling, her head resting on his head. She awoke at six-thirty that evening. Lucy and Jack were knocking on her door, Lucy holding a bottle of champagne. Jack said, "What the fuck, Bec?"

"What the fuck to you."

"Lucy got a part in the new Mercer film."

"No shit." Becca was sleepy and dirty and turned her back on her neighbors standing in the doorway—waiting for their invitation to join her. She said, "I need to clean up. Grab some glasses." While she showered, Jack and Lucy walked around the big room, looking at the wet canvases perched on easels and second-hand tables. There was paint splattered on the glossy hardwood floors, and when Becca came back into the main room, her white robe tied about her waist, her hair black cherry in the fading light, Jack said, "They're going to freak when they see the floors."

"I know it sounds fucked up, but my dad will pay for it. That's what he does. He pays for things. He pays for love and he pays for art and he pays when his only daughter destroys things. It's only right I give him something to pay for." She laughed and took a glass of champagne from Lucy. "That's so cool about the movie. What kind of role is it?"

"It's nothing big. I'm in this department store. Okay, but it's still pretty cool. Really cool. I mean it's a speaking part and everything. I'm in this department store, and the main character . . . Okay, get this. Get this! Played by Johnny Depp! He comes in and says, 'Excuse me, miss,' or something, and then, 'Where's the women's department?' and I say, 'Upstairs,' and I point and smile and maybe they're going to let me spray him with some men's cologne. I don't know yet, but it's a speaking role and I got it! I got it!"

Becca's phone rang. Her father was calling from San Francisco. He said, "I miss you," and she thought he sounded strange. There was something in his voice that she had never heard before, and it sounded like insecurity. She said, "I miss you too, Dad. Is everything okay?"

Look at photographs of lightning. The images are extraordinary. They're deadly beautiful. I've seen pictures of cloud-to-ground lightning, spreading and spiraling over soybean and cotton fields. I've seen pictures of one lightning bolt fork into eight directions—like spider's legs. I think about Zeus and the gods when I see these pictures. I think about this force of nature as something I will always be at odds with, and I will never win. I know that. Neither will you.

32

QR66, 1989

Rowan sat on a mahogany bench in the antechamber of a San Francisco courtroom.

Atkins and Thames's newest vice president, a twenty-something man named Billy Abernathy, patted his thigh. "We've been over this. Tell the truth." Billy Abernathy had been with Rowan for the past three days. Their hotel rooms at the Gypsy Spa connected. For three days, over breakfast, lunch, golf, and in-room massages, Billy advised Rowan to listen to the attorneys, and above all else, tell the truth. "Susan Copper's lawyers have the documents, so tell the truth."

Waiting, his palms moist with perspiration, Rowan said, "I don't see why *I* have to testify."

"Look, Rowe. This is all about money. Nobody put a gun to that woman's head and said she had to smoke two packs a day. Put on a good face in there. Nice suit, by the way."

Rowan looked at the sleeve of the pinstriped suit that one of the lawyers' flunkies had picked out for him. "Thanks." It was a nice suit. He couldn't remember the last time he'd worn a suit. Maybe that cocktail party last year. No, he'd worn jeans and a sports jacket. Until this trial, he'd almost forgotten that he was associated with Atkins and Thames, except for those checks. The large door swung open. The bailiff, a short Hispanic woman with a scowl, said, "They're ready for you now."

"Tell the truth," Billy Abernathy said. "You're fine."

Rowan was sworn in. Sitting in the witness box, he remembered what Billy Abernathy and the attorneys assured him: This is only a pre-trial. Tell the truth. There's nothing to worry about. We have one hundred and fifty lobbyists in forty-seven states.

Still, thought Rowan, if this "pre-trial" were nothing to worry about, why had he been escorted around San Francisco for three days by Billy Abernathy and an entourage of attorneys?

The plaintiff's lead attorney, Betty Solznick, a young red-headed woman in a crisp peach suit, approached the witness box. She put her hands on the box and cleared her throat. She looked to the judge, then to the plaintiff, Susan Copper, wheezing away, her face browned and carved with wrinkles. Then she looked at Rowan, her hands still on the witness box. "A few questions for you, Mr. Burke. Please state your occupation."

"Chemist."

"Your employer?"

"Atkins and Thames."

"And what do you do at Atkins and Thames?"

"I'm a chemist."

"Specifically, what do you do at Atkins and Thames?"

"I develop cigarette additives."

"Did you *develop* QR66?"

"Yes."

"And what's in QR66 exactly?"

"Hydrochloroloxinate."

"What does hydrochloroloxinate do?"

"It's an additive."

"Yes, we understand. What does your additive do exactly?"

"It enhances the flavor of a cigarette."

"Is that all that it does, because we've already heard testimony from Dr. Daniel Witzel that hydrochloroloxinate, QR66, the additive *you developed,* triples the addictive effects of nicotine in the bloodstream. Is that a fair statement?"

"I don't know about triples."

"What about quadruples?"

"I don't think that's been proven." Why hadn't his attorney spoken up? Wasn't Betty Solznick out of order? Rowan pushed his graying hair back. One strand after another drooped its way onto his forehead. The woman at the salon had used too much gel. His head felt greasy. He smoothed his widow's peak.

"Are you a shareholder?"

"Yes."

"How much did you receive last quarter in dividend checks, Mr. Burke?"

"Objection."

Finally, Rowan thought.

One of the Atkins and Thames attorneys, a man Rowan's age, but with a nasally voice that made him sound like he was whining, rose from his chair. "The witness's dividend check is irrelevant."

"Sustained," said the judge, who appeared to Rowan to be at least eighty years old.

"Is QR66 addictive?"

"Yes."

"Did your employers, specifically the executive officers at Atkins and Thames, know that QR66 was an addictive additive?"

"Objection, your honor. That's hearsay. The witness has no way of knowing if the executives at Atkins and Thames were aware of the addictive nature of QR66."

"I'll rephrase the question. Were you ever present when your employers, specifically Roger Billingsworth, Franklin Thames, and Max Childress, were discussing the . . . I guess we should say addictive qualities of QR66, hydrochloroloxinate?"

"Yes."

Betty Solznick smiled.

Rowan testified for more than an hour. He would not do this again. *Never again,* he thought. The gate to the witness box slammed shut as Rowan stepped down and started for the double doors.

The bailiff grabbed his elbow. "Wrong way," she said, pointing to a side exit where another bailiff held the door open for him.

The subpoenas poured in. There were more trials, not just pre-trials, but grand-jury trials and state trials and then Rowan had to testify before the House Commerce Committee. He was always asked the same questions, and he always answered truthfully. The legal team of Atkins and Thames, thirty-six strong, ever vigilant, telling Rowan to be honest. Tell the truth. They wouldn't be asking about QR66 if they didn't already have the proof. Internal documents had been smuggled out of the company. Rowan thought, *That fink—whoever took those documents should be shot. Look what they've done to me.*

From his hotel room in San Francisco, Rowan phoned Becca in New York. It was six West Coast time. Nine o'clock in New York, but his daughter sounded drunk. Music blared. "How's the apartment?"

"Good," she said. "How's Patty?"

"She's good." He clicked the TV off and sat up in bed. "I'm just calling to say I miss you."

"I miss you too, Dad. Is everything okay?"

No, thought Rowan. *Nothing's okay.* "Are you having a party?"

"Sort of. My neighbors, Lucy and Jack—I told you about them. Lucy just got a bit part in this movie they're filming in Murray Hill."

"Tell her congratulations." He'd never heard of Lucy or Jack.

"Will do." Becca relayed, "My dad says congratulations."

"We'll see you at Christmas," he said.

"Will do."

Eight months later, walking down Sixth Avenue on her way to the train, Becca stared at her father's picture on the April 15, 1990, front page of the *New York Times*. The headline read, "Atkins and Thames Contends Chemist Lied." She turned to page A12. "Franklin Thames, CEO of Atkins and Thames, testified before the House Commerce Committee, 'Rowan Burke did not make us aware of QR66's adverse effects. There is no documentation that myself or the Board of Trustees was ever informed of the addictive enhancement QR66 has on nicotine. In fact, documents show that QR66 was an additive meant to improve the cigarette's flavor. Nothing more. Rowan Burke is a liar.' "

Becca read and reread, "Rowan Burke is a liar." She tore page A12 into shreds and walked on, the scraps of newspaper trailing behind her.

Excerpt from
THE HANDBOOK FOR LIGHTNING STRIKE SURVIVORS

No one deserves to die.

33

Sue's Gallery, 1989

Early on, Sue said, "I take fifty percent, but we'll help with the installation." Having first spoken with Sue in May, Becca already had her first gallery show. It wouldn't have been so quick, but to use Sue's words, "The artist we scheduled flaked and burned his canvases. I don't know why every artist thinks he has to be fucking nuts to make art." She paused. "I don't mean you. It's been a long week." Becca had a long September, painting every night until well past midnight. And it just figured that the second Friday in October had to be Friday the thirteenth. She didn't believe in bad omens or jinxed numbers, but just the same, her friend Lucy advised, "Try to postpone. It's bad luck. This dude burns his paintings and you get his show, and the show's on Friday the thirteenth!"

"I can't postpone." Becca couldn't. This was a once-in-a-lifetime opportunity.

On the phone, Sue told Becca to call Mark Kelly. "He prints the price list and the programs."

Two days before her opening, Becca, Paulo, Jack, and Lucy met Sue at the back door to her gallery. The foursome unloaded Becca's canvases from Paulo's pickup. Becca was sweating. Sick with anticipation, not so much about the work itself but about the opening, about possibly having to talk about her paintings, she could barely speak. Jack and Lucy, who'd seen Becca's paintings in the making, had said things like, "I think it's good. I like

that color" or "That one's neat." Their opinions and their obser-
vations were in some way insulting. They didn't understand that
her soul was painted into each canvas. They couldn't understand.
Becca wondered if anyone could.

Becca pulled an old bedsheet off *Fish, Number Twelve* in the
high-ceilinged gallery while Sue watched. Becca said to Sue, "We
shouldn't take long." Becca wore a pair of cutoff Levis and a red
T-shirt embossed with the logo BUILT FORD TOUGH. Down on her
knees in front of *Fish, Number Twelve*, she smiled at Sue. "I really
appreciate this opportunity."

Sue handed Becca a copy of the *Lightning Fish* program and
price list. Half of Becca's paintings were reproduced on the thick
paper in one- and two-inch squares, the titles underneath. Sue
said, "Mark does a nice job."

"He does."

"I'll be upstairs if you need me." Sue was brunette, older, but
well coiffed and made up in bright pink blush and blue eye
shadow.

Paulo and Jack were still carrying Becca's canvases into the
gallery.

As Sue's heels tapped the oak steps, Lucy said, "You look like
you're going to hurl."

"Do I have to come to this thing?"

"You probably should."

Sue's intern, Johnny Bosworth—who was a few years older than
Becca—was supposed to help with the installation, but Becca said
no. She wished that she could hang each of the paintings herself,
but there wasn't time. For months, there hadn't been time for anything but painting.

Panicked about the impending opening, Becca had telephoned her mother the night before. She'd said, "What if nothing
sells? What if no one comes? What if they don't like it or they
don't get it?"

"How old are you?" her mother asked.

"Twenty."

"You have your own show. You're twenty. That says something. That says a lot." Becca knew that if she hadn't threatened to tell Apple Pie's wife about their affair, she wouldn't have met Roderick Dweizer, and if she hadn't met Roderick Dweizer, she wouldn't have a gallery opening. She wondered if she deserved her own show.

Becca hung ten of her fourteen canvases. She said, "There's a smudge here," staring at the wall. "Do you think she painted in here?"

"Of course she painted," Lucy said.

"There's a gray spot here. See it."

"That's a shadow, Becca. They'll fix the lighting."

"There's a glare on *Fish, Number Twenty-two*."

"They'll fix the lighting before Friday. Calm. Remember calm? Take deep breaths."

Lucy was a blond waif with doll-baby blue eyes and thick eyelashes. Jack, her effeminate steady boyfriend, was also blond and blue-eyed with thick eyelashes. As a couple, they were often mistaken for brother and sister. They were Becca's closest friends. Lucy the wannabe actress and Jack the waiter. Jack was content as a waiter. Having grown up in Newark, New Jersey, his only aspiration was to leave Newark and live in Manhattan. He was twenty-five and he had achieved his lifelong dream. Lucy, on the other hand, was, as Paulo would say, "mad with the acting." She had complex dreams and aspirations that included living in Hollywood and being interviewed on *Entertainment Tonight*. She was funny and bubbly and always smiling. Becca could never tell when Lucy was acting or being her real self, or if Lucy *had* a real self. It seemed to Becca that Lucy's onstage persona was forever and permanently mixed in with her real self. Lucy and Jack were like all the friends Becca ever had—other than Carrie Drinkwater. They were acquaintances. Becca knew deep down that she would never really know these two, but they were her closest friends, and as such, they would escort Becca to her first opening at Sue's Gallery on Friday.

As she installed the last painting, she thought about Carrie. She wanted to telephone Carrie in Chapel Hill, but Carrie had a daughter (she knew this from her crazy poetry-writing mother), and people who have kids, people with husbands and jobs and mortgages, don't much want to hear about other people's paintings.

With each of her paintings mounted on the walls and the sun setting, casting shadows on the glossy gallery floors, Becca stared uncomfortably at what she had spent the last year creating. She cried. She didn't mean to cry. Lucy said, "Let's get a drink."

Paulo, a thirty-year-old Columbia graduate, who at one time had fancied himself an artist (but gave it up, he explained, "because it was too much work for too little money"), offered to treat them to martinis at the Gypsy on Fifty-ninth. Paulo, clearly smitten with Jack, worked at Macy's in the men's department. That's where he'd met Jack and thus met Lucy and thus Becca.

Sipping her martini at the Gypsy and making an ugly face (she loathed vermouth), Becca was hopeful. She was the antithesis of her dejected father, who sipped an airplane cup of chardonnay on his way to a deposition in St. Louis, Missouri.

The night of her first opening, Becca rubbed her hands down the front of her vintage cherry-printed dress. A tear escaped her left eye. *Shhh. Don't cry. Not here.* With Indian summer making an appearance, the doors to the gallery were propped open.

Buckley blew his nose on the 6-train and shifted in the orange plastic seat. He leaned forward and held on to the silver pole for support as the train jerked on the tracks. Mia said, "This'll be fun. You know Paulo. He'll be there."

The sky outside grew black and the wind picked up, whirling

trash on the sidewalk. Becca paced inside the gallery while Paulo ate grapes from the hors d'oeuvres table. He said, "You got those nails clean."

"Don't think it was easy. Sometimes I think my hands will be permanently stained."

He popped a grape in his mouth.

She smacked at his hand. "Don't do that. It's not seven yet."

Sue, her arms folded at her waist, whispered to her intern, Johnny Bosworth, "It figures it'd rain." Johnny Bosworth, who fancied himself a much better artist than Becca, grimaced at *Fish, Number Fourteen*. He said, "So there's a lightning storm that kills all the fish in the sea? How original."

Sue said, "Be nice, Johnny." She pointed to the front of the gallery. "Close the doors. It's moist."

"She hasn't even graduated," Johnny griped.

"Get the doors."

Becca watched Johnny pull the doors shut. Nervous, she wondered if there was still a chance she might slip out the back. Thunder cracked and she took a deep breath.

Roderick Dweizer was the first to arrive, and Lucy, knowing to what extent the old man had helped Becca, met him at the front door. She said, "Did Becca tell you I'm an actress?" The rain had already begun, and he shook out his umbrella, the water sprinkling Lucy's brown skirt. "So sorry," he said.

"Don't apologize." Lucy's lips shone pink in the gallery light.

Roderick Dweizer, Lucy jabbering at his side, made a beeline for his favorite artist, Rebecca Burke. "Don't worry," he said, patting Becca's arm. "It's going to be a great success. That worry of yours is in the paint."

"I guess so."

"Enjoy tonight." Roderick fixed a plate of brie and crackers and said to Becca, with Lucy still hanging on, "I'll tell you a secret, Becca Burke." He leaned close, a smidgen of cheese on his lower lip. "Sue knows nothing about art. If it weren't for her wealthy husband and my taste, she would not be in business. She is not as smart as she thinks." He tapped his temple with his pointer finger. "We will surprise her tonight when everything sells."

Becca blushed. Roderick Dweizer had no motive to help her. She had done nothing for him but given him one painting because he appreciated it.

"You are magnificent." He kissed her cheek.

The gallery filled with Sue's regular Friday-night crowd, including Apple Pie and his preppy wife.

Fanning herself with the program, Becca hung by the buffet table. She didn't want to mingle. She didn't want to see Apple Pie or his ridiculous wife. More and more people filled the space despite the pouring rain.

Mrs. Apple Pie approached Becca, her husband following close behind. She said, "Wonderful show."

Apple Pie nodded his agreement.

"Thanks."

"I particularly like *Fish, Number Twenty*, I think it is. The one with the little girl." She turned to her Apple Pie husband. "Didn't you like that one, honey?"

"It's fine."

Becca knew that "it's fine" was all she'd ever get from Apple Pie.

Apple Pie said, "I think I'll get another glass of wine. Anybody need anything?"

"I'm fine," Becca said, thinking, *We're all fine. The paintings are fine. Your Betty Crocker wife's fine. I'm tee-totally fine. You're a fine jackass.*

Mrs. Apple Pie, who of course knew nothing of Becca's affair with Apple Pie, said to her husband, "I'll join you." With her hands in fists like a cheerleader's, she said to Becca, "Just wonderful. Really wonderful."

As Mr. and Mrs. Apple Pie walked away, Becca heard Mrs. Apple Pie say, "This is one of the best shows I've seen. Really compelling."

"Jesus Christ," Becca said, grabbing on to the edge of the buffet table. It had been only seven months since Apple Pie. Remembering the pills and the late-night phone calls, how pathetic she'd been, unnerved her. What had she been thinking?

"Mingle, mingle," Sue said, taking Becca's hand in hers. "We've got quite the crowd. Mingle, mingle." Sue patted the back of Becca's hand. "Good show. Really good show. Smile."

Mia, wearing a black skirt and her standard Dr. Marten boots, and Buckley, in a pair of khakis and a sweat-stained oxford, ran down Broome Street toward Sue's Gallery. Thunder boomed in the distance. Neither Mia nor Buckley had foreseen rain when they left the Bronx, so by the time they reached the front door of Sue's, they were dripping wet. Buckley thought it was perfect. *An art show about lightning in a thunderstorm.* Mia and Buckley entered laughing and were promptly handed the *Lightning Fish* program. Before he saw the one- and two-inch reproductions of Becca's paintings in the program, let alone the paintings lining the gallery walls, he saw Rebecca Burke's name printed in Courier font on the program's cover.

She was the *only* person who had ordered his book out of a magazine, and she was the *only* purchaser of his book to write him a letter, and here she was, Rebecca Burke, lightning strike survivor. *I don't believe it.*

Buckley, his loafers squishy with rain, stumbled. Reaching for the gallery wall to steady his feet, he crumpled the program in his fist. He felt dizzy, and Johnny Bosworth, Sue's flunky, said, "Watch it. Watch it." He asked Mia, "Is your friend all right?"

"Are you okay, Buckley?" Mia reached for Buckley's hands to ground him. "Are you okay?"

He dropped the program. "I should go."

"Why? It's 'Lightning Fish.'"

"I don't know." Buckley bent down for the program. "Is she here?"

"Who?"

"The painter. Is she here?"

"Of course she's here," Johnny Bosworth said. "You know her work?" After all, it was his job as studio and gallery assistant to sell Becca's work. The gallery took fifty percent. Johnny would one day show his own work at Sue's. It was a matter of time.

"I'm not a fan. I'm wet. My head hurts." Buckley glanced up and saw *Fish, Number Fourteen*. He saw the lightning striking the ocean, the red zigzag across the sky, the white translucent furious line touching and illuminating the black water. The yellow streaks twirling north and south. The dead fish on the beach. He approached the painting. Mia followed. She shrugged as they left Johnny Bosworth to clean up the puddles of rain they had deposited at the gallery entrance. Johnny knelt down with a roll of paper towels.

"We should find Paulo," Mia said. Buckley was speechless. He remembered his mother, the stagnant water, reaching for her arms.

He said, "I want to buy it."

Mia said, "Good luck. Have you seen the price list?" She held the program open. "It's three thousand dollars. I don't think she wants anyone to actually buy anything at these prices. Jesus God. You'd never know this was her first show. I'm going to get some wine. See if I can't find Paulo."

The crowd seemed to twirl in front of Becca like ballroom dancers—one partner spinning another, the group as a whole circling round and round, dizzying her. She had a third glass of wine and felt her face flush. She felt safer. She asked Lucy, "What time is it?"

"Quarter to eight."

"This isn't so bad." *I don't have to do anything. I stand here, and Sue brings people over, and they say things to me like what Jack and Lucy have said for the past year: "I really like it," "It's dark," "It's bright," "The medium's impressive."*

My soul is in the paint. She sipped her chardonnay. *They don't know. My soul is in the canvas.*

"Maybe you should lay off." Lucy pointed to Becca's glass.

"I'm fine, really." As she took another sip from her glass, Becca saw the stout fellow standing in front of *Fish, Number Fourteen,* cocking his head right and then left, walking forward and then backward, reaching his hand out and actually touching the titanium white wash of lightning on the canvas. *He's not supposed to do that,* she thought. *He's not supposed to touch my painting.* From her position in the gallery, she could see that he was sopping wet, with a wavy head of dark brown hair. *Rumpled,* she'd say, between the hair and the clothes. *Rumpled.* She left Lucy standing by the buffet table.

As she made her way toward the rumpled man, one person after another in their fall hues of sap green, yellow ochre, and burnt umber stopped her. The star of the show, the centerpoint, she played along, responding, "Oh, thank you. Thank you. I'm so glad you like it."

She tapped the rumpled man's shoulder. She tapped his shoulder again. "Excuse me!"

He turned and faced her.

"I'm the artist." What did she expect from him? Praise? "I'm the artist"? *I sound loony.* She immediately reconsidered. "I'm Rebecca Burke."

"I know who you are now."

"Excuse me?" *Very creepy.* "Don't *touch* my painting."

"You wrote to me."

"I don't think so." Becca looked around for Paulo or Jack or Lucy or Sue. She suddenly imagined the rumpled man a homeless person, a derelict.

"I'm Buckley R. Pitank. I wrote *The Handbook for Lightning Strike Survivors.*"

Becca dropped her glass of wine. It shattered.

"Oh my god. I'm so sorry," Buckley said. He bent and began

picking the large shards of glass from the floor, slicing his thumb on the stem. "I'm sorry. Did I startle you? I shouldn't have touched the canvas. It's hard not to touch it."

Becca saw the red blood on his hand, a shiny new blood, like rose madder, her favorite red paint.

Johnny Bosworth and Sue approached. Sue said, "It's all right. Everything's fine. The show's a big success."

To Buckley, she said, "How are you? Looks like you've got a nasty little cut. Come with me. Come on." She pulled Buckley's hands away from the broken glass. "Johnny, please take care of that." To Becca, she said, "I'll have someone get you another glass of wine."

Becca knew from Buckley's book that his mother was struck by lightning when he was just fourteen. She had titled the painting *Fish, Number Fourteen*. Was it subconscious? She lingered in front of the painting while Johnny Bosworth swept glass around her feet. She said, "Sure. I'll have another glass of wine." It was a delayed reaction. Someone was already handing her a glass.

Buckley R. Pitank's Handbook. *I read it on the train ride to New York. He's like my brother. Can I have a brother? Am I allowed that? Can I adopt family members?*

If she had had the opportunity to ask Buckley that very question, he would've been delighted. He would've said, *Yes, absolutely, but don't adopt me. I hurt people.*

Hugging her from behind, Paulo said, "What's going on, fair artist?"

"I met Buckley R. Pitank."

"Mia's weird neighbor friend. Oh, good."

"I read his book."

"I didn't know he wrote a book. That's impressive."

"It's a handbook for lightning strike survivors."

"How very strange."

"I was struck by lightning."

Paulo looked around the gallery. "That explains it."

"I'm serious."

Becca looked for Buckley, but the twirling crowd was like a maze. She said, "He sliced his finger, and Sue took him for a Band-Aid." Becca took Paulo to *Fish, Number Twenty-one*, a painting of two severed fish heads. "Buckley Pitank's blood was the color of rose madder." She pointed to the blood-streaked fish.

"That's a little strange, Becca."

"I know." Becca scanned the crowd for Buckley. She wanted to talk to him. She asked Johnny, "Have you seen him?"

"Sue's getting him a Band-Aid. He came with punk rock goth girl."

Paulo interrupted. "Mia. She went to Columbia."

The night vibrated with electricity. Becca felt the energy and light pulsating, moving from one end of the room to the other, from one person's hand to another, and her canvases were the perimeter. With the rain falling outside and the scent of it filling the gallery like a clean perfume, Becca was walking around inside one of her paintings. *Buckley R. Pitank and* The Handbook for Lightning Strike Survivors, she mused. *Life is strange.*

Buckley's thumb was wound tight with Band-Aids, one on top of another and crisscrossed. Mia bumped her hip into his. She sipped a glass of wine and said, "It's just a little cut. He's okay. Right, Buckley?" Mia bumped him again and again, like she was magnetically attracted and repelled by Buckley's hip. "It's great to meet you," Mia said to Becca. "I think this shit's amazing."

That's more like it, thought Becca. *My shit's amazing.*

Paulo rolled his eyes.

"You know what I mean?" Mia said. "It's really good. God, Paulo, I'm a fucking painter. It's shit. That's what it is. Becca knows what I'm talking about. It's in your head. You don't have to be all 'school' about it."

Paulo said, "Okay, Mia. I'm going to find Jack."

"I'll join you," Mia said. "That kid Jack ought to be afraid of you."

Becca said to Mia, "Thanks for coming."

Mia leaned in close. "It's so good. Really. It's the shit. You're amazing."

Buckley stood across from Becca with a finger in the top groove of his ear, running it back and forth. He stared at the gallery floor. "I'm sorry you got struck by lightning."

Sue waved from across the gallery, calling Becca over. Becca held up a finger to indicate *Just a minute* (as her father used to do), and then she said to Buckley, "I'm sorry your mother died."

"I like your paintings." He kept running his finger in the top groove of his ear. "I can't believe we're meeting, and you painted these pictures."

"Thank you for *The Handbook*. I felt like a freak until I read it."

"You're not a freak."

"No one believes you," she said, "or they act like it didn't happen."

"You're a survivor."

"Thank you for writing me back." She was flustered and jumbled. Sue waved again. "Look, I'll be right back. Don't go, okay?" But Becca wasn't right back because she got shuffled from one interested person to the next, and when she looked for Buckley R. Pitank and his bandaged thumb, he was gone.

Buckley rode the train home, thinking it was a bit of good luck meeting Becca Burke, meeting someone who had read his book, meeting her face-to-face. He was hopeful—which he hadn't been in a very long time—that he would meet her again.

Excerpt from
THE HANDBOOK FOR LIGHTNING STRIKE SURVIVORS

NASA scientists monitor lightning worldwide, and although lightning rarely strikes the ocean, it happens. The number of fish and marine animals that die is dependent on the voltage of the strike and the number of animals near the water's surface.

Lightning flashing cloud to cloud can appear orange or pink over a black ocean.

34

The Damicis and the Jesus and Mary Chain, 1989

It was a dreary November.

Carmine saw the thin man through the plate glass and unlocked the door. "How's it going?" he asked. "You want a drink or something?"

The thin man didn't say anything. He pulled a cassette tape from his back pants pocket and slid it into the tape deck on the bar.

The music started and Carmine said, "What the fuck's this shit?" When the thin man didn't answer, Carmine said, "She wanted it, man. I'm telling you. It was mutual."

The thin man turned the volume up.

In the kitchen, Buckley heard the menus slip one after another like playing cards from the tabletop. He heard Carmine mumbling and the *tap-tap* of menus being restacked. "Hurry the fuck up!" It was after midnight. "I ain't got time for this shit."

Buckley dropped the Tupperware bowl of mozzarella trying to seal it shut, and the white brine sloshed across the tiles. He was down on his knees, his fingers milky with cheese, when Carmine called, "Did you mop out here? It doesn't look like it." Mr. Damici, Carmine's father, still didn't trust Buckley to lock up.

Buckley thought, *Of course I mopped the floor.* Carmine was a real jerk. Buckley tossed the mozzarella balls into the trash and wiped the floor with a rag. He wasn't going to mop the kitchen floor again. He checked to make sure the grill was off, and then he heard the music. It was a Jesus and Mary Chain song, "Darklands." He knew the song—had heard it in Mia's apartment only a week earlier. It was a strange song, Buckley had thought. It was stranger now.

He liked Mia a lot, despite her weird music, like the Jesus and Mary Chain. Despite her punk rock clothes and eccentric friends, like Paulo and Sheila. Mia had taken him to see Lightning Fish. If it weren't for Mia, he wouldn't have met Becca Burke or seen that painting with the fish on the beach and the lightning. He was going to get in touch with Becca Burke. Buckley thought, *I'm glad I met Mia. I'm glad she harassed me. I'm* not *glad about Sheila.* Sheila wrote him poetry that didn't rhyme. She said he was her "dark lord." He needed to stay clear of her.

Buckley still had to wrap and label the other cheeses, the left-over spinach, and the asparagus. He shouted, "I need ten more minutes," but Carmine didn't answer. Buckley liked the song "Darklands," but he couldn't imagine why Carmine was listening to it. It was no secret that Carmine liked classic rock like Led Zeppelin and Jethro Tull. Buckley had worked for the Damicis long enough to know the tastes of everyone in the family. "There's no album better than *Houses of the Holy*," Carmine had told Buckley a month ago when Buckley was closing up.

"Do you like the Pixies?" Buckley had asked. Mia and her friends liked them. So did Buckley.

"Is that faggot music?"

Buckley had resumed sweeping.

Tonight, Carmine was listening to the Jesus and Mary Chain and Buckley was rushing so Carmine wouldn't knock him in the back of the head with an open palm. Carmine had picked up his father's habits of endearment. Buckley put the spinach away, checked the stove one more time, and flipped the light switch. Then he heard the pop. Not a loud pop, but a muffled pop like one firework exploding far away. With his apron still in his hand, he ran into the dining room. There was a tall thin man, scruffy-faced, bedraggled, no more than twenty-five, thirty at most, pointing a handgun at the air where Carmine had presumably stood, and Carmine was dead and bloody on the floor with a hole in his new Louis Vuitton shirt, a hole just above where his heart would be. Buckley thought, *Treat the apparently dead first.* The music still played. The gunman, who wore leather driving gloves, turned to Buckley.

Buckley thought, *I am going to die. I am going to die*, and part of him thought, *Finally. Finally.* It had come to this: He would die in a restaurant on the Upper West Side of Manhattan at the age of thirty. He was ready.

The gunman said, "He raped my sister," and unscrewing the silencer from the gun, set the pistol and the silencer on the bar beside the gold-tasseled menus. "Carmine raped my little sister."

Buckley said, "The night deposit bag is beside the register."

"I don't want money."

Buckley was a witness to a murder. He was going to die.

"My sister's name is Margaret."

Strange as it might sound, Buckley said, "That's a pretty name."

"She's a pretty girl." The killer with the sister named Margaret picked his gun and silencer up, and Buckley closed his eyes.

"I got no beef with you," the shooter said.

Buckley opened his eyes.

The shooter secured the gun in the waist of his jeans, exposing his thin torso. With his trigger-happy hand, he stopped the cassette deck and slid the Jesus and Mary Chain tape into the back pocket of his jeans—from whence it had come. He shrugged as he picked up the night deposit bag: *That's not why I'm here, but sure, I'll take it.*

The shooter left the way he'd come in—through the front door.

• • •

Frank Damici shouted, "Why Carmine and not you?! You're fucking worthless! A waste of life. A waste of breath, you fuck!" He slugged a shot of something dark and slammed the glass on the bar, and one of the detectives, an older man, said, "Frank, it's not his fault."

Another detective said, "This is a goddamn crime scene, Mark! Take it outside. Now!"

The restaurant was framed with yellow police tape, much in the same way that Carmine Damici's body had been framed with white chalk on the floor of the restaurant, and Buckley was taken to the Twenty-fourth Precinct, where he was questioned by Detectives Jones and Smith (*really*, Jones and Smith). The two men whispered five feet from where Buckley sat at a table alone. Jones folded his arms. He said, "The guy's a little slow."

Smith said, "What is it they call it? Functionally retarded?"

"My wife teaches those kids. It's *educated* mental retardates."

"He's slow."

Jones patted Buckley's back and then both detectives sat down, asking Buckley again if he wanted some coffee. No, he didn't drink coffee, but he wouldn't mind a candy bar. "Something with nougat."

Smith said, "We can do that." He got Buckley a Zero bar from the vending machine.

Jones and Smith asked the same questions over and over, including "Do you like your job?" "Is the candy bar all right?" "Do you like your boss, Frank Damici?" "How long have you worked for Frank?" "Where you from?" "What exactly did you see?" "What'd you hear?" "Tell us again what you were doing when you heard the shot." "Take us through step by step." "Can we get you a glass of water?" "So, you heard music and then a shot?" "What's the Jesus and Mary Chain?"

Buckley's answers to the police included the following: "I've worked for Frank and his family for eight years. Since 1981. Carmine and I were friends." "I heard this music, this song by the

Jesus and Mary Chain, which was strange because Carmine likes classic rock, and then I heard the shot and when I ran into the restaurant, he was there on the floor, shot in the chest. When I opened the front door, I saw this person in a black overcoat running away. I was going to chase after him, but I knew I needed to call an ambulance." "The candy bar was good." "I didn't know what to do. Did I do the right thing? Can I have a glass of water?"

"How do you know our shooter is a him?"

"I think it's a him, but I don't know. The shooter was tall."

"How tall? What color was his hair?"

"Not like a giant or anything. It was dark. I don't know the hair color."

"So the shooter played the music? Is that some kind of punk rock stuff?"

"I don't know."

Buckley heard Jones whispering to Smith, "Carmine's a known heroin user and small-time distributor."

"Frank's boy?" Smith shook his head. "Fucking unbelievable. You give your kids everything, you know."

Jones said, "The shooter took the night's deposit."

"Why would a drug dealer play a tape and walk through the front door? It doesn't make sense."

"It doesn't."

Carmine was not a junkie. He was a cokehead. Frank Damici didn't know. He thought Carmine drank too much espresso. That's all.

Carmine Damici's funeral, an elaborate two-day affair, was held at St. Michael's Cathedral. Buckley would have wished as much for his mother or Clementine, but then again, maybe not. Carmine, like the others, was dead, and dead is dead.

On Friday night, Buckley sat in a back pew for the prayer vigil, where Frank Damici eulogized his own son, and the Damici clan, five dozen or so, along with their friends and friends of friends, packed the cathedral. Frank said nice things about his son

Carmine, like "He was a good boy," and then the crowd hushed, so the first person heard to cry out was Carmine's mother, Christina Damici.

On Saturday morning, with the silver mesh trash cans spilling over onto the sidewalks, the sky gray, Buckley walked thirty-six blocks to Carmine's funeral liturgy. He watched row after row rise and take Communion. He had to shift in his seat to let the good Catholic mourners pass, and he waited in the pew with the little kids who were not yet old enough for their First Communion, for the Body and Blood of Our Lord Jesus Christ. A little girl in his pew, maybe five or six years old, went, "Psst, psst." Buckley looked at her. She said, "Your hair looks funny." He felt the top of his head, and sure enough, a tuft of his thick brown hair was sticking straight up. He smoothed it with his hand, and whispered back, "Thanks."

"You're welcome."

He didn't understand the singing or the organ music, but it was nice in a dark way, much like that band the Jesus and Mary Chain. He thought the Reverend Whitehouse could've learned something about reverence from the Catholics. He wondered if the reverend had ever been to a Catholic Mass before.

He did not follow the body of Carmine Damici or the Damici family to the cemetery, because when Frank Damici saw him in the cathedral, he shouted from his pew at the front of the church, "It should've been you! It should've been you!" and the siblings of Carmine Damici had to physically restrain their father. Mrs. Christina Damici wept louder. Frank Damici was still shouting, "It should've been you."

Buckley left the church. Even outside on the front steps, he could hear Frank Damici wailing: "It should've been you!"

Buckley didn't think so. Not this time.

He walked home and finished packing.

The police questioned him once more. "More of a formality than anything else," they explained. "For Frank. For the family."

Jones said, "We talked to Frank. He said you couldn't have done it. You're not a killer. He did say . . ." But Buckley could imagine what else Frank Damici had said, and Jones didn't finish the sentence. Rather, he smacked Buckley on the back and winked at Smith.

Two days after leaving the Twenty-fourth Precinct for the last time, Buckley called Rebecca Burke, even though he hardly knew her. He left a message on her answering machine: "This is Buckley Pitank. I wrote *The Handbook for Lightning Strike Survivors*. We met at Sue's in Soho. I'm, uh . . ." he stuttered, and wished he hadn't called. "I'm uh . . . leaving New York today. I'm going to Wanchese. You probably don't know where that is. It's in North Carolina." The message was already too long. "If you're ever there, I mean in Wanchese, not North Carolina. Wanchese is on the coast. It's a fishing village. It's supposed to be nice." The answering machine beeped and shut off. He called back, "Just, if you're ever there, in Wanchese, give me a call."

Buckley hugged Mia goodbye in the stairwell. He said, "Take care of yourself," knowing full well that she could never understand the gravity of those four words: *Take Care of Yourself.* He told Mia that she could have whatever she wanted from his apartment, and then Buckley R. Pitank left the Bronx, his home for eight years, with one red and black checkered suitcase.

Buckley took a bus from the Port Authority to Elizabeth City, North Carolina, and slept most of the way. He woke in a sticky, dry-mouthed fog here and there and thought about the song "Darklands." He had been to those lands. He had walked there among the "river of disease" where heaven is too close to hell, and he was tired from the darkness. He couldn't save Carmine. No one could, and he had no doubt that Carmine had raped that man's sister. Carmine had probably done much worse in the eight years Buckley had known him. Buckley thought, *I lied to the police. I let a murderer go free. I saved a man's life. My mother would be proud.*

At one point, as the bus headed south down I-95, an old

woman's silver-haired head wobbled onto his shoulder, her temple heavy and furrowed. He didn't care. Buckley fell back asleep. Fifty miles west of Elizabeth City, he woke again—this time to the sound of rain. At first just metallic pitter-patters, drip-drops, like a spring rain falling on an old tin roof. Clementine's roof. But then a full-on tempest, and the old silver-haired woman, awake now, saying her Rosary, ran the tiny red beads through her wrinkled fingers. The wind blew the rain in sheets from the west, as if God stood on the ground hurling pellets at Buckley's window.

The streets in Elizabeth City were flooded with a foot of water, and the bus seemed more like a boat to Buckley than an automobile on tires and road. He felt the rushing water beneath his feet through the rubber-covered floorboard, and he wondered for a moment if he'd die on a bus. His mother died with one foot on a boat. He didn't want to die. *Revelation*: He did not want to die.

Despite the flood, Paddy John was there at the Elizabeth City bus depot, water pooling on and dripping off the rim of his canvas hat. He shook Buckley's hand. Tide also reached for Buckley's hand, but Buckley, overwhelmed from his long journey or maybe by seeing Tide all grown up, pulled Tide to him and gave him a hug. Tide smelled of bourbon.

Buckley released Tide, patting his back. "I never would've recognized you."

The three men, sopping wet and quiet, walked in the dark evening across the parking lot to Paddy John's pickup. Buckley sat between Paddy John and Tide. As they passed the green mileage sign on Route 158 indicating WANCHESE 27 MI., Buckley said, "I meant to tell you a long time ago: My mother never loved John Whitehouse. She loved you. She told me." Buckley shifted in his seat. "I hope you knew that."

Paddy John had hoped, but he hadn't known. Not for sure. Not until now.

. . .

The thin man hid the night's deposit under his bed and worried for weeks that he would be picked up for murder.

Then he joined the U.S. Marines.

He never counted the money, but landed in Saudi Arabia in a sandstorm, where he eventually saved two men from Iraqi border fire. He was awarded the Navy Cross Medal for saving Private John Winston and Corporal Adam Myers.

Upon the thin man's safe return to New York, he gave the contents of the night deposit bag to his sister Margaret, who had just turned eighteen. Margaret had actually turned out all right despite being raped at sixteen. She was glad almost every day of her young life that someone had murdered Carmine Damici. She was starting college in the fall. She didn't know that her brother had killed Carmine Damici, but then again, she never asked.

Her brother the thin man was a hero.

It doesn't do any good to ask, "Why did I survive?" You survived. The question to ask is "What now? What am I going to do now?"

If you feel yourself slipping into a depression, thinking you don't deserve to be alive, remember that life is a gift. It can be taken in one flash. Do something meaningful.

35

Victoria, 1989

Rowan wanted to sit in his Adirondack chair on the Core Sound and read. He wanted to take his yacht, the *Rebecca,* out on the water and watch the seagulls and the pelicans swoop overhead. He wanted to drive his Alfa to Manteo Island and eat lunch on the waterfront. He wanted to make love to his beautiful blond Patty-Cake wife. He wanted to extricate himself from the antitobacco furor that grew daily so that he could do all the things he *wanted* to do.

Instead, he spent four months in 1989 meeting with attorneys from Atkins and Thames, testifying on the effects of QR66, "telling the truth." He was tired of being a tobacco chemist, tired of telling the truth, tired of *telling* anything, for that matter. *If it will end sooner, let me lie. Just let it be over.* He didn't know he was a scapegoat.

In November he flew to Chicago. He was exhausted and feeling old. Back in North Carolina, Patty flew to Puerto Vallarta by way of Raleigh and Dallas. She said, "Just for the week. We'll both get home at the same time. Then we can have missed-you sex. I will miss you." She smiled. "It'll be over soon. Don't worry."

"You could come with me."

She weighed the options. "Puerto Vallarta or Chicago? Sorry, pal." She kissed him on the cheek. "You'll do great. When all this is over, we'll spend a month in Mexico."

She was his rock.

In Chicago, he met with Atkins and Thames's attorney, Victoria Petersen. He smacked his forehead on the table. They sat in a large conference room. "Why am I here? I can't take this anymore."

She said, "There are multiple lawsuits. I was under the impression that everything had been clearly explained to you." She was a twenty-something up-and-comer. She wore glasses, her hair in a tightly wound bun, an oversized jacket. *She'd look better in something fitted*, he thought. Her figure wasn't bad.

He finished testifying in two days. Patty wouldn't be home for five.

Could he still entice a twenty-something woman to bed?

He booked a suite at the Knickerbocker and plied Victoria the attorney with chocolate and champagne. He slid off her flats. She explained, "I don't wear heels. They make my corns ache. I've got this thing." He plied *himself* with champagne. He massaged her feet, her back, her inner thigh.

They had sex in five different positions. Victoria said, "You're the best lover I've ever had." Rowan didn't know that Victoria Petersen had been a wallflower in college. She'd only had three men before him, and one was her second cousin.

He bought her a tailored suit before he flew home. "This will look great on you."

She said, "Thank you."

"I probably won't see you again." She'd seen the wedding ring, but he showed it to her again.

"I understand. You're happily married." She wished him a safe flight before he left the suite. *Their* suite. She called her dad at home in Morgantown. She didn't tell him what happened. Instead, she said, "I'm lonely," which was his cue: He said, "You'll find the right man. You deserve someone extra special. You're a princess and you should be treated accordingly." Victoria looked at herself in the mirror. She looked at their bed, at the half-eaten strawberries, at the fitted suit he'd bought her, at the new high heels that didn't hurt her feet. *Rowan said I was beautiful. He said, "If I weren't married. If I didn't already have a family . . ."*

He reminds me of my dad, not in a sick incestuous way, but in a normal, every-woman-is-looking-for-her-father kind of psychological way. Maybe he's my prince.

She'd never had an orgasm before Rowan.

A week later, Victoria telephoned Patricia Burke. She explained what had transpired between herself and Rowan. She was very descriptive, saying, "I think I love him." Adding, "If it weren't for you, I think he'd marry me."

Patty said, "You can have him!"

Patty Burke would never be made a fool. Rather than confronting Rowan, she plotted her exit. Telephoning banks, attorneys, airlines, and Mediterranean villas for rent, she built up her resolve. She loved Rowan. This wouldn't be easy.

After Victoria the attorney telephoned him at home the first time, Rowan told her to *stop*. He even used profanity, which was not in his makeup. She telephoned again. He wrote a short letter to Victoria the attorney: *I'm not leaving my wife ever. I made a mistake. I love my wife. I'm sorry if I misled you.*

In January, Rowan was where he wanted to be—finally—on the back deck of their Cedar Island home, sipping a mug of coffee, feeling relaxed for the first time in a very long while, when Patty said, "I want a divorce."

At that exact moment, a gull defecated on Rowan's hand. "Fuck!"

He said, "Patty-Cake, don't do this! I need you."

She said, "There's bird shit in your coffee. Good luck with that psycho." No matter her feelings, this relationship was over. "See you in court."

Patty-Cake left in a taxicab already waiting in the driveway.

Rowan was alone.

Excerpt from
THE HANDBOOK FOR LIGHTNING STRIKE SURVIVORS

More than 220 tall British ships
were damaged by lightning during the
Napoleonic wars. The easiest solution
was to install lightning rods, but since
Benjamin Franklin, traitor to England,
had invented the device, His Majesty's
navy, under the rule of the lunatic
monarch George III, refused.

It's strange to think how many famous
men are mentally unstable. My mom used
to say, "Some elevators don't rise to
the top floor." No fooling.

36

A picture is worth a thousand words,* 1990

Colin's three-story house, named Sunnybrook, had a formal dining room, a great room, a kitchen, and one bathroom on the main floor. Upstairs, there were five bedrooms and three baths. On the basement level, there was a game room, a laundry room, and Brittany's studio. Except for the basement, the ceilings were high, the rooms well lit, the walls white. The first thing Colin hung on his stark walls was the Yeatesville photograph he'd bought from the Belle Tara Gallery. He hung it above the mantel in the great room.

Next, he hung reproductions of children's artwork from Terezín, Brittany commenting, "That's morose." She jingled, walking from one room to the next. Sometimes he heard her bubbling. His therapist said he was projecting his want of verve and life onto her. His therapist said, "No woman actually bubbles." He wanted to hang his vibrant wife's art on the walls. *She does bubble!* But Brittany wouldn't let him enter her studio.

He hired a photographer to take Brittany's picture. He hung those pictures on the white walls. He hung paintings by lesser-known artists Thomas Van Auken, Anne Chamblin, and Melinda

---

*The saying "A picture is worth a thousand words" was coined by Fred R. Barnard and first appeared in an advertising trade journal in 1921. Though the term is often attributed to Confucius, Barnard wanted to encourage advertisers to use images on streetcars.

Thacker on his walls. He hung his mother's picture. Quickly, he filled the bare walls with the images he loved.

In 1990, Susan Cruisenberry (Sue of Sue's Gallery) sent him the program for Lightning Fish. Right away, Colin purchased *Fish, Number Fourteen,* hanging it beside his mother's photograph and requesting Becca's contact information from Susan Cruisenberry. She said, "I can't do that, but I will tell her you inquired."

Colin didn't want to seem weird, like a stalker. Telephoning Susan right back, he said, "Forget it. Please send me any future programs."

"You bet."

Colin touched Becca's brooch to his lips. He hadn't mentioned Becca Burke to his therapist. Maybe he should do that.

When Colin became suspicious of what Brittany was doing all day in her studio, he used a screwdriver and jimmied the lock. On a white stool, he found a stack of eight-by-ten photographs of his naked wife; his naked wife and the naked photographer, his naked wife, the naked photographer, and the photographer's naked wife; his naked wife having sex with the photographer's naked wife; and his naked wife having sex with the naked photographer. Colin was not interested in making it a naked foursome.

Aside from the photographs, Brittany had also completed some stick-figure drawings. He imagined he'd save one as a testament and reminder to why this marriage was a mistake.

Brittany got a good attorney. She assumed she would need one, with the damning pictures, but she didn't. Colin didn't care about the money.

Isolated pointy-shaped objects are the most likely targets for lightning. Do not seek shelter near a barbed-wire fence, metal or wooden bleachers, in a convertible, or under a gazebo—wrought iron or otherwise.

As a rule, stay away from tall pointy things.

37

Wanchese, 1994

Buckley boarded the Tide, Paddy John's thirty-six-foot North Carolina sportfisherman, at four in the morning to prepare the day's tackle, rods, and bait. His thumbs and biceps ached from the previous day, when he'd had to brace himself in the fighting chair and reel in that Ohio lady's blue marlin. His head hurt too because after the trip the three couples who'd chartered the boat had offered to take the captain and his first mate out for beers. Buckley cursed Paddy John, who knew Buckley couldn't drink. Buckley should've refused outright, but Paddy John was a stubborn old man these days and wouldn't take no for an answer from anybody.

Buckley, Paddy John, and the three vacationing couples sat at the Wanchese Marina's bar, Pirate's Way, drinking draft beers until past ten o'clock. Paddy John told one story after another, and Buckley kept saying, "We should go. Joan and Sissy come tomorrow."

"We're fine," Paddy John said. "Have another beer."

In the cabin, Buckley popped two aspirin and sat in the recliner. He couldn't believe he'd been in Wanchese five years now, watching the sun rise, watching the sun set, fishing for marlin and yellowfin tuna, king mackerel and wahoo. Watching the seagulls and the pelicans and the silver fish circling his fingers in the greenish brown muck of the Wanchese Marina. Buckley never thought he would live by the ocean, not after what had happened to his mother, and he told Paddy John as much that first day, riding from the bus depot in Elizabeth City to Wanchese. Paddy John said, "There's a time when you have to let go."

Now, according to Paddy John and evidenced by the tips Buckley raked in from the grateful fishermen, Buckley was a topnotch first mate. Paddy John said, "You're as good as Tide ever was." Paddy John was quiet then. It had been a long time since Tide had been good at much. It'd been a long time since Paddy John had spoken to his son. Buckley, on the other hand, kept in touch with Tide, but he knew enough to keep quiet. If he told Paddy John that he was still helping Tide with his bills and rent, Paddy John would be disappointed. It was better that Paddy John think Tide was making his own way in the world.

Buckley's brown hair had grown shaggy and golden in the North Carolina sun. His stocky frame had grown muscular from life on the water. He was often mistaken for Paddy John's son, and Paddy John never corrected the mistake. "Buckley," Paddy John often remarked, "has grown up to be a good man." He told Buckley, "Your mother would be proud of you." There was nothing better, Buckley thought, than hearing those words and believing them true. She had loved the ocean. Now he did too, making it his home.

Today, Buckley was eager for the day to end and it hadn't even begun. He looked forward every year to the two-week vacation he and Paddy John spent with Sissy and Joan Holt. They didn't go anywhere or do much of anything. They rested. They sat on the deck of Paddy John's beach house, a house built from cedar in 1946. They watched the ocean, the rise and fall of the tide, the stars' and the moon's reflection on the water. They walked the beach. Buckley read Paddy John's dusty paperbacks, and each evening, Paddy John manned the grill while Buckley mixed tropical drinks, keeping Sissy and Joan happy. Joan Holt was very old. Ninety-something. Buckley guessed a hundred. She talked incessantly before nodding to sleep in the rocker while Sissy rolled her eyes at Joan's musings. Joan rattled on about Wally Holt and her own mother—who survived the 1900 hurricane that killed more than eight thousand in Galveston, surviving with baby Joan swaddled and bound to her chest. It was a great story, but Sissy had heard it a hundred-plus times. Joan rattled on about the carnage of the sea oats; about the kids today, who no longer respect nature. Her mother had seen Mother Nature at Her most furious, and she'd taught Joan to respect Her.

Paddy John told Buckley, "Sissy won't make it after Joan dies."

Buckley wouldn't think about Joan dying.

Paddy said, "She's had a good life."

Buckley tuned him out. *Joan's life is not past tense.* He knew more than anyone the inevitability of death. *We are born. We live. We die.* But he wouldn't anticipate anyone's death, no matter how old the person was.

Joan was wrinkled from the Texas sun, so wrinkled that someone who didn't know her might turn away. Sometimes she didn't make sense, but the sound of her voice was like the sound of the ocean to Buckley. It soothed him.

This year, thought Buckley, wiping the salt from the captain's bridge, *will be our best yet.*

At five-thirty, Paddy John boarded the *Tide.* He said, "They're calling for gale-force winds offshore. I'm not going to risk it."

Buckley emerged from the cabin, his head still foggy with last night's beer.

"I thought you'd be glad. Let's close her up."

"Are there really gale-force winds?"

"There can always be gale-force winds." Paddy John, his face cut deep with age, smiled. Birds chirped as first light appeared. "Get to work."

Buckley rinsed out the big coolers and set the minnows in the well free. He carried the rods into the cabin and unfastened the fighting chair. He grinned.

For the past five years, Buckley R. Pitank had been happy—winning at the game of life. He helped out on the boat and around the house. In the fall, he boarded the windows when the National Weather Service called for nor'easters and hurricanes. He and Paddy John huddled in the living room, a bottle of whiskey and a candle between them. The island evacuated while he and Paddy John remained. After the storms blew through, Buckley was on the ladder, a pouch of nails at his waist, pulling down boards, reattaching shingles and siding, doing what needed to be done. It felt good to be needed.

When the storms devastated the island, Buckley and Paddy John delivered bottled water to many of the locals, who, like them, had chosen to stay.

For these five years, Buckley walked the cool sands of South Nags Head at night. He walked the beach just below where the sea oats rise and fall in the salty wind, watching sea turtles trek from the ocean to the dunes, watching ghost crabs scamper before his bare feet. He walked for miles thinking about nothing but the feel of sand on the soles and balls of his feet, the taste of salt on his lips. When the thunderstorms came, he watched the lightning play on the black water and remembered Becca Burke's painting, *Fish, Number Fourteen.*

Excerpt from
THE HANDBOOK FOR LIGHTNING STRIKE SURVIVORS

My mother loved the water. She loved that the ocean was vast like the sky, and she loved the sand. We were going to go sailing the day she was struck dead, and I always think that it should've been me, not her, who died, but I know what she would say: "Stop taking the blame." And I know that sometimes it's harder to be the survivor.

38

Christmas in New York, 1990

The moppy head of black hair that Becca remembered from only a year ago was now salt and pepper. Her father, who'd always been handsome and self-assured, seemed beat down.

More than a year had passed since Becca's opening at Sue's Gallery, and inside her loft, she had new charcoal and graphite sketches of snapper, trout, bluefish, and croaker thumbtacked to the high-ceilinged walls. She was eager to show her new art to Patty and her dad. In the kitchenette, lit up by the waning December sun, she had oil pastels of chrysanthemums and Shasta daisies and renderings of bright storefronts like Martha's Flowers and Arturo's Italian Restaurant. The oil pastels, brighter than any of her paintings, were accented with scarlet lake and cadmium yellow barstools, flowers, and drunken faces. Last Christmas, her father hadn't asked about her show at Sue's Gallery, and she hadn't bothered to tell him, but this year she felt more secure. She wanted to tell him about her art. She wanted her father to know that three of her paintings had sold. She was a real artist.

Leaving his suitcase just inside her front door, Rowan took off his gloves. "It's freezing in here. Can I have a glass of water?"

She wondered if he'd notice the once glossy hardwood floors now stripped of lacquer and spotted with dark paint. Becca tossed her knit cap on the kitchen counter, and grabbing a glass from the red cabinet, filled it from the sink. "Why didn't Patty come?"

"Do you have bottled water?"

"The water's not bad here."

"I'd like bottled water."

"Is Patty sick?" She handed him the glass of water. "I don't have bottled water."

"We're getting a divorce."

"What! Why?"

"She's crazy." Rowan took the glass from Becca and gulped the water down. "It's freezing in here."

"What happened?

"She thinks I'm cheating on her."

"Are you?"

"How can you ask that?"

"You cheated on Mom."

He set the glass on the counter. "I can't believe you'd say that."

Becca shrugged. She wasn't sorry.

"Your mother was very sick."

Becca thought, *You're right. You're so fucking right—as usual*, and she felt a wave of heat spread into her chest, rising up her esophagus. *My mother was very sick, and I was the lucky one who stayed home and took care of her while you ran off with Patty.*

She chucked her winter coat, a secondhand army jacket, onto the sofa. "I thought we'd stay in and order Chinese."

"I'd rather go out." Rowan hadn't taken off his coat. He sat down beside Becca.

For the past three years, Rowan *and Patty* visited every Christmas. Every year, it was Patty who did the talking and Patty who decided what they'd do for dinner, what Broadway shows they *had* to see, what art exhibits and which jazz musicians weren't to be missed. It was Patty who praised Becca's art. It was Patty who, despite Becca's understandable resistance, tried to make friends.

Becca and Rowan sat, quiet, on the sofa, both of them missing Patty. Becca looked around at the walls, waiting for her father to ask about school or art, waiting for him to comment on the bright sketches strewn about the loft, but he got up and refilled his glass.

She'd settle for a comment about the ruined floor he'd eventually have to pay for. He said, "The water tastes like metal."

"Don't drink it." Becca stood up. "Where do you want to go?"

"Anywhere."

"Well, you said you wanted to go out to eat."

"Surprise me."

Rowan put on his gloves, Becca her army coat. She pulled the bright red hat that Jack had knitted for her—an early Christmas gift—down over her ears.

As Becca and Rowan walked along MacDougal on their way to Bleecker, an older man, his blue-black skin in creases and folds, played saxophone under the streetlamp. Beside him, a white sheet of loose-leaf paper marked *TIPS* was safety-pinned to a top hat. Becca stopped. Rowan kept walking. She tossed two dollars into the hat. The saxophonist dipped his head as she passed.

As she caught up with her father, who was already half a block away, he said, "You're only encouraging him."

"Encouraging what? He's a musician."

"He's a beggar and a bum."

"Okay, Dad." There was no point arguing. She said, "You'll like this place. It's a jazz club, but they do fresh pasta from five to nine."

"What's it called?"

"Club Plenty."

Rowan picked up the red candle between them and set it back down. "I talked to your Auntie Jane. She wants us to drive up to Connecticut for Christmas. I was going to rent a car."

"Who's Auntie Jane?"

"Becca, you know Auntie Jane."

"No, Dad, I don't."

"My mother's sister."

"Then she's *your* Auntie Jane."

"She's invited *us* to spend Christmas Eve and Christmas Day in Connecticut."

"We're spending it in New York."

He shrugged. "I thought it'd be fun. Something different."

"I don't know Auntie Jane." Becca picked up the red candle. "Do you know what you're going to get?"

"What are you having?"

"I'm not all that hungry. Maybe some pasta marinara."

"Me too."

Becca and her father ordered their pasta, and Becca ordered a bottle of the house red. After her first glass, she said, "You could've told me about Patty. When did it happen?"

"January. I didn't see the point."

"Last January!?"

He nodded.

"And you didn't see the point?" Becca twirled the long spaghetti noodles around the tines of her fork. "I'm not going to Auntie Jane's."

"Why not?"

"If I wanted to spend Christmas with family, I would've gone to Aunt Claire's with Mom. We're supposed to do Rockefeller Center and Macy's and the Rockettes. Christ, Dad, I can't believe you didn't tell me what's going on with you and Patty and these lawsuits, and now you want me to pack up and ride to Connecticut with you to see some old woman I don't know."

"She's your Auntie Jane."

"She's *your* Auntie Jane, not mine."

"I don't need this, Becca."

Becca pushed her plate of food to the corner of their table. "I've sold three paintings."

"That's wonderful. I've sold two photographs this year."

"Are you kidding me?"

"What? What did I do now?"

"It's all about you. Can it ever be about me?" Becca gulped her wine, refilling the short juice glass.

"I didn't come here for this. I came here to have a nice time with my daughter. Look, I have to fly to Nevada the day after Christmas."

"To testify again? What did you do, exactly, Dad? I mean, let's be honest here."

"I didn't do anything. I made glues for cigarettes."

"I'm not going to Auntie Jane's with you." Becca began to cry. "Did you see my paintings in the loft?"

"Piddle, don't cry."

"Did you see my paintings in the loft?"

"I saw them."

"Then why couldn't you say anything?"

"Well, I was going to."

"Why couldn't you say anything now?"

"I just got here."

"Why can't you see who I am?"

"You're being overly dramatic."

"Why couldn't you be there for me?"

"Calm down."

"Am I embarrassing you?" Becca's breathing quickened. She blew her nose into her dinner napkin.

"Calm down, Piddle."

"Don't fucking call me Piddle."

"We'll get the check." Rowan got up from the table to look for their waitress, and when he returned, Becca was gone. She had left the key to her loft, which she kept on a beaded silver chain, on Rowan's bread plate.

When Tripp, a no-last-namer like Chris, who lived on Lafayette Street, saw Becca, her freckled cheeks caked with mascara, he said,

"I thought you wouldn't see me again? You gotta wait three weeks to come knockin'? Is that like the don't-call-somebody-within-forty-eight-hours rule? Your rule is three weeks?"

"Shut up." She stepped past Tripp into his apartment and leaned with her back against the exposed brick. "Can I have a beer or a shot or something?"

"You're presumptuous."

"That's me."

She swigged two shots of tequila, drumming her paint-stained fingers on the bar in Tripp's small kitchen, wanting to explode. "Can I use your bathroom?"

She washed her face and blew her nose.

Back at Tripp's bar, drumming her fingers again, she said, "My dad's a dick."

"My dad's a dick and Merry Christmas. Get in line. Whose dad isn't?"

"Will you fuck me?"

"Of course I'll fuck you." He smiled. He was handsome. She could fuck him, his dark eyes, his pink lips, his strong back, his strong hands, and he would *love* her, and then she would leave . . .

Except this time turned out different. This time it was no good. She heard the rubbery squeak of the condom. She envisioned the folded black skin of the saxophone player and remembered her dad taking her to Bobbie's to buy a new watch. She saw her mother passed out on the kitchen floor and Bob and his cheating whore wife across the street, watching the Burke family. She saw Carrie walking away from her, yellow lockers on both sides of her best friend. "I don't trust you," she remembered. She saw her father driving away from her. She tried to feel Tripp inside her. She wanted so badly to feel nothing else. She said, "More! Please! I can't feel anything." He pressed her bare back against the exposed brick of his fireplace, her right leg around his thigh, the toes of her left foot on the hardwood floor, and she let go. Her chest sweaty, she slid from beneath him. She had really let go.

"What are you doing?"

She crumpled to the floor and cried.

"Did I hurt you?"

"I have to go." She fumbled around Tripp's place, grabbing her jeans and sweater. "My hat. Have you seen my hat?"

"What hat?"

"My friend made it."

"I didn't see a hat."

"Bye."

"Wait a minute."

"I can't."

"Did I do something?"

"It's not you, Tripp. It's me."

On the walk back to the Village, Becca remembered the saxophone player's face. She mixed the paints in her head. She saw Old Man John, his skin blue-black, digging a grave for Bo, and old Bo, blue-black and charred in the pouring rain. The blue-black blood of the dead fish when she split them open. And then she saw herself, who she had been—a firefly charmer dancing with the stars. Minnows darting between her thighs beneath breaking waves. A little girl haloed with fire in her eyes. Becca, all grown up now, remembered the red roses in a crinkly bag of pork rinds. She remembered Grandma Edna laughing at her own funeral, and Becca, all grown up now, mixed the paints in her head. She felt that the Winnie-the-Pooh watch hands had quickened. It was time to slow down.

Inside Becca's loft, her father paced the floor. He flipped through her record albums and wondered why life had to be so difficult. He wanted to see Auntie Jane. He thought it would be a nice change. He hadn't seen her since his own mother's funeral. He missed his Auntie Jane. With three fingers on his jaw, he walked around the loft, looking at Becca's paintings and sketches, wondering what he could say about each of them to make things better, to make things less difficult with his only child. He liked the picture of the chrysanthemums because it was bright. He didn't like the pencil drawing of the fish head. He liked the storefronts. He thought they were well rendered. He thought, *I'll say this one's my favorite because it looks so much like a real flower, or I'll lie and say I like the fish head because it's dark and if I were to be honest, if that's what she wants, I'll say the fish head's disgusting. It's disturbing.* He paced the loft and waited.

The door was locked. Becca knocked. When her father opened the door, he was smiling. "I'm glad you're okay."

"I need to paint."

"We should talk."

"I don't want to talk any more, Dad." She set her coat on the kitchen counter and rolled her sleeves up.

"Are you drunk?"

"You mean like Mom?"

"That's not what I meant."

"I need to paint."

"You can paint. Don't let me stop you. As a matter of fact, I was looking at your paintings and some of your drawings. You're quite the artist."

Becca ripped a sheet from her sketchbook and, remembering the face of Old Man John, she began with his forehead. She had seen his face in the saxophone player, that same level of dignity. Something she had lost. Something she wanted back.

Her father said, "I like the flowers in this picture. They're so bright."

Becca stopped her pencil. "Dad, no offense, but I really need to work."

"Go ahead, honey."

"Look, I'm supposed to have another show in six months."

"Did you ever have that other one you were telling me about?" Rowan sat on the sofa, his hands between his knees, his voice as insecure as it had been when he'd telephoned from San Francisco.

"Over a year ago."

"How'd that go?"

"It went swell."

"Tell me about it. Did you sell any of your paintings?"

"I already told you. You weren't listening!" *My paintings*, she thought, *have no more to do with you than the men I've fucked and forgotten.* Becca said, "It's late. Take my bed, and we'll talk in the morning."

By morning, the loft floor was strewn with sketches, and Becca slept, her narrow waist and shoulders beneath an old quilt on the sofa, her father rubbing circles on her back. He whispered, "Bec. Hey, Bec."

"Are you leaving?" She stretched out her legs, arching her back.

"I guess so."

"I think you should. Go to Auntie Jane's."

He sat on the edge of the sofa. "Are you sure?"

Becca squinted up at him before rubbing her eyes. "I have a lot of work to do."

"I left your Christmas present over there."

There was no reason to look. She knew it was cash since there was no more pretty Patty to buy her things she didn't need.

Rising from the sofa, her father squeezed her shoulder. "You know I'm proud of you."

She smiled. He could be anybody.

"I'll see you soon, sweetheart. I love you."

"Bye, Dad."

He left with his suitcase and Becca fell back asleep. For the first time in a long time, she slept soundly.

"One fellow called me stupid. I ain't stupid. I was fishing at this pond up near Luray when the rain started. I did what the cows did. I went to the nearest tree for cover. Wouldn't you know it: Me and the cows and the tree get zapped and I'm off my feet, my left side aching. An hour later, the wife comes to get me. I limp over to the truck. 'Where the hell have you been?' I asked. She said, 'What are you talking about?'

'Woman,' I told her. 'Do you want me to die in a thunderstorm?'

She said, 'It weren't storming where I was.' Sure enough, just five miles down the road, nothing but blue sky.

Seeing me in pain, she thought I better go to a hospital, but I felt all right. Just a little sore, and I didn't have no insurance. That was the first time I got struck. Since then, I've been struck four times. I'm not afraid no more. I told my grandson, 'Your Pa-Pa is Lightning Man. I'm a goddamn superhero.'"

Account by Jimmy A.

39

Redemption, 1995

Winter had a beef stew simmering in the Crock-Pot. She was making biscuits. John Whitehouse came up behind her, putting his hand on her back. "It smells good." She felt his breath on her neck.

With a palm full of peanut M&M's, he said, "A sweet for my sweet."

She smiled. "Your *sweet?* You're plumb out of your mind." She loved John Whitehouse, the man her daughter rejected. She was seventy-four years old, and she loved him more than she'd ever loved Joe Pitank. She couldn't much stand Joe—she could now finally admit.

After Abigail was born, he'd always favored his daughter over Winter. It'd been his idea to name her Abigail. Winter had thought Summer would be more appropriate—what with her own name being Winter. He hadn't liked it.

Joe spoiled Abigail while Winter washed laundry, while Winter worked her fingers red and hard. She hadn't much mourned his passing, she remembered. He died a lifetime ago. Abigail was another matter. For Abigail, she still felt guilt. She could have loved her more. Abigail might not have strayed and had a bastard child if she'd been a more attentive mother, but she saw Joe in Abigail. She could admit that now too. She was old.

As for Buckley, she wondered about him—what had become

of him, if he was alive. She felt that she and John Whitehouse had done right by him. And off he'd gone, disappearing like his mother tried to do.

Sitting across the table from John in their same cinder-block house, he slid a letter to her. "I've already read it," he said. "Couldn't resist."

The letter was from Buckley. She hesitated before pulling the stationery from the envelope.

He wrote, *I'm living at the ocean with Padraig John—the man my mother loved.* He wrote, *I'm happy. Life is like a card game. You either play or you fold. I'll never fold.* Winter wondered what in God's name Buckley was talking about. Playing or folding. He was as nuts as ever. Still, she was glad to know that he was happy. The letter continued: *I'm never coming back to Mont Blanc. I plan to avoid the whole state of Arkansas.* (Buckley had laughed when he wrote that particular sentence.)

He needed to say goodbye to the reverend and Winter once and for all. As long as they were ignorant of his feelings, he felt haunted by them; like they could come and get him anytime they wanted. He was a man now. He didn't want to be afraid. He wrote: *I don't think either of you treated my mom with love or kindness, which is a shame, because I know now that the love she gave me in just fourteen years of life has sustained me.*

Finishing the letter, Winter scratched her face. "Do you know what he's talking about?"

"Not really."

She dug into her stew. "He's a bastard," she said, "and it sounds like he's judging us. What nerve!"

Buckley and Paddy John sat across from each other eating Shake 'n Bake pork chops and applesauce on a red checked table-cloth, and Buckley said as nonchalantly as he could, "I know where

Tide is living. It's only two miles from here. What if we sent him to one of those drug treatment places?"

"Pass the salt."

"Or we could have one of those interventions?"

"Tide is old enough to do as he pleases."

It was hard for Buckley to watch anyone kill himself, let alone Tide, but Buckley was only a boy of thirteen when he'd first met Tide, and Buckley didn't know then and he didn't know now that up until he was five, Tide lived with his "unfit" mother, Judy, in a three-room dump. Buckley didn't know that Tide remembered sleeping on a dirty Coleman sleeping bag while his mother, high on heroin, had sex with Big Lime, her supplier, in the next room. Buckley didn't know that Tide ate dry cereal and cold Franco-American Spaghettios almost every day for a whole year and that he still remembered their metallic taste. He didn't know that Tide, desperate for his mother's love, sometimes went into the room while Big Lime was on top of Judy.

Big Lime grunted, and his mother's eyes rolled up white, and Tide sat down beside her on the mattress, the coils squeaking, her breasts lolling one to each side.

Tide didn't know enough not to be there beside her, and he still remembered the smoky, moist smell of her brown hair. He remembered Big Lime telling him to "get the fuck out," but Tide kept coming back. Finally, Big Lime gave in and let Tide stay.

Even while Big Lime sweated and heaved and grunted on top of Tide's mother, Tide held her hand.

Like Buckley, Paddy John didn't know what Tide had seen, but he knew there was a time to let go of the past, and he thought it was well past time for Tide to let go of his.

In Galveston, Judy McGowan, fifty-four this month, still worked at Trina's whorehouse. She took her methadone. Some habits you don't break. You only replace. She no longer serviced Big Lime or any other man unless he paid cash up-front.

She didn't want to see or know her son, Tide. She carried the guilt only a mother can carry, and she never wanted to confront it.

Some people can't be saved. If you
administer CPR but the brain has been
severely damaged by lightning, the
victim will probably die or exist in
a vegetative state.

40

Starving, 1994

In 1991, Becca moved to East Ninety-ninth Street in Spanish Harlem. On the weekends she walked Central Park to breathe in something other than bus fumes and turpentine. She did not graduate from the School of Visual Arts, but dropped out three credits short. If you asked Becca why and she liked you enough to tell you the truth, she'd say, "Degrees don't matter. Jealous egomaniacal professors make students jump through hoops, and for what? For what? So you can get some job working for some advertising firm after you graduate, doing what you never wanted to do in the first place, or so you can kiss so much ass trying to get your work seen and get so wrapped up in so much bureaucratic bullshit that you forget why you started painting in the first place?" That's what Becca would say if she liked you. That's what she explained to her mother.

Becca stopped taking her father's money and took the subway to and from a full-time job at the Corner Drugstore on Fifty-seventh Street. She worked days as a cashier, catching the grimy coins tossed across the narrow countertop. She said, "Have a nice day," and sold Fleet enemas and candy bars and cigarettes. She wore a blue smock with a name tag, REBECCA embossed with a plastic label maker. At the beginning of each shift, she used the handy-dandy label maker to give herself a new identity, like CATHERINE for Catherine the Great. Her manager, Spencer, who took his job far too seriously, told her, "It has to be your real name. You're not 'Joan of Arc' or 'Catherine the Great.'" Becca didn't care. He could fire her. She could get another low-paying job.

At night, she painted in her one-bedroom apartment and listened to her neighbors, Jose and Maria, shout at each other and their two kids. She couldn't imagine four people living in a space not much bigger than the space she occupied.

She kept in touch with Jack and Lucy, but neither of them came to visit. ("Spanish Harlem," they said, "is a little too close to *the* Harlem, and a little too scary all on its own—what with all the Latinos and the gangs and those bandannas they wear. And what's with those creepy Jesus candles they sell in the bodegas?") Mostly, they just spoke on the phone. Lucy still got bit acting parts. Things hadn't worked out as well as she'd anticipated with Johnny Depp. Her speaking role got turned into a nonspeaking role, and she didn't get to spray him with cologne. Jack was still happy about not living in Newark. He still worked at Macy's with Paulo, who made a habit of visiting Becca Burke. Paulo latched on to the talented whenever possible.

Her paintings sold. For a pittance, much of the time, but they sold. To Paulo, Becca was the quintessential starving artist. He said, "If my father were rich, I'd take him for every penny he's worth. You should absolutely do that. You should consider what he owes you."

Sometimes it was hard to talk to Paulo. She said, "I don't want his money. He's a liar."

"All the more reason to take it."

Her father called once a week to ask about her paintings and to offer money. Oftentimes she said, "I'm just on my way to work." Oftentimes she lied. He asked if there was anything he could do to help. Her answer: "No."

She telephoned her mother in Chapel Hill and said, "I don't know how you ever put up with his shit. No wonder you drank."

Her mother said, "I don't know how I put up with him either." Of course, Mary knew. She'd been in love with the man, and love is a scary thing. If not reciprocated, it can turn a person into a monster. Mary had recovered, but the wounds ran deep.

Each year, like clockwork, Becca showed her work at Sue's in Soho. She wasn't the star artist anymore; in fact, most years she was relegated to a back corner of Sue's, where she could hang only a few paintings. Each year, she sold one or two, and Sue took fifty percent, but still, she was painting, and that's what she wanted to do. That's what she *needed* to do. Occasionally she saw Roderick Dweizer—the man who had given her her big break—but he was no longer interested in her paintings. She wasn't painting fish anymore. Instead, she painted black men, dogs, old women, and hillside funerals. Not for him, but thank you.

Becca knew from eavesdropping at the gallery that there was a buyer from North Carolina who bought one of her paintings each year. She assumed it was Buckley R. Pitank, but there was no way to find out. Not without traveling to Wanchese, North Carolina, and she had no intention of leaving New York. Nor did Becca have fond memories of the Outer Banks of North Carolina. Additionally, she didn't really know Buckley R. Pitank.

Paulo said, "You should go. Take a vacation. He told you to look him up."

"I can't afford it."

"Yes you can. I'll come with."

Her father was in agreement. He knew Peggy at the Seaside Gallery. Becca should send Peggy some photos of her paintings. Becca didn't want her father doing her any favors. "That's okay, Dad."

"But it's about your paintings, Becca. It's not about me. You should call her. She doesn't take fifty percent. She takes thirty."

Becca worked days at the Corner Drugstore. She painted at night. *Life is good without waves.*

Then Sue telephoned. "I've known you a long time, so I won't beat around the bush: I don't have the room this winter, Becca."

"Not even for one?"

"I don't want to seem harsh, but your paintings border on pastoral. There are all these farmlike images. I'm sorry. There's the guy in North Carolina who we can count on to buy one, but to be honest, I don't want the work in my space. It's not worth the check. I'm sorry. You need to do something new. Something exciting. Do you remember Johnny Bosworth? He used to be my assistant."

No response.

"He's painting Russian prostitutes overlaid with fairy images. It's fascinating. Remember Lightning Fish? *That* was fascinating."

The next day at work, Becca's manager, Spencer, said, "You took thirty-five minutes at lunch. You need to stay five minutes past six." He was short and bossy, with mousy brown hair, a fat wife, and a fatter kid.

Fucking breeder. "I don't need this," she said.

"You don't need what?"

"This!" She took off her smock. About to drop it on the counter, she remembered her name tag. This morning, she'd used the label maker, becoming WONDER WOMAN. She slipped the name tag into her pocket and stuffed the smock in Spencer's hands. "I quit."

"I was struck while golfing at the White Hill Country Club in Schubert, Indiana. After the incident, no matter what I did, I couldn't stop feeling like I was going to die. My heart raced, but when I went to the cardiac specialist, he said my EKG was normal. He said it was anxiety and prescribed Valium.

I felt like I couldn't breathe. I felt like I couldn't swallow.

I've never been an anxious person.

I wasn't badly injured. There were no marks and no burns on my body, only bruises. The lightning shot me ten feet from my golf clubs, rendering me unconscious. My heart didn't stop. I didn't think I'd been hit until someone told me what happened. I was embarrassed. I'm still embarrassed. It's only because of the wife that I went to see the doctor.

After one month, I left Schubert. I was tired of feeling strange and sick. Now we live in Eugene, Oregon, and I do feel better. I gave the Valium to the wife."

Account by Daniel P.

41

All about the paint, 1995

Mary picked up the telephone. "Hello." Silence. "Hello." She thought, *Fucking telemarketers.*

"Mrs. Burke."

"Can I help you?"

"It's Carrie. Um, Carrie Drinkwater."

"How are you, Carrie?"

"I'm all right. I was actually calling to see how Becca's doing."

On March 25, 1995, Carrie Drinkwater Kingsley drafted and redrafted a letter to her old friend Becca Burke. The letter she finally sent read:

> *Dear Becca,*
>
> *I know it's been a long time. I just wanted to check in and see how things are going. I think about you every year around this time with your birthday coming up. Your mom told me you're painting and doing well in New York. I'm glad.*
>
> *Mike and I are getting divorced. He's suing for custody of our daughter, Alice. There's not an easy way to write that.*
>
> *I know it's been a long time since we've spoken, and I wanted to call you, but I didn't know if you'd want to hear from me or not. I would really like to hear from me. I hope*

you'll call. Maybe the next time you're back home we could go
for a cup of coffee or something and just talk. I miss you.
   Your friend,
   Carrie

In New York, Becca read and reread Carrie's letter before picking up the phone and calling her.

"Hello."

Becca heard the TV in the background.

"It's Becca."

Carrie tried not to cry, not right away at least, but succumbed just the same. Then Becca started. They talked about their lives, the highs and lows. Becca talked about her art. They laughed about stupid Kevin Richfield. Carrie said, "I hate that guy."

Becca said, "Yeah. Me too."

"I can't wait for you to meet Alice."

"Me either."

It was like they'd never been apart, except there was a new person, a next generation, in their midst.

Becca handed her mother a paint roller. Her father leaned against the plate-glass front of the Seaside Gallery. "Can I help?"

"We've got it," Becca said.

Between rolling zigzag strips of white paint on the gallery wall, Becca gawked at eight-year-old Alice, the spitting image of Carrie at Alice's age. Becca still remembered that first day she met Carrie, her insta-friend, the little girl with the grape Kool-Aid smile, the little girl Becca had loved more than anyone.

Alice bounced a rubber ball on the concrete floor and blew a pink bubble, which popped on her bottom lip.

Rowan said to Carrie, "I could take Alice to get an ice cream next door." The Seaside Gallery was in a strip mall on Beach Road. It was not what Becca expected, but Peggy, the owner, was only taking thirty percent and she promised a good turnout, a good crowd. She was nothing like Sue in Soho. She said, "This is your show. It goes how you want. You're in charge." Becca swept an annoying curl from her face.

"Can I, Mom?" Alice asked. "Can I get some ice cream?"

"Sure." Carrie dug into her shorts' pocket.

"It's on me." Becca's dad pulled the door open. "I like butter pecan."

"I like mint chocolate chip."

"Becca liked mint chocolate chip."

Becca thought, *You liked mint chocolate chip. I liked vanilla.*

After the door closed behind Alice and Rowan, Becca cleared her throat and said, "I can't believe he's fucking here."

"That's your dad," Mary said.

"This is why I didn't want to do this. It's got to be his thing."

Carrie said, "He's not so bad. I think he wants another chance."

"A little too late."

Mary didn't say it, but she thought, *It's never too late, Becca. Never.* She wasn't thinking about herself and Rowan. It was much too late for them, but for Becca and her father, there was still time. Mary wished her own father had made some effort. Anything. Even if she hadn't forgiven him, to know that he had tried would mean something. But he hadn't.

Rowan, like Becca, thought it was a little too late. He was old. There were no more chances. His daughter didn't approve of or like him, and he knew it. When he looked at his own life now, he felt regret. He wondered *What if?* every day. What if he had stayed at UNC? What if he'd tried to work things out with Mary? What if he'd spent more time with Becca? What if he hadn't slept with Victoria the attorney? He'd still have his Patty-Cake. He pined for that woman.

Every day, he felt like crying.

His therapist said, "*What if* gets you nowhere, Rowan," but Rowan couldn't help it.

His therapist said, "You have your photographs," but Rowan countered, "My claim to fame is Atkins and Thames. I caused the deaths of hundreds, if not thousands, of smokers. After all, it was *my* additive. No mistaking that."

His therapist said, "You can't beat yourself up," but Rowan didn't know how to stop. He got up every morning, took his prescribed antianxiety medication, and tried to feel better. The pills only made things bearable. Besides, his need for the drugs was the ultimate weakness. Rowan would agree with Becca: It's too late. *I ought to start smoking.*

The caterers were late the Friday night of the opening.

In a yellow daisy sundress, Becca paced the concrete floor. It never got easier. The jitters were always there.

In South Nags Head, Buckley fumbled with his tie. Paddy John looked at Buckley in the mirror. He untied and retied Buckley's tie, his wrinkled hands working the yellow silk. He said, "I'm eager to meet your friend."

"She's not really my friend."

"She sounds like a friend."

Buckley said, "She read my book. She's a lightning strike survivor. I told you that."

When Buckley read that Rebecca Burke, "a successful painter from New York," was showing her work at the Seaside Gallery in Kill Devil Hills, he could not believe it. Joan and Sissy were visiting from Galveston. Buckley told them about meeting Rebecca in New York, about her wonderful paintings of the fish and lightning. "She wrote to me," he told them over and over.

Paddy John turned Buckley to see himself in the mirror. "You are a handsome young man."

Thirty-six-year-old Buckley touched the silk tie. "I look a lot better than the last time I met her."

"You look good."

Paddy John wore a long-sleeved shirt and jeans. He was too old to dress up for anybody. Buckley didn't mind.

He and Paddy John could hear Sissy and Joan Holt in the living room, quarreling over who should drive. Sissy was saying, "I'll drive," and Joan Holt was saying, "I'm tired of riding around with you. You're like to kill me. Let Paddy John drive."

"I'm a good driver," Sissy said.

"Says who?"

Buckley and Paddy John laughed. Buckley said, "You should drive."

At the Seaside Gallery, Becca's paintings were hung with wire from picture molding. Her father said to her, "This is my favorite collection."

"I'm sure it is."

"It's like your soul's in the paint."

"What did you say?"

"Your soul: It's in the paint." He pointed to one of her paintings, a graphite drawing of a man washed with turpentine, faint splashes of yellow ochre, and sap green.

Becca said, "I'm going to get some air."

"Let me know if I can do anything to help."

Outside the gallery, Carrie was smoking a cigarette. "You doing okay?"

Becca took a smoke from Carrie's pack. "I don't get the big sudden interest in my life. I can't deal with my father."

"Do you have to get it? He's taking an interest."

Becca's father knocked on the glass to let Becca and Carrie know that the caterers had arrived. At the same time, Becca's mother and Peggy entered the gallery through the back door.

Ten miles away, Joan Holt, Sissy, Paddy John, and Buckley rode in Sissy's station wagon toward the Seaside Gallery to see a collection of paintings by Rebecca Burke entitled Visions. Sissy drove.

By seven-thirty, the gallery was crowded with people, and Becca was amazed at how relaxed she now felt even though her father, her mother, and her best friend were in Kill Devil Hills, North Carolina, for her latest unveiling. It was almost surreal. The crowd twirled round and round, but unlike the dancing art lovers at Sue's, who'd sucked her in and spit her out, these people were family. Becca was used to being alone even in a crowd.

Over and beyond the mishmash voices of the crowd, Becca heard the low-pitched boom of fireworks. She pictured the red and blue plastic launchers littered on the sand, and then she saw Buckley R. Pitank. Even with his hair long, she couldn't mistake him. What luck! She knew he had to be the buyer from North Carolina. *I'll thank him,* she thought. *I ought to marry him. I wonder what he sees in the paint.* She smoothed the wild curls at her temples, but because of the humidity they spiraled again. Handing her plastic cup to Carrie, she said, "Be right back."

"Want some more?"

"I'm good."

Becca twirled with the crowd crossing the concrete floor. She tapped Buckley on the shoulder, much as she'd done in New York, except this time Buckley was looking at a painting of a barn loft scattered with fireflies, the moon full through an open window— not a beach lit up and strewn with dead fish.

Seeing her, Buckley said, "You remember me?"

"Of course."

"This is Paddy John. This is Sissy. This is Joan Holt." Buckley introduced his friends like he and Becca were old friends themselves. Brushing his shaggy hair from his face, he smiled. Becca thought, *We are old friends. Buckley and I are old friends of sorts.* She remembered the day *The Handbook* came, the day she realized she wasn't alone.

Sissy extended her hand. She had long, brittle white hair and wore a T-shirt embossed GIRL POWER. Forever the feminist. No bra. Joan Holt had circles of pink rouge on her brown cheeks. No bra. She said, "Look who it is! I never forget a face."

Paddy John said, "I remember you. We've met before. You were just a kid, but I remember."

Joan Holt said, "It's Flamehead."

Becca said, "Who's Flamehead?"

"A girl I knew in Galveston," Buckley said. "No, Joan," he said. "It's not Flamehead."

"I'm Becca Burke," she told Joan. "Nice to meet you. I like that name: Flamehead." Becca remembered Paddy John—even without his beard. "Captain," she said.

Buckley said, "This is the artist, Becca Burke."

"We got that, Buckley," Paddy John said.

Becca hugged Buckley. He patted her back. He didn't want to get too close. He was sweating and worked his hair again, tucking the golden-brown strands behind his ears. "How do you know Paddy John?"

"My dad had this boat and Paddy John was his captain. Long story. I'm so glad you're here. It's a small world. I got your message when you left New York. I'm glad you called."

"I didn't know if I should."

Mary, who would never forget the fateful day her husband's lover and future wife showed up at Barnacle Bob's, rushed over and said, "Paddy John."

Like Buckley, Paddy John fumbled when Mary tried to hug him. He too was sweaty. He said, "I ain't seen you since . . ."

"A long time."

"Not by the look of you. And don't waste your time going to Galveston. The best part of the town's here now." He introduced Mary to Sissy and Joan.

Becca took Buckley's hand. "Thank you for taking an interest in my career."

"When I saw your name in the paper, I knew I couldn't miss your show."

"You must have four or five of my paintings."

"What do you mean?"

"The paintings you bought."

"I wish I did. I don't have that kind of money." His hand was moist in hers. He took it back, sliding it in his pocket. "You and your mom should come over after the show." Buckley turned to Paddy John, "Don't you think they should come back to the house?"

"A fine idea."

Becca took Buckley's other hand, but he pulled it away. "Sorry," he said. He wiped his palm down the front of his khaki pants. "I'm sort of sweaty."

"I don't care." She took Buckley from one numbered painting to the next. She said, "You bought some of my paintings. I want to know about it. I want to know why." They were looking at painting number one, *Edna,* and he said, "I love your paintings, but I didn't buy any." Becca took him to the second painting, a shiny bag of pork rinds with red roses painted into the bag's crinkles. She folded her arms at her waist and shook her head. "I don't believe you."

The third painting, titled *Falling Down,* depicted a boy on a wrecked bike, but the bike's handlebars and the boy's arms were elongated like the road itself, leading to a skyscraper. The fourth painting, titled *The Edge of the World*, showed an old woman and a black dog walking through a field of wildflowers in front of a barbed-wire fence. In all, Becca had fourteen paintings in her Visions collection.

In the gallery program she described the collection as "A glimpse into childhood."

Buckley said, "When I saw your paintings in New York, I wanted to buy the one with the lightning on the water and the fish on the beach, but it cost three thousand dollars."

"Yeah. I overpriced everything on purpose. I don't know why. I was—"

Buckley interrupted, "It doesn't matter."

Around eight o'clock, Becca got a glass of wine. Her mother jotted down directions to Paddy John's house. Carrie, who had a babysitter for the night, was talking with Buckley, fascinated that he'd self-published a book to help lightning strike survivors. She'd never met a real writer before.

Peggy touched Becca's elbow. "There's someone dying to talk to you," she said. "He's a huge fan of your work."

The man was at least six feet tall. Just below his chin, he cupped his wine in both hands. Smiling close-lipped at Becca, he was balding with blue-gray eyes. She did not recognize him.

He said, "I think your work's amazing."

"Thanks."

"We knew each other."

"At SVA, right? I think I remember." There was no telling, really. There were so many years when there were so many men: *SVA? A club? A bar? A bathroom? A boy from Whitby's Academy?*

"No. Not at SVA." Reaching into his pants pocket, he said, "I have something that belongs to you." He pulled out the long-lost butterfly brooch. The twenty-eight amethysts were still in place. The setting gleamed. He said, "I'm Colin Atwell from middle school. Remember me?"

Of course she did. She remembered him standing in her kitchen, the rain outside, her mother sticky and drunk on the linoleum. The sirens. Her neighbors gawking. Her dad not there. She remembered Colin Atwell bobbing her knee, making her fall. Chasing her through the woods. He had her brooch. She felt uncomfortable. She was not, until recently, one to search the past for anything.

Taking the brooch, she said, "I remember you." She pressed it between her palms. "It was my grandmother's brooch. Where'd you get it?"

"I found it in the woods. I tried to give it back to you at school, but you wouldn't talk to me."

"You could have given it to Carrie or just handed it to me."

"I know, and I don't know why I didn't." He sipped his wine. "I put the brooch in my sock drawer and forgot about it. I found it again when we left Chapel Hill. I figured if I ever saw you . . ." He pressed two fingers to his pink lips, shifting his weight from one foot to the other, adding, "I'm not a stalker or anything weird like that. I just always thought about you. Not always, just sometimes. You know how you do when you think about somebody and you wonder whatever happened to so-and-so, and then five years ago I saw one of your paintings in a gallery brochure. What a small world! That sounds cliché. Sorry. I swear I'm no stalker weirdo." He took a breath. "Are you married? Is that an appropriate question? I swear that I'm not always like this. I'm bumbling, aren't I?"

Colin Atwell bumbled sometimes—like when he married Brittany—but he was a good boy. He grew up with a single father telling him, "Girls are crazy," and as he grew older and taller, his father reminded him, "Women are just as crazy," and for Colin Atwell, that proved to be the case. He latched on to one crazy woman after another—none of them comparing with crazy Becca Burke running through Morgan's Woods during a thunderstorm.

Five years ago, he looked at the Lightning Fish program, and, retrieving Becca's butterfly brooch, pressed the stones to his lips. He liked the feel of the cold smooth amethysts. In his mind, the brooch, platinum and amethyst, metal and rock, still smelled like rain. He telephoned Mortimer Blake, one of his financial advisors, explaining to Mortimer that he wanted to buy one of Becca Burke's paintings. The cost was three thousand dollars. Mortimer advised, "It's a bad investment."

Colin countered. "It's not because of money." Didn't Mortimer know him? *It's because I remember freckled Becca dripping in the rain: Rebecca of Sunnybrook Farm; her corduroy dress that felt like velvet to me; her legs in tights sliding across the linoleum; Becca Burke, struggling to lift her mother's head; Becca's pride; Becca's grace.* He remembered wanting desperately to kiss her, teasing her instead, the two of them sitting on the Coker Arboretum lawn.

He was twenty-six now, like Becca. Married and divorced. Tonight, he was nervous. "I just wanted to say hi and return your brooch."

"Thanks. So what have you been up to?" she asked.

He told her about Brittany, about his money, about the paintings he collected. Hers included. He said, "My dad lives with me," adding, "It's good. We sail together. He helps me stay clear of crazy women."

"It's a good thing he's not here tonight."

He laughed. "You're not crazy. You're talented. I speak from experience. There's a difference. Imagine walking into a studio and finding stick-figure drawings of yourself labeled *dumb-ass*. It's quite the eye-opener."

"I bet. Sometimes I pretend I'm Wonder Woman."

"I love your art. I love Wonder Woman."

"Did you ever find your mom?"

"As a matter of fact, I didn't." He didn't know what else to say. How much should he reveal about himself? His passions? "I bought the picture of you and the watermelon truck."

"You're kidding!"

"It's in the den. I like to collect things. Art mostly. Old stamps. Coins. And this is sort of strange, but wedding bands, really old ones. I go to estate sales and antique shops. I have a glass case of platinum and gold bands. They're magnificent. It's the history they hold."

"Wow."

"You should probably mingle."

"No, I don't have to do that. Keep talking."

"I've been to Terezín, to Theresienstadt, to the site of the concentration camp where the Nazis sent artists and children, where they successfully tricked the Red Cross into believing the inmates were living normal lives. The children there were taught art. I am working to preserve the art that remains from the camp. The children's teacher, before he was taken to the gas chamber, hid the artwork in suitcases that were found a decade later. The drawings are safe now, but I want them not just safe but reproduced. I want the world to remember."

Becca was speechless. As a girl, art had been her salvation.

Like Becca's father, Colin was a collector. Unlike Becca's father, he was a sentimental collector.

Staring at the brooch in her palm, Becca repeated, "It was my grandmother's and then my mother's."

"I'm glad you have it back."

"I'll show you my new paintings." Becca pointed to *The Edge of the World*. "That's my grandma and her dog, Bo. Grandma Edna had these long freckled arms." Colin studied the painting. Becca said, "Sue in New York . . . Obviously you know Sue, having bought my paintings, but anyway . . ."

He interrupted. "I don't actually know her. I have a liaison."

"Anyway," Becca said, "she thinks my new stuff is too sentimental and pastoral. There's not enough blood. I should be painting prostitutes and fairies. Some bullshit like that."

"She's an idiot."

She showed him each of her paintings, telling him about the first lightning strike and the second. She told him about the second hand moving backward and about the fish on the beach. She told him about Buckley R. Pitank. She told him about her time spent as a drugstore clerk, about her dad and Patty-Cake. Then she said, "I'm all grown up now. I had to paint these pictures in order to realize something that simple: I grew up."

Later that night, as Peggy swept the concrete floor and Becca boxed the leftover wine to take to Paddy John's, her father said, "I'm going to buy the painting of the barn." From across the room, Mary watched him talking to their daughter, pointing at one of Becca's paintings, hopeful that Becca might forgive him or at least give him a chance to make amends.

Becca told him, "Dad, don't buy my painting. I'll give it to you."

"No, I want to buy it." He put his arm around his daughter's shoulder, and rather than pulling away, Becca put her hand at his belt. It was a small gesture, but it was the most she could do. He kissed her forehead. "You're a great artist."

She showed him the brooch. "I'd lost it."

Mary approached, taking the brooch from Becca. "I thought you lost it."

"I had."

She handed it back. "Keep it for a while."

"Thanks, Mom."

Mary looked at Rowan. "Are you coming to the after-party at Paddy John's?"

"I can't."

Becca said, "How come?"

"I'm driving back tonight. I have a busy day tomorrow. I have to let Shug out." Shug, short for Sugar, was his new dog, his best friend. A Chesapeake Bay retriever, she was loyal to Rowan, which Rowan admired, having had difficulty his whole life with loyalties.

"I love you." He kissed Becca's cheek.

"I love you too, Dad." It was strange for Becca to witness her dad's insecurity. Maybe he had changed. Maybe he was trying to change. Trying, all by itself, was a change.

Skin tingles and hair stands on end
when lightning is about to strike. If
there is no shelter close by, immediately
crouch low to the ground, shielding the
head. Do not lie flat on the ground
because this can do more damage to the
body, and remember: Treat the apparently
dead first.

42

The Handbook, 1995

Becca and Buckley stood on the beach.

"What did it feel like, Becca?" he asked.

"I don't really remember the first time, except for the noise. It was so loud, I thought I was dead, and then the second time, it felt like I was a caterpillar squished under a fist, and it looked translucent white everywhere. It was really clean, but then it was deep too, like the whites of your eyes. You fall into it. *Zap*. There's no way out."

They stood in front of Paddy John's house where the black waves swept the shore. The wind blew hard off the water. Becca said, "How long did you live in New York?"

"Eight years."

"It's eight for me too."

"I was hiding," he said. Buckley dug his heel in the wet sand. The waves washed over his feet and calves. The rolled cuffs of his khakis were stiff with salt and spray.

"From what?"

"This." He looked up at Paddy John on the balcony and back out to sea. The wind whipped his hair. "You should get out of New York. There's too much concrete."

Becca took a deep breath. "I like concrete."

"No one *likes* concrete."

On Paddy John's deck, Carrie was drunk on gin and tonics. She sat beside Joan Holt, who had nodded off, her chin on her bony chest. They rocked on a wood-slatted swing.

Paddy John sat in a straight-backed chair beside Mary, who leaned against the warped railing. Paddy John and Mary drank bottles of Budweiser, and Mary said, "I will never forget when you told the bartender to give me a shot."

"Well, you needed it."

Mary laughed. "I did."

Paddy John's rusted chimes clanked in the wind. Mary pulled a strand of salty hair from her mouth. Paddy John said, "It's good seeing you again. You doing all right?"

Mary told him about her job. About going back to school. She said, "I couldn't be better."

"That's apparent." He rested his hand on top of hers, and Mary heard that voice again, the voice from fourteen years ago, telling her, *This is the kind of man I was supposed to marry.* And then, *It's the beer talking. Maybe.* His hand was coarse and strong from hard work.

Inside, Sissy washed dishes. From her place at the window, she could just see the white of Buckley's shirt on the beach.

Out on the beach, Buckley said, "You want to head inside?"

"You know," Becca said, playfully punching Buckley on the arm, "we need to keep in touch." She squinched sand between her toes.

He playfully punched her back. "I agree."

"I'll race you."

Buckley felt the electricity first. The hairs on his arms and legs stood up. He saw Becca's hair electrified about her face. He heard the crackling. His skin pinpricked. He shouted, "Get down! Get down!"

Becca dropped to the sand. She thought, *Please, no! Not again!* The black sky turned bottomless and split open white and blinding. The sky lit up. Becca saw Buckley through her eyelids. The electricity sparked. In that fraction of a second when the world froze, Becca thought she'd dreamed Buckley. She'd dreamed Buckley the way she dreamed Grandma Edna and Bo, the way she dreamed fish. As the electricity shot to the ground and back to the heavens, she thought she was dead.

From Paddy John's deck, the sky, the water, and the ground melded fuming white. Inside the kitchen, Sissy saw nothing but translucent brightness and her hands glowing pink in dish soap.

The first drops of rain fell. Becca cowered at the edge of the dune. She heard her mother's voice. She heard Paddy John. She was not dead. She ought to be dead. The rain felt good on her back. She couldn't move. Then she felt her mother's hands on her back and on her shoulders. Her mother's hands, the touch of skin—so unlike the feel of electricity. She heard the sky open up. She heard her mother say, "Becca, honey, are you all right?"

She heard Paddy John say, "Goddamn it," and before she raised her head, she knew.

"Come on, Becca," her mother said. In the wind-driven rain, Becca crawled toward Buckley's burned body. She took Buckley's right hand in hers. The lightning had split his palm open, and in the rain, his palm was sticky with blue-black blood. Paddy John cursed, "Goddamn it." Buckley's ankles and his feet were burned. Paddy John, on his knees, clutched fistfuls of wet sand. The lightning touched down all around them. Carrie froze on the dune. Paddy John shouted, "Motherfucker! Motherfucker!" Ambulance sirens sounded in the distance, and Becca screamed, "Somebody call 911!"

Mary said, "Sissy's calling. Sissy's calling."

You've read excerpts of *The Handbook for Lightning Strike Survivors*, so you know that witnesses to lightning strikes suffer from shock similar and sometimes comparable to the victim's shock. As a matter of fact, witnesses are often conduits, like parallel transformers, their bodies transporting the positive electrical charge returning to the cloud or the negative charge meeting the ground. In simpler terms, the lightning had touched them all.

Becca thought, *Call a fucking ambulance. Call a fucking ambulance. It should've been me.* How many thoughts can fill someone's head in a matter of seconds, like a bad pop song that won't go away? Becca thought, *Call a fucking ambulance. Call a fucking ambulance. Call a fucking ambulance. Call a fucking ambulance* was mantra. It was rhythm. It was the pulse of electricity traveling through Becca's veins.

Mary said, "Let's get you inside. Come on, Bec." She saw her daughter's toes. Jesus, honey. Jesus."

Becca's toes were scorched deep purple. The sky cracked white and orange and gold down the beach. The light played across the water in red circles. God's fireworks. In Becca's head, clusters of fish washed up gaping on the beach. The wet sand struck Becca's back like a million prickling toothpicks.

She moaned. She pressed her cheek to Buckley's chest to feel his breathing. To feel his heartbeat. Nothing. She thought, *It should've been me*, and *Call a fucking ambulance.* Paddy John held his fistfuls of sand. "God can't do this to me."

Mary said, "We need to get off the beach. Come on." The lightning played around them, pounding and sputtering and splitting the sky white.

Call a fucking ambulance, call a fucking ambulance. The pop song in Becca's head turned to *Treat the apparently dead. Treat the apparently dead first.* Becca straddled Buckley's waist. With two fingers, she traced his bottom rib until she found that knot of cartilage. She was afraid. She counted two fingers up. With one hand on top of the other, she pressed down two inches deep into his chest. *One*, she counted. *Two, three, four*, and up to fifteen. She got off and pressed her mouth to his wet lips. One breath. Another breath. His lips were warm despite the rain, and she was methodical. Her mother pulled at the straps on Becca's dress. "We have to get off the beach." Becca pressed down and counted again. The ocean and sand melded white in a deafening blast. Becca's mother shouted, "Becca! Becca!" but Becca heard, *Treat the apparently dead first, and one, two, three, four . . . One breath. And another.* She counted and she breathed into Buckley's mouth.

She heard the sound of her breath forcing its way into Buckley's chest. She heard the five words over and over again: *Treat the apparently dead first.* As the lightning played around them, Becca's mother pulled again on Becca's dress and the yellow daisy shoulder straps tore loose. The straps were in Becca's mother's hands. Becca wouldn't stop. She was Buckley's heart. Paddy John grabbed Mary. The sky cracked open translucent violet. Paddy John saw Mary's hair electrified about her face. Mary said, "Buckley's dead. Buckley's dead." She remembered Bo: her daughter sopping wet, covering the body of a dead dog. "Becca, Buckley's dead."

Mary, breaking free from Paddy John, grabbed Becca's right arm and her wrist. Becca pressed down on Buckley's chest, turning to Paddy John, the old man dripping gray in the flashing light and darkness. She said, "Get her away from me."

Becca breathed for Buckley. She pumped his heart.

The paramedics rushed the beach. Their orange pant legs swished in the dying rain. One of them cupped Becca's body from behind, wrapping his arms around hers. He grabbed ahold of her wrists. She realized that her back ached. Her lips were numb. "That's enough," he said. "That's enough. We got it." The rain drip-dropped onto the beach. Lifting Becca up, he shouted over the dune, "We need two stretchers."

"Don't stop!" she screamed.

The paramedic held Becca against his chest.

"Don't stop! He can't die."

The paramedic shouted, "Stat."

Excerpt from
THE HANDBOOK FOR LIGHTNING STRIKE SURVIVORS

10% of lightning strike victims die.

A direct cloud-to-ground strike, lightning entering and exiting a person's head, almost always results in death.

Paramedics are not miracle workers. When a heart stops beating and won't start again, there is nothing anyone can do.

To the survivors reading my book, I offer this advice: Don't feel guilty. Lightning is random. Don't feel embarrassed. Don't feel afraid. You are no closer to death than anyone else. You are a survivor.

43

Aftermath, 1995

Today was day four. Becca, her toes wrapped in white gauze, hobbled down the sunlit corridor of Norfolk General Hospital. The streams of light played on the patients' hospital room doors like black and ivory piano keys, and Becca saw a blue-tipped angel flit across the tiles. With a squint, she saw that the blue-tipped angel was Carrie, a cardigan draped over her shoulders, the sleeves loose about her arms like wings.

In Becca's room, the two friends lay on their backs, Carrie gonging her sandal heels into the metal bed frame. Becca unwrapping a piece of bubble gum, her freckled arms like two lightning rods above her head. Carrie's heels gonged. The sun cast shadows of willow tree leaves on the beige hospital wall.

With good friends, with best friends, it's all right to be quiet.

Flowers and cards, which had started arriving day one, crowded Becca's hospital bureau. Her mother had phoned practically everyone in Becca's address book to say, "I just thought you should know . . . Becca's in the hospital. She's been struck by lightning." In addition to receiving a card and a bunch of daisies from Lucy and Jack, Becca got flowers from Paulo (with an attached note—*I can't fucking believe you got struck by lightning! Your mom says you're going to be fine. I miss you. Get well soon. Love, Paulo*) and a card from Sue of Sue's Gallery (a standard get-well wish, despite the circumstances). And even her old boss Spencer

sent a ridiculous hospital gift-shop bear wearing a hat that read
GET WELL SOON.

Aunt Claire and Uncle Tom sent yellow tulips and a card with
a picture of Grandma Edna inside. After so many years, Becca still
missed her Grandma Edna.

On the morning of day one, Becca swore she saw Grandma
Edna leaning forward at the foot of her hospital bed, Edna's freckled hands pressed into the white blanket. She said, "Buck up! Are
you feeling all right? Of course you're feeling all right. So, you
won't wear toenail polish for a while. So what!"

Becca said, "I miss you." Mary was stroking Becca's hair then, and
the doctor said, "She's fine. The painkiller in her IV's pretty strong."

Paddy John was there too, and he said, "I told you she'd be all
right, Mare."

Becca said, "Where's Bo?"

Grandma Edna whistled. She said, "I have to go," but she didn't
go right away, not before Bo leapt onto the bed.

"You're a good boy," Becca said, feeling the dog's bristly snout
at her cheek.

The doctor said, "The painkiller," explaining Becca's apparent
hallucinations, and Mary said, "You're going to be good as new,"
stroking her daughter's arm.

Grandma Edna smoothed the hospital blanket with her spotted
hands, which smelled of some sort of fruit, and Becca fell asleep.

On day two, Rowan, who was testifying yet again, this time in
Washington, D.C. (and who was not the first person Becca's
mother notified about the lightning strike), sent a lavender and
gold orchid, a flower Becca would certainly kill trying to trans-
port it back to New York. *The man has no common sense*, she
thought as she tore open the card's envelope. He had written:

> *Bec,*
>   *I thank God you're all right. Your mom said you're a hero.*
> *I told her I already knew that.*

When they let you go home, please come to Cedar Island.
Don't go back to New York. You know my house is too big for
me. We could go fishing on the sound. You could paint. There's
plenty of space for a studio. Mi casa es su casa.
   I love you, Piddle,
   Dad

She'd been a real waterfall since Buckley was struck, since her
toes were burned, since the nurses filled her full of painkillers.
That was the only explanation. She thought, *Goddamn him*, and
then she cried.

On day three, she opened and closed her father's card again and
again. She'd like a big bright studio. It might be fun to go fishing or
skiing. Maybe just a week or two—not long, and then, as if her
mother's voice filled her head, she thought, *It's not too late. Not really. Not yet.* Maybe when he wrote that note her dad had thought
the same thing. Besides, Colin Atwell had been hanging around,
asking how she was, when he might see her.

When the doctor finally let Colin visit Becca, he said he hadn't
brought flowers because they die. Rather, he wanted to make a
donation in her name to her favorite charity. "What's your
favorite charity?" He wanted to take her out to dinner when she
felt better. If she was up to it. If she wanted to go. "Would you go
out with me?"

She laughed at him. "Yeah, sure." She liked the idea of dating someone who'd made his fortune in condoms, even if they
weren't the brand of condom she preferred. There was something horrifically honest about this man. Something that ap-
pealed to her.

Down the hall, Buckley had lost time. He'd lost Clementine,
and he had only vague remembrances of a piggish man with a zucchini nose. He remembered the feel of his mother's hand and the
shine of her hair, and he remembered the New York Public Library
and the Thin Man. No Martin Merriwether. He remembered how

to rig a tackle and bait a hook, and his neurologist, Dr. Nicholas Cave, said there was no way of knowing what memories would return. He still remembered Galveston, Charlie Zuchowski, Flamehead, and the nine-page Barbi Benton spread.

Buckley remembered Becca Burke.

He did not remember being struck by lightning.

He suffered third-degree burns on the bottoms of his feet and felt numbness in the right palm of his hand where the lightning made an exit wound. He knew that he would never feel the wet sand on the balls or soles of his feet the same way again, but he looked forward to sifting sand through his fingers. Like his mother, he loved the ocean.

Paddy John sat at Buckley's bedside. "You'll be coming home soon," he said. He thanked God he hadn't lost Buckley. Buckley *was* his son.

Buckley sipped Orange Crush through a straw. His dark hair was newly shorn, having been singed by the lightning, and he wore a hospital gown. He watched the TV mounted on the wall now and again—old episodes of *Bewitched*—and Becca sat at his waist on the bed. Her toes were still wrapped in gauze and her feet dangled.

Buckley said, "You're supposed to keep them elevated."

"I have a surprise for you."

Colin Atwell, grinning, with his sleeves rolled up, his shirt untucked, entered Buckley's hospital room. He carried with him *Fish, Number Fourteen*. Becca clapped. "Do you love it?"

Buckley reached out his bandaged hand, and Becca remembered that first night she and Buckley met, that rumpled man dripping rain, his arm outstretched, touching her painting.

Colin carried the canvas closer to the bed, and Buckley fingered the white-tipped black waves with his scarred hand. He said, "I love it. I do."

Buckley saw his mother in there, in the paints. Not in the

gaping, dying fish suffering and littered on the beach, as you might imagine. No. Buckley saw his mother, Abigail, in the glossy dark waters and white foam, and he saw her higher up in each painted brushstroke. Oh, how she'd loved and sustained him. He saw and felt her there in the cracked, forgiving sky.

Endnotes to
THE HANDBOOK FOR LIGHTNING STRIKE SURVIVORS

I wrote this book for my mother—who
did not survive.

If anything I've written is inaccurate
or disputable, I apologize. This book was
written out of grief and love. My mother
wanted to see me grow up and be a good
man. I hope I didn't disappoint.

They were each, in some way, touched by
lightning—connected and transformed by
the heavens.

In case you are wondering what became of them . . .

Kevin Richfield flunked out of the University of Florida. Returning to Chapel Hill, he landed an entry-level position with a marketing conglomerate. By twenty-five, he had four children he couldn't adequately support. He regularly suffered nightmares in which he, not Becca Burke, was struck by lightning.

A few years after his tryst with Becca Burke, Christopher Lord, a.k.a. **Apple Pie,** fell hard for a student, Joy Parker, who was already married. Her husband, a bounty hunter, discovered the lovers together. He broke Apple Pie's nose, his left thumb, his pointer finger, and three of his ribs. With Apple Pie's eyes black and blue, his fingers bound, and his torso taped, his colleagues chuckled as he walked past, knowing that he'd picked the wrong student (or at least the wrong student's husband), *finally.*

Mrs. Apple Pie remained married to him, telling her girl-friends, "I feel sorry for him." He was, they all agreed, "pathetic."

John Whitehouse died from a sudden and painful heart attack—leaving Winter a widow (of sorts) once again.

Winter spent her last years knowing that she was right about everything and everyone else was wrong about everything. She attended the funerals of the Mont Blanc townsfolk she hardly knew, and when someone happened to ask, "Whatever happened to your grandson?" she said, "I never had a grandson."

Mike Kingsley lost his fight for sole custody of Alice

Kingsley. He and Carrie Drinkwater, civil to each other—for the sake of their daughter—shared custody. Carrie eventually remarried, this time to a pediatrician and vegetarian who played guitar for the band Pumpkin Seeds (folk and bluegrass). Alice Kingsley learned acoustic guitar.

When Tide went to prison, Paddy John wrote to him.

The afternoon Tide was released, Paddy John brought him home, saying "I don't understand you" and slamming his fist into the refrigerator. Buckley urged him to calm down. Paddy John shouted at Tide: "You have to shoot up drugs? What the hell is wrong with you?" A tear rolled down his old cheek. "Goddamn it!"

Paddy John stared at his son. Tide stared at the floor.

With the sound of the ocean audible through the screened door, Paddy John walked over and took Tide's forearms in his hands. "This is what we'll do," he said. "Stay here, just temporary, and get yourself together." He patted Tide's back. "You'll get better. You got time." Leaving the kitchen, he added, "You know I love you." He turned to face his son. "You know it?"

Buckley said, "Of course he knows."

Tide said, "I do now."

Richard Martin played basketball and worked in the laundry room at a low-security federal prison in Dade County, Florida, where he served a thirty-year sentence. Occasionally, he wondered if Abigail Pitank had been telling the truth. The baby might have been his. He considered this notion in the same way one considers what to cook for dinner. It doesn't really matter.

Joan Holt died in 1998. Nearly all of Galveston attended her funeral, Paddy John and Buckley among them. Sissy was inconsolable for a time, but the world was a mess. No denying that. There was still work for her to do, battles to fight. Joan would want her to fight the good fight. Idealists are an uncommon breed.

Mary Wickle Burke became Mary Wickle Burke McGowan in a sunny June ceremony on the sands of South Nags Head. Buckley was best man. Despite being barefoot, he still couldn't feel the sand on the bottoms of his feet. At the ceremony, Sissy wore a see-through blouse, no bra. Becca was maid of honor. Aunt Claire, matron of honor. Surprisingly, there were fewer than ten people in attendance. Mary didn't have many friends, and Paddy didn't think to invite anyone but Sissy and Buckley.

Paddy John McGowan never stopped loving Abigail Pitank. In Mary, he found a first mate, a seasoned partner to spend his days and nights with, to laugh at, and to laugh with. He loved her, but not the same way he'd loved Abigail.

Rowan begged Patty-Cake for forgiveness, but she wouldn't take him back. He continued to take photographs. He was learning to talk with his daughter. He was learning to listen. **Patty-Cake** took a Spanish lover, Paco, who was rightfully enamored of Patricia Heathrow. Amazingly, Paco—owner of a leftist bookstore, accomplished chef, and percussionist—equally charmed Patty. For the first time in her life, Patty desired a man as much as he desired her. It was unsteady ground, but it was so worth it!

In Wanchese, **Buckley** returned to work. He felt the same as before, except now he dreamed of Abigail wearing a key lime skirt. *Vivacious. Tremendous.* Not bloody, not hurting. *Beautiful.* In his dreams, she said, "I knew you'd grow up to be a good man. You were always a good boy." She took his hands in hers. He woke knowing she was with him. She'd always been with him. "It was never your fault," she told him. On the beach, he sifted sand through his fingers.

Becca moved in with Rowan on Cedar Island and immersed herself in her art. In the late 1990s, she and **Colin Atwell** traveled to Czechoslovakia to visit Terezín. They met one of the camp's few survivors: Anya—a child then, she was a great-grandmother now, a woman with many friends and passions, a pianist. She told them about her girlhood; about losing her mother and father, her brother and sister; about her nightmares; about the ugliness. She told them about the young woman, Marta, who'd shared her bed in the camp. When Marta was sick, she gave Anya her bread. She told Anya to survive for the both of them. Anya said that Marta used to trace little hearts on her inner wrist (she showed them). Anya said, "Marta would tell me, 'I'm glad that we're together. I lost my daughter and you lost your mother, but now we have each other.' When I cried, Marta told me, 'There's no reason for tears. You're a beautiful girl, and you're strong,' and she wiped my tears away. She said, 'When you're free, you will make the world beautiful.' "

Anya told Colin and Becca, "I believed everything Marta said to me. I would survive for both of us. I knew it. I believed it. I had faith."

Without hope . . . without faith . . . no one survives.

Acknowledgments

Thank you to Michelle Brower for championing my debut novel, to Sarah Knight, my editor, for her passion and hard work. To my mom—for teaching me faith. To Brigitte McCray, Gemma Driver, Tom De Haven, Tommy Van Auken, Carol Stone, Joy Payne, Bill Tester, Kim Lavach, Peter Young, Sal-Baby, my friends and family. Thank you to Christopher Robin for insight, and thank you to Danny Stone for everything.

About the Author

Michele Young-Stone is a lightning strike survivor. She earned her MFA in fiction writing from Virginia Commonwealth University in 2005 and currently resides in Virginia with her husband and son.